# BROKEN LIGHT

**JOANNE HARRIS** is an Anglo-French author, whose books include 18 novels, three cookbooks and many short stories. Her work is extremely diverse, covering aspects of magic realism, suspense, historical fiction, mythology and fantasy.

In 2000, her 1999 novel *Chocolat* was adapted to the screen, starring Juliette Binoche and Johnny Depp. She is an honorary Fellow of St Catharine's College, Cambridge, a Fellow of the RSC, and in 2022 was awarded an OBE by the Queen.

Find out more by visiting her website: www.joanne-harris. co.uk or follow her on Twitter @joannechocolat

# JOANNE HARRIS

# BROKEN LIGHT

ORION

First published in Great Britain in 2023 by Orion Fiction
an imprint of The Orion Publishing Group Ltd
Carmelite House, 50 Victoria Embankment
London EC4Y 0DZ

An Hachette UK Company

1 3 5 7 9 10 8 6 4 2

A CIP catalogue record for this book is
available from the British Library.

ISBN (Hardback) 978 1 3987 1082 5
ISBN (Trade Paperback) 978 1 3987 1083 2
ISBN (eBook) 978 1 3987 1085 6
ISBN (Audio) 978 1 3987 1086 3

Typeset by Born Group
Printed and bound in Great Britain by Clays Ltd, Elcograf S.p.A.

www.orionbooks.co.uk

To Fred Harris,
the best man I know.

# Playlist

# INTRO:

---

## A Kind of Magic

# 1

*From the LiveJournal of Bernadette Ingram (marked as Exhibit BI 1): March 26th, 2022*

The first seven years of my life are a blank. I don't remember a thing before that. Most children remember something of their early years, but not me. No favourite toy, no lullaby, not even a fall down a flight of stairs. My memories start at six-thirty on September 12th, 1981, and I remember what happened then with cut-glass crystal clarity.

It was my birthday, and my parents had taken me to see a magician called The Great Carovnik. I remember everything about that evening. The long, red-carpeted staircase, the red velvet seats, worn peachy with time, with the opera glasses fixed to the back. I remember the scent of smoke and the lights of the auditorium, and the musicians in the orchestra pit, and the cherubs on the ceiling. Every detail is fixed in my mind, except for one thing. Katie was there. There's even a picture of us both; a slightly faded photograph taken in the foyer. In it, we look like sisters. We have the same dark, jaw-length hair, the same fringe, the same vivid faces. We are even wearing the same kind of dress, though mine is pink, and hers is blue. But although there can be no doubt that this was the night of the magic show, I don't remember her being there at all. It's as if she was snipped from my memory.

But I do remember everything else. The lights, the music, the hush of the crowd. The rabbit from the black top hat. The glass box and the seven swords. The scary Sphinx's head in the box. The paper flowers and fluttering doves. But most of all, I remember the magic trick with the table. That, and the way she looked at me, and what she whispered in my ear. That is what I remember most. That's where the real magic happened.

It began with a dining-room table, laden with dishes and silverware, with branches of candles and glasses of wine atop a damask tablecloth. The Great Carovnik spread her arms to indicate the scale of it: the bowls of fruit, the covered plates, the delicate bonbon dishes. The back of the stage, I remember, was all hung with mirrors, reflecting the lights. I could even see myself in the front row of the audience, suspended magically in mid-air, my small pale face like a bauble hanging from a Christmas tree.

A drum roll, loud as thunder. The lights went down. There was a hush – and then she flipped away the cloth so fast that you could barely see, leaving every candle lit, every piece of glassware in place – except for a single glass of wine, which somehow ended up in her hand, raised in a toast to the audience. And behind her was the table, every dish and glass in place: but in that second, she had somehow managed to turn the dinner table around so that it faced the other way: the branch of candles at one end now burning at the other . . .

I was so very young at the time. And yet I remember it perfectly. The woman's face in its greasepaint. Her outfit – silver frock coat, black boots, top hat at an angle – the smile she sent me over her glass; the tiny, delicious sip of wine she took – *Here's to us* – as her eyes met mine.

I must have been staring. She saw me there, watching from the front row. And as the stagehands raced to remove the heavily laden table, she moved to the front of the stage and knelt to whisper softly in my ear. And then she stood up, and drained her glass in a single mouthful, and winked at me, and took a bow, and the applause was thunderous.

I told my mother, when we got home, that I wanted to do real magic, just like the silver lady on stage. My mother laughed.

'Oh, Bernie,' she said. 'Magic's not *real*. It's just a trick with mirrors. And The Great Carovnik is a *man*. That lady was his assistant. The man in the suit and the black cape – *he* was the magician.'

Well, of course I'd seen the man in the suit, pulling rabbits out of hats and changing handkerchiefs into doves. But the woman was who I remembered. She was the one who deserved the name. She was the one who counted. Even when they both stepped up into the spotlight to take their bow, I only ever had eyes for her. The way she spread her arms, as if to say: *I did this. I'm amazing.* The way she claimed her victory, smiling all the way to the gods. So many women never claim their achievements openly. So many women are eclipsed – sawn in half, or stabbed with knives, or made to vanish into thin air – as if that were so unusual. After all, it's hardly news. Women vanish every day. But The Great Carovnik had shown me this: that we need never vanish. She had shown me that you could take the spotlight if you wanted to, even from the man in the suit, with all his smoke and mirrors. Of course, it took me many years to fully understand this. But that was where it started, on the stage at Malbry Lyceum, with the footlights reflecting in my eyes, and her voice in my ear as she whispered:

*Little girl. Make them look.*

# TRACK 1:

---

# Girls Just Want to Have Fun

Hey, goddesses! Feeling washed-out? Hot flashes
getting you down? Strap in, grab a smoothie,
run a warm bath with essential oils. Light a
scented candle. This is your time to shine, shine,
shine. The party's just beginning!
*(DeeDee LaDouce, Mybigfatmenopause.com)*

# I

*Extract from* Class of '92, *by Kate Hemsworth*
*(published by LifeStory Press, 2023)*

When we were children, Bernie and I, magic was easier than
sums. It was the kind of magic children never think about; the
kind that adults don't notice. I remember I could change into
a pony, a rabbit, a bird – anything I wanted to be. Even a boy,
if I wanted. That's what Bernie told me.

In those days, the world was infinite. All our doors were
open. A lifetime of possibility, where all the choices were
mine to make. I don't remember much of it now. But I do
know it was real. And I know the moment I lost it for good,
and the one who took it away from me, the way so many
men take away the power they find in women.

But I'm not going to talk about him right now. He isn't
a part of my story. Even writing his name gives him power,
and he was small and ridiculous, and doesn't deserve our
attention. And yet, this is why we're here, I suppose. Even
though what happened was terrible, let's not pretend that's
not why we're here. Because Bernie Ingram wasn't a freak.
She could have been any one of us. In some ways, maybe I
think she was. Maybe she was that part of us that still believes

in magic; in change. Yes, I know what she did. But I can't find it in me to blame her. A part of me would have done the same. A part of you would have done it, too.

Don't think I don't know what we're doing here. I know why I was chosen for this. I'm nicely middle-of-the-road. Readers can relate to me. I'm still reasonably attractive – at least, as attractive as a woman can be when she's approaching fifty. I could be your next-door neighbour. I could be your mother, your sister, your wife. My life looks appealing on the page, but not enough to provoke too much envy. I'm not a doormat, although I'm not any kind of activist, and I certainly don't want to be a man – which is what so many of you think poor Bernie really wanted. And, of course, I knew her back then. I can tell her story. But not for you. Because of her. Because I owe it to Bernie.

Let me introduce myself. Kate Hemsworth – mother of Sadie (15) and Ben (19), wife of Lucas Hemsworth, and graduate of Pog Hill Class of '92. Born right here in Malbry; educated at Mulberry House, then at Pog Hill Sixth Form College, just like Bernie Ingram. She was Bernadette Moon in those days, and I was Katie Malkin, and we were best friends when we were small, although by the end of junior school, I didn't have much to do with her. Even then, something was wrong. Even then, she was different.

Our junior school was Chapel Lane, two steps away from Mulberry House. A small community of no more than a hundred pupils, but with a good reputation. About two thirds of the pupils there went on to attend independent schools – Mulberry House for the girls, St Oswald's or King Henry's for the boys. I liked it there. I had nice friends. After the first year, Bernadette Moon, with her long dark plaits and her look of never quite knowing what day it was, was no longer among them. To the rest of us, she seemed childish – the kind of girl who still has invisible friends. And she was always pretending things – prancing around like a pony, or being a princess, or a jungle explorer, or someone out of Greek myth, or running and barking like a dog – which seemed, from the height of my eight months' seniority, both absurd, and slightly insulting. No one bullied or called her names – Chapel Lane wasn't that kind of school – and yet she was somehow set apart. Kids can sometimes be cruel, and girls are especially quick to pick out any visible difference. But there was nothing visibly weird or different about Bernie. It wasn't her accent, or her clothes, or any of the other things that sometimes mark kids out at school. In a way, that made it worse. Bernie was weird from the *inside*, more so than I ever imagined.

And yet, we might never have realized, except for that birthday party. It was her eleventh, and we were both entering our first year at Mulberry House. Mulberry House was much grander and more imposing than Chapel Lane, and Bernadette, still young for her age, was now in danger of getting a shock unless she really tried to fit in.

Her mother must have known that. The party was all her mother's idea. Bernadette's eleventh birthday happened to coincide with the start of the autumn term, and her mother invited the whole form, in the hope that Bernie might make new friends. It was a kind of desperate move, and I rightly saw it as trying too hard – never a way to be popular.

It had been over three years since I had believed in magic. Now I believed in Toyah instead, and dreamed of being a teenager. I noticed boys in passing, but secretly worshipped Adam Ant, and practised swaggering dance moves in front of my bedroom mirror. My mother thought it was charming, but my father didn't like it. 'She's growing up too fast,' he would say. 'She needs to enjoy her childhood.'

No one said that about Bernadette Moon. In fact, as far as she was concerned, she wasn't planning to grow up at all. But my mother was friends with hers, and I was in her form that year, and so, when the invitation came (on a handwritten card, with silver stars), I ended up agreeing to go. And so I arrived at the party that night, dressed in my sparkly T-shirt and jeans, only to find that I was one of only three guests in attendance. The other two were Grace Oyemade, a new girl from the Red City estate, and Lorelei Jones, whose parents ran the party shop, which made the whole thing both sad and ironic.

The saddest thing of all was, it should have been a great party. There were tables laden with food: sandwiches, jugs of lemonade, cakes, jellies, ice cream. There was a three-tier birthday cake, topped with pink and white icing. There were twenty-one goodie bags, one for every girl in the class, and a mountain of party hats and balloons. There was a pile of videos, a wide-screen TV, and chairs and beanbags all around the living room. One bedroom was a disco room, with coloured lights and a mirrorball. There was a crafts station for making candy bracelets, and paper lanterns for when it got dark. And there were games – Pass the Parcel, and Spin the Bottle and Twister – all set up and ready to play. It should have been a big success. Instead, it was a disaster.

The worst part was that Bernie didn't really seem to notice. I remember her greeting me at the door, in a tiara and a white ruffled party dress, her eyes all hopeful and shining, as if she were having the time of her life. I'd brought her a present – a Yardley talc-and-scent set from Boots, chosen by my mother – which I already knew was all wrong. Bernie was a My Little Pony girl. You could tell that just from looking at her.

'We're having a magic show!' she said, dragging me inside by the hand.

'A magic show?'

'You remember.'

For a moment, I thought I did; something from a long time ago, from those days when magic was easy as maths. Then it was gone, like the words of a song you haven't heard in years, leaving nothing in its place but a sense of vague discomfort.

'We've got snacks. This is going to be fun!' She talked like that, all exclamations: like a child in a book from the fifties. I followed her into the living room, where Grace and Lorelei were sitting in front of a long table piled with snacks, and crisps, and little sandwiches, and in the middle – to my surprise – a blindfold next to a little cut-glass dish of Opal Fruits. It didn't much look like a magic show, not even when Bernie reached under the table and produced a top hat and cloak, which she proceeded to put on over her ruffled party dress, and a plastic fairy wand with a silver star on the tip.

I was a bit disappointed. I'd expected an actual *magician*, like the one Jenny Kite had at her birthday, but it seemed as if Bernie was going to try to demonstrate the trick herself.

'So – what do we do?' I said.

'You know. It's just like playing House. You start. Just take an Opal Fruit, and put it in your mouth, and chew.'

I looked at her. 'What do you mean, *playing House*?' I didn't see the connection between playing House and a magic show; besides, playing House was for *little* kids. Surely she didn't mean for us to play with Barbies all night long?

Bernie shook her head impatiently, making her long plaits fly. 'Go *on*!' she said. 'Just take a sweet. Don't show us what you've chosen, though.'

I shrugged and selected a strawberry sweet, turned away to unwrap it, and popped it into my mouth. I remember it well – the sharpness, the juice. I'd always loved Opal Fruits. It was the last one I would ever eat.

'Now for the blindfold.' She picked it up. 'Let me help you put it on. We don't want any cheating.'

Still confused, I played along. I heard the rustle of Bernie's cloak as she moved behind me.

'OK. Can you taste it now? Now – go!'

For a moment, I heard them all, whispering and giggling. 'Now what?'

'Now I'll tell you what Katie chose.' She paused for effect. I imagined her waving the wand and swirling the cloak. 'Are you ready? She chose – *strawberry*!' The others whispered and giggled again.

'Big deal. You probably saw me.' I reached up to take off the blindfold.

'No, don't take it off,' she said. 'We haven't got to the good bit yet.'

More whispering and giggling. I could sense more movement around me, and the sound of cutlery on a plate. I was starting to feel annoyed; as if they were secretly mocking me.

Then, Bernie's voice said: 'This one.'

Lorelei: 'No, *this* one.'

'Ewww!'

'Shh!'

'*Shhhhh!*'

Someone giggled uncomfortably. Once more I sensed, rather than heard, someone moving towards me. And then Bernie took hold of my arm. It could have been anyone, I guess. And yet somehow I knew it was her. And then –

Remember, I was eleven years old, where memory works

differently. And it had already been three years since I'd been close to Bernie. I had grown a foot taller since then. I had lost my baby teeth. I had made new memories. I was almost a different person.

A moment of connection. *Flash.*

'*Abracadabra!*' said Bernie.

I can't be certain what happened next, or if I remember it accurately. But as she touched me, I recall a strange kind of sensation, as if something in me had been turned around. And it seemed weirdly familiar, too, like something from a recurring dream.

'What can you taste now?' Bernie said. She sounded as if her mouth was full. 'Think. What can you *really* taste?'

'Strawberry Opal Fruit,' I said. 'This is stupid.' I was annoyed. I didn't like the blindfold, or the giggling, or the feeling that the others were sharing a joke from which I was excluded. I reached once more for the blindfold. 'What did you even think I'd –'

And then, suddenly, the taste in my mouth was brutally over-ridden. The sharp acidic tang of fruit gave way to something different. A different flavour and texture; familiar, but so unex-pected that I could barely identify it. Nothing had been put into my mouth: I had been sucking my sweet all the time. And yet, it was there, unmistakeable: something salty and fatty and strange –

It felt like a violation.

I started to choke and gag in alarm. I started to pull at the blindfold.

'No! That's cheating!' said Bernadette. 'What can you taste?'

'I – d-don't know. P-pork pie?'

Bernie laughed in delight. The other two laughed with her, though I thought they sounded uncomfortable. Someone took off my blindfold. Bernadette was still laughing. She was holding a half-eaten piece of pork pie between her fingers. *I was eating that just now*, I thought. *I could taste it. Feel it there.* But there was nothing in my mouth except a half-eaten Opal Fruit. I spat it out into my hand. I didn't trust it anymore.

I know. It's difficult to explain. I suppose it's difficult to hear, especially coming from someone like me. But I need you to understand. I wasn't a suggestible child. I wasn't especially imaginative. I was a team player, which made me as susceptible to peer pressure as any other girl at a new school wanting to fit in and be popular. But what I'd experienced wasn't like that. I wasn't going along with the crowd. There *wasn't* a crowd. Just Bernie Moon. I didn't need to impress *her*. And yet, it happened all the same – that thing we now call *The First Incident*.

If I'd been older, I might have assumed that she'd somehow hypnotized me, or even slipped me some kind of drug. But I was not as streetwise as I would have liked my friends to believe. All I could think of at the time was: *She can make you feel things, somehow. She can make you feel what she feels.* What else could she have made me feel? A headache? The urge to pee my pants? Instinctively, I sensed that she could have done both those things – maybe even more than that. And in the wake of my surprise and fear came burning anger. I threw the half-eaten Opal Fruit at Bernie.

'You're disgusting!'

She looked surprised. 'Don't be like that. Don't you like pork pie?'

'That isn't the point!'

'But that's the magic,' said Bernie, as if what I'd just experienced was completely normal. 'Don't you remember *anything*?'

'Remember what?' I was trembling now. Once more came that fugitive gleam of recognition in my mind, like a shard of memory, working inwards to my heart.

She sighed. 'Come on. Let's try again. We'll do Lorelei this time. You were last, so you can choose.'

'Choose what?'

'What she gets to *taste*, of course. That's the magic. You know that.'

I glared. The thought that Bernadette Moon could somehow have made a strawberry Opal Fruit taste like a mouthful of pork pie was still too much for me to take, but I had been badly frightened, and I felt a need to retaliate.

'You're so weird,' I said spitefully. 'No wonder no one else turned up to your stupid party. Why couldn't we just do *normal* stuff?'

For a second, she looked at me, and I saw that my words had struck home. The light of excitement in her eyes dimmed, then seemed to darken. I was suddenly half afraid – of what she might say, of what she might do. Suddenly, I seemed to hear a sound like an approaching train, and feel something breathing against my neck, and I saw the fine little hairs on my arms rise in response to some primal fear –

And then Bernie's mother came in with a tray, calling out in her too-bright voice: *How's it going, girls?* and offering jugs of lemonade, and by the time we'd helped ourselves, the moment had passed, and Bernie was back as she'd been before; looking like Wednesday Addams dressed up in her granny's wedding dress, hopped up on sugar and atmosphere, but no longer strange or menacing. By the time I'd finished my glass, everything was normal again, and I could almost convince myself that Bernie's mysterious party trick was just my imagination.

I looked at Grace and Lorelei to see if they knew what had happened. Grace was very shy, and seemed not to have understood the 'trick'. But Lorelei seemed quite relieved not to have had to take her turn. She and I spent the rest of that party watching *The Muppet Movie* and whispering to each other behind our hands, while Bernadette tried in vain to interest us in a series of normal activities. Eventually, she and Grace settled down to watch the movie in silence, while Lorelei and I pretended not to see or hear her.

Meanwhile, from the kitchen, her mother looked on with an unhappy smile, coming out at intervals to ask if we were enjoying ourselves, or if we wanted more lemonade, and leaving with a sad look on her face, as if she, and not her daughter, were the one whom the class had rejected.

I only saw her father once, quite near the end of the party. He came into the kitchen, where Bernadette's mother was cleaning up, and looked into the living room, where we were still watching the movie. Behind him, Bernie's mother said something, and he turned and said: *I told you so. Bloody waste of money, Jean.* Bernie's mother shut the door then, so that all I could hear was the rise and fall of their voices through the glass, but I could tell that she was upset, and that he was angry. It made me feel guilty, and more so when, as I left the party, Bernie's mother insisted I take home the whole top tier of the birthday cake, as well as some extra goodie bags.

'I'm sure your mum would like one,' she said in that bright and hopeful tone. 'And maybe your sister would like one, too? There's a little make-up kit in there, and some stickers, and sweets, and a friendship bracelet.' Once more, that wide, heartbreaking smile, a little too like Bernie's. 'I made a few too many, I know. But it's good for Bernie to have friends like you. You're such a good influence on her.'

In the end, out of guilt, I took four goodie bags, the cake tier and a parcel of sandwiches. Grace and Lorelei took their share, and Bernie waved goodbye at the door, bugling: *See you on Monday!* as if she couldn't bear to see us go.

But, by Monday, everyone knew that the party had been a disaster. Lorelei must have spread the word, and although she omitted to mention the magic show, the story she told was already enough to establish Bernie as unpopular and weird. I kept away from the subject – partly out of embarrassment for Bernie, but also because I didn't want to be thought of as weird by association. And if I found myself dreaming about things I'd never dreamed before, things that belonged to that vanished time when magic had been as easy as maths, I managed to convince myself that none of that had ever been real, and that Bernie's mysterious party game was nothing more than one of those dreams.

But something was beginning to grow, silently across the years. Something that would take four decades to reach its full potential. Something that sounds like breaking glass and smells like burning rubber. And it starts as all these stories do.

With blood.

# TRACK 2:

---

# Manchild

# I

*From the LiveJournal of Bernadette Ingram (marked as Exhibit BI 1):*
*March 26th, 2022*

I had my music turned up loud. The man's voice cut right through it. I tried to ignore him. I wasn't afraid, and yet I could feel his aggression, like heat. I lengthened my stride from a jog to a run. Too late. He yanked out my earphones. I felt his hand grab my shoulder. I knew I should be frightened, and yet, somehow, I couldn't feel it. Maybe it was the music still playing tinnily into the night – Neneh Cherry, and 'Manchild'. I always liked that song, you know. Martin laughed at me for that. Hip-hop wasn't his thing at all. Kate Bush was his girl. And that *other* Kate, who still lives in his passwords.

*Don't you dare ignore me, bitch. Don't you fucking ignore me!*

Some dreams are so intensely real that they defy even reality. This one dragged me from Martin, and my memories of him and Kate, to that other place, that parallel world, where I was not myself, but some other woman, a woman alone and in terrible danger, telling herself that it's all a dream, that none of this can possibly be happening –

She's thinking about her living room. The pastel pictures on the walls. The oatmeal-coloured throw on the couch. The bookcase, with its colourful rows of paperbacks. Her children. There they are. Maddy and Sam. Their photographs, there on the mantelpiece, their faces rosy and smiling. She thinks, *Nothing bad can happen to me. This is my world. I'm safe here.*

But she is wrong.

His hand is still there. This stranger's hand on my shoulder. I can hear his voice, loud and strange. I can smell the aggression on him. *I'm talking to you. Don't ignore me. Don't you dare ignore me.*

I try to turn. But his other hand has already moved to my throat. Too late, I try to scream – to *breathe* – but too late. He has moved in closer. The stink of his rage is overwhelming. A sense of suffocation, a pressure on the side of my neck, and a thought – *This isn't happening. This isn't how it's supposed to be, I was going to make pizza tonight, I was going to read to the kids, and maybe have a long, hot bath, with lavender oil, that's good for stress, and oh, this can't be happening, oh, let me live, oh, let me breathe –*

And then, there's a feeling of slipping away, like a train going into a tunnel, and a muddled, half-waking memory of darkness, and the cold night sky, and the petrichor scent of soft damp earth, and the tinny ghost of Neneh Cherry playing into nothingness. And after that, for a time, I was dead, with his arms still clasped around me; dead, and yet still somehow aware of the damp earth under my body, and of his breathing, harsh and slow, and the smell of decomposition. And it felt like an eternity.

They call it *sleep paralysis.* I've had it half a dozen times, since the onset of menopause. I'm told it's not uncommon, but that doesn't make it less frightening. It feels like being buried alive in the basement of a haunted house; a basement long-abandoned, filled with relics of another life. It only lasts a few seconds, I'm told. But this morning it felt like forever. Lying there in the darkness; listening to the sounds from above; the footsteps of the living. Because that's the worst thing about being dead. Everyone else goes on living. The sun keeps shining. Years come and go. People fall in love, and out. But not you. That's over for you. Your life – that brief, bright, shining thing, barely glimpsed or understood before it was snuffed out – is at an end.

I tried to open my eyes, but I was dead. The sheets were cold. The earth was damp beneath me. *He's going to bury me*, I thought, and for a moment, I didn't know which of the two women I was – myself, or the other one, rapidly cooling on the ground, and I wanted to scream, but I was dead, and the walls of the house were collapsing –

And then I opened my eyes at last, saw daylight through the curtains. My bedroom curtains, dark blue, with a pattern of silver stars. My bedroom, with its familiar clutter of pictures and ornaments. *My* house, and *my* man, not hers, lying warm beside me –

The bedclothes beneath me were sticky and damp. My cotton nightshirt was wringing wet. For a time, I could still smell the ground, and that house, and the stagnant water, and now, a terrible butcher's-shop reek, like raw meat steeped in loose change. And I thought: *It wasn't real. Thank God. Thank God, I'm still alive.* Except for the blood. The blood was real, soaking the mattress beneath me.

I looked at the clock. It was six-fifteen.

What a way to start the weekend.

Gingerly, I rolled onto my side, and peeled myself free of the mattress. It made a kind of tearing sound, like ripping off a Band-Aid.

'Fuck's sake, Bernie,' Martin said, tugging at the duvet.

Martin likes to sleep in late, especially at weekends. I try not to wake him when I get up to go to work. I stood up, looked down at my nightshirt, butcher's-aproned black with blood, feeling blood run down my leg and into the bedroom carpet.

'Holy *fuck!*' He sprawled out of bed as if I'd stuck him with a cattle prod. 'What the fuck, Bernie? What happened?'

I shrugged.

'I thought all that was over?'

*All that.* Meaning, I suppose, what my mother used to call *The Curse*. But yes. He was right. I haven't bled for six months. I thought I knew what that meant. The end of my life as a mother and the beginnings of cronehood. Plus, the wild changes in thermostat; the food cravings; the night sweats; the sudden attacks of exhaustion; and now the terrible nightmares and attacks of sleep paralysis. At least the blood was over, I'd thought. Or, at least, I'd assumed until now.

'Jesus, Bernie.' He made a face. 'The bed looks like a crime scene. I'll have to get a shower.'

Martin showers twice a day, sometimes for twenty minutes or more. He says it helps him to relax. But he's a very tense person. He grabbed his clothes and vanished, leaving me to strip the bed. The blood had soaked all the way through the sheet and deep into the mattress, leaving a stain shaped like a semi-colon.

*That's never going to come out,* I thought. No point even trying. No amount of scrubbing or bleach would bring it back to its virgin state.

*Fuck!*

*I'll just turn over the mattress. Martin will never notice.* Martin never makes the beds. It's part of our arrangement. I take care of the garden, the house; Martin, the garage and the car. I decide what meals we eat; he keeps hold of the TV remote. I make the beds; I change the sheets, and sometimes, in an emergency, I turn the mattress over.

*Slut*, came a voice from the back of my mind. The voice of my inner critic. Some women have inner goddesses: I have my inner critic instead, who sounds something like my mother. *Good girls don't do that*, she said. *Only sluts cut corners.* Odd, how promiscuity in women is linked with untidiness in the home; as if a woman who enjoys sex must also dislike vacuuming. As a matter of fact, I enjoy neither. Both are household chores, designed to keep the home in order. Not that Martin is especially demanding in that respect. As long as the floors are clean, he doesn't seem to care much about the sex part. I used to think he might be having an affair. But now I don't believe he is. He's just the kind of man who finds it really, really hard to relax.

I remember what it was like when we first met as teen-agers. We really believed we were different then. We wanted to share everything. Kissing him for the first time felt like looking into his soul. Everything we did had meaning. Song lyrics existed for us alone. In films, we were the heroes. We fantasized about growing old together; chose the names of our children. We wanted to disappear into each other, like Salmacis and Hermaphroditus. But it's really all just hormones, you know. That joyous surge. The power. The *blood*. Love is a complex cocktail of dopamine and oxytocin, released by the hypothalamus via the pituitary gland. That's where the magic comes from. That's how Nature's trickery works.

Nowadays, my dopamine comes from checking my social media. A medical website I often visit says: *Social media mimics human connection, releasing dopamine when we get likes and comments.* Perhaps that's true. It's the first thing I do – at least, it is on normal days. On normal days, it starts before I even get out of bed. I turn on my phone and go online to find out what my friends have been doing. Of course, I know they're not *really* my friends. But the chemicals in my brain react to their images anyway.

In the bathroom, I could hear Martin moving around, slamming the shower cubicle door. I waited for him to finish, then showered (he had taken most of the hot water) and looked around for tampons. I managed to find a couple of packets of Maxi Pads at the back of the laundry cupboard, but was alarmed to see how fast the first one soaked through. I caught a glimpse of myself in the bathroom mirror as I fixed it on, and turned away with a shudder. Who the hell wants a mirror in their bathroom, anyway?

By now, it was nearly seven o'clock. Too late for me to go back to bed. I don't sleep very well nowadays and, of course, I work on a Saturday. Martin had gone to the guest room to finish his Saturday sleep-in. I always keep the bed made up there, just in case Dante comes home. I put the bed sheets in the wash, made tea, did my pelvic-floor exercises, then went online and googled *bleeding*, cross-referenced with *menopause*.

Look for *menopause*, and you'll find roughly eighty million hits, including medical websites, blogs, articles, research papers and a website called My Big Fat Menopause, run by an (unfeasibly slim and pretty) American influencer called DeeDee LaDouce, featuring mostly what she calls *Life Hacks*, as well as pictures of herself in a number of dream locations, alongside a series of affirmations designed to help women *live their best lives*.

On the subject of bleeding, DeeDee says: *Hey, goddesses! Remember to top up on iron for those days when the cardinal drops in unannounced! And, good news, there's as much iron in a square of dark chocolate as in a plateful of spinach!*

The medical website puts it rather more soberly: *Women may experience an increase in the amount and duration of bleeding episodes, which may occur at various times throughout the menopausal transition. These dramatic changes can be disconcerting and often provoke questions about whether something is wrong.*

No shit. Thanks to Google, I know all about what my mother (never at a loss for a phrase) rather ominously calls *The Change*. Not that she ever discussed it with me, just as she never really prepared me for menstruation. Instead, I learnt about it at school, in Biology, with Mrs Harding. She told us very little about the symptoms of menstruation – the pain, the mood swings, the hormones – but kept our attention focused on the *purpose* of this physical change: a purpose that expresses itself every twenty-eight days, in blood.

*Every month, until menopause, your body prepares for pregnancy.*

That made me think of the guest room at home, made up every week in case someone happened to stay over. No one did. During the whole of my childhood, it was only used a handful of times. And yet my mother kept changing the sheets; airing the room; preparing it for an occupant. Otherwise, why have a guest room at all? My body is like that, I told myself; preparing for pregnancy every month, only to find that the guest room is once more unoccupied, with nothing but more blood to clean up.

Of course, when I had Dante, that changed. The guest room suddenly came into its own. The plans we had made, Martin and I – to go to university together, Martin to study Marketing, me to study English – were suddenly, brutally overturned. Instead, we got married at eighteen, and I cared for our son at my parents' house, while Martin went to Leeds alone, pursuing his ambitions. And, in spite of my disgrace, and my mother's disappointment, the guest room was finally occupied. At last it had a purpose. My mother had always wanted a son. My son would be payment for the shame that I had brought on her. And she made it clear that my mothering skills were far below her own standards.

'You coddle him too much,' she'd say. 'You'll make him into a sissy.' And so *she* mothered him instead – and saw to his meals, and his nap times, and shortened his ridiculous name – so that by the time we left Malbry, he was already three years old, and, at the prospect of leaving her, cried all the way down the M1.

Now, Dante's old room has assumed the role of guest bedroom in our house. The last time Dante used it was three years ago, at Christmas. Since then, I've changed the bed every week; aired the sheets; brought flowers. I suppose that's what being a mother is. Most of that effort is wasted.

But no one told me this at thirteen. Mrs Harding made it sound as if we were training for the Olympics. *You are becoming young women*, she said. *That means preparing for pregnancy.*

I wondered what a woman became once she reached the menopause. Whatever it was, Mrs Harding didn't seem to find it worth talking about. Menopause is the end of life: the end of a woman's fertility. And when I had my first period, at the end of that dreadful Sports Day, it came with the sick realization that this would happen every month, for years and years, *until I was old* –

Of course, I don't feel old inside. Inside, I don't feel nearly fifty. Although DeeDee LaDouce makes fifty sound like the entrance to an amusement park, filled with great sex, cashmere throws, winter cruises down the Nile and luxury loungewear in pastel shades that never need dry-cleaning, inside, I'm still that eleven-year-old who never wanted to grow up.

I made some coffee and checked my phone. I do like social media. Like the Lady of Shalott, watching the world through her mirror, it often seems safer than real life. And online, I can watch those I love without being too conspicuous.

First comes Martin's Facebook. In it, he is intelligent, funny and approachable. Of course, he can be those things in real life. But online he seems more relaxed, more friendly, funnier, more familiar. Facebook is like a person's front room, tidied and cleared for visitors. There's no place for anger here, or rudeness, or indifference. Here, there's always something new: a joke, a conversation. Here, there are stories, and pictures of cats, and greetings from around the world. Here, he is always charming; always attentive and present. Like DeeDee, Martin's online self is airbrushed, and upbeat, and smiling.

I checked his private messages. He has no idea that I do this, just as he would never think to check for blood under the mattress. And, to be fair, I seldom see anything to concern me. But I still look from time to time, just for reassurance. His password is *DreamgirlKatie*. This too, he thinks is private.

No private messages today. A note to Dan about Easter. A debate between two of his colleagues. A political cartoon. A funny cat meme. A selfie, showing him at work, with one of his more famous authors. Nothing suspicious. Nothing strange. There was, however, this invitation from his friend, Lucas Hemsworth:

*30-year sixth form reunion! Pog Hill, class of '92! June 4th, 7.30, at Pog Hill Sixth Form College, Malbry. Nineties music, cocktails and more!*

Martin has already accepted the invitation. Nothing strange there – Lucas and Martin have always been close. Nineteen other people have already said they will attend. Linda Kite and Lorelei Jones, and some other names I recognize. Lucas, of course, and Katie. Katie Hemsworth, as she is now. I wonder what it would be like to see them again; what might have changed. I wonder if they remember me with scorn or with affection. I wonder if going back to Pog Hill would awaken the ghosts, or put them to rest. I wonder what I ought to wear.

Someone has posted some photographs. *Pog Hill, Class of '92*. Most of them were taken the night of the party we called the *Pog Hill Prom*. Here's Martin, looking impossibly young, and Lucas, and Katie, and the band. I do not feature in these, of course. I kept out of the spotlight. But there is one shot of me. It isn't a flattering picture. I think it must have been taken near the end of the evening. My hair is lank, my posture poor, and yet, I realize – too late – that this was the time at which I was at my most attractive. What a sad age is seventeen. So filled with self-hate and uncertainty. Desperately wishing for firmer breasts, better legs, a total absence of body hair. So grateful to be loved by him that you would have done anything. Sex is less of a pleasure and more of an affirmation. This is what it feels to have power. To provoke this kind of reaction. I wonder what it feels like now, to still have that power. I wonder if Katie Malkin ever understood what she had.

I made some more coffee and drank it while checking Dante's Instagram, which is mostly pictures of food. From this, I know that Dante enjoys Tex-Mex, and pizza, and fried things with cheese. I see that yesterday he was at a cocktail bar with friends. I didn't recognize any of them, but I thought my son looked happy.

DeeDee LaDouce says this about dealing with feelings of menopausal sadness. *Hey, gorgeous goddesses! Got the blues? Did you know exercise releases almost the same feel-good chemicals as sex? So try a walk in the park today! Or stay in bed with your special person and beat the blues the old-fashioned way!*

Oh, DeeDee. Not an option. And after that dream, the thought of the park fills me with apprehension. The damp ground. The scent of leaves long-dead. The sound of traffic, baffled by leaves. Some dreams are so very specific that they cling to the waking consciousness. Last night's dream was like that, I thought; a slice of discarded memory.

I opened Twitter. That's where I find all my news. Martin still buys paper newspapers. But Twitter is enough for me; and I tend to graze there accordingly. On there I am *@theberniemoon*, and I tend not to interact very much, except as my work persona, *@KafkaTheBookshopCat*. Salena, my boss, co-runs that account, so I tend not to use it from home. I looked down at the trending topics. One headline instantly caught my eye, marked in my settings as *Local News*. *Finchley Mother-of-Two Found Dead After Jogging in Park*. On a different day, I might have scrolled right past. I don't go online to bask in bad news, and there's already so much of that. But this time I clicked, for two reasons. First, I live two streets away from the park where she was murdered. The second was, I recognized her. I'd sold her a book less than two weeks ago.

I felt the approach of a hot flash, gathering under my armpits. I shouldn't drink coffee, I told myself. But, dammit, I *like* coffee. And today, I need the energy that my caffeine fix delivers.

I clicked on the photo. Yes, that was her. Jo Perry. Thirty. Mousy-blonde hair, rather closer to pretty than plain. Looking a little tired that day, in a denim jumpsuit and platform shoes. She'd asked for something escapist. *Something by a woman.* I suggested *The Hundred Thousand Kingdoms* by N. K. Jemisin. She came back the following week to buy the rest of the trilogy. That was the Tuesday before she died. I told myself that if I'd known, I'd have picked something shorter.

The hot flash swept over my face, leaving beads of sweat that rolled into the creases of my neck. I hadn't even put make-up on, and already I felt disgusting. Not that I usually bother with trying to use make-up much. My mother thought it was slutty, and the last time I tried a lipstick that wasn't my usual pale pink, Martin said I looked like a clown. Now, I don't even need to try. Nobody sees me anymore.

I scrolled through the piece. It was very brief. Jo had been to a Pilates class at seven o'clock at her local gym. She had decided to take a run around the park before heading home. She never arrived. At 6 a.m., a jogger discovered her body. Jo had been wearing leggings in a jaunty raspberry-pink, and a grey sweatshirt with the slogan: *Feminist Killjoy*.

I wonder if that was what caught his eye. A joke by day, perhaps, it acquires a sinister meaning by night.

*Woman Found Dead After Jogging* implies that jogging itself is dangerous. Women – or so we are led to believe – are not murdered for nothing.

I seldom read the comments, but this time I couldn't stop myself.

*@goonr1966: Shouldn't of been out at night.*

*@runninghilda1975: I always run with a buddy. It's common sense.*

*@whitey2947: Why was she wearing that sweatshirt? She must have known it would piss people off*

You forget, though, *@whitey2947*: Jo Perry is the victim. The man who stole her life is to blame. Murder is not an accident. Ready access to victims doesn't make an innocent man any more likely to commit a crime. And yet, some of these comments seem to suggest a world in which the reverse is true:

a world in which women are fair game, like money left lying on the ground. Loose women, like loose change, awaiting some man to pick them up.

I can almost see him now. One of those middle-aged white men who run to fat in their forties. Joggers, vest and running shoes – gear that can confer a kind of invisibility to a man alone, in the evening. He smells of sweat and Lynx body spray. His face is hidden in shadow. He steps directly into her path, forcing her to move aside. And I can almost hear his voice, raised as the woman turns away.

*Don't you dare ignore me, bitch!*

The hot flash has now become a shower of sparks across my skin. They prickle there like electrodes, delivering an intermittent current. I should drink a glass of water, I think. That often tempers the worst of it. But I am unable to move, or to react to the surge of sensations.

*Don't you dare ignore me!*

Funny, how dreams can seem so real that they are almost memories. This one is like that. The scent of damp earth; the lights from the street; the comforting sound of the music that comes to her through her earphones. *Ignore him. He's a creep*, she thinks. *Ignore him, just keep running.* To Jo, the situation feels at the same time mundane and deeply surreal. The stranger in his joggers. The song, from a playlist she made up last week, mostly nineties electronica, with a cheery smattering of hip-hop. *And besides, who dies to a soundtrack like that? Who dies running a stupid 3K?*

The comments on the little screen kept scrolling in time to the memory.

*@whitey2947: It's tragic, but why was she out there at night?*

*@radfem_Bonnie95: She was only running.*

*@jimfromthegym69: not fast enough, apparently* 🌀

*@radfem_Bonnie95: not funny, asshole*

*@jimfromthegym69: relax, can't you take a joke?* 🌾

*@theberniemoon: She's a woman, not a punchline.*

*@jimfromthegym69: if you can't see the difference between a joke and murder then you're the one with the problem, babe*

*@theberniemoon:*


It feels like a hot flash, but now I'm beginning to understand what it really is. There's something about a woman's rage that feels very old, very primal. A man's rage may be more physical, but a woman's rage is born from centuries of violence. It calls across cultures. It calls across race. It is old, and hungry, and dark, and does not know its power. *Yet.* But wielded correctly, it can reduce men to snivelling little boys. I know. I've seen it. A long time ago, but somehow it feels like yesterday. And it feels somehow terribly dangerous, like a bomb that has been hidden in the foundations of a house since some forgotten, unspeakable war, unearthed now by accident, all rusted and ominous and filled with horrific potential . . .

*Jo, a primary school teacher, leaves a grieving husband of nine years, David, and two young children, Maddy and Sam.*

Pictures in a haunted house. Reflections in a laptop screen. The flash of something glimpsed from afar, at night, in a rear-view mirror. The scent of dead leaves; the traffic sounds. A siren in the distance. The memory of how it felt, now crammed into a box on a shelf, along with all the others.

*There.*

He choked her from behind. I know. It doesn't take long, if you know the technique. In any case, Jo Perry was unconscious in thirty seconds. He kept the hold for five minutes more, just to be certain. And it felt good, lying on top of her on the grass, face pressed hungrily into her hair.

I don't know how I know these things, but I know them as surely as if I'd been there. Just as I know that this morning's dream – and the blood – wasn't just a coincidence. Just as I know that Jo Perry was going to make pizza on the night she was killed. Just as I know that her children's names are Maddy and Sam. And just as I know that the last thing she heard as she slipped into the dark was Neneh Cherry, and 'Manchild'.

# 2

Instincts gained in childhood never completely disappear. That way of flinching at certain sounds, certain familiar gestures. The ominous, sinking feeling of dread when you feel you've done something shameful. The desire to fill the inner void with *something* – food, social media, love – anything to try and appease the swirling vortex of emptiness. The inner critic, with its more-than-familiar roundelay of complaints, reproaches and warnings:

*Bad girl! Bad girl! You promised you'd never do that again!*

The thought comes accompanied by a scent of dead leaves, wet grass and petrichor, and something else, unexpectedly sweet. The smell of synthetic strawberry.

*Abracadabra!*

*No, not again. You said you'd never do that again. His arms. The cuts all down his arms. Never again. Never again.*

Martin was still in bed when I left. I'd been considering phoning in sick. I was feeling sore and washed out, and I had the start of a headache. On top of that, the murder of a young woman half a mile from my door – on top of that strangely *specific* dream – had left me feeling shaken and strange. But

Saturdays are busy at Salena's Books, and however bad I felt, I couldn't leave her to cope alone.

Salena is not quite a friend, but she is maybe the person I talk to most. She's thirty, lives with her parents, and runs the bookshop on their behalf. I suppose that, technically, makes her my boss, although it doesn't feel that way. Maybe it's because she's so young – about the same age as Dante. Martin thinks the business is financially unsustainable, but then, his branch of publishing is built on a different model. LifeStory Press is quick to point out that it is not a vanity publisher, but authors pay between five and ten thousand pounds for the LifeStory package, which advertises regularly in *Saga Magazine* and *The Oldie*, and mostly publishes memoirs and illustrated children's books. Salena does not stock their books. This does not play well with Martin. And yet, I do enjoy my job. It's close to the house – twenty minutes on foot – and it gives me the chance to meet people. So I took two paracetamol and set out at a quarter to nine, hoping the fresh air would clear my head and banish the lingering after-effects of this morning's unpleasant start.

Wrong. I was barely halfway there when the hot flash hit me. Of course, I should have known it would. I shouldn't have skipped breakfast. I was passing the gates of the park where she died – gates which are locked today, and tied with the black-and-yellow tape that marks it out as a crime scene. Perhaps that's what triggered the hot flash. But suddenly I felt terrible; weak, and shaky, almost in tears, pulse racing, close to exhaustion.

*His arms. The cuts on his arms.*

The smell of synthetic strawberry was suddenly over-whelming. No, not just the scent, the *taste*. Fasting induces a catabolic state, as it starts to use up the energy stored in the body's fat cells. But flavour is stored in those cells too, releasing the experience of things you tasted a long time ago. Today, the taste of something I hadn't eaten since I was a child suddenly overwhelmed me.

*Abracadabra. She chose strawberry!*

This isn't happening, I thought. It's just that I didn't have breakfast. Blood sugar can fluctuate wildly during menopause. DeeDee LaDouce recommends low-carb meals regularly throughout the day. A handful of edamame beans, or maybe a courgette brownie.

There was a café across the street. Its name was Priscilla's Pantry. I crossed and went to the counter, and looked at the display of pastries. None of them looked like the kind of thing DeeDee LaDouce would recommend.

*Be careful. You'll get fat*, said the voice of my inner critic.

Whose voice is that, anyway? I've heard it ever since I was a child; that spiteful voice, that tells me that I'm too ugly, too lazy, too fat — but too fat for what? Too fat to be loved? Too fat for my space? Too fat to deserve attention? Or was it the other way around? Was I afraid of being accused of somehow attracting attention, of stealing the spotlight away from those who might be more deserving?

There was a man in front of me, lingering over his choice of cake. A big man in a sleeveless shirt, occupying his chosen space with the comfortable conviction of someone who has never been told that a piece of cake must be earned, rather than just enjoyed. He didn't notice me, or seem concerned that I was waiting. I'm used to this, of course. I watched him linger between a slice of coffee cake and a doughnut. Eventually, he ordered both, along with a caramel latte. The pink-haired girl at the counter served him, while, behind her, a girl in a hijab operated the coffee machine. There came the sound of rushing steam, and the smell of fresh-ground coffee. I found myself craving a latte, but dismissed the thought regretfully.

The pink-haired girl smiled at the man and said; 'Hungry this morning, love? Good for you!' as if she were speaking to a child. It occurred to me then how often men – like children – are praised for doing everyday things. Doing the washing-up. Minding the kids. Choosing to eat a piece of cake. I doubt the girl would have said the same if I had done the same thing. I might even have got a raised eyebrow: I've put on half a stone since Christmas.

My Big Fat Menopause has this to say about weight gain: *I know it's hard to admit to yourself that you'll never fit back into those size 8 jeans. But hey! You gorgeous goddesses! You're beautiful, whatever your size! Flaunt your curves! Embrace your sensuality! Your man certainly will!*

I sense that DeeDee LaDouce does not have much experience of weight gain. If size 8 jeans are her problem, then she doesn't have much of a problem at all. And how exhausting she must be to her friends. All those exclamations. All those cups of herbal tea and pomegranate salads. All that lounging by the pool. All that sex and yoga.

I finally ordered breakfast tea and a skinny muffin. The hot flash was thankfully over by then, although my shirt was glued to my skin. I could feel sweat pooling in the hollow of my back. I hadn't even made it to work and already I needed a shower.

'Eat in or take out?'

'In, please.'

The girl rang up my purchases with a thin, professional smile. Maybe twenty-two; sullen mouth; a piercing in one eyebrow. A name tag on her uniform gave her name as IRIS. For a second, our fingers touched as she handed me the change, and I felt a sudden electrical charge, like those people who claim to pick up radio signals through their teeth. For a second, I saw myself, as if reflected in window glass: sour-faced, unfriendly, old.

*Another one who can't give a shit. Too busy even to say hello.*

For a moment, I thought she had spoken aloud. 'What did you say?'

'Nothing.' But I thought she sounded uncertain. For a moment, her gaze held mine: troubled, no longer indifferent. I wondered if all women were torn between feeling invisible and feeling horribly exposed; as if the gaze of the world were a lens that could burn you up as easily as blur you out of existence. I felt a sudden, poignant sympathy for her: under-paid, discontented, unnoticed, and, like most women of her age, unaware of her beauty.

I smiled and said impulsively; 'Iris, I love your hair.'

Again, that look of uncertainty. But this time her smile was genuine. 'Thank you! I thought I'd treat myself.'

'You did right. It suits you.'

I took my muffin and tea to an armchair by the window. I brushed past the man with two cakes as I passed, sitting facing the counter. I could see the back of his head, the gym muscles in his fleshy arms revealed by his sleeveless sports shirt. Being next to Iris had felt like suddenly seeing a light come on in a stranger's house, and hearing their conversation. Now it was gone. What had it been? Brain fog? Sugar imbalance? Or worse?

*You read her mind, Bernie.*

*I didn't. It was an accident.*

*You know where this leads. Remember? Remember his house. The basement. Remember the way he used to flinch whenever you came near him. Remember the state of the house, the walls. And the cuts. The cuts on his arms.*

The medical website has this to say about hormonal changes in menopause: *Hormone imbalances cause many women to overreact to things that never used to trouble them. Beyond the physical changes you may be going through at this time, you may also be dealing with empty-nest syndrome, ageing parents, grief issues, infidelity, or generally looking back on your life.*

My Big Fat Menopause says this: *Hey, you gorgeous goddesses! Hot flashes and stress getting you down? Try to think of it this way instead: You're in for a craaaazy Hot Girl Summer!*

Both DeeDee and the medical site then go on in their different ways to advise women to lose weight, to eat more seeds, to load up on antioxidants, to take the stairs whenever they can, to de-clutter the house, to consider antidepressants, and to make sure to make some time for themselves, whether that's sitting down with a good book, having a relaxing bath, or taking up a new hobby. It also makes sure to mention making an effort for your partner, and writing things down to avoid forgetting them. Nowhere on either website, however, does it tell women how to tell whether or not they've developed mind-reading skills. Hormones aren't meant to work that way. Hormones are at the same time something that changes everything, and something of a joke, just as hormonal women are a joke; over-dramatic; untrustworthy.

I bit into my muffin. It was dry and unpleasant. *I should have had the doughnut*, I thought. *If I'm going to have extra calories, they might as well be good ones*. I could see the doughnut man eating his. It looked delicious. I could almost taste the cream; the sweetness of the strawberry jam against the softness of the dough.

*Good girls don't eat doughnuts*, my inner critic reminded me. As if I needed reminding. I had a sudden image of myself eating the doughnut, nevertheless; living my best life; flaunting my curves; not caring what anybody thought. *Visible women flaunt their curves. Invisible ones steal your doughnut.*

I closed my eyes. I could taste it now. The jam was black-currant, not strawberry. I could feel sugar around my mouth; sugar on my fingers. So real, I thought. Almost as real as if I were biting into it myself. Once more, there came the sensation of lights coming on in a darkened house, the reflection of an intimate scene. A man eating a doughnut. A pink-haired girl at a counter.

*I'd give her one*, said an inner voice. *I bet she's a right little goer.* What?

Automatically, I reached to brush the sugar from my lips. At the same time, the monologue – no longer my inner critic, but something else entirely – seemed to grow more persistent.

*She likes me too. She called me love. I wonder when she gets off work? Got to be careful, though. Play it cool. Not like last time. That wasn't me.*

Of course, it was nothing so flat and precise. The words are a kind of translation. But the feelings, the sentiment – all that was real and utterly three-dimensional; as real as if I'd opened a box and let a cloud of moths escape. Suddenly, I was no longer looking into a house. I was *there*, awash with sensations. The man's reaction to Iris. (The other girl barely registered.) The smell of his caramel latte. The effortless feeling of taking up space. The pleasure of physicality, of biting into a doughnut –

*And it feels good, doesn't it, Bernie? It feels so good. Because it's wrong.*

Once more, I reached up to brush away the sugar from around my mouth. The taste of blackcurrant jam was still almost overwhelming. And now I could smell Lynx and old sweat, and feel the roughened palms of his hands all sticky with sugar and sweet whipped cream, and feel his slow confusion as he finished his doughnut in one bite, and turned round abruptly to stare at me as if I'd prodded him in the back.

I let my eyes drop to my plate; made a show of pouring tea. Those phantom sensations were gone again. (Or had they really been phantoms?) The house was once more in darkness. But the voice of my inner critic had risen to a hysterical scream:

*Bad girl! Bad girl! You weren't going to do that anymore!*

I felt a prickling of shame, like a hot flash across my chest. The inner voice was right, I knew. I'd opened a box from the past that had been safely and properly tidied away, and now the box was open again, the box I'd put away for good. And inside the box was the dream of last night: the scent of stagnant water, and the cool breath of the night air, and the distant sound through her headphones, playing Neneh Cherry –

*You went in. You flipped him. Like Mr D –*

*That was years ago. I was a child. It wasn't real. In fact, I can hardly remember –*

Except that I can. I remember it all. That box was never completely sealed; only ever hidden. Just as the secrets of childhood were eclipsed by the gift of womanhood; of blood; the gift that keeps on taking. Women and blood have always been close. Wise blood; profane blood; forbidden blood; spilled blood. Blood that is at different times both primal and accusing; disgusting and exciting; provoking horror, shame and lust – and, sometimes, the promise of something else. Something stronger than womanhood. Something I believed was lost, until I felt it again today. Something almost like *power*.

# 3

People are like houses. We all have public spaces. Well-lit façades; neat gardens. Pictures of loved ones on the walls. A mirror over the mantelpiece. These are the carefully chosen things that other people are meant to see. But, most of the time, we're inside the house, and what happens there is private. Not all of it, not always. Sometimes we let friends inside. People we trust absolutely. Sometimes we show those people around. Sometimes we even build rooms for them. But there are places where no one goes. Attics filled with lumber. Cellars filled with boxes. Crawl spaces crammed with broken things. This is where we hide those things that we don't want other people to see. Sometimes – very often, in fact – we don't even want to remember them.

To understand what happened today in Priscilla's Pantry, I have to go back a long, long way, to a place I'd almost forgotten. I have quite a lot of these places. I've collected them over the years. But some of them are hidden away deep in the foundations of a house that has acquired many, many storeys since then.

As a child, my house was child-sized. Simple. No cellars or attics. No labyrinth, peopled by monsters. Playing House was so easy then. There were no forbidden rooms, no broken mirrors, no dead space. And playing House is one of the things that little girls learn early. It seemed so very normal then. To go to a friend's house to play; to rearrange their furniture. To share their toys, their games, their lives. That's how it started with Katie. As a harmless childhood game. Later, it grew into something else. But, at the start, that's all it was. A blanket fort around us both. A pastel-coloured playhouse of dreams.

I remember Katie Malkin as a little round-faced girl with black hair and an invisible friend called Mog. Except that Mog wasn't invisible, not to either of us, then. In those days, we both saw him. In those days, we were inseparable. Our mothers were friends. We'd known each other since birth: we'd been on holidays together. We wore each other's clothes; we answered each other's sentences. And playing *House* was as much a part of our world as *Play School*, or milk at break times. It needed no explanation. We'd shared it since we could remember. Katie and I were two halves of a whole. People mistook us for sisters. And we shared *everything* in those days. My bedtime stories. Her imaginary friend. We swapped the taste of my Milky Bar for that of her Opal Fruits; her broccoli cheese for my apple pie. And I *liked* being in Katie's house. I liked it better than my own. It felt safe in Katie's house, as if nothing bad could ever happen there. I wanted to stay there forever, surrounded by pastel ponies with fairy wings, and enchanted castles, and secrets, and Mog.

Our friendship went on throughout primary school and right on into junior school. We always sat together in class; we walked home after school hand in hand. And although we were opposites in some ways – she was pretty, I was less so; she was good at sports, while I was an avid reader – we always *completed* instead of trying to compete with each other.

During that time, our special game had become increasingly part of our lives. We used it to help each other at school. To talk to each other without using words. It was fun; and it meant that we were never told off for talking in class. And when it was lunchtime, and one of us didn't like what we'd been given, we just flipped the taste for something else, so that the dinner ladies wouldn't notice.

And then, along came Adam Price. The new boy, arriving among us like a lit firework in a Christmas stocking. No one was ready for Adam Price at that nice little school, but Katie and I, with our special game, were especially unprepared.

We were in our first year at Chapel Lane Junior School. Katie was nearly eight years old: I was eight months behind her. It was December, and we had snow; snow of the kind you only see in movies and in childhood. All of us had come to school in boots and scarves and woolly hats, and we had brought indoor shoes to wear, to avoid bringing snow into the classroom. We weren't expecting a new boy – the term was almost at an end – but there he was one Monday, two weeks before the Christmas break, waiting to be introduced to the class by Mrs White, our teacher. He was a small and wiry boy with hair and eyelashes so pale that they looked almost tinselly, and one of those pinched, angry faces I associated with Sunnybank Park, and the streets of pebble-dashed houses on the estate we called White City.

I don't think the concept of *poverty* was something we really understood. But there was *something* about the new boy that made us feel uncomfortable. Perhaps it was his ill-fitting clothes, or the shape of his mouth, or his accent. Perhaps it was the perpetual rage that came off him like a fever. It was too late in the year to make friends, even if Adam had wanted to. But when Mrs White introduced him, she said he might be feeling shy, and urged us all to be kind to him, and we were curious to know about the new boy's history.

Adam wasn't feeling shy. He was one of those bony, under-sized boys who compensate by being aggressive. He glared; he swore; he kicked his desk; and that very lunchtime he picked a fight with Matthew Sweeney – a big, slow boy who had been quietly building a snowman – apparently just because he was bored and angry not to be involved. By the time Mrs White intervened, Matthew's nose had been bleeding, and there was a trail of red in the snow. Adam, who hadn't been wearing a coat, was looking more pinched than ever. Mrs White at first assumed that Matthew had upset him somehow, but we already knew better. Adam Price was a ticking bomb, and however much we avoided him, it was only a matter of time before Katie or I got in his way.

It happened to be Katie. It could just as easily have been me. But this time it was Katie, who usually got along with everyone. There was a dressing-up box in our class, all filled with different costumes and props. We loved that box, but we always took turns to share it with the other kids. That lunch-time, we were dressing up as pirates in the costume den, when gradually it became clear to me that Adam Price was watching.

He'd been at the school for just over a week. During that time, we'd had ample occasion to judge him. Everyone else had a pencil case; but Adam didn't have pencils, or a bag, or even a handkerchief. His nose ran, and his upper lip was always sore and reddened, and when he saw something he wanted, he always took it, and never said please. Looking at it now, I know that Adam was a damaged child, an unhappy child, maybe even an abused child: but all I saw then was a mean boy, a dirty boy who said bad words and wouldn't share the toy box.

'Get out, you. I want to play.' He talked like that – in bullet points, and in a flat kind of monotone. 'Playing pirates isn't for girls.'

'It is so for girls,' said Katie. 'We play pirates all the time.'

'Girls are stupid,' Adam said. 'Girls can't even pee standing up.'

'They so can!' said Katie, who even then was bolder than I was. 'Girls can do anything boys can do.'

Adam said: 'Prove it.'

She said: 'I will.'

The taste of a strawberry Opal Fruit for that of a mouthful of pork pie. A table, turned on a mirrored stage. A house, flung open to the winds. One moment Adam was standing there scowling by the dressing-up box; the next, he was grinning and dancing around, saying: *Look! Look at me! Look at me! I'm a girl!*

Beside me, Katie was staring. Her face looked somehow blank and unformed, like a Katie-mask that allowed someone else's expression to show through. Horror and disbelief were splashed all over her like paint.

'Stop it,' she said in a low voice.

But Adam kept singing and dancing about. 'Look at me! I'm a girl! I'm a girl!' He picked up a princess crown from the box and put it on his head, all the time, singing: *Look! I'm a girl! I'm a princess!*

'Stop it,' said Adam, in Katie's voice.

'I can do whatever I like! I'm a *pirate* princess!'

'Please,' said Adam, whose features under Katie's black hair no longer looked even a bit like hers. That pinched and angry look was there for anyone who cared to see – and in that moment I wondered what Adam had seen, what reflections Katie had glimpsed of him from inside his house.

I felt a sudden sense of dread.

*Abracadabra.*

*Get out, Katie. Now!*

I tried to attract her attention. But everything was turned around. The blanket fort; the invisible friend. The rooms filled with pastel daydreams. Now I was looking into a house of dreadful confusion, as if the Great Carovnik's trick had collapsed as she turned the table, leaving her with nothing but shattered crystal, broken plates.

And then she and Adam both went very still, looking at one another. For a moment, no one moved, or even seemed to be breathing. Adam's face slid back to its old expression of rage. Katie sat down hard, as if her legs had suddenly given way. And then Adam was on top of her like a bear with a headful of bees, pushing her face into the floor, hitting her again and again, crying and panting and using words that Katie and I didn't even know —

*Bitch! Cunt! Fucking whore!*

When do boys and men learn those words? Did Adam even know what they meant? Or were they just magical formulae, designed to rob girls of their power? Once more, Mrs White intervened. Adam was crying and flailing so hard by then that he gave her a black eye. Katie had a bloody nose and a scrape on her chin, but luckily, the carpet had prevented too much damage. I went to comfort her, but she pulled away, and Mrs White took her to the nurse, while Adam went into the Quiet Room, where children sometimes went to calm down.

It took him over half an hour. I watched the time on the big round clock that hung over the classroom door. Mrs White tried to cover the noise by reading us a story, but we could all hear Adam next door, swearing and crying and thumping the walls. It was frightening. He didn't sound like a seven-year-old boy. He sounded like a monster from a scary story, a ravening monster that wanted our blood.

His mother was called in that day to talk to the headmaster. Katie's parents came in too, but Katie refused to say what she'd done to upset Adam so badly. She just said we'd been playing a game, and that Adam had pushed her. She did not speak to me at all, or look at me, or even acknowledge I was there. Her house was shut tight. The lights were all off. Mog was nowhere to be seen.

We never saw Adam at Chapel Lane again. I understood from scraps of overheard conversation that he'd been taken into care because of his family's circumstances. Katie stayed away from school for the last few days of term, and didn't speak to me over Christmas, not even in the regular way. Her mother, Maggie, came to our house for lunch, but Katie stayed at home, and her present stayed under the Christmas tree when all the rest had been opened. Then, when we came back to school, she pretended not to understand when I asked her what was wrong, but, instead of taking her usual place at the desk next to me in class, she went to sit with Lorelei Jones, and walked home with her arm in arm, and told the others to tell me we weren't best friends anymore.

*What happened? What did I do?*

Her eyes were dark; unreadable. Her house, so open to me before, was plastered with signs reading: *WARNING: KEEP OUT: PRIVATE.* Even her front room was dark. I tried to touch her hand, but she turned away, shaking her head so fiercely that her black hair was a blur.

'Please. I just want to talk to you.'

Once more, she shook her head.

'I saw something really funny today. I'll show you if you let me in.'

She turned and fixed me with a gaze as sharp and cold as a hunting hawk's. 'I don't want to do that. Ever again. Go away, and leave me alone.'

I cried myself to sleep that night. The next day, Katie ignored me. I told myself that she would come back eventually. She had to. She was my best friend. But no amount of trying, of heliographing of messages, ever got me a response. We continued to see each other at school, and when our parents socialized. But the thing we had shared – the game we called *House*, our magical friendship – was over.

Childhood is filled with such everyday woes. Small dramas. Small betrayals. No one paid much attention to mine, or questioned Katie's defection. Except for my mother, who seemed almost as upset about it as I was. Maggie, Katie's mother, had always been a part of our lives, and both of them had always assumed that our friendship would grow alongside theirs. *Friends are so important*, my mother used to say to me. *I've been friends with Maggie since long before I met your dad*. It's something she still says to me, now that Dad's gone. *Our friends outlive our marriages. That's why you need to keep them close*. Perhaps my lack of close friends is part of the disappointment I hear in her voice whenever we happen to speak on the phone. My emptiness, her disappointment. Two sides of the same dismal currency. As if Katie Malkin had been the glue that kept us both together. But by the end of that first year at school, Katie and I had grown so far apart that even I hardly remembered the closeness that she and I had shared. And, of course, by that time, *House* had evolved into something different.

*House*. It sounds so harmless. But like so many children's games – *Ring a Ring o' Roses, Murder in the Dark, Mr Wolf* – it had a sinister side. Children are like animals: through play, they acquire the skills that they will need in later life. Boys play with weapons. Girls play House. And sometimes, with each other.

*You stole his doughnut, Bernadette.*

No. That isn't possible.

*You did. You flipped him. Just like before. Just like Katie flipped Adam Price.*

That wasn't real. That was a dream.

*It wasn't a dream. Remember –*

Sometimes, it comes in blood. Sometimes, it comes in memory. And sometimes, it comes like thunder in the taste of a jam and cream doughnut, a fugitive glimpse of memory –

# 4

Memory is a curious thing. Nothing is really forgotten. It lives on, persists in a million ways, it hides in your muscles and synapses; in cells you thought were dormant. It shows itself sometimes in dreams. Its triggers are often sensations.

*Proust had his madeleine*, I thought. *I had a jam and cream doughnut.*

That's how it started. That doughnut. But that's not where the memory lives. It lives somewhere else, somewhere darker. And now I was in this other's house; this man, with his caramel latte and his uneaten piece of coffee cake, my mouth still full of the taste of his unfinished blackcurrant doughnut.

*Get out, Bernie. Get out, now!*

But I couldn't. I was there. The thing I'd been dreading for thirty years was finally upon me at last, and I was frozen; helpless; feeling the weight of that memory like a ceiling about to collapse –

Not that it looked like collapsing just then. And honestly, there was nothing there to suggest that I was in danger. His house looked a lot like my mother's house – or, at least, the front room did. Knick-knacks on the bookshelves; pictures on the walls. A mirror over the mantelpiece, reflecting the interior. And behind the showroom, the *real* house: the storerooms and backrooms and basements.

Of course, it's nothing as simple as that. Houses are more like assemblages of feelings and thoughts and memories than actual furniture. A scene through a lighted window. A glance in the dark, from a passing car. To me, it still *seems* like a house, just as it did when I was a child. But an adult's house is so much bigger and more complicated than the houses we build in childhood. And this man's was the first adult house I'd been in since I was thirteen. I didn't want to be in it now, but something had triggered a response as I was sharing his doughnut. Something that was warm as blood, and cold as a distant memory.

*This isn't happening*, I thought. *This is a menopausal fugue, brought on by stress and sleeplessness. DeeDee would probably recommend a glass of iced cucumber water, or maybe some gentle stretching.*

My laughter echoed eerily. I flinched. *I can't be here*, I thought. *Whatever I'm doing, it's dangerous.* But the thing I'd felt as I touched him – that sense of wrongness – persisted. I hadn't just *seen* him, I told myself. For a moment, I'd *been* him. Everything had come from that. The memories, the reflections, the fears. From the taste of a blackcurrant doughnut.

*Magic isn't real*, said the voice of the inner critic in my mind.

And yet it *is*. As real as blood. As real as his thought: *Not like last time.*

*It's none of your business, Bernie*, said the voice of the inner critic. *This man has nothing to do with you. Get out, before you do damage. You know that happens. You've done it before.*

And yes, this time my mother was right. But there was something about this man that made it difficult to leave. The way he'd looked at Iris, the pink-haired girl at the counter.

*She likes me too. She called me love. I wonder when she gets off work?* And underneath it, that afterthought: coloured darker in his mind: *Got to be careful, though. Play it cool. Not like last time. That wasn't me.*

*Bad girl! You shouldn't be here!* By now, the inner critic sounded almost hysterical. I sent her to the Quiet Room – my equivalent of the room in which turbulent pupils were sent at school – while I looked into Doughnut Guy's house. Of course she wouldn't stay there – I could already hear her cries of outrage, dimly, through the walls – but it would give me a little respite.

*OK. What are you telling me?*

There's something about being in someone's house. It's like a physicality. When you break a bone, you know. When I was pregnant with Dante, I knew. When I awoke this morning in a caul of blood, I knew. When I passed the gates of the park and saw them closed with crime-scene tape, and felt the hot flash seize me in its burning claws, I knew. Just like that other man, years ago. I could feel it, just as I could feel the heat of the coffee cup in his hands, the doughnut sugar on his chin. My body was telling me *something*, with every nerve and synapse. But my mind didn't want me to hear.

*His arms. The cuts on his arms.*

*Shut up!*

I slapped the laminate table hard enough to hurt. Doughnut Guy looked around, and I realized from the look on his face that I was back where I belonged. I felt the blood rush to my face – not a hot flash this time, but a rush of simple embarrassment. I pulled out my phone, and pretended to look at it. Doughnut Guy was still watching me. I felt a sharp prickle of anxiety, followed by the stinging sensation that always heralds a hot flash. *Was* it a hot flash this time, or a reaction to what

I'd seen? Either way, I could feel it now, surging hungrily over my skin. I was sure he could see it too; like some kind of luminescence.

I turned my attention deliberately to my uneaten muffin. I could see every poppy seed standing out individually, like boulders on a landscape viewed from an impossible height. I reached to pick up my teacup and saw that my hand was shaking.

Doughnut Guy got up from his seat and came over to my table. For the first time, I saw him clearly. Mid- to late forties; muscular; head shaved to hide a bald patch; a broad and not unpleasant face, lit by a pair of bright blue eyes. For a moment, he stood there, watching me. Then he grinned.

'It *is* you, isn't it?' he said.

I stared at him. Did I know this man? I could feel myself burning up. My armpits prickled. My face was hot. I could feel a trickle of sweat forming in the small of my back. I felt excruciatingly exposed, like in one of those dreams, when you step onto a stage to find yourself naked in front of an audience of thousands, and worse still, I was suddenly sure that what I'd seen in his house had been nothing but a momentary fugue; just an extravagant episode of menopausal brain fog.

He said: 'You're Marty's wife, right? Birdie, isn't it?'

'Bernie,' I said.

'That's right. Bernie!' The grin widened. 'Jim Wood. Woody. Jim from the gym. Remember me now?'

And yes, I did. Suddenly, all my self-belief came crashing down around me. I *hadn't* looked into this man's house. I *knew* him. I'd actually met him before. I'd even seen his comments this morning on my Twitter feed: *@jimfromthegym69*. Of course. I'd projected all my discomfort – the cramps, the hot flashes, my vivid dream, the shocking news of a murder, plus the equally troubling fact that I'd once met the victim – onto this man, who just happened to come into the same café that morning.

My face burned. 'Jim, from the gym. Of course. How could I forget you?'

Some years ago, Martin had decided he was putting on too much weight. He'd hired a personal trainer to help him work out. *Jim from the gym*. At first, we'd laughed. Martin and he had nothing at all in common. Jim Wood had been addicted to protein shakes and cardio. Martin sometimes went running, but only as an excuse to listen to audiobooks. Nevertheless, the two became friends. And although Martin's good intentions had been, at best, sporadic, he had maintained the friendship, although I'd only met Jim Wood once. And yes, I do remember it well.

It must have been three or four years ago. Martin had arranged to meet two of his gym buddies and their partners for lunch at a local sports pub. But the 'partners' had turned out to be two yoga instructors, who had settled down with the other two to watch a match on the wide-screen TV, while I picked at my pizza slice and tried to look invisible. It wasn't at all difficult. The girls were both in their twenties, blonde and pretty and slim-hipped. I could have been their mother, I thought. Next to them, I felt like a buffalo.

Jim Wood said: 'You're looking well.'

'Thanks.'

And now that I really saw him again, I could picture that afternoon, with the smell of beer and second-hand smoke wafting in through the windows, and the deafening sound of wide-screen TVs, blaring out different channels. He had been wearing a sleeveless T-shirt emblazoned with a picture of a woman in a wedding veil shooting a kneeling man in the head, above the caption: *Some vows are made to be broken.*

*You can call me Woody*, he'd said. *I'll leave it to Martin to tell you why.*

I remembered vaguely disliking him. His shiny face and his booming laugh – not to mention that awful T-shirt. I'd disliked the way he ate, the way he flirted with the girls, his jokes, his shouting at the screen. Most of all, I had disliked who Martin became in his company. The self-possessed, thoughtful man I loved had become someone else for the afternoon; reflecting the other man's boorishness, laughing at jokes I knew he despised, using words like *ripped* and *dude*, words I'd never heard him use before. I still see him interacting that way with Woody on social media: on Facebook, where they are friends, and sometimes even on Twitter.

'How's Marty?'

'Oh, he's fine.'

'Still working out?'

'You mean at the gym? Sometimes,' I said. 'But, you know, his work –'

'He married his job.' I could still feel Woody's eyes on me, intense and not quite friendly. 'Now, if I had *you* to come home to –.'

I smiled. It was a meaningless smile, designed to acknowledge a compliment. We do that so often, don't we? Women try so very hard to spare the feelings of men. We have to pretend to feel flattered, even when the attention is unwelcome. We smile when a man makes a comment, or whistles at us in the street. We laugh when a man makes a dirty joke, even when it's at our expense. And if we have to reject a man, we smile, we lie, we apologize. We give out telephone numbers with the digits reversed. We pretend to have headaches. We fabricate urgent appointments. And when all else fails, we claim to be already spoken for – *so sorry, but I have a boyfriend* – as if the only way to reject a man is to tell them another man got there first. Men are territorial. Men understand protectiveness. But their pride is so easily hurt. And when they are bruised, they often lash out. I thought of the man in last night's dream. *Bitch. Don't you dare ignore me.*

He put a hand on my shoulder and grinned. My face and throat were still burning. Some men like to provoke unease. Some men like vulnerability. And at that thought, all my earlier fears came rushing back like a tide of blood, along with a tremendous urge to get out of his presence, to lose myself in the safety and anonymity of the high street.

'Can I buy you a coffee?' he said.

I gave another meaningless smile, and looked at my watch. The need to be polite, even now – even to him – was too much to ignore. *Good girls are polite*, said my inner critic, right on cue. *Good girls never make a scene.* Would it have helped Jo Perry, I thought, if she'd tried to make a scene? What would have happened if, instead of walking on, of ignoring her attacker, hoping he would leave her alone, she'd screamed and kicked him in the shins, and run away as fast as she could?

'I'm really sorry. I'm late for work. It was lovely to see you, though.'

*Lovely.* By now I was panicking. Now I could smell his aftershave, and his sweat, and the cake he'd been eating, and the coffee he'd drunk, and the cigarette he'd smoked last night, late, alone in his bedroom. And behind it all was the soundtrack of his interior monologue, a wordless rosary of thoughts that somehow still translated as words: *She looks nice. She could be the one. I wonder when she gets off work?* And under that, the constant rhythm of the counter-melody: *Not like the last one, though. That wasn't me. But some girls can be real bitches.*

'Are you sure?' He smiled again. His hand moved to the small of my back, but his eyes were somewhere else. I realized they were on Iris, the pink-haired girl who'd served him. *He's using me as cover*, I thought. *He wants an excuse to watch Iris. To watch – and maybe more than that.*

'No, really, I can't,' I said.

'Oh well. Tell Marty I said hi.'

'Of course.'

And now I was screaming, screaming inside. Red with the effort of trying to hide the knowledge that was burning me up. *Woody is a predator. Jim Wood – Martin's friend from the gym – is thinking of harming that woman.* I could still feel his hand on my back, all mixed up with the feel of the sweat that had cooled above the band of my underwear. I wondered if he could scent my fear, whether that attracted him. I pulled away with too much force, and fanned myself with comic emphasis.

'Sorry, hot flash. *Hello, menopause!*'

Men are always uncomfortable when women bring up the subject of their own anatomy. In the same way, at Mulberry House, period cramps always got me off Games. He took a step away from me. Averted his eyes from Iris. From inside his house, I sensed his disgust, like a clanging door deep in the basement. But there was something else, too – something like an echo – that whispered: *Maybe I'll see you tonight.* And I knew that whatever temporary diversion my presence had caused, that inner eye was still on the girl, watching her, *assessing* her –

'Well, give old Marty my love,' he said. 'And tell him to drop by and see me sometime!'

And then he was gone – thank God, he was gone – the link between us severed as if it had never existed.

*Abracadabra.*

I half walked, half ran down the street without looking back, clasping my handbag to my chest like a piece of armour. My heart was still pounding; my face was still flushed, but the further I left him behind me, the more my doubts began to return. What the hell had happened back there? What the hell had happened to me?

*The sharp taste of blackcurrant jam. The shadow of a sugar moustache. The way he looked at Iris. The hungry way he looked at her. And in his mind, the memories of women he had taken home, women he thought of as fair game –*

I tried to dismiss the memory. I'd had *drinks* with him, for God's sake. He was a friend of my husband's. How much more likely was it that whatever I'd felt in Priscilla's Pantry had been a momentary fugue?

And yet, as I reached the bookshop, I still couldn't get him out of my mind. That smile, that didn't quite reach his eyes. His hand against the small of my back. The way he'd looked at Iris, sizing her up the way he had the pastries on the countertop, claiming her without a thought, just as he had the doughnut. What if it hadn't been a fugue? What if I was actually *right*?

# 5

I know how naïve all this must sound. But you need to understand. *What if I was right?* isn't a question I ask myself very
often. Most of my life has been spent hearing men dismissing
my instincts and feelings as wrong. Men are the keepers of
common sense, of reason and of balance. Women, on the other
hand, are over-emotional, hormonal. Martin often uses this as
a reason to dismiss my opinions. He considers himself a logical
man, whereas I am governed by feelings. He used to find this
attractive, once. He said I made him human. Now, it often
annoys him. My feelings are an annoyance.

I arrived at the bookshop five minutes late, and out of
breath from running. Salena had already opened up, and was
working on one of her window displays. She wears her dark
hair natural, and this morning the sun through the window
gave her a corona of fire. A pile of coloured tissue paper lay
on a table nearby. Paper flowers, hearts and birds bloomed
between her brown fingers.

'You OK?' she said. 'You look a bit –' *Tired? Flushed?* (I
could see her trying to find a word that wouldn't make me
feel old.)

64

I smiled. 'I just need coffee.'

There is a galley kitchen at the back of the bookshop. Salena went in for a minute or two, and brought out two cups of camomile tea. 'Coffee's the last thing you need,' she said. 'Here. This'll relax you. I've already done the socials. I just need to update Kafka.'

Salena is mostly in charge of the bookshop's social media. Business has been slow this year, and we have been relying on social media to encourage sales and boost interest. Salena has succeeded in doing this, via a number of clever ideas, though none more so than her daily portraits of Kafka, the bookshop cat. Kafka was a street cat, one of several animals that Salena insists on feeding. Since then, he has grown from a tattered stray into a well-groomed feline with white paws and a neat white bib, who is now a permanent resident, and often sleeps in the window display, to the delight of passers-by. He has his own Twitter and Instagram account, as well as a YouTube channel with over eighty thousand followers. There's even a PayPal account called *Buy Kafka a Book*, which generates enough money per month to pay for his food and vet's bills.

'I'll do it, now I'm here,' I said.

'OK.' Salena vanished back into the window display, and left me to find Kafka, photograph him with my phone, and upload the picture to Instagram and Twitter, along with an update on *What Kafka's Reading* (today, a biography of Nelson Mandela).

I made the mistake of lingering on Twitter, where Jo Perry's name is trending. The Met police have issued a warning to women not to go out alone. I wonder when they will issue a warning to men to stop preying on women. I typed:

*@theberniemoon: Why should women have to change? Why not men?*

*@whitey2947: It's common sense. It takes two to make a victim.*

*@theberniemoon: The victim isn't to blame.*

*@whitey2947: I'm not blaming her, just saying that if she hadn't been out alone, she would still be alive today, and two kids would still have a mother.*

I started to compose my reply, then closed the app and took a breath. I could already feel myself beginning to prickle with heat. It's pointless getting involved in debate; no one changes their mind online. And yet, we're taught as children that a woman's patience can tame a beast. What the stories all omit is the strength of a woman's anger.

'Are you OK?'

My tea had gone cold. Salena was watching me with concern. I started to tell her that I was fine, but I wasn't. I was angry. Angry, and suddenly close to tears from everything that had happened.

Salena saw my expression, stepped in, and silently gave me a hug.

Such a simple gesture. A hug. I'd almost forgotten how it feels. Salena smells of the coconut oil she sometimes uses on her hair; a scent that reminds me of summer, and Dante, as a little boy, building sandcastles on the beach.

I started to cry. 'I'm sorry.'

'Why?'

'I'm fine. I had a bad night, that's all, and this morning I'm all over the place −'

'You're *not* fine, Bernie. Take the day off. I can manage without you.'

I shook my head. 'It's the weekend.'

'So? We sold a grand total of six books last weekend. And

forgive me for saying, but you look like shit.' The kindness in her voice took any possible sting from her words. 'What happened?'

'Nothing. Just hormones.'

'Don't minimize. Hormones are everything,' she said. 'Now, go wash your face, I'll make some more tea, and this time, you're going to drink it.'

I went into the bathroom and looked at myself in the mirror. Salena was right; I looked terrible. I felt it, too: pulse racing; tearful; on a razor's edge. My doctor says it's normal to experience these symptoms, but offers no solutions. According to Dr Lovett, it's best to *let Nature take its course, unless there's a real problem*. According to Dr Lovett, crashing exhaustion, mood swings, weight gain, hot flashes, sleep paralysis and night sweats aren't a real problem, although he did ask me if I'd noticed a drop in my interest in sexual activity. I told him no. *My* interest was never really the problem. Once more, it occurs to me that Martin might be having an affair. The late nights. The mood swings. The showers. The rage. Male menopause exists, they say. If so, you'd think they'd acknowledge ours.

I ran some cold water, washed my face. Then I changed my Maxi Pad. It was already soaked through. According to My Big Fat Menopause, that means that I'm allowed a square of dark chocolate today. *One whole square*. I smiled at the thought, and realized that I was hungry. The half-eaten muffin seemed as if it had happened to someone else. I looked at myself in the mirror again. My make-up was gone, my face was scrubbed pink, but I thought that perhaps I looked better.

I went out to find that Salena had opened a packet of biscuits. 'The *good* biscuits? Wow.' I took one. 'I'm sorry. I didn't mean to cause such a drama this morning.'

'You're allowed to feel your feelings,' said Salena, looking at me. 'That's what my friend Leonie says, and she should know; she's been in therapy half her life.'

'Oh. I'm sorry.' I don't know much about Salena's social life. In fact, given the time I've spent working here, I don't know much about her at all. Her social media sometimes reflects fragments of her home life, but the little space we inhabit – the shop, the cat, the customers – might as well be the whole world.

'No need to be sorry,' Salena said. 'Leonie's the most balanced person I know.'

I smiled. I was feeling better. I took another biscuit. The tea was something herbal, a blend of liquorice and mint. 'This is the kind of thing I imagine DeeDee drinks, by the poolside. Maybe after Pilates.'

'Who?'

I explained about DeeDee LaDouce, and My Big Fat Menopause.

'I'm pretty sure that's pronounced *LaDouche*,' said Salena, taking a biscuit.

I laughed. 'You realize I'm always going to hear that now?'

She grinned. 'You can thank me later.'

By four today, Salena's Books had had eleven customers. Five came in to pet the cat. Only one made a purchase. That's the problem with independent bookshops; people love the concept, but they don't like paying full price for books. They come in, browse the shelves, talk to Salena about their reading choices, listen to her recommendations, then fake a phone call and step outside to order the books from Amazon. One guy didn't even bother to pretend he was taking a call; just scanned the codes straight into his app, then left, leaving the door ajar.

*What a dick.*

*At this rate,* I thought, *the business will be on its knees by Easter.*

I checked my phone. Martin was online. I looked into Facebook, and found him discussing the Pog Hill reunion. Over a hundred people have already replied to Lucas's post. No word of the Jo Perry murder. Perhaps he hasn't read the news.

I said: 'You'd think there'd be more police around, after what happened last night.'

Salena looked up. 'Jo Perry?'

I nodded.

'Don't worry. They'll catch him. A case like this? They can't afford not to pull out all the stops.'

She's right, of course. Jo Perry – young, attractive, white – is considered newsworthy. She had value. She was a wife; a mother of two children. So many women of colour die at the hands of violent men without even making the news. So many women's lives are not considered enough of a loss to report.

Salena lifted Kafka out of the display window. 'They were at the gym today. Trying to find out if anyone there could have been a stalker.'

*A stalker.* I thought back to *Jim From the Gym*. The way he had looked at Iris, assessing her as if she were no more than a pastry on a tray. And once more I thought: *What if I was right? What if Jim Wood is a predator?*

I knelt to stroke Kafka, who rolled over, purring. I took that as consent for me to stroke his underbelly. Kafka sometimes likes to be stroked. When he doesn't, he lets you know. I smiled at the unexpected thought. It isn't a difficult concept, I thought. Anyone who has a cat understands the importance of consent.

'If you suspected someone you knew might be in danger,' I said. 'What would you do?'

'What kind of danger?'

'A stalker, perhaps.'

Salena looked at me, alarmed. 'Jesus, Bernie. Is this you? Have you been to the police? Good God, after Jo Perry —'

I shook my head. 'It's not like that.' I suddenly felt exhausted. How could I make her understand? 'You can't go round accusing men of being stalkers just because they make you uncomfortable.'

Salena frowned. 'That's true,' she said. 'But don't ignore your discomfort. Have you told your friend how you feel?'

I shook my head.

'Then tell her,' she said. 'Maybe she suspects him, too. At least that way she won't be alone.'

Once again I shook my head. I couldn't speak to Iris. I didn't even know her. Nor could I go to the police. There wasn't a shred of evidence that Woody was planning anything. A menopausal woman, blaming a man for her hot flash? They'd think I was a crazy person. They might even arrest *me*.

And yet, Salena was right, I thought. Too many women ignore their discomfort. Too many women are afraid of seeming rude or hysterical. Too many women hide their abuse behind a veil of politeness.

'I guess I could go back,' I said. 'I could go back, and —'

*Stop him.*

That voice. Who does it belong to? It was not the hectoring voice of my inner critic, but of someone who was almost a friend. *You know you could,* she told me. *You knew, the moment you saw him. But you were taught your feelings don't count. That good girls shouldn't make a fuss. But you're not a good girl. Are you?*

I turned to Salena. 'You're right,' I said. 'Could I maybe leave early tonight? The café shuts at five o'clock, and if he decides to wait for her —'

'Of course,' said Salena. 'Do you think he'll turn up? The creep, I mean. The stalker.'

I shrugged. 'I hope he doesn't.'

*Liar*, said the inner voice.

*Bad, bad girl*, I thought. And smiled.

# 6

*Saturday, March 26th*

It was just after five o'clock when I reached Priscilla's Pantry. The sign on the door already said CLOSED, but the lights were still on inside, showing Iris cleaning up, wiping tables and stacking chairs. There was no sign of Woody. The gym in which he works is just a couple of streets away from here. *Not* Jo Perry's gym, but one of those little studios that offer women's yoga classes and man-to-man personal training. So easy for Woody to watch the place, to check out when Iris is working there. *So easy for him to follow her. To do what he has done before.*

I crossed the road and chose a place from which to watch the café. The orange street-lamps were already lit, and a small, fine rain was beginning to fall; not enough to soak me through, but enough to throw a veil of fine droplets over my hair. In a way, it was pleasant. It took the heat away from my face. Maybe he wasn't coming, I thought. Maybe I'd dreamed the whole thing. That was the more likely scenario, I told myself as I stood on the street. Bernie Moon, daydreaming again. Bernie Moon, still wrecking everything since 1992.

*And what will you do if he does turn up?* My inner critic was back again, sounding like my mother.

*I could stop him.*

*Could you?* she says. *You sound very certain of that. Of course, you've been certain of things in the past. How did that work out, again?*

I have to admit she has a point. I'm the girl who got pregnant too soon and wasted her opportunities. Who failed her mother. Who failed her man. Who failed her son. Who failed her friend. Why was I so sure of *this*? What was I even doing here?

Then I saw him approaching on the other side of the street. He'd changed his gym clothes for a fresh white T-shirt and a leather jacket. I already knew that he had showered; that he was wearing aftershave. I already knew why he was there. I had known he'd be there from the moment I looked into his house.

I stepped into the shelter of a nearby awning. An instinctive, but unnecessary precaution – women like me are invisible. Unless I made an effort to attract his attention, I could follow him unseen for as long as I needed. I watched as he went to the café door; tried it. It was bolted. He looked through the window at Iris, who was now mopping the floor. He knocked at the glass. Iris looked up, and indicated the sign on the door: *Sorry, we're closed.*

Woody smiled. I could tell it was meant as a friendly smile, but I guessed how fast he could turn mean. He gestured at Iris, palms raised up. *Let me in. I'm a friend.*

I saw her hesitation. To a woman alone at nightfall, no strange man is ever a friend.

Woody smiled again and mimed: *Just one minute. Please?* – by holding up one finger, then clasping his hands in a gesture of comic entreaty. He was pretty good, I thought. Playing the clown to seem harmless. I wondered how often he'd done it before.

I silently willed her to refuse. To just turn away and ignore him. But she must have recognized him. Maybe he was a regular. She moved to the door and opened it, and Woody followed her inside. I waited for a few minutes there, feeling the soft fine rain on my face. What should I do? Should I go in? My heart was racing; my fists were clenched. Not for the first time, I wondered whether I was losing my mind.

Suddenly, my mobile rang. The sound of Whitney Houston singing 'I Will Always Love You' came from the depths of my handbag. I swore, and fought to retrieve my phone. Anyone else, I might have simply muted it, or turned it off. But that ringtone was Dante's. It's the song that was topping the charts on the day he was born.

'Dante?'

'Mum?' My son's voice remains eerily like that of the little boy he was, only an octave lower. He sounded distracted, almost surprised, as if he'd been expecting someone else. 'Damn, I think I butt-dialled you. Sorry. I must have put my phone in my back pocket without locking it. Sorry.'

'It's OK.' That explains it; Dante never calls me. Just as long as there's nothing wrong.'

'No, I'm fine. Everything all right?'

'Of course.' I sounded bright and false. 'Just walking home. It's been a long day.'

'OK.' He sounded keen to go. 'Well –'

'What are you doing right now?' I suddenly, desperately, wanted him to stay on the line; to talk to me. To tell me about his day at work; what he was making for dinner. What he was wearing; where he had been; what he was watching on TV. Dante always used to be such a talkative little boy, always talking to himself, to his toys, to everyone. Adolescence

74

took that away. Now he is a man of few words, most of them simple; all of them dear.

'Nothing. Making burritos.' A pause. 'Mum, are you really all right? You sound a bit – tense.'

'It's nothing,' I said. 'You know there was a murder, right? Just over the road, in Victoria Park. She was jogging. They found her today.'

'Of course.' I could hear the relief in his voice. 'No wonder you got weirded out. Listen, everything's going to be fine. Just go home and get some rest. Call you later, Mum, OK?'

'What kind of burritos?'

'Chicken. Look, I have to go –'

'Of course. Goodb—'

He cut me off before I could say *I love you, or take care, Dan*. My son is uncomfortable around casual expressions of feelings. I wonder if I did that to him. I wonder if it's my fault. I wonder what he would have said if I'd told him: *I'm not in the least bit OK. I'm standing outside a coffee shop, waiting for a man to come out. And I think I might be losing my mind.*

The lights in Priscilla's Pantry were out. There was no sign of anyone. I realized that while I was talking to Dan, I'd allowed my surveillance to slip. The rain was falling steadily now from a sky the shade of dark denim. A bus passed by, then another, sending up a fuzz of spray. I lingered there uncertainly, watching the traffic, feeling the rain. A prickle of anxiety ran over me like a centipede. Could I have missed them? Had they left while I was talking to Dante?

*Maybe that's a good thing*, said the inner critic. *Maybe Dante's phone call stopped you from making a big mistake.*

And then I saw them, moving away, some fifty yards down the main road. Iris was wearing a pale raincoat and holding an umbrella, but even at that distance, I recognized the pink

75

of her hair. I started to follow rapidly, watching from the far side of the road.

*Big mistake*, said the inner voice.

I banished her to the Quiet Room. Crossed the road behind them. Moving rapidly along the High Street, collar turned against the rain, I could have been almost anyone. I overtook them on the left, stepping abruptly towards them to avoid a skirt of rainwater from the passing wheels of a car, and walking by, just brushed against his extended elbow –

I felt that small electrical charge, like something making a connection. Saw the reflections from his house, like something glimpsed from a passing car.

*Good*, I thought. *I can do this.*

I paused in the awning of a shop, as if to check my mobile phone. Woody and Iris passed me again, walking at a leisurely pace. I caught her scent as she went by; something light and floral that reminded me of home.

Woody's house was open wide. I could see into his front room, all lit up for guests. I thought: *He's making an effort for her. He's trying to be charming.* From what felt like a long way away, I heard him laughing, and heard her small, polite response, like a good girl at the birthday party of someone she doesn't much like.

*I can do this*, I told myself. *And I'm not losing my mind.*

Then, I took a deep breath, and silently let myself in.

# 7

*Saturday, March 26th*

No man ever really believes, deep down, that he is a predator. Some abusers blame their wives for their sexual frustration. Some blame their mothers for the way they were raised. Some men even tell themselves they are acting out a *biological imperative*, effectively blaming Mother Nature herself for their lack of self-control. There's always a woman to blame behind every crime against womankind.

With Woody, it's the feminists. They are the ones who have ruined things. Before that, he thinks, there were certainties. Men and women knew where they stood. Men were the providers, the protectors, the heroes. Women wore frocks, and respected themselves. A man came home to a clean, tidy house, and dinner on the table. Everyone was happy. Nowadays, you can't even tell whether some people are girls or boys. Now, it's all about *#MeToo*, and genderqueer, and trans, and tattoos. *I bet she's got tattoos. Still* – with a sideways glance at the girl – *you have to pretend to play the game. To speak the language of wokeness. And this one could be beautiful, if only she took care of herself. If only she could learn to relax* –

Through his ears, I heard Iris say: *I'm pretty tired. Some other time?*

He must have asked her out, I thought. This was her way of letting him down without making him feel rejected. I didn't need to be in her house to know how it worked. He was an unknown quantity. He'd made an effort to please her. And she had been ready to be pleased – at least, when she was on duty. Pleasing the customers came with the job. But now she was off duty. Her time was no longer paid for.

*Just one drink*, came Woody's voice. *I came all this way to see you.*

*I've been on my feet all day. I really don't feel up to it.*

*One little drink. I promise. Please?*

These men. They wheedle like children. Dante was the same as a boy. My mother raised me differently. *I want never gets.* Are all women raised this way? To put men's needs before their own?

*OK. Just one.*

The sound of his satisfaction is like the sound of a man sitting down to an especially tempting meal. His inner voice, which sounds like a smaller version of his own, says: *That's right, babe. One's all it takes.*

*I was right to do this*, I think. *This man is most definitely not a good guy.*

I looked around his bright front room, with all its props and knick-knacks. Photos of himself on the walls. Sporting trophies and pin-ups. But it was a stage set, filled with the kind of furniture no one ever uses. Behind it, in the theatre, there were the levers and pulleys that made the curtain go up and down; and beyond that, the rooms filled with costumes and props, reaching down into the darkness. Except that in this theatre it wasn't props, but memories, and secrets, and porn, and muscle magazines, and fitness gear, and health food, and pictures of himself, all piled up alongside conspiracy theories, casual racism, sexist jokes and *Boy's Own* dreams of adventure, charged with a sense of nostalgia for an imagined past in which men got the respect they deserved, and women and foreigners knew their place.

I'd almost forgotten how banal the inside of a predator's house could be. This man wasn't violent, or evil. He was a friend, a brother, a son. He told bad jokes at parties. He went to karaoke. All of his close friends were men, and they never saw those one-night stands (with girls who had been *very* drunk) as anything more than the healthy male's pursuit of female company. There was a general feeling that he'd been unlucky with women so far – his last three girlfriends were *crazy* – but there was an overwhelming sense that Woody was one of the good guys. A bit of a rough diamond, perhaps, but underneath, a good guy.

I wonder if Jo Perry's murderer has friends who think he's a good guy. People are so much more complex than social media would have you believe. Evil is not a uniform, or a mark of Cain. Evil is not extraordinary. Evil is someone you know. Someone you could never imagine doing anything wrong, because they're your friend, and you're a good guy.

I don't have to imagine. I know. I've seen in his basement. There's no evil there either, just a lot of outdated porn, splashy teenage crushes, some blurry, drunken encounters, a buried sexual fantasy about his best friend's mother, some creepy Twitter sock puppet accounts, and that unpleasant little joke about Jo Perry that morning –

*@radfem_Bonnie95: She was only running.*

*@jimfromthegym69: not fast enough, apparently*

79

For one terrible moment, I wondered if there was more to be found. But Woody had barely noticed her, lingering over the news of her death on his way to somewhere else. *Silly bitch got herself murdered*, he'd thought, lingering for a second on the photo under the headline. *Pity. She had kids as well. Shouldn't have gone running alone.* Further investigation revealed nothing more than slight distaste for the shirt she'd been wearing, and under it all, a subconscious thought that the woman was probably asking for it.

I felt a moment of relief. This was not the man of my dream. And yet, I'd seen enough of his house to know that there was something wrong. Those drunken encounters, where the girl seemed barely even conscious. The pleas for them to *just relax*. The photos he'd taken afterwards, the trophies of his conquests. And, time after time, the hopeful thought – *not like last time* – positioned right next to *just in case*, half optimistic, half resigned to do whatever was required.

He buys the pills from eBay. It's easy to slip one into a drink. And he's had plenty of practice. It's only a muscle relaxant, he thinks: it doesn't do them any harm. It makes them happy. It makes them forget the stresses and worries of modern life. It brings them back to their natural state of feminine trust and dependency. It makes them warm and affectionate. Calling it rape is ridiculous. He knows he isn't a rapist. But feminists think all sex is rape. Feminists ruin everything.

*How many more men are like this?* I thought.

I'd continued to follow in his wake, keeping at a distance, still aware of the train of thought that ran alongside his consciousness. Iris walked beside him, looking like a polite little girl at a party she doesn't know how to leave. From time to time, I heard her voice. But his was a constant monologue, self-satisfied and avuncular, covering everything from politics to his fitness regime, humour to nutrition, and requiring nothing by way of response but occasional validation.

After ten minutes or so, we reached their destination. A half-timbered, mock-Tudor gastropub of the kind that Iris would never choose, but where Woody could pass unnoticed. I knew exactly what he meant to do. Now all that remained was to find a suitable way to stop him. I could go inside, I thought. Try to catch him in the act. But, even then, would they believe me? Would Iris believe? Or would she assume I was crazy, making unfounded accusations against a man I barely knew?

I waited outside. By then, it was dark. A thin, light rain was falling, and my hair was plastered to my skull. From *inside*, I watched as he ordered drinks, then slipped the dose into her glass. He was quick. He'd practised his move before trying it out for the first time. This wasn't the first time. He knew what he was doing. The question was, did *I*?

*I've done it before.*

*Yes, and look what happened.* The inner critic is back again, sounding like Katie Malkin, which makes her voice very hard to ignore. Katie, who was there from the start; Katie, who had disappeared from my memory the day of The Great Carovnik.

I said: *I was young. I didn't know. I couldn't have known –*

*And you liked it. Didn't you?*

And there it is. My inner voice speaks from a place more intimate than the heart, where lying is impossible; morality, irrelevant. There is no way to ignore that voice; no way to disbelieve it. *The cuts on his arms. The way he flinched whenever a girl came near him.*

And yes, I liked it. I liked it a *lot*.

Besides, he had it coming.

# 8

*Saturday, March 26th*

When I was still at Mulberry House, I learnt how Archimedes prevented a Roman attack on Syracuse by using mirrors – polished shields – to reflect sunlight onto the enemy ships, causing them to catch fire and burn. The story may be apocryphal, but the science behind it is sound. Reflected sunlight *does* create heat. And thoughts are also reflections.

*Wait.*

Rohypnol takes twenty minutes or so to take effect. I waited fifteen. Then I went in after them. I knew they'd be in the corner. Woody likes corner tables best. It's easy to watch the room that way. Iris was drinking rum and Coke – good choice for the person spiking it. You slip the drug into the can, or sometimes straight into the glass. The colour of the liquid, as well as the quantity of ice, makes it easy to camouflage any residue.

Iris had almost finished her drink. I knew she'd be impatient. *One drink, that's all*, she promised him. She despises herself for that. But sometimes you have to give a little, if only to keep the peace. I looked, but only far enough to know what the girl was thinking. Her memories were private. I didn't want to see them. Looking further without her consent would have made me no better than Woody.

*OK, Sleeping Beauty.* The dose of Rohypnol in her drink was starting to take effect now. She was feeling floaty inside, like a yellow birthday balloon. I caught a reflection of being very small, and watching a yellow balloon float away into a sky like summertime. It was a small, harmless memory, and I was glad it had found her. I didn't want her to feel afraid, or to struggle against me. I stayed beside her as she went further into the soft, warm trance that Woody thought of as *her natural state*, and then I opened the door that led into that dangerous part of him, the room in which the predator lived.

*Abracadabra.*

How easily it all comes back. The spotlight, the mirrors, the tablecloth. The trick, performed so perfectly, in the blink of an eye. That's how the magic works, you know. With mirrors. My mother was right about that. That trick the Great Carovnik had pulled is called *The Turning Table* among practitioners of the art. And it's done with nothing but mirrors and lights. The table with the silverware was never in any danger. Nothing ever got broken that way. Not even in rehearsal. Not so with people, I'm afraid. Mirrors can be dangerous. Especially when you can only guess at the angles, the perspectives.

*The cuts on his arms.*

That memory is never far. It feels like a tiny shard of glass in my eye; a constant reminder of the fact that I am not a good girl.

*You made him look. You did that,* says the voice of the inner critic. *You got angry. You lost your cool. And that's why little girls shouldn't play in the toy box meant for boys.*

I thought of The Great Carovnik. Her top hat and her silver smile. The way she turned the table with a single fluid gesture. *She* had played in the toy box. *She* hadn't lost her cool. *She* had eclipsed the magician on stage. And now I found I remembered the scent of the auditorium – the library scent of the velvet seats, like dusty old books in the darkness; the reek of powder and theatre smoke; the popcorn and the chocolate. The inner critic heckled and railed. I banished her to the Quiet Room. I was OK. I was in charge.

*Look at me.*

*Abracadabra.*

I'd chosen the perfect moment, when Iris was sleepy and trusting, still dreaming of that yellow balloon; Woody not yet suspicious; focused on the task in hand. There was only just time for a moment's surprise as he saw me enter the room. He raised a hand automatically, but I saw his expression flicker from complacency to annoyance.

*That bloody woman again.*

I smiled. Then I reached out to touch his arm, and at the same time, I took Iris' hand. For a second, I had a foot in both their houses. Hers was soft and sleepy as pastel cashmere, his was a marauder's maze, all barbed wire and stacked garbage. For a moment, I reached out; heard the hush of the audience, heard the drum roll, saw the lights fade over the auditorium –

And then I used the mirrors to turn the tables on both of them. It happened in less than a moment. In less than the time that it takes to shake hands, I exchanged her sleepy semi-consciousness for his state of hyper-vigilance. *Boom.* Easy as exchanging the taste of a strawberry Opal Fruit for a bite of pork pie. No dishes smashed; no secrets spilled. My heart rate barely quickened. He slipped gently into sleep, like a child up past his bedtime, and she stood up, abruptly alert, and crackling with nervous energy.

'What happened?' she said. In her house, I could see all the lights suddenly blazing. In Woody's, everything was dark. The Rohypnol had finally kicked in. 'Who are you?'

'I'm Bernie.' I smiled at her. 'Everything's fine. You'll be OK.'

'But he's —'

'He'll be fine. I promise.'

Now that the danger was over, I could feel the familiar prickle of an impending hot flash sweeping up my body. Suddenly it was much too hot; the air inside the crowded room seemed all breath and no oxygen.

Iris looked at me, frowning. 'Are you all right? You look as if —'

'Hot flash.' My smile was ghastly. 'Hello, menopause!'

'I'm sorry.'

'No need.' I sat on the bench, feeling the hot flash rise to my face; to my scalp; to my neck; to the roots of my hair. My throat was suddenly very dry. I picked up Woody's discarded glass and drained it. Iris was still watching me. For a moment, she looked like an animal, glimpsed across the campfires of some mythical jungle, and I glimpsed her thoughts; among them, the realization that only by a fortunate twist had she escaped the hunter.

She glanced at Woody, then back at me. 'They say you shouldn't do that,' she said. 'Drink from someone else's glass.'

'You're right. You shouldn't.'

'Is he OK?'

I nodded. 'Don't worry. He'll be fine.'

The dose he had slipped into her drink would keep him asleep for a couple of hours. But I'd kept it under control. Nothing damaged, nothing smashed, nothing lost forever. Only an innocent, dreamless sleep, from which he would awaken, refreshed, no longer a danger to women. It was perfect.

Iris was still watching me. Before, she'd been sleepy; child-like. Now, she was fully adult; in charge. I found myself responding instinctively to her air of quiet authority, as if I, and not she, were the victim.

'What did you do?' she said.

'Nothing.' I hated my defensiveness. 'Look, he drank a little too much. He's fine. But we should get you home.'

'What are you even doing here? Do you know him?'

'Enough to know that he'll be fine. Come on, before someone notices.'

Once more, Iris looked at the sleeping man. Her expression was thoughtful, almost sweet. She stooped as if to kiss him goodnight, then, reaching inside his jacket, she pulled out his wallet, removed a wad of twenties, then replaced the wallet before turning to me.

'We should get a cab home,' she said. 'He can afford it, don't you think?'

I nodded. I was troubled, and yet I didn't dare comment. Rearranging the furniture in a person's house can sometimes have unexpected consequences, and I didn't want to interfere any more than I had to. I don't know what I'd expected. Maybe a little confusion. Tears. A sense of relief at her escape. A need for maternal comfort. Friendship. I'd been prepared for all of that, Maybe I'd even looked forward to it. Since Katie Malkin, I haven't had friends. Not one friend. Only Martin.

But this was different. This was strange. This was like seeing the housecat that sits on your knee, purring, during the day transform into a hunter at night; lethal and unfathomable. I looked around uneasily. The pub was getting crowded. Soon someone would notice Woody, asleep, and link him to the two of us. There was very little chance of anyone remembering me, but Iris, with her pink hair, was likely to stand out in the crowd.

'Please, Iris. We have to go.'

She looked at me and shrugged – *OK* – then followed me into the street. I felt a rush of warm relief: not quite a hot flash this time, but close. I realized I'd been sweating: under my light jacket, my shirt was plastered to my skin. But the night was damp and cool, and there was a distant scent of smoke. No one came after us from the pub; from inside came the distant drone of music and conversation.

Against the wet tarmac, the passing cars lit up the road with their headlights. I scanned the oncoming traffic for a cab. A black cab drove past, empty, ignoring my attempt to flag it down.

'The fuck,' said Iris. 'Here, let me.' She stepped out into the road, arm raised. Once more, I was struck by how different she seemed; how fully in control of herself. She had no fear of the traffic; no expectation of being ignored. The next cab stopped for her at once. She held the door open, unsmiling.

'Get in,' she said. 'I'll drop you off. We can talk inside.'

'Oh, no, I –'

'Just get in,' she said. 'What? Don't you want me to know where you live?'

Well, I'll admit it had crossed my mind. 'Of course not. It's just –'

'We need to talk. Come on. I'm not going to eat you.'

I got into the black cab, feeling increasingly uncomfortable. It smelt of perfume and cigarette smoke.

Iris took the seat opposite, and fixed me with her direct gaze. 'Right,' she said. 'Now it's just us. Tell me exactly what happened back there.'

I shook my head. How could I explain? I'd expected to be in charge; to have to pick up the pieces. Instead, she was whole, and I was the one who felt broken inside, and uncertain.

Iris seemed to sense it. 'You'll be OK,' she told me, putting a hand onto my knee. 'My mum has hot flashes. She takes evening primrose oil. Says it helps.'

I nodded. 'Evening primrose.'

'Yeah. She buys it from the health-food place.'

I nodded and looked out at the street. Neon signs and shopfronts, watercolours in the rain.

'Take your time,' said Iris.

She wasn't going to let it go. I'd have to tell her something. 'The man you were with,' I said at last. 'He's a creep. I've met him before.'

Iris grinned. 'You're telling me. He made me promise to go for a drink. Wouldn't take no for an answer. I thought I'd never get rid of him. Then, you arrived – and he just passed out.' She looked at me closely, curiously. 'Come on. Tell me. What did you do?'

'Nothing,' I said.

'Don't give me that. I felt it.' She leaned closer. I caught a simple, wholesome scent, like lily-of-the-valley. 'It's like I'm suddenly awake. Like I'd been asleep for twenty years. What was that? Did you give me something?'

Once again, I shook my head. I'd only deployed my mirrors; reflected her mental state at him, exchanged her somnolence for his wakefulness. The Archimedes strategy, but without the conflagration. But now I wondered if I'd reflected more than I'd intended. The theft of the notes from his wallet. The unapologetic look. The way she occupied her space, where once she'd shrunk into her shadow.

'He spiked my drink, didn't he?'

I nodded. 'Yes. He's done it before.'

'So, how did you know? And how did you –'

'Iris. Just forget it. You're safe, and that's what matters.'

She gave a low and breathless laugh. 'Oh, no. You're not going to give me that. Something happened in that pub. That guy was going to hurt me. But we stopped him. We did it together. I felt it, like a sudden light going on at the back of my mind.'

I nodded. That's what it felt like.

'So what I want to know is this,' Iris went on. 'What did we do to him, Bernie? And *how soon can we do it again?*'

# 9

*Saturday, March 26th*

I finally managed to placate Iris by giving her my number and promising to call her on Monday. I dropped her off at her little flat, and got home to an empty house and three missed calls on my mobile, all of them from my mother.

*What a day.*

*What a fucking day.*

Now that I was home again, everything felt like a blur. Priscilla's Pantry. Jo Perry. My dream. The blood on the mattress. *Jim From the Gym*, and how I'd flipped his state of mind for Iris'. All that seemed incredible now, like something that happened to someone else, years ago, when magic was real. My body ached, and I could feel dull pain in my lower abdomen. I went into the bathroom and took two paracetamol. I became aware that I was cold and trembling, as if in the wake of a terrible shock, or a catastrophic sugar crash.

In these cases, DeeDee LaDouce (now forever *LaDouche*) recommends turning off all screens, then a warm bath, with essential oils, and maybe a glass of iced cucumber water if you're feeling especially stressed. I had to make do with

Epsom salts and a large glass of Merlot, but turning off the phone felt good.

I sank into the bath, and let the hot water do its work. Steam rose into the air and hung in sheets at the windows. I thought: *Maybe none of this happened. Maybe all of today has been nothing more than a case of menopausal brain fog.*

*But Woody passed out,* I protested.

*So what? He'd been drinking. Hardly front-page news, is it?*

The wine had gone to my head by now. I felt untethered; weightless. The painkillers had started to work, and the cramps were beginning to recede.

*See? You needed to relax. All this is just hormones.*

The inner voice had softened now, becoming almost affectionate. And yet, I thought, how often we hear the phrase; *it's just hormones.* As if hormones were not the most powerful force in the human body. Hormones tell us what to do; when to grow; when to sleep; when to eat. Hormones regulate temperature; fertility; muscle development. Hormones trigger every stage of the body's development. Hormones dictate our mental health. They drive our personality. They are the source of all power, all change in the body and the mind.

I opened my eyes. The water was red. I felt a surge of self-disgust. But at the same time I also felt a kind of validation.

*Blood remembers,* I thought. *The body remembers. Just as the mind sometimes refuses to see the truth. Because the truth is sometimes too bright to see. What if all of it was real? What would I do with a power like that?*

All our stories begin with blood. I see that now. The blood that marks; that sets us apart; that thinks for itself; that walks alone; that sometimes sings; that provokes so much fear and horror that men have to spill it again and again, just to be sure that women remain weakened enough for their purposes.

Because if men could see what we really are – the strength within us, the burning rage – they would never touch a woman again.

Some women might welcome this.

Some women would go further.

# TRACK 3 :

---

# All I Really Want

And moving thro' a mirror clear
That hangs before her all the year,
Shadows of the world appear.
*Alfred, Lord Tennyson, 'The Lady of Shalott'*

'Visible women flaunt their curves. Invisible
women steal your doughnut.'
*From the LiveJournal of Bernadette Ingram (marked as
Exhibit BI 1): March 26th, 2022*

# I

*Extract from Class of '92, by Kate Hemsworth
(published by LifeStory Press, 2023)*

I wish I could give you more details about *The Second Incident*.
But I was just thirteen years old. I had troubles of my own.
Mulberry House was the kind of school where girls were
expected to do very well. Every year, the Honours Boards
boasted a double row of Oxbridge successes. I had three lots of
homework per night; twice as much at weekends. And I was
an average student at best; fairly good at English and Games,
enthusiastic in Drama and Music, but bottom of the class in
Maths, and scraping the bottom in both Latin and French.
My form teacher, Mrs Laramie, made it clear that I had to
improve. My parents had hired a Maths tutor, which added
to my workload, and I was conscious of their need to see my
grades improve quickly.

Only Games was stress-free. Mr Davis was athletic, relaxed;
good-looking and approachable. He had once been a Premier
League footballer, and he now ran the school athletics club,
and wore shorts instead of a tracksuit, and all the girls adored
him. Mr Davis never had lunch in the cafeteria with the other
teachers. Instead, he ate his sandwiches out on the fields or

by the track. Sometimes he would run laps, and we would watch him from afar. There was a little gang of us – *Mr Davis' Special Squad* – who would join him at lunchtimes in the gym, or out on the field if the weather was fine. Lorelei Jones and I were both regulars, as was Grace Oyemade, who could already run a hundred metres in close to twelve seconds, and who trained after school at the local athletics club, and who – so Mr Davis said – might one day go to the nationals, even, perhaps, the Olympics.

The rest of us were a bit jealous, I think, because Grace was his favourite. But you couldn't really be jealous of Grace. All you could do when you saw her run was marvel at the way her movements seemed somehow to charge the air, like something born to a different world. She was the tallest girl in the class, with legs too long for the rest of her, and a narrow head, with close-cropped hair, which made her look more adult, somehow, less like the rest of the girls in the class. I think it made her self-conscious; she often slouched to disguise her height. But when she was running, all that changed. When she ran, she became something else; something more than beautiful. Watching her run, you could almost believe that girls could be cheetahs and gazelles. And, although she never said, you could tell she had a crush on Mr D. She had a look – a kind of glow – whenever Mr D was around.

Bernie Moon never had that look. She never even watched him run. But she watched the rest of us, although she never took part herself. Maybe I should have noticed it more. But what did we know, at thirteen?

It was our last term in Lower School. Next year, we would be Middle School girls. As the summer weather grew fine, my friends and I spent more time outside, hanging out with Mr D. Bernie would come to sit on the grass with her little packed lunch – always the same thing: a Blue Riband biscuit, a peanut butter sandwich and a Granny Smith apple – whenever we were training, but she never looked at us, or joined the conversation. Instead, she just watched us run, with a strange intensity that made me quite uncomfortable. I can't really tell you why it was weird. It just *was*. Her face would go pink. Sometimes her breathing would quicken, so that by the end of the race she was as out of breath as any of the runners. Lorelei Jones thought she might be a dyke, and spread the word around Lower School that she was getting off on watching girls run. I told her that was kind of mean, and we even fell out over it for a while, but Bernie Moon seemed not to care. She just went on watching as before – at least until that Sports Day.

Sports Day at Mulberry House came at the end of the summer term. Every girl in the school took part: from the eleven-year-olds in Reception to the leaving sixth-formers. There were all kinds of sports, from track events to tennis, culminating in an 800-metre race, in which every girl in the school took part. Parents were invited to watch from stands overlooking the track, while girls sat on the grass with their friends, and talked, and shared the snacks they'd brought, and cheered for their Houses, and made daisy chains, and enjoyed the summer sunshine.

It should have been a perfect day. Exams were over, and teachers had abandoned all pretence at teaching, so that lessons had deteriorated into a series of quizzes and games. I'd been picked for three events in my category – the 400 metres, the relay race and the 100-metre hurdles. My mother and Bernie's were coming to watch. Plus there was a special guest: Dame Hettie Randall, who had been one of our old girls, and had won a silver medal for the 100-metre sprint in the European

Championships, years ago. But I'd sprained my ankle, messing around on the monkey bars, and Mr Davis had banned me from running. I had only myself to blame. All the same, I was feeling low. Not that I was expecting to win a race against Grace Oyemade, but I had to sit with the other girls who couldn't take part in Sports Day, on the row of folding chairs that we called *Losers' Corner*.

My friends were sitting all the way across the other side of the track. I could see them, sharing what looked like a little picnic. Lorelei, especially, seemed to be having a good time; her laugh was penetrating and, I thought, a little mean. From time to time, she looked across at me and the handful of other girls – Amy Watts, who had cerebral palsy, Josie Fletcher, who had a broken ankle, and some girls who were on their period – and the laughter seemed to intensify. I didn't like it. I've never liked the feeling of being excluded. For a moment, I thought to myself: *Bernie must feel like this all the time*, and felt a furtive kind of shame.

Bernie was sitting on the grass fifty yards away from me. There was a space around her, as if she were a stone that had been thrown into a puddle. Beyond it, the other girls sat in groups, or talked, or did stretches. For the first time in three years, I felt a little sorry for Bernie.

Then came the 400 metres. Mr D called through the loud-speaker for the runners to take their places. I saw Grace get up from the grass. Her long brown legs were lean and strong under her navy-blue school shorts. Bernie stood up, and touched her arm, and said something to her. It could have been *Good luck*, I suppose – although, knowing Bernie, it was probably more likely to be something about horses, or books, or which superpower you'd choose, invisibility or flying. But there was something about her expression. Something intense, almost *angry*.

For a moment, Grace looked uncertain, as if Bernie had said something weird, then she went to stand at her mark. The rest of them joined her; Lorelei Jones, and Kate Lindsey, Jenny Ashford, Linda Kite – all the good runners in Lower School. Mr Davis wished them all luck. The starter pistol went off, and Grace took the lead, like she always did. I mean, she was a natural. We'd long since stopped expecting anyone else to win a race. There was hardly any point competing, except that you got points for your House, and besides, nobody wanted to come across as a bad loser in front of Mr D.

And then, the incident happened. I say *incident*. The truth is, nothing much happened at all, except that Grace just stopped running. I was too far away to see her face, but I remember the way she stopped – abruptly, as if she'd hit a wall. Some of the other girls slowed down too, then speeded up reluctantly, like cars in the wake of a motorway crash. Jenny and Lorelei kept going, crossing the finish line in a dead heat, but Grace just walked right off the track, picked up her sports bag, and made for the gate. Some of the girls tried to follow her, but Mr D waved them aside and went running after her. By the time he reached her, she was already outside the gates and in the parking area. I could just see them between the cars. Mr D put a hand on her arm, but I saw her shake him off. I caught the sound of her voice on the wind, shouting: *Never! Never again!* Then she was running down the road, leaving poor Mr D looking awkward and dejected. Later, he would tell us that Grace had had an attack of nerves, but we never saw her again at school, and the next year, we would learn that she had left Mulberry House, and had moved on to Sunnybank Park, the big comprehensive across town.

By now, I could see the other girls, crowding around Mr D. But not Bernie. She was standing there alone in her little circle of space, a forlorn figure in tracksuit pants, with long plaits like a little girl. She was holding both hands to her lower belly as if it hurt. Then, she walked across the grass to Losers' Corner.

'Are you feeling OK?' I said. Seeing her up close, she looked as pale as a Polaroid.

'It hurts,' she said in a low voice. She put a hand on my arm, and I felt a strange and vivid sensation. It was as if someone had opened a door to a darkened cellar and shown me a childhood toy I'd once loved, now broken and forgotten. And with it came a sympathetic aching in my pelvic floor, and a scent of something like pennies in dirt, and I knew what Bernie was feeling, and why.

'It's probably just your period.' I guessed this must be new to her. Of course. She was eight months younger than I was, and at that age, every month counts. It wasn't as if she didn't know what periods actually were (we'd had the talk at the start of the year), but sometimes there's a difference between knowing and knowing what to do. 'Is it your first time?' I said.

Bernie nodded silently.

'OK. Come with me. We'll get you a pad from the office.'

She followed me to the school office, where the nurse gave her a sanitary pad from a cheap old-fashioned pack. We went into the girls' toilets, and I explained how to put on the pad, feeling pleasingly mature. Bernie might be weird, I thought, but that didn't mean I had to be like Lorelei Jones. Once more, I felt a vivid flash of sudden, inexplicable guilt, and once more came the sense of looking behind a door into a darkened cellar, where the discarded toys of my childhood lay, unloved and abandoned.

'Thank you,' she said, from the cubicle. 'Are they always this big? I feel as if I'm wearing a mattress between my legs.'

'You'll get used to it,' I said.

'That's what I'm afraid of.'

When Bernie came out of the cubicle, she looked a little better. Again I thought how young she seemed, in comparison with the rest of us.

'What do you think happened back there with Grace and Mr D?' I said.

Bernie shrugged.

'The way she lashed out. It doesn't make sense. I always thought she liked him.'

'Maybe she did,' Bernie said. 'Maybe that was the problem.'

'What do you mean?'

She shrugged again. 'Maybe she realized he was a creep. Maybe she saw what he's really like.'

'He's not a creep,' I protested. 'He's pretty much the only teacher here who isn't boring.'

She smiled, a little sadly, I thought. 'You've grown a lot faster than I have.'

That flash of guilt. Where was it from? I didn't understand it at all. Hadn't I done everything right? Hadn't I looked after her?

'You should cut your hair,' I said. 'Plaits make you look like a little girl.'

I didn't mean it to sound unkind. But there was something unnerving about the whole situation. I could see her reflection in the mirrors above the sinks; her face under the overhead lights was like an untethered white balloon. She gave me one of her strange looks, and I wondered why I'd thought she looked young. She looked very old to me then – as old as a circus monkey.

'If this is growing up,' she said, 'I think it's overrated.'

'You'll change your mind soon enough,' I said.

'I don't think so,' said Bernie.

The next term at Mulberry House saw the departure of Mr D, under circumstances that can only be described as gruesome. But no one linked it to Bernie Moon; who stayed as solitary and as uncommunicative as ever.

# 2

*From the LiveJournal of Bernadette Ingram (marked as Exhibit BI 1): Sunday, March 27th, 2022*

I awoke to terrible menstrual cramps of the kind I haven't had since school, and a sense of dazed relief: *It was all a dream, after all. Of course it was. How could I have thought otherwise?* I stretched out under the covers. My muscles felt sore, my joints stiff. I felt as if I'd run a race – except that I'm not a runner – and I wondered if that, too, was another symptom. Martin was in the spare room again: he came in late last night, and didn't want to disturb me, he says, though I think perhaps he is disgusted by the bleeding. Martin is very fastidious. I've known him throw a shirt away because of a stain under the collar. *No one would know it was there*, I say. *I would know*, he answers.

I got up and changed my Maxi Pad. I was wearing two last night, and they were both completely soaked. I thought: *How many squares of dark chocolate is that?* and turned on my mobile. There were two texts from Iris.

*7.15: Hey, Bernie! Call me as soon as you get up.*

*8.02: Babe! Are you still asleep? Call me, OK?*

That was when I knew for sure that it hadn't been a dream. That was when it all came back – Iris, the café, and Woody's house, and how it had felt to be there, watching from inside. The way I had somehow *flipped* them both, like Janus, looking both ways at once. Two texts made it sound as if Iris didn't want to wait until Monday. I was just thinking of how to reply, when my mobile rang.

It was Iris. 'Where are you?'

I explained that I had just woken up.

'Then grab a coffee and come over here. Didn't you get my messages?'

'Sorry. I didn't. Are you OK?'

'I'm fine. But we need to talk.'

'Can't we talk tomorrow?' I said.

'Come over. I'll buy you breakfast.'

In the end, I agreed to drop by after I'd taken a shower. I used to be able to roll out of bed with last night's mascara under my eyes and start the day not looking like the victim of a crime. Nowadays, it takes longer to show a presentable face to the world. But Martin wouldn't be up for a while. I could afford to go out for an hour. And so, at ten, I left the house and went to Priscilla's Pantry.

The café was deserted, except for Iris, who eyed me impatiently and indicated a table, where a plate of iced buns was waiting. There was no sign of the other girl. Maybe Sundays were slow, I thought.

'Have you heard from Woody?'

'Why do you ask?'

'Here. Have a listen to this.' She handed me her phone. The display indicated several saved messages. I heard:

*Saturday, 10.02 p.m.: Iris, it's Woody. I enjoyed our date. I'm sorry I –*

I frowned. 'You gave him your number?'

'Please, Bernie. Just *listen*.'

*Sunday, 4.05 a.m.: Hey, Iris, it's Woody. Thanks for last n —*
*Sunday, 7.21 a.m.: Er, Iris —*

'Was there something wrong with his phone?'

'That's what I thought at first,' Iris said. 'Here. Have a bun. They're fresh, for a change.' She picked up one of the buns from the pile and ate it in quick, wolfish bites. 'I'm starving. I've been starving ever since it happened.'

'Since what happened?'

She looked at me. 'You know. What you did to Woody.'

'I think you're reading too much into this. He doped you. You recovered. That's all. The rest is just the effect of the drug. And I just happened to be there.'

She laughed. 'Yeah, right. Great story. It's what you should say if he ever tries to make trouble. But don't forget, I know what you did. It felt like you'd shone a spotlight on me. No – right *into* me. One moment I was dopey as hell, and the next I felt like I'd drunk ten espressos. Nothing works that fast. If it did, every coffee shop in London would go out of business.' She took another bun, and said: 'What if it *keeps* happening? What if every time he even thinks about doing something bad to a woman, he passes out like he did last night?'

That was quite a leap, I thought. And yet –

*What could you do with a power like that?*

I shrugged. 'What matters is, you're safe. Just – keep out of his way, that's all.'

'Keep out of his way? Jesus, Bernie. He's the one who should be keeping out of our way. I think we should both go over to his. See if he faints at the sight of us.'

I smiled to hide my anxiety. 'Look, Iris. I understand. I know you'd like to challenge him –'

'Fuck that,' she said with an evil grin. 'I want to see him shit himself. I want to fuck him up, the way he tried to do to me.'

At this point – and to my relief – a customer came in. I finished my coffee and stood up, but Iris put a hand on my arm. 'We need to discuss this properly. How about a drink? Just one. One drink, and a chat. I swear.'

'OK,' I said, though the irony of her phrasing wasn't lost on me. But I needed to deal with her before she did something impulsive, and I couldn't think of another way to talk her down. 'OK, but not this weekend. How about Friday, after work?'

I named a wine bar a few streets away. Martin and I never go there, so there's less chance of being recognized. And I do hope that by Friday, Iris will have calmed down enough to start to question her story. In any case, she doesn't seem to have suffered from her experience. Quite the opposite; she seems to have gained forcefulness and energy. As for Woody, I hope that cleaning up his house won't lead to anything more than a lifelong aversion to date rape. But mirrors only reflect the truth. If his own image burns him up, then why should I feel responsible?

*Bernie. He had it coming.*

Now the inner voice sounds more than a little like Iris. Not the Iris from the café, but the Iris who pocketed Woody's cash and strolled off coolly into the night. And Iris' voice is persistent, drilling into my consciousness: *What if it keeps happening? What if every time he even thinks about doing something bad to a woman, he passes out like he did last night?*

What could you do with a power like that?

*Anything you wanted to.*

I walked home via the little park along the street behind our house. Not the one where Jo Perry was killed, but a green space no more than a couple of hundred feet across, with a little children's playground, and a bridle path against a hedge. There was a bench by the playground, and I sat there for a few minutes, listening to the birdsong and checking my social media.

Dan has posted on Instagram: a picture of a taco.

Nothing on Martin's Facebook. I'm guessing he is still asleep, although there is this from Lucas, on the *Pog Hill Reunion* thread: *What do you think about hiring a band? Or should we have a DJ instead? Or the original line-up?*

Martin hasn't played in a band since the night of the Pog Hill Prom. I sense that the coming reunion is meant to recapture that evening. A highlight for many, but not for me. I wish there was a way for me to refuse to go, but I know Martin wouldn't understand. I can already sense his excitement. Is that because *she* will be there? In thirty years, Katie has barely changed. Two children have not thickened her. I suppose she dyes her hair, but to me it looks just as it did when we were eighteen. And will she wear that lamé dress, and step up to the mike, and sing? Like so much else about this event, it seems bleakly inevitable.

On Twitter, the Jo Perry murder continues to trend. A commentator suggests that Jo might have been followed from the gym, prompting calls from Gender Critical feminists for women-only gyms, and protests from men, pointing out that not all men are murderers. Many men are keen to do this. Not all men are predators. It's almost as if every man online feels the need to defend himself, like a boy at school shouting out: *Wasn't me!* – when the class misbehaves. Why do they do this? Why is their first instinct to deny the crime, instead of denouncing the criminal?

I closed the app. I felt suddenly cold. March is a month of changes, veering unpredictably from unseasonal mildness to cruel chill. A man approached me on the path, eating a sausage roll from a paper bag. I realized I hadn't had breakfast. Iris had eaten all the buns.

*So just take his*, came that inner voice, not so much a critic now as a confidant, almost a friend. *Take his. He'll never notice.*

No. That would be dangerous.

*Why?* That new voice was stronger than ever today, almost drowning out the voice that always tells me that I'm wrong. *Because of something that happened years ago?*

Well, yes. It got out of control. I got angry.

*Well, you're not angry now.*

That's hardly the point, I told myself. With Woody, I'd *had* to intervene. I'd done it to protect Iris. But this – this was asking for trouble. My curious ability – which left with the arrival of my first menstrual blood, and has returned now, with the end of it – is something that even I barely understand. It can be good, even harmless. A looking *inside* other people. But it's a lens that can also burn.

*Has it ever occurred to you that the way to fix that is practice? Like yoga. Or pelvic-floor exercises. Come on. Besides, you've done this before. Remember Woody's doughnut?*

My mouth was beginning to water. A prickling heat began to ignite around my skull like a burning cap. I hadn't been hungry a moment ago, but suddenly I was ravenous.

*Go on, Bernie, it's dream food. No calories in dream food. Focus.*

I watched the man with the sausage roll as he approached. He was quite young; nondescript; wearing a navy-blue raincoat. A pair of earbuds in his ears. His path would lead him right past me. I leaned forward, pretending to look at my phone, and, very casually, allowed my hand to brush against the back of his raincoat as he passed. A sharp sense of *connection*, like something finding a signal. Then, almost instinctively, I reached for the sensation –

I haven't had a sausage roll in years. Far too many calories. But this one was hot and greasy and good; and it was good to enjoy it from inside this passing stranger's house without the smallest sense of guilt. There are whole rooms in my house devoted to guilt and self-hatred; whole galleries of unflattering selfies; forbidden fruits; whole food groups labelled *Danger*. This man's house was different. Eating was something you had to do. From inside his house, I could taste the salty, fatty texture; feel the warm physicality of being at home inside one's skin; the satisfaction, the fullness of having slaked an appetite.

*I wonder, could I keep it?* I thought. *Take that feeling away with me?*

In Priscilla's yesterday, I had shared Woody's doughnut. But could I really have *stolen* it, replaced it with my muffin?

*And if he doesn't realize, then is it even stealing?*

I watched as the man with the sausage roll crumpled his paper bag and dropped it onto the footpath, and felt a small stab of vindication.

*The guy's a dick. He deserves it. Besides —*

*It feels good. Doesn't it?*

I could still feel the pastry in my mouth; the hot grease on my fingers. And yes, it felt good. It felt *deserved*. I pulled away from the sausage-roll man, leaving him to go on his way. But I held on to the feeling. For a moment, I sensed his puzzlement: *Wow, that hardly touched the walls. Should have bought a couple more.* And then I was back on the bench again, and our connection was broken.

I was no longer hungry. The crushing fatigue and the menstrual cramps I'd felt on waking up were gone. Even the alarming signs of an impending hot flash had vanished. Instead, there was a feeling of warmth and well-fed satisfaction, a feeling I'd taken from the man as he continued on his way. I felt a surge of fierce triumph, followed by a sense of unease. What had I given him in exchange for what I'd taken from his house? My hunger? My fatigue? Something else? I watched him walk on down the path, half expecting him to stumble, to fall, but nothing happened. He looked fine. There was no sign of fatigue or unease. He hadn't even noticed me. I watched until he turned off the path, and vanished from sight behind a hedge.

*Wow. That was easy.*

I picked up the ball of paper he'd dropped and put it in the litter bin. I could feel the awareness of what I'd just done – the monstrous *significance* of the thing – working its way into me like ink through a glass of water. The two conflicting voices – that of my inner critic and the new one, as yet unidentified – took it in turns to tell me: *It was nothing. It was everything.*

I sat for five minutes more on the bench, with the sound of the birds ringing in my ears and that feeling of warmth and contentment working its way through my body. *Forget social media*, I thought. *This is the* real *dopamine.*

I stood up, still feeling that curious sense of strength and satisfaction. It lasted all the way home, where I enjoyed a second, more tangible breakfast of toast, and fruit, and coffee. But the headache and cramps were gone for good, although, as I checked my Maxi Pad, I found that, once more, it was completely soaked through.

*That was easy*, I thought again.

*I should have tried something harder.*

# 3

*Sunday, March 27th*

Martin and I have a Sunday routine. It goes more or less like this. I get up at eight o'clock, go for a walk, take a shower, maybe do some quiet housework, like dusting or washing the windows. Then I spend an hour or so checking my social media, until Martin gets up and has breakfast. After that, I start getting lunch ready, while Martin works on his laptop in his little office. We sometimes have lunch together, or sometimes he eats at his desk. Then, in the afternoon, we read, or watch a film, or talk, or sit, he on his laptop, me on mine, until it's time to make dinner. Then, in the evenings, we watch TV; maybe open a bottle of wine. I go to bed early, he goes to bed late. This is how we spend our days.

Today was different. I came home to find that Martin was already online. I can always tell when he's stressed; this morning he seemed to crackle with a kind of furious energy. Hunched over his laptop, he did not look up as I came in, but I could see by the speed at which he was typing that something had put him on the alert. The coffee I'd left to percolate in the kitchen was untouched. I went to kiss him good morning, and he waved me aside with a gesture.

'No time. This is important.'

He doesn't see this as a rebuff. Martin is very focused. Sometimes, feelings must take second place to the things that really matter. His job, for instance. Recently, LifeStory Press has been under attack for publishing a memoir by a literary novelist called Jared Noonan Philips, author of a book called *The Sphinx*, now largely remembered for his far-right opinions, misogyny and championing of the kind of 'free speech' that has never really been under threat. Following his 'cancellation' by a previous publisher, in the wake of multiple complaints, he decided to take up with LifeStory Press, publishing his latest *oeuvre* wholly unedited, under the proud banner of freedom.

Today, a minor Twitter account by the name of *@YoungPretenders*, run by ex-publishing employees, posted the following Twitter thread:

*@YoungPretenders: When I worked in publishing, I was struck by the casual misogyny dominating the industry. JNP was notorious. I know personally of at least 5 people he sexually harassed or assaulted.*

*@YoungPretenders: All of them were juniors: 4 publicists and a sub-editor. Complaints were ignored by the management. One girl was actually told that she 'needed to get streetwise', implying that this came with the job.*

*@YoungPretenders: And yet, he's still being platformed. He still gets invited to festivals. No word from LifeStory's CEO. Still, I guess he'll be safe enough there. Vanity presses don't have publicists.*

Martin is mostly incensed by the fact that they're calling LifeStory a vanity press. It is a hybrid publisher, he says, with some well-known authors on its books. However, these well-known authors all share a certain point of view, giving credence to the belief that LifeStory is a *far-right* vanity press, devoted to tales of misery and cancellation by the woke.

*@theMartinIngram: I would have thought that anyone who has actually worked in publishing would know the difference between hearsay and fact. Please delete your defamatory statement.*

*@YoungPretenders: So you're accepting a predator's word over that of his victims?*

*@theMartinIngram: I'm saying that unless you have proof, you're just another troll account spreading malicious rumours.*

'It's Twitter,' I said. 'Not the real world.'

Martin kept on typing. 'You have no idea what this is about.'

As a matter of fact, I do have *some* idea. Jared Noonan Philips once came to sign stock at Salena's Books. He wasn't a LifeStory author then, and he arrived with a very young publicist, who seemed more than usually anxious. Philips spoke to Salena once, to ask for a cappuccino, and when he had finished signing his books, left the shop without a word, as if we'd been invisible. I think, maybe to him, we were. Martin describes him as *difficult*, but sees his work as signifi-cant, and my aversion to the man as irrational, and therefore unimportant.

I said: 'You forget. I've met the man.' I could feel my own tension mounting. The warm and comforting dopamine rush I'd experienced in the park had subsided. In its place, I could feel a mounting sense of danger, like the approach of a thunderstorm, and with it, the return of that rage, like a dog that has been fed before, and needs no more encouragement.

'*And?*' said Martin, still typing furiously on his laptop.

'And I thought he was a dick,' I said, putting down my coffee cup. 'Now, are you going to spend all day arguing with strangers online, or can we just sit down and enjoy the one day a week we have together?'

Martin sighed. 'For fuck's sake. What's wrong with you this morning?'

*Be careful*, said the inner voice. *Don't get angry. It's dangerous.* 'Nothing,' I said.

'Because if you're going to be like this, I might as well be in my office.'

His eyes did not leave the computer screen, with its scrolling display of messages. Martin seldom makes eye contact. There's always something more urgent to look at. I felt a sudden, vicious urge to scream, to swear, to throw crockery. *Anything to make him look –*

The medical website says this on the subject of hormonal imbalance: *Menopausal mood swings can mask a variety of more serious symptoms, from anxiety and depression to full-blown psychosis.* Or, as My Big Fat Menopause puts it: *Feeling under the weather today? Go mad! Embrace the crazy! Your man will thank you for it!* The accompanying picture shows DeeDee, nicely airbrushed and wearing a pink kimono, kneeling on an enormous bed, and having a pillow fight with Jules, the man she describes as *My Everything.* Jules is handsome, dark and muscular; just the kind of man you'd expect someone like DeeDee to end up with. Similarly, her menopause is exactly the kind of inspirational and photogenic menopause that ends up with her looking fit and slim, and having more sex than ever before.

I had to smile at that. The thought of Martin having a pillow fight, or of doing anything frivolous, seems like a distant memory. Martin is moody; complicated. He thinks about mortality more often than he thinks about sex. When we were eighteen, that made him seem profound and sensitive. But nowadays he is constantly stressed, constantly judgemental. By comparison, I am lightweight, relying too much on my feelings. I wonder what he'd make of my gift. Whether he'd even believe it.

'Jared Philips is a product of his generation,' said Martin. 'A straight white man who's had a long and quite controversial career. Nowadays, that makes him a target for a certain kind of troublemaker.'

According to his Facebook account, Martin believes that the #MeToo trend has been taken to extremes. A woman can ruin a man's career just by dropping a casual hint. I try to point out that this isn't true, but he feels it strongly nevertheless. Women are getting their own back, he says. There's bound to be an injustice.

'I know,' I said. (I *didn't* know.) 'But Twitter's not the place for this. All you can do is make things worse.'

Martin gave a percussive sigh. His mouth tightened like a fist. He stood up, slammed the laptop shut and stuck it under his arm.

'You don't have to go,' I told him.

But he was already halfway to the door, heading for his study. His gaze did not even flicker for a moment towards me. I already knew that his house would be nothing but shuttered windows and bolted doors. Not that I've ever looked in his house. Would I even want to? The thing that I feel for Martin is snarled in complications. Anger is a part of it – anger, and a kind of shame. What would happen if I looked into the room marked *Katie*? Would it awaken the monster within? Or would it simply confirm my fear – or that of my inner critic – that there's no place for me there anymore?

But hers is not the only voice that speaks to me this morning. My inner demon has shown itself, and its voice is very persuasive. The critic says that I should stay, make Sunday lunch, wait for Martin. But now, the inner demon says:

*Fuck that. Let's get more of that dopamine.*

# 4

Now I understand what they mean when they say 'like a child in a sweetshop'. As a child, I was not allowed sweets. My mother always watched my weight, and made sure I never forgot it. But today, my mother's voice takes second place to the inner demon that urges me to follow my joy, and not my guilt. I deserve a little joy. And besides, it doesn't do any harm, as long as I stay in my lane; as long as all I do is look, and share, and stay invisible.

It's not so different, after all, to watching social media. Here too are windows. Here too are friends. Here too is the intimacy of a shared experience. Here too is the chemical hit: igniting the part of the brain that responds so readily to addictive drugs. I know all this. I've been there before. And I know where it can lead. But now I am no longer a child. I can learn to control my gift. With practice, I can make it safe. I can make it better.

The thought is unexpectedly sweet. It smells like synthetic strawberry. I know that scent, and the memory that always comes with it; the memory of my eleventh birthday party, and of my little magic show. I'd been so sure that Katie would understand, and join in the game. So sure that she would remember. But she'd said – *You're disgusting!* – and thrown the Opal Fruit in my face. It had felt like a violation to her. My gift was a violation.

*That was a mistake*, said the voice of my inner demon. *Little kids make mistakes all the time. You're not a little kid anymore. Stop blaming yourself for everything. Get out and start enjoying life.*

Iris' voice is very clear, very persuasive in my mind. Of course, spending time in someone's house does create an intimacy. Perhaps the thing we shared last night has given me this connection; maybe this could be the start of an actual friendship.

*Way to go, Bernie*, says Iris. *Go on. Live a little.*

But where to start? There are so many minds, so many pleasures to choose from. A man, drinking a latte. A child, eating an ice cream. Two young people, a boy and a girl, walking hand in hand on the grass. I need to make contact to look inside – although, with practice, I think that could change. I pull a glove from my coat pocket. I walk up to the two young folk and tap the girl on the shoulder.

'I'm sorry, did you drop this?'

She's even younger than I'd thought. Seventeen, maybe eighteen. Long, dark hair tucked into the hood of an olive-green parka. Her young man is about the same age; maybe they are still at school. She smiles at me and shakes her head – *No, sorry* – before turning away.

All it needs is a touch. Hiding a smile, I slip the glove back into my pocket. The pair moves on, still hand in hand, but I am already with them: elusive and invisible. I stole a sausage roll because I was feeling hungry. And now I am so hungry for love, and this feels so right that it's dangerous.

Her house is a perfect bubble of light, swirling with iridescence. There are no visible doors, no walls, nothing like a front room at all. It feels at the same time small and secure, and yet filled with tremendous potential, like the egg of a mythical bird. And inside, there are photographs, and memories, and private jokes, and nicknames, and invented words, and rainbows, and kisses, and walks in the rain, all of them gilded with meaning; mystic with significance. They spin and dance around the room, reflections from a mirrorball. And at the heart of it all there he is: her beloved, her everything, his presence filling the whole world; shining like the heart of the sun.

For a moment, I felt it with her. That feeling of immortality. The utter certainty, that he too feels exactly what she feels. *This cannot change*, it tells me. *Love like this can never grow old. Time will make an exception for us. Death himself will pass us by.* And for a moment I long to take some of it away with me, to steal from her store of sensations. *Just one kiss. One moment. She'd never even notice.* But this is not a sausage roll or a doughnut, lifted in passing. This is a woman's first love. To take it would be monstrous. And so I tear myself away, still incandescent with borrowed light, and look around for another house. There are so many to choose from. No one suspects when I let myself in. No one feels my presence.

A striking woman saunters by. I take from her the satiny texture of their glances. From a child, feeding ducks by the stream, I snag a bright thread of excitement. It's easy, once you get used to it. Easy, like social media. Little flashes of their lives, reflected through their windows. Here, a lick of borrowed ice cream. There, a powerful memory of surfing in Hawaii.

*This could become an addiction.*

Well, yes. But it feels *good* to be someone else, to live inside another mind. All I need to do is to avoid dark places, forbidden rooms. Mr D was an accident, born of inexperience and rage, the kind of rage that a child can only release in violence. But now, I can learn to control my gift. Now that I am older. Now that I am experiencing what my mother calls *The Change*.

It sounds so ominous, put that way. And I'll admit that when it began, it seemed like the end of everything. The sudden hot flashes. The brain fog. The rage. The death of my visibility. But now I come to realize that change is a two-way mirror. Imagine if I embraced it. Imagine if, instead of being bereft, I learnt to understand my strength. And instead of taking my invisibility as a sign that I have reached my expiry date, I can see it for what it really is.

A superpower.

# TRACK 4:

---

# Strange Phenomena

She knows not what the curse may be,
And so she weaveth steadily,
And little other care hath she,
The Lady of Shalott.
*Alfred, Lord Tennyson, 'The Lady of Shalott'*

# I

*From the LiveJournal of Bernadette Ingram (marked as Exhibit BI 1):*
*Monday, March 28th, 2022*

On Mondays, Salena's Books is closed. I have the whole day to myself. Usually, this tends to involve housework, or ironing, or batch-cooking, or any one of the many tasks that it falls upon me to complete. Today was for important things. Today, I wanted to *practise*.

Martin came downstairs at eight, after a third night in the spare room. I'd prepared his breakfast and mine – coffee, fruit and warm croissants – and was sitting in the front room, checking my social media. There is still no suspect for the Jo Perry murder. CCTV footage shows her about an hour before she died, buying a bottle of water from a little shop near Victoria Park. The footage is in black and white, but you can still read that slogan. *Feminist Killjoy*. Stills from the footage have prompted a number of – largely critical – memes. Several hashtags are trending, including *#NoCurfewForWomen* and *#SheWasOnlyRunning*.

On Instagram, DeeDee LaDouce has discovered the secret to a perfect night's sleep. All you need is Egyptian cotton sheets, a memory foam mattress, great sex and maybe a handful of goji berries, *if you're feeling naughty*. Dan made chicken fajitas last night, and posted a picture to prove it. And Martin must have been awake until about one-thirty: I saw that he had replied to a message from Lucas, then added a comment to a debate about Jared Noonan Philips. Nothing about Katie yet. Nothing about the reunion.

'You're up early today,' he said.

'I thought I'd get an early start.'

'Yeah, the windows need washing, I think. Might as well do it while you've got time.'

*How quick he is to decide*, I thought. *How easy it is for a man to determine how a woman's time should be spent.* I felt a twinge of annoyance. *Here it comes again*, I thought. But maybe there was something left of yesterday's hit of dopamine, because I smiled at him and said:

'I don't think I'll have time today.'

'Whatever. I might be late tonight. I'm having drinks with a client.'

'Jared Noonan Philips?'

He shrugged. 'He's an important author, Bernie. I don't have to agree with everything he says or does, but he's having a rough time, and loyalty matters.'

'OK.'

He gave me a sideways look, as if to check that I wasn't being sarcastic. Then he shrugged again. 'Well, see you later. Don't stay up.' He dropped a cool, dry kiss on my cheek, and suddenly, I felt the most tremendous urge to look into *his* house – to see what his front room was like, and whether *she* still lived there, the way she lives in his passwords. *DreamgirlKatie.* I wondered what it might be like to be somebody's dream girl. To step into the spotlight and shine, like something you were born to do.

I pulled away. 'Have a good day.'

'Oh, and Bernie – your mother called. Yesterday, while you were out.'

*Damn. I'd forgotten those messages.* 'What did she want?'

He shrugged. 'Who knows? Anyway, better call her.'

I watched him go, and felt the last of my dopamine evaporate. I didn't want a conversation with my mother right now. All I wanted now was to go out and enjoy the day. But I always call her on Mondays. I knew she would be expecting me. And she had phoned me while I was at work, which very seldom happens. So I poured another coffee, even though it's bad for me, and braced myself for the ordeal.

She answered at the third ring. 'Oh, it's you.' Even when she's expecting my call, she always manages to sound both surprised and vaguely resentful, as if I have interrupted something important.

'I'm sorry. I got your messages. Why don't you use the mobile?'

'You know I don't do mobiles. Besides, it's fine. Dan called me.'

'Oh, right.' Of course he did. Even now, it's hard to suppress that little twinge of resentment. Pocket-dialling aside, Dante speaks to his grandmother more often than he speaks to me. 'He must have guessed it would be a shock,' she went on. 'Having that happen so close to your house. Thinking that the murderer might even have been someone you met.'

For a moment, I was confused. 'You mean – Jo Perry's murder?'

*Of course*, I thought. It makes perfect sense. My mother has lived all her life in a town of small events and small people. To her, London seems like a vast hotbed of crime, and still she assumes that I must know everyone in my neighbourhood. I decided not to tell her that I had met the victim. And as for telling her that I might even have dreamed of the murderer –

'They're saying he might be a stalker. He might have followed her from the gym. Is that *your* local gym, Bernie?'

'There must be half a dozen gyms within a mile of our house,' I said. 'Besides, you know I don't go to the gym.' My mother uses the local gym as her private social club. She feels that I should do the same, stalkers notwithstanding.

'I don't know why you don't,' she said. 'I go to my step class every week. Then there's the pool, and the yoga. I go there with Maggie. And Katie, of course. It's nice. We make a day of it.'

My mother likes to remind me that Katie Malkin has remained in the place where she was born; close to her mother; her old school friends. She likes to remind me that Katie often sees her mother, even goes with her to the gym. That they are friends.

*Here it comes.*

I shouldn't have had the coffee. The tension that always gathers when I speak to my mother on the phone had become the start of a hot flash, clawing at my breastbone. I forced myself to breathe deeply. This anger. Where does it come from? What am I meant to do with it?

'Katie goes running,' my mother went on. 'Of course, she was always a runner.'

'Yes, she was.' The hot flash had spread, and once more I felt a dull ache in my lower abdomen. Even with painkillers, these menstrual cramps are the worst I've had since school. Maybe evening primrose will help. I promised myself to buy some. But really, it might be better just to ignore my mother.

'And at your age, it's easy to put on weight. You should think about taking up yoga, or Pilates.'

My mother has a difficult relationship with her weight, and with mine. When I married Martin – not at St Luke's, but in Malbry Town Hall, with only six guests in attendance – I wore a plus-size wedding dress bought from a local second-hand shop, and my mother wept throughout. Not at losing me, but because I was too big for *The Dress*. It was my mother's wedding dress, and her mother's before her; a floor-length sheath of handmade lace over a slip of oyster silk. It had always been understood that I, too, would wear it one day. But women in the twenties were small. My mother had to diet for months to manage to fit into it herself. And by the time Martin and I were wed, I was seven months pregnant. *The Dress* might have fitted, but for my sin. Smallness in a woman is a measurement of virtue.

'Come up at Easter,' my mother said. (She knows I won't come up at Easter.) 'I could get you a day pass to the gym. Spinning, step, anything you fancy. Or you could just try the sauna.'

The cramp again, like a burning hand, clawing at my insides. I wanted to scream. The sauna. *Why bother with the sauna*, I thought, *when you've got the menopause?* I said: 'Listen, Mum. I've got to go. I need to wash the windows.'

'Of course,' she said. 'I'll let you get off.'

It's the kind of excuse she understands. The myth of my domesticity is one that my mother likes to believe. '*Will* you be coming for Easter?'

'I don't think Martin can get the time off.'

'Well, if ever you change your mind –'

'I'll let you know. Goodbye, Mum.'

I sat for a moment, feeling that unfocused anger begin to subside. I know I'm being ungrateful. It isn't her fault she's like this. But after the past few days, I think I can cut myself some slack. I drank a large glass of water (another of DeeDee's

*Life Hacks*) and then headed off to the park again in search of some hacking of my own.

It took me maybe half an hour to regain my earlier sense of well-being. But, today, I wanted more than just the taste of a stolen doughnut. My glance into the teenage girl has given me an appetite for more of the same, and a curiosity to see of what more I am capable. Could I go back to a person's house without having to touch them again? I sense that perhaps, with practice, I could. Could I even go without having touched the person at all? So far, I have no idea of the limits of my newfound skill. But something tells me that it must extend further than just baked goods. And on a day like this – clear and sunny with the promise of spring – the possibilities are endless. People are always eating.

I avoided Priscilla's Pantry – I didn't want to have to deal with Iris today – but managed to snag an almond croissant from a businessman on the way to work, then a turmeric latte from a woman coming from yoga. In both cases, I took the sensation with me as I left. Neither of them noticed. DeeDee would probably say something about the importance of mindful eating, but I've realized that most people are very far from mindful. They ignore so many sensations; so much of their experience. Caught in the worry-groove of their thoughts, they forget to live in the moment.

Another takeaway was the yoga class the woman had left. I've never really tried yoga before, and she won't miss the session. In fact, she'll probably tell herself that she was concentrating so hard that she achieved a state of temporary bliss, thereby wiping out much of the memory. From my perspective, however, I learnt not only what it feels to achieve perfect body alignment, but also (perhaps more importantly) that I can take away recent past experience as well as mere sensation.

Victoria Park has reopened. A fenced-off area under some trees is marked as a crime scene by the police, but the rest of the park is available. A pretty young woman in running gear, wearing Wi-Fi headphones, happens to drop her water flask within easy distance of my bench. A moment of contact. A smile. *Thanks*! And then she runs on, with the easy stride of someone at home in their body, feeling the quiet enjoyment of well-trained muscles and youthful joints, little knowing that she has picked up an invisible passenger.

It has been a long, long time since I travelled in this way. Katie was a runner, and so was Grace Oyemade. I ran with them both in secret, around the track at Mulberry House, feeling the wind against my face, the flexing of my muscles. As a girl, I avoided sports, except in this clandestine way. I hated my body; my puppy fat; the way the other girls looked at me. Most of all, I hated the way Mr Davis looked at me: the boyish, blue-eyed charm of him, the way his gaze would linger. The male gaze is all entitlement. It sizes up girls like bakery goods. And the other girls *liked* it. Even Katie liked it, fluttering her eyelashes and playing with her hair. Katie had *liked* it, even though she knew how to look into his house, and see what he was hiding –

*Did you think you could win her back? Is that what you were thinking?*

I banish the voice to the Quiet Room. Things are different for me now. Now I simply take what I need, reflecting nothing but blind space. This woman will never know I was there, but will assume that she has zoned out, listening to her music. No 'Manchild' for her, but the soothing tones of Schubert, and the regular, easy strides as she runs, and her calm and powerful breathing. She is thinking about a fun run in memory of Jo Perry. *All the girls will be there*, she thinks.

*We'll show those bastards we're not afraid.* I feel a strong sense of hope in her that the murderer will be found, and that the woman's family will be able to grieve in peace. And then there is nothing but Schubert, and the silky momentum of her stride, and the air that rushes past her face, and the joy of losing time.

I stayed with her for half an hour, until she came to the end of her run. I was pleasantly out of breath, but nowhere near exhausted. And throughout the whole experience, I was aware of my true self, sitting there on the park bench, looking out into nothingness. If anyone had spoken to me, I would have heard them, and come back, as if from deep reflection. But no one did. Why would they? A middle-aged woman on a bench, wearing jeans and a pea coat. No one stopped to look at me. No one asked me anything. No one would remember me.

I went back home – I was feeling cold, in spite of the unusual exercise, and dream food can only take you so far. Filled with the kind of endorphins only a runner feels, I went online and bought myself a pair of new trainers, and a sports bra in a cheery raspberry colour that I would never have chosen otherwise. Then I made a light lunch, checked my social media, and sat down to the second part of today's experiment.

Travelling is just the start.

Now to see if I can go back.

# 2

*Tuesday, March 29th*

Her name is Steph. She is twenty-five, currently single, but dating. Her Tinder profile shows her at a beach party in Tenerife, wearing an ochre print sarong and a crochet bikini top. She looks like every girl in every magazine you've ever seen; but unlike DeeDee LaDouce, she is calm, sincere, and thoughtful. I can see this in her house, although I do not venture far: I stay clear of her private spaces and her painful memories.

But yes, now I know the answer to the first of my questions. I *can* return to a person's house without making physical contact. It's easy; once I know a house, I can locate it on the map of streets and houses in my mind. I visited Steph several times last night. I watched her take off her running gear. I watched her making dinner. We went on a night out with her friends. I drank two strawberry daiquiris. I borrowed the memory of that beach party in Tenerife, and the feel of the ocean on bare, tanned skin, and the wonder of being in a body that seemed at ease with its nature. I did *not* look into her sex life, although I did take a look at her large and bewildering collection of vibrators, then later, when she was in bed (and

Martin was in the guest room), I shared her use of one of them (a sugar-pink object she thinks of as *The Magic Wand*), before drifting into sleep by her side, and waking up in the afterglow of being another person.

This could become an addiction. I know. I'll make sure that doesn't happen. But getting up this morning in my own, sad, middle-aged body, with the sweat of another hot flash pooling under my breastbone, I can still recall the thrill of how it felt to be twenty-five, and confident in my body. I never felt that way myself. At twenty-five, my life was a mess. There were no cocktails, no runs in the park. No holidays in Tenerife. No supportive circle of friends. At twenty-five, I was already a woman in free fall, lost and afraid, the mother of a six-year-old, the wife of a man whose heart was elsewhere.

He only fucked her once, he said. He thought I should be grateful for that. And, in a way, I suppose I was. Men have such a low bar to reach, compared to most of the rest of us. And after all, he has stayed with me. Surely that counts for something. Surely, that must matter more than a fleeting infatuation. I tell myself these things when I want reassurance. My inner critic repeats them to me with just the right level of sarcasm.

*It's nothing*, she tells me, in that voice that reminds me of my mother. *Only a child would still resent a one-night stand from decades ago. You have the marriage, the house, the son. Let him have his fantasy.*

But what about *my* fantasy? Maybe I could have one, too. And although my newfound talent might seem disturbing – *intrusive* – to some, no crockery was broken. No one was harmed. All mirrors and smoke. Nothing but reflections.

Martin left early this morning, without even stopping for coffee. The meeting with Jared Noonan Philips last night seems

not to have eased things as much as he'd hoped. He tells me
nothing, of course, but Facebook is always forthcoming. It
tells me that Noonan Philips is once more being interviewed
on TV on the subject of his cancellation, and that he will be
part of a debate on no-platforming later next month at the
Oxford Union. The thought occurs that for a man who has
been rejected by his industry, he is still getting more than his
share of attention. His name was trending on Twitter today,
above the Jo Perry murder. There's something desperately sad
about this: that a young woman's death has been eclipsed by
a man's discomfort.

One of the publicists who accused him of harassment has
been identified online, and is receiving abuse from his readers.
It seems that Noonan Philips's readers feel that she is ungrateful,
sly and attention-seeking; using the *#MeToo* movement to
further her publishing career. The *@YoungPretenders* account
has disappeared from Twitter. I'm not surprised: these are
junior staff. Noonan Philips is a monolith. It will take more
to topple him than a few allegations of sexual misconduct.

I check Dante's Instagram. (Sausage and mash.) I like these
glimpses of his life. I know they are trivial, but it makes me
feel as if I'm with him every day. And DeeDee has written a
new post, entitled: *Let Your Inner Goddess Fly!* – which includes
many photographs of her on a kind of garden swing or trapeze,
long hair flying like a flag, with Jules standing ready to catch
her. There are also *Goddess Recipes*, including multi-seed Cobb
salad, sugar-free ginger lemonade, and cucumber granita, all of
which seem designed to give me a craving for carbohydrates.

Before heading out to Salena's Books, I made for Priscilla's
Pantry. Iris was at the counter, with Rahmi, the girl in the
hijab. Iris was wearing hot-pink jeans under her nylon overall,
and a silver stud in her nose.

She grinned as she saw me. 'Hey, Bernie! I was just thinking you might pop in.'

'How are you?'

'Great! The muffins are fresh. Yours might have been a bit chewy last week.'

I returned her smile. 'That's good to know. I'll have one, and a pot of tea.'

I sat at a table, and drank my tea, watching the people come and go. Iris was right: the muffins were fresh. *Should have ordered two*, I thought.

'Do you want another?' she said. 'This one's on Priscilla.'

I was surprised. Coincidence? Or had I reflected the thought at her accidentally? I glanced, very cautiously, into her house. I saw a glimpse of bright colours; some cheery disorder; a TikTok account; some *Marvel* comics merchandise; a guinea pig; a tattooist; a sense of being young and filled with hope in the face of a rapidly changing world. No damage. No sense of violation. No anxiety, no fear. Nothing to suggest that my intervention had done any harm. Nor was there any remaining trace of Saturday night's misadventure. No mental or physical sign of stress. No unusual behaviour. Maybe whatever changes had happened to her were wearing off. I hoped so.

'Thanks,' I said. 'Where *is* Priscilla, anyway?'

'Sorry to disappoint you,' said Iris, setting the muffin in front of me. 'There is no Priscilla. Instead, there's a guy called Dean Potts who manages a bunch of different bakeries and coffee shops around London, and who I see maybe once a month. Dean likes me to sell *all* the cakes, no matter how chewy they're getting.'

'Dean sounds like a prince,' I said.

'You can put him on the list.'

'What list?'

Iris grinned again. 'You know. The *list*. Of all the guys who need – *you know*. A bit of the old VIP treatment.' She made an expressive gesture.

*Oh.*

I felt a flash of anxiety. I'd been so concerned about Iris that I'd almost forgotten how quickly she'd adapted and moved on. Katie had been traumatized by what she'd seen in Adam Price. She'd even been disgusted by my little trick with the Opal Fruit. And later, she'd been devastated by what had happened to Mr D. Thus I'd expected Iris to be confused, afraid, revolted. Instead, she had embraced it all – *accepted* it – with alarming speed. Not just that: she'd *liked* it. Liked it, and she wanted more.

I swallowed. 'Iris. There isn't a list.'

'Isn't there?' said Iris.

'Absolutely not,' I said.

Iris shrugged, still grinning. 'We'll talk about that on Friday,' she said. 'I've already got some ideas. You'll see. Then you can tell me how it works. This is going to be a *lot* of fun.'

I finished my muffin in silence, now feeling very uneasy. Contrary to my expectations, Iris has not changed her mind about what had happened on Saturday. If anything, her certainty has become even stronger. I doubt now if I could make her believe that she imagined the whole thing.

*You could, though. You could change her mind*, the inner demon told me.

I pushed the thought away. No. Iris, in spite of appearances, is processing a traumatic event. To interfere in that process could have dangerous consequences.

And yet, the question remained. Could I *really* change someone's mind? Make them pick an almond croissant instead of a chocolate doughnut? Something inside me told me I could, although my inner critic protested that it was wrong, it was *dangerous* –

*Never again, you said. Never again.*

I banished her to the Quiet Room, and sat there, enjoying my second muffin. A couple of customers came and went, one a woman buying croissants to take away, the second a man in his seventies who ordered a cup of black coffee. I hooked an arm over the back of my chair. He brushed against me as he passed. I felt that crackle of energy, like a hot flash, without the discomfort. And then came the click of connection, and a familiar surge of dopamine.

*Could* I have made him buy something else?

I glanced at his house. It was open. His front room was colourless, lonely and spare. A widower's house. No children. A portrait on the mantelpiece of a woman, gilded with love. A collar and lead beside it, from a dog that died some years ago. A sense that the woman, too, had died many, many years ago. A sense of resignation, of waiting for something to happen. A powerful air of nostalgia, like the scent of potpourri.

I sent him a tiny suggestion. Something like a little note, left on top of his mantelpiece, saying: *Go on, treat yourself* – and the taste of my lemon muffin.

From the corner of my eye, I watched him. Saw him look around, as if he'd heard an unusual sound. I held my breath, half expecting him to say something to me. Then he stood up.

'Excuse me, young lady. I've changed my mind. I think I'll have one of those,' he said.

Iris smiled. 'Lemon muffin? Good choice.'

I felt a sudden rush of triumph. *I can do it! I changed his mind!*

From the Quiet Room, I sensed the inner critic protesting. But the dopamine rush was still strong in me. I glanced at

Iris. *You next.* What would it take to make her give up her suspicions about me?

A note, maybe. A note that says: *Forget about Woody*. Or: *Life goes on*. Nothing deep or probing. Just a friendly, casual hint.

I looked into her front room again. Iris likes bright colours and the energy of disorder. Her house is filled with shiny things, make-up palettes, vintage clothes. She loves super-heroes, especially Wonder Woman and Ms Marvel, but her house is filled with other figures that I do not recognize: women with names like Rogue and Storm, Mystique, Jean Grey and Kitty Pryde. Her guinea pig, Ralph, features heavily in her inner décor, as does her houseplant, Henry (an avocado she grew from a seed). She has a boyfriend, but he scarcely warrants a mention: the last in a handwritten list of men Blu-tacked to the living-room wall, the names crossed out in lipstick and marked: *Douchebag Exes*.

There are many reflective surfaces – more than I remember. And on the mantelpiece there is a light-box, decorated with holographic palm trees. As I approach to leave my note, it flashes:

*Hello, Bernie!*

*She knows I'm here. How can she know?* Perhaps it's the link between us. Iris knows how this trick works. She's seen it in operation. She knows when I'm trying to misdirect, and refuses to co-operate.

I finished my muffin, stood up and brought my tray back to the counter.

'Thank you, Iris.'

'Any time.' She grinned. 'I'll see you on Friday.'

# 3

*Tuesday, March 29th*

I arrived at Salena's Books to find a poster in the window, carefully lettered in rainbow script, embellished with drawings in a style I recognized as Salena's.

*FUN RUN*
*Victoria Park, 9.30 a.m.*
*Sunday, 3 April*
*#RunForJo*

This must be what I saw in Steph's house as she ran through the park yesterday. According to Twitter, running clubs all over the country are holding similar events. While Salena was making tea, I checked the hashtag *#RunForJo*, which happens to be trending.

Comments are mostly what you'd expect:

*@whitey2947: Feminists have persuaded women that they can do anything. This proves they can't. You can't fight biology.*

*@brrrrrro2156231: Women should get a male friend to go with them when they go out. It makes sense.*

138

*@Irisnoir23: Or maybe men should stay indoors unless they have a female friend to keep an eye on them. #NoCurfewForWomen*

Ouch. I scrolled through the angry replies. *@Irisnoir23* has no fear, and responds to even the worst of the comments with a humour that is often profane. There's something about the style, too, that seems oddly familiar. I clicked onto the bio, and read: *Poisonous flower. Blooms at night.* There is no photograph. A search through her feed shows most of her posts consist of pictures of make-up, tattoos, hairstyles, her guinea pig, and shots of a miniature dachshund belonging to her tattooist. But over the past forty-eight hours, she has become visibly more combative, especially on the subject of violence towards women.

*Iris?*

My glimpses into her house suggest that, yes, it's likely to be her. Maybe I'll ask her on Friday. Maybe I should warn her, too. I don't think she's as tough as she sounds. The need to protect her still feels very strong. I wonder why I feel this way. It's surely nothing as basic as the mothering instinct. And yet, there's something about her that draws me – that *attracts* me. Maybe it's just that I've seen who she is without the usual filters.

'How do you like my poster?'

That was Salena, startling me out of my social media haze. She was carrying two cups of tea and a plate with two almond croissants. *At this rate, you'll be as big as a house,* warned my inner critic, although the part of me that perpetually craves baked goods gave a cheer.

'I like it. Do you run, then?' *I've known her all this time,* I thought, *and yet it never occurred to me to ask how she spends her free time.*

She nodded. 'The Finchley Fliers. You should join us. Reclaim the park. Take the curse off what happened there.'

I smiled. 'I'm not a runner,' I said.

*And yet, you chose to follow Steph. You bought running shoes and a sports bra. Could it be your subconscious telling you something, even then?*

'No one's a runner, until they start,' said Salena. 'Try it. Surprise yourself.'

I wondered what Salena would think if she knew how much I've already done that. Steph has already shown me so much. With her, I can experience the dopamine of a runner's high. I could even learn how it feels to run the London Marathon. And yet, the part of me that bought those running shoes and sports bra feels a twinge of rebellion. *You could do those things* yourself, it says in a tiny, needling voice. *You don't need smoke and mirrors.*

'How many people have signed up?'

'Over a hundred women so far.'

'Wow.'

Sometimes my skin seems to understand my feelings more readily than I do. I felt a hot flash sweep over me, rising from my throat to my cheeks, bringing fear, excitement, and that familiar rush of adrenaline. I tried to imagine the scene. The women in their running gear, the ushers, the leaflets, the laughter. I could feel my heart beating a little faster at the thought. Once more, I thought of Tennyson's Lady of Shalott, watching the world in reflection. What if, instead of watching from the safety of another's house, of sharing their borrowed experience, I tried to make some of my own?

*That didn't work out too well with the Lady of Shalott,* says a distant voice from the Quiet Room. *Better stick with what you know.*

And yet, the words have a resonance. *I am half sick of shadows.* Maybe I'll put my name down today. After all, as DeeDee says, *you are whatever you want to be.*

# 4

Nine customers this morning. Three cat-lovers, four browsers, and one of our regulars, Peggy Griffin, who already owes Salena for her last book, and somehow keeps forgetting her credit card in her other coat.

The last one was a woman with a little boy of about six, who excitedly made for the children's corner, only to be shooed away from the book he was holding, in favour of another one chosen by his mother.

'But I want *this* one!'

'That one's for girls, Olly. You can tell. It even has a pink cover.'

'Why?'

Salena looked up from her display. 'You know, he's right,' she said with a smile. 'We only sell books for everyone here. Otherwise, Kafka feels left out.'

The woman gave Salena an unfriendly look. I could tell she didn't approve of her. Some people are like that with Salena. They assume – because I'm so much older (and whiter) than she is – that I'm the bookshop manager.

'We'll just take these,' she said to me, holding out two paperbacks by a (male) celebrity children's writer. I sighed

141

inwardly, and smiled, and rang up her two purchases. There's really no point in trying to reason with a personal prejudice. And yet, I wanted to tell her that boys who don't value girls' stories eventually grow into men who don't value women's rights. I looked at her as she rummaged in her handbag for her credit card. My face was suddenly very hot.

*None of my business*, I told myself, in the voice of my inner critic. *She's the one with the credit card.* The customer is always right, even when they're totally wrong. The little boy – Olly – stood by her side, looking mutinous. He'd left the book he'd chosen on the table in the kids' corner. I couldn't see the title, but the jacket was pinkish-purple.

'You know, that's not really pink,' Salena told Olly with a smile. 'The name of that colour is *heliotrope*. It's from the Greek. It means: "turns to the sun". It's a mineral, too, called *bloodstone*. It's worn as a sign of courage.'

Olly's face lit up. 'Wow!'

His mother's expression tightened. 'With the prices you charge here, you're lucky I buy anything. If I didn't want to support my local high street, I'd just go online, like everyone else.'

I gave another inward sigh. I wasn't planning to interfere. I didn't even touch her. But still, there came a flash of heat, a buzz like bottled lightning; a crackle of activity across the channels of my mind.

Her house was lit. As if through a glass, I could see inside it. And this time, I looked beyond the front room, to a door that led into a narrow arcade, lit by stuttering neon signs, clanging with insecurities. Racism has a resonance. So does homophobia, and internalized misogyny. I could hear them chiming away, in that place beyond consciousness, like radio signals in the dark, sending out the same primitive message.

For a moment, I listened for a specific frequency. And then, very gently, I reached inside, and made a few adjustments –

That's how Katie and I played *House*. Making up rooms, leaving messages, swapping little trivial things from one house to another. The taste of one thing for another. Or maybe the clang of bigotry to something more melodious. It was easy. Instinctive. I barely knew I was doing it. That heat, the colour of anger, was beginning to subside, leaving in its place the warmth of a human connection.

I smiled, and said in a quiet voice: 'Let him have his book, Ruth.'

She looked at me in sharp surprise. Then her expression softened. 'Of course. My name's on my credit card. What did you say?'

I smiled again. 'How old is Olly?'

'Seven in May. But his reading age tests as nine.'

'That's wonderful,' I said warmly. 'It means he's ready for something more than mass-produced clichés and stereotypes.'

She nodded. 'Absolutely.' From inside her house, I sensed a shift from suspicion to acceptance. The harmonies were changing. The neon signs shifted from red to blue. Gently, I introduced a suggestion that there was no cause for fear; that reading books with pink jackets instead of blue ones would not stop her son being who he really was. And then I left a note for her on the mantelpiece of her front room: *A mother loves her child for who they are, not for what she thinks they should be.*

I went on: 'Reading diverse authors helps a child develop their social skills. You're making a wonderful investment in your little boy's future.'

She nodded again, looking relieved. 'Of course. That's what every good parent wants.' Once more, she turned to the child. 'Run and get your book, Olly.'

Olly grinned and scampered off to retrieve his book. His mother watched him indulgently. I caught a glimpse of his house from afar, reflected in the window glass; a fairyland of unicorns, and pastel dreams of flying.

'Not a bad day,' Salena said. 'We sold a dozen books online. And Kafka got over eight hundred likes. If he gets over a thousand, I'm going to buy him a catnip mouse.' She paused to check the arrangement of a stack of books in the window. 'You were great today,' she said. 'You're really good with the customers. I think maybe things are starting to change.'

I smiled. 'Thank you, Salena.'

Maybe she's right, I told myself as I walked home past the park where Jo Perry died. Maybe things *are* starting to change. I stopped at the chemist to buy another couple of packs of Maxi Pads. I have the feeling that over the next few days, I am going to need them.

# TRACK 5:

## Fight like a Girl

And sometimes through the mirror blue
The knights come riding two and two:
She hath no loyal knight and true,
The Lady of Shalott.
*Alfred, Lord Tennyson, 'The Lady of Shalott'*

# I

*Extract from Class of '92, by Kate Hemsworth*
*(published by LifeStory Press, 2023)*

What most people didn't know was that the *Second Incident* came in two parts. Part One was Sports Day. You know about that. Part Two came later, and as far as anyone knew, Bernie Moon had nothing to do with it.

They were wrong.

After Sports Day, Grace Oyemade left school. She dropped right off the radar. We didn't think much about it at the time. There was so much already happening – end-of-term parties, books to give back, special Assemblies, House awards, as well as all the usual Mulberry House drama – that we didn't give much thought to one girl's disappearance. Most of us assumed that Grace had simply lost it for a while – too much pressure, too much work, too much Sports Day atmosphere – and that she'd be back at the start of next term. But by the time September arrived, we found that she had vanished for good into the frenzy of Sunnybank Park, where pupils wear sweatshirts instead of uniforms, and bunk off to the amusement arcade. No one said why she had left, but I think we assumed that her parents couldn't afford to pay the school fees. Some of us spoke of looking her up, but we never got around to it. We never saw her at the athletics club anymore, either; apparently, that part of her life had also vanished without trace.

Meanwhile, Bernie Moon went on as she always had before, spending her breaks in the library, or walking alone around the edge of the playing fields, like a stray dog. No one was actively unkind, but no one made much of an effort to be friends with her, either. I used to see her around sometimes, in her home-knitted cardigan and Wednesday Addams plaits, but, to be honest, most of the time, I never really thought about her.

It was three weeks into the new term that we started to really notice that something had changed about Mr D. He turned up late to lessons. Where once he had been fit and well groomed, he now looked increasingly scruffy. He started to wear his driving gloves all the time, even indoors. He no longer ran laps outside, or chatted to his Special Squad. We wondered if he'd been working too hard. There were rumours he'd been drinking.

We tried to cover for him at first. We started lessons without him. When he arrived at the gym fifteen minutes late, holding a cup of coffee and looking harassed, he would find us running laps, or getting the equipment out, or skipping, or doing exercises. But some days he never turned up at all, and finally, just before half-term, Ms Langley happened to walk into a third-year gym class one day to find no member of staff in charge, and that was when the whole thing came out.

Apparently, Mr D had been having what Ms Langley called 'episodes'. What that meant, Ms Langley did not specify, but we got a new teacher after that, and Mr D went on sick leave. He never came back. There were rumours – a nervous breakdown; a mini-stroke; a reaction to illegal steroids; an illicit affair with a pupil – but we never found out what had happened.

Lorelei favoured the sex-scandal theory. But Mr D didn't look like someone having an affair. He looked like he slept in his clothes every night. He smelt of stale cigarette smoke and booze. He looked like a drunk or a homeless guy, and we felt let down, embarrassed because we'd once looked up to him. And when he left, school life went on with all its other dramas, and we forgot him, because, to us, what happened outside our world wasn't real. Adults were like shadows to us, looking out for us, telling us what to do, but we never saw them as human beings who might have dramas of their own.

Six months later, he made the news. Not just the *Malbry Examiner*, but some of the nationals, and Yorkshire TV. For a time, he was everywhere. One picture showed him at Sports Day: tall, good-looking, surrounded by girls. The other, taken by some kind of security camera, showed a scruffy old man with white hair who might have been fifty, or older. He looked so different in that shot that we wouldn't have recognized him. And then came the pictures of his house, stacked floor-to-ceiling with old magazines, cardboard boxes, rubbish bags; the windows nailed shut from the inside; ripped-up carpets pinned over the doors. We heard he'd stayed there since leaving his job, never venturing outside; having his groceries delivered rather than walking the hundred yards down the road to the corner shop. His electricity supply had been cut off when he didn't pay the bills. When the police finally called, after several reports from neighbours, the man had been dead for at least a month, the groceries left on the inside porch in a soft grey cushion of rot.

The cause of death was uncertain – opinions hovered between starvation, suicide, drugs, or maybe some kind of infection – but it was clear that his state of mind had been unbalanced for some time. It was a shock to all of us. Ms Langley offered counselling. Most of us declined – it would have meant missing Drama – but all the same, something had shifted. Maybe it was something to do with adolescent hormones. Maybe it was the shock of his death. Or maybe it was Bernie Moon, and the way she looked at me.

I started to remember things. Not all at once, but in flashes that whipped me around like a spinning top. Tiny fragments of memories, like reflections in broken glass.

*Choose a sweet. Don't show me which one.*

*It's our secret. Best friends share.*

I didn't talk about it, though. None of my friends would have understood. I briefly considered Lorelei, but after Bernie's party she'd been so quick to dismiss any kind of weirdness that I didn't want to confide in her. There was a mean side to Lorelei, popular though she was at school, and if she was in a nasty mood, there was no telling what tales she might spread. And I *enjoyed* being popular. I liked being on the hockey team, and being part of the Drama club. I liked being invited to the kind of parties that everyone wanted to go to. I couldn't afford to remember Bernie Moon, or her weirdness.

For a long time after his death, Mr D's house remained empty. Children sneaked in once in a while, to see where it had happened. I went there myself, once, alone, in the summer holidays. Someone had spray-painted *NONCE* on the door, in an aching, metallic blue. Inside, the peeling walls were covered in spray-painted messages; tags from local graffiti artists, but mostly the same words, repeatedly. The same words the officers had found crudely tattooed onto his hands and chest, and then scrawled into his inner arms, probably using a razor blade.

*Never again.*

# 2

*From the LiveJournal of Bernadette Ingram (marked as Exhibit BI 1):*
*Wednesday, March 30th, 2022*

Somehow, I've already managed to get through two packs of
Maxi Pads. I think perhaps the worst of it is coming to an
end – at least this morning I didn't wake up to a crime scene
between the sheets. And both my running shoes and sports
bra arrived this morning. Martin was just leaving the house,
and signed for the delivery.

'Thinking of taking up running?' he said. 'Well, if it helps
you lose the weight –' Martin is always very aware of other
people being overweight. He's always been tall and skinny,
but now he has to watch what he eats, and he is forever self-
conscious of his slightly increased waistline. 'Maybe you should
try one of those day passes first, before we waste money on
a year's gym membership you'll never use.'

'I don't want to join a gym,' I said. 'I thought – I might
join a running club.'

He looked surprised. 'Really? Well, as long as you don't
do it at night. You heard about that woman, right?'

'Jo Perry.'

'Right. You should get one of those apps. The ones that

track you through your phone. And maybe try a self-defence class. I think they do one at Woody's gym.'

I shook my head. 'Not there, no.'

'Why not?'

'I just don't want to.'

He looked at me curiously. 'What's wrong? You've been acting weird for days. Is it still the –' He made a sweeping gesture in the general direction of his belt buckle, which I think was meant to convey either 'bleeding' or 'menopause'.

'I'm fine,' I said. 'I just don't want to hang around your creepy friend's gym.'

The words were out of my mouth before I could stop them. The changes of the past few days have brought my emotions into sharp relief. My words are no longer cushioned, but edged, like tiny shards of broken glass. And it feels good to say it at last, to let out some of my anger. Strange, but I never knew there was so much anger in me. Who is it for? I'm really not sure. I've never thought of myself as an angry person. And yet, there it is, like an old friend, back after years of absence.

Martin gave me a strange look. 'Creepy? That seems very unfair. You can't have met him more than a couple of times.'

I shrugged. 'I know he's your friend, but –'

'He's going through a bad time right now. You should try to cut him some slack.'

I stopped. 'What kind of a bad time?'

'Health issues.'

'Oh.' I wonder what *health issues* Woody is experiencing. I wonder whether hot flashes feature, or changes in libido, or brain fog, or night sweats, exhaustion, or insomnia. I somehow doubt it. If he were going through something like that, someone would have noticed.

My skin seemed to understand how I felt. It prickled with a sudden heat. I could almost visualize the anger shifting over me, like colours on an octopus.

*Yes, let's all feel sorry for Jim Wood. Let's try to cut the rapist some slack. Because people like Woody deserve a free pass from the consequences of their actions.*

I kept it in check until Martin had gone, but I can feel it in me still. Rage, yes – but rage against whom? My Big Fat Menopause says this on the subject of menopausal rage:

*No, you're not going crazy, although some days it may feel that way! But make sure you have a plan for those days when you just feel like biting someone. Have a bath, or go for a run, or work on those yoga exercises. Replace coffee with herbal tea. And if all else fails, there's always my number-one way to relax! Remember, it burns calories, too!*

By which she means having sex, I suppose. In DeeDee's world, sex cures everything not cured by baths, or sheet masks, or breathing deeply. Personally, I'd rather have tea. But running seems like a good idea. Maybe I can channel my energy into something healthy. Meanwhile, there's always the borrowed thrill of someone else's sensation. Dopamine is a gateway drug, and there's no shortage this morning. Breakfast snagged from a passer-by who pushes past without an apology. A hug from a mother with her child as she plays with him in the park. The memory of great sex last night from a young woman in a wheelchair. The feeling of having completed the final level in a challenging game from a girl in school uniform. And I no longer need physical contact to look into these people. I can make the connection just by getting close to them.

A man bumps into me on the path. At first, I assume it's an accident. I was in someone else at the time, and the sensation is slightly delayed, like a brief loss of signal. I find myself saying *sorry* even as I feel the impact – an impact that sends me spinning. My shoulder is aching fiercely. I have bitten my lower lip. Then I see him running, fast: a young man in a baseball cap, clutching my bag under his arm, and the inner critic has time to say: *This is what happens when you* – and that rage lashes out like an animal.

*STOP!*

There was no time to look into his house. No time to get to know him. No time to formulate the words; instead, I flung them into his mind like a stone through a plate-glass window.

*STOP RIGHT THERE!*

He stopped. My skin was burning. I could feel the sweat running down my face; stinging my armpits. I could feel the rush of adrenaline – more addictive than a runner's high – making my muscles tremble. I looked at the young man on the path, some hundred yards away from me. A young man in a baseball cap; black sweatpants; nylon jacket. My bag was still tucked under his arm. I could see him shaking. He hadn't moved. His back was still turned, but even at that distance, I could see the tension that held him in place on the footpath.

Very slowly, still trembling, I started to walk towards him. The young man in the baseball cap stayed exactly where he was. As I came closer, I saw his face contorted with exertion.

I put my hand on the bag. 'Give that back.'

The young man nodded; reluctantly held it out towards me.

'Now, apologize,' I said.

He whispered something inaudible.

'I asked you to *apologize*,' I said, a little louder. Sweat was streaming down my face and into the band of my sports bra, and yet it felt good. It felt *powerful*.

'I'm sorry,' the young man whispered.

I took the bag from his outstretched hand and slung it over my shoulder. I felt as if I'd run a race; endorphins flooded my body. *Eat your heart out, DeeDee*, I thought. *This is my kind of menopause.*

'I'm sorry,' repeated the young man. 'Please, Miss. I'm sorry.'

'All right,' I said. The rush of heat was slowly starting to dissipate. The young man's eyes were fixed on mine like those of an abused animal. For a second, I thought of Dante. Then I thought of Adam Price, with his perpetually runny nose, and his angry fists, and that pinched, white look that spoke of malnutrition. I wasn't angry anymore. Instead, I felt like crying. I tucked the bag protectively under my arm, looked back at the young man and said: *'Now never do that again.'* Then I walked on without looking back, into the sunny spring morning.

# 3

'You look different this morning,' said Salena as I came in.

'Different how?'

'You're glowing.' She grinned. 'You look as if you've just had either great sex, or a *really* good breakfast. Or both.'

I laughed, although my face was hot. '*Definitely* the breakfast.'

'Oh well.' She grinned again. 'There's time.'

And yes, I'm feeling good today. Not just because of my encounter with my would-be assailant. There's something in the air today; a sense of *possibility*; something that smells of fireworks, and burning paper, and ozone, and change. I feel as if, for the first time, I could take control of my life: be the hero of my story, instead of a sad little footnote.

While Salena was making tea, I googled the Finchley Fliers. Their Facebook header shows a group of women finishing a race together. Salena is among them. They are laughing; red-faced, unkempt. They meet three evenings a week at a sports shop called Finchley Allsports. I tell myself I don't have to join, but it won't hurt just to see what they're like. A tiny, hopeful part of me says, *You might even make a friend.*

156

A friend. Now there's a crazy thought. I try to imagine myself with a friend. Going running together. Maybe having a coffee together, or going to the cinema. Talking. Going shopping. It feels as strange as science fiction. And it feels somehow disloyal, too, as if Martin should be enough for me. I suppose that's the problem with marrying your child-hood sweetheart. You sometimes miss out on having friends. You're too wrapped up in each other to think that one day the other may not be enough.

And then, there was Dante. When he was a boy, I simply didn't have time for friends. I wanted above all for my son to know that he was cared for and loved. I wanted to be there to wave him goodbye, and to greet him when he came home from school. I wanted him to have time with me, to help out in the kitchen. I wanted to read him stories. I suppose I thought that my influence would make him into the sensitive, imaginative child I had always believed he would be.

I was wrong. Dan was impatient with books. He hated being in the kitchen. In spite of all my attempts to nurture my son's softer side, he remained stubbornly, predictably masculine. He shook off displays of affection. He liked toy trucks and soldiers. He got into fights with other boys. I loved him – and I still do – with a fierce kind of desperation, but my mother's influence remains the dominant one in my son's life. She is very proud of him. He travels to see her four times a year. He sleeps in my old bedroom, which she has redecorated to suit him. He even goes to church with her, although we never did at home. Inevitably, she indulges him. Thirty years old, and she treats him like a little boy, cooking all his favourite meals, waiting on his every need. I wonder what she would have been like if I'd given birth to a girl. I wonder what she would have been like if I'd been more like Kate Malkin.

Time for another dopamine hit. Thinking about Dan makes me sad. And I am in the perfect place to practise my redis-covered skills. Amazon Guy is back again. This time I send him a message that high street bookshops need support. He buys three books, and leaves with the sense of having done something righteous. Yes, I suppose I manipulated him. But where's the harm? Everyone benefits. And really, it's so easy to adjust a person's choices. To put them right. To leave in place a suggestion to buy in bookshops, and not online; to try a woman author instead of a man; a Black author instead of a white one. It's just a form of tidying: of clearing out the rubbish from an otherwise acceptable space. Of setting a card on a mantelpiece, with the message: *Buying Books is Fun!* Or *Never Steal From a Bookshop!* Or *Support Your Local High Street!*

My inner critic squawks alarm. I send her to the Quiet Room. No one's getting hurt, I say. No one sees me doing it. It makes Salena happy. And it's fun to have a secret. To look into their lives unseen. To share in those flashes of memory; those briefly tasted pleasures –

Nineteen customers today: twenty-four sales between them. Salena thinks it's the weather. I smile, and agree that it must be. Let her think that. And if she starts to suspect something, I can always put her right.

'Have you thought about the park run, then?' she said, as I was cashing up.

I shook my head. 'I don't know.'

This morning's adrenaline rush has died down, and the thought of actually *joining a club*, of *running with other women*, seems like a dream I had as a child. I thought of my new running shoes, of that ridiculous raspberry bra. I wondered how I could possibly have imagined I could wear them. And then I imagined what Martin would say when he saw the unopened shoebox gathering dust under the bed; and I felt my skin prickle with sudden heat.

'You ought to come,' Salena said. 'Check us out. It might be fun.'

I thought of the man in the baseball cap, and the way he had whispered, *I'm sorry*. I thought of the way I'd used my rage as a defensive weapon. Then I thought of Jo Perry, and the way she'd tried to placate her murderer. I thought of the way I'd *apologized* to the man who'd attacked me, assuming that I was at fault. These instincts we have as women, conforming to expectations.

Then I nodded. 'Maybe I will.'

Maybe it's time to make a change.

# 4

*Thursday, March 31st*

Martin came home late last night. A text at around eight o'clock
read: *Sorry, crisis at Woody's. I'll get back when I can. M.*

I waited for him until ten o'clock, then went to bed and
read a book. I wondered what kind of a crisis could have kept
him out so late. Martin's social life is sparse. He goes out with
friends maybe twice a month, usually for drinks after work, or,
sometimes, to a football match. But a crisis at Woody's sounded
serious. I couldn't help thinking it might be connected with
what happened on Saturday night. Remembered Iris saying:
*What if it keeps happening?* Of course, that's absurd. It won't
happen. But I wondered what Woody remembered about that
night. What he had said to Martin. Did he remember that I
had been there? Did he connect it with Iris?

Finally, just after twelve, Martin came in, looking exhausted.
'I had to take Woody to A and E,' he said. 'He just passed
out on me. He says it's been happening since the weekend.
Like narcolepsy, or something.'

*Oh.*

I managed a look of concern. 'Did he say what he thought
it was?'

'He doesn't know. I left him there. The hospital's going to run some tests.'

I shrugged. 'Well, he's in the best place for that.'

Martin nodded. 'I think he's really worried, though. Hasn't had a day's illness in his life, and now, this, out of nowhere. He thinks someone might have slipped something in his drink the other night. Maybe some kind of a sedative. He just passed out, in a crowded pub. He hadn't even been drinking much. Good thing there were people around. Imagine if he'd been alone. He could have been robbed, or anything.'

I felt a hot flash rising, and fanned myself with a magazine. Martin's concern for Woody is ironic, to say the least. 'Wasn't he with anyone?'

He shook his head. 'He didn't say. He wasn't making a lot of sense. I think he was meant to be on a date, but she never turned up, or something. In any case, I wouldn't have believed it if I hadn't seen it with my own eyes. We were at his place, just talking. He just stood up to pour us some drinks. He was telling me some kind of story, and suddenly poof! – he just passed out. No warning. Poor guy. I can't imagine how frightening that must be.'

'What kind of story was it?' I said.

'One of Woody's jokes. You know.'

Yes. I am aware of Woody's jokes. I heard enough of them that afternoon at the sports pub. *What do you say to a woman with two black eyes? Nothing; you've already told her twice.* Or: *What's easier to pick up the heavier it gets? A woman!* All delivered with the kind of sideways smirk that challenges you to take offence, and often punctuated with the phrase: *Only joking!* As if that made a difference.

The hot flash had spread to my belly and chest, making my nightshirt clammy. I tried breathing deeply (DeeDee's solution to most things is *Let It All Go, and Breathe!*), without success. The heat that shimmered across my skin was alive with conflicting emotions.

Martin glanced at me and said: 'Are you OK? You look a bit feverish.'

I shook my head. 'Hot flash, that's all. I think I'll get a shower.'

Showers are DeeDee's solution to the things that deep breathing doesn't solve. Preferably by candlelight, and using many overpriced shower products. In DeeDee's case, her *Everything* will usually join her. I make do with a bar of soap, and sensible overhead lighting. But when I got to bed at last – at something like one in the morning – I found Martin back in his usual place on the left-hand side of the bed; caught his scent, like tobacco and salt, and felt him turn, sleepy, towards me –

*There he is*, I told myself. *There's the man I married.*

*So look into his house*, said the voice of my inner demon. *See what's really on his mind.*

But Martin's news of Woody had filled me with a new alarm, and when I finally went to sleep, I dreamed of Mr Davis' house, awash with guilt and garbage; with broken mirrors in every room; and *Never Again* carved into his arms, and scrawled over the peeling walls.

# 5

*Thursday, March 31st*

Twenty-eight customers today. Salena is ordering more stock, especially of children's books, and of today's surprise bestseller, *Managing the Menopause*. It was Kafka's Choice last week, which explains its popularity. At least, that's what Salena thinks. I happened to think that all men (yes, *all* men) should know at least something about these things.

I came in this morning with my new running shoes and some leggings in a gym bag, which I hid in the stock cupboard until it was time to leave. For some reason, I felt reluctant to say anything to Salena. My inner critic was vocal today, sending me hot flashes that snapped at my skin like elastic bands. *You're really going to do this?* she said. *You'll make yourself ridiculous. And, by the way, what about Woody? What harm has your intervention caused? Imagine, thinking you could make a difference to anyone. Imagine, trying to change someone. You can't even change yourself.*

I pushed her into the Quiet Room. *I can't deal with your bullshit today.* Then, as soon as the shop closed, I went to check out the Finchley Fliers. The sports shop – Finchley Allsports – was a half-hour's walk away. It was closed when

I arrived, but I could distinguish movement inside. I looked in at the window. It's one of those trendy running shops that sells high-end shoes, and backpacks, and gloves. I doubted it would be right for me. A club calling itself The Fliers, whose members met in a place like this would be younger, fitter (*better*) than I could ever pretend to be. They'd take one look, and laugh at me, just as they had at Mulberry House. Why had I come here at all? I turned away, and almost bumped into someone standing behind me.

'Bernie! You *came*!' Salena said.

'I was just having a look. That's all.'

'What's with the bag, then?'

'Just some stuff.'

'*Running* stuff,' said Salena. She took hold of my arm. 'That's great, Bernie! Come on in, let me introduce you.'

She pressed the bell by the side of the door, and ushered me inside the shop. A half-dozen women were already there, in an alcove out of sight of the road. Some were pulling on tracksuits, or tying up their running shoes. I was surprised and cheered to see a far broader range of ages and body types than I'd expected.

'Don't worry if this is your first time,' Salena told me warmly. 'We've all been beginners at some point or another. Some of us run the circuit, others walk and run, or just walk. But Alex keeps an eye on everyone, and makes sure no one comes last.' She raised her voice; 'Hey, everyone! Say hello to Bernie!'

A blur of faces. *Hey, Bernie!* First glimpse of the women who might become friends. A younger woman, slim and blonde, seemed to be in charge of the group.

'That's Alex,' said Salena, rapidly taking off her jeans and changing them for a pair of leggings. 'She runs the shop and keeps us all together. Then there's Daisy, and Helen, and Abi, and Leonie, and Rahmi, and Steph. Don't worry,' she said, seeing my look. 'You'll have plenty of time to get to know everyone. Just get changed for now, and we'll go.'

The shop smelt of floral deodorant, and the biscuity scent of running shoes. I pulled on my new leggings, feeling absurdly self-conscious. Sports kit always makes me feel like an imposter, somehow, as if there might be someone waiting in the wings to shout: *Bernie Moon runs like a girl!* I had to smile at the thought. When we still believed in ourselves, we just thought of it as running. But now, doing anything *like a girl* means simply doing it badly. When did we learn to think that way? Who taught us?

I pulled on an oversized sweatshirt to hide my too-tight leggings, then put on my new shoes. I looked up from lacing them to find the young blonde woman watching me.

'Bernie, I'm Alex. I'm so glad you came.' Alex looks uncannily like those yoga instructors of Woody's: young, athletic and ready (or so I imagined) to pour scorn on women like me. But there was no scorn in her voice, and her eyes were smiling. 'I hear you want to start running?'

'I really don't know. I just thought –'

'Yes, she does,' Salena said. 'She's a friend. I'll look after her.'

*A friend.* Am I really? Some people use that word to mean anyone they slightly know. Even people they know online. Perhaps I have a higher bar. I have made it a high one. And yet I wonder how it would feel to be part of a group. To have friends. To hear my laughter mingled with theirs.

I became aware of the other women putting their bags and clothing in a cupboard at the back of the shop. I did the same. A young woman with brown skin and a gold stud in her nose looked my way and smiled. She had changed her hijab for a kind of stretchy black snood, but I recognized her anyway.

'It's Rahmi, isn't it?' I said. 'You work at Priscilla's Pantry.'
She smiled. 'I thought I'd seen you before. First time runner?'
I shook my head. 'Oh, no. I'm not a runner at all. I'm just –'

What am I, exactly? Curious? Lonely? Ridiculous? Mad?
All of the above? My inner critic thinks so. But the part of
me that has been unlocked – that has blossomed – over the
past few days thinks otherwise. I am no longer a schoolgirl. I
am no longer *Weird Bernie*, who used to watch Mr D's *Special
Squad* from her lonely place on the edge of the track.

'That's terrific,' Rahmi said. 'Don't worry, you'll be fine.
We're none of us professionals. And Alex will look after you.'

I followed the others into the street. I couldn't remember all
their names. One – a woman younger than me, but consider-
ably larger, with curly dark hair and a smile that went all the
way to her eyes – introduced herself as Leonie.

'I was nervous as hell the first time I came,' she said. 'I
was sort of expecting it to be all show ponies and Karens.
But everyone here's really great and supportive. Alex sees to
that. You'll be fine.'

'Where are we going?'

'Just to the park. Twice around, and then back here. Alex
always runs ahead, then when she's finished the circuit, she
runs back to pick up the rest of the group. No one ever gets
left behind. We'll make sure you're OK.'

The women around me began to break away from the
group, some already jogging, some walking at a warm-up
pace. With a sudden jolt of surprise, I recognized Steph among
them; she gave me a brief and welcoming smile, then set off
ahead of the others. For a second, I felt a flash of unease at
our previous intimacy. Then came the sound of Schubert
through the windows of her house, and then she was gone,
like the memory of a half-forgotten dream.

Salena and Leonie stayed with me. 'We'll get you started,' Leonie said. 'We'll start you on short intervals of running, then some walking. That's how everyone starts off.'

It sounded suspiciously easy. I wondered how long it would take before someone noticed my baggy shirt, my brand-new shoes, my lack of co-ordination. The girls in Mr D's Special Squad had always noticed everything.

'So what made you want to start today?' Leonie said. 'What's your story?'

I shrugged. 'I don't know. I —'

'Bullshit. Everyone has a reason,' said Leonie. 'People run to gain confidence, or strength, or endurance, or to outrun their ex, or to say "*fuck you*" to cancer. There's always a reason. Hold on to yours. It'll keep you coming back.'

There came a sudden shout from the road. I saw a young man on a scooter. 'Get running, Tubs!' he yelled as he passed. I flinched.

Leonie flipped him the bird. 'You're the one riding a kid's toy, mate!'

I laughed, and felt guilty laughing. 'That's one of the reasons I was nervous of coming here,' I told her. 'I've never been much good at —'

'At what? Telling douchebags to fuck off?' She grinned. 'Relax. Just go with the flow. I guarantee you'll amaze yourself.'

I smiled. I was beginning to feel as if this might not be the ordeal I'd anticipated. Leonie is large in every way; and yet she occupies her space with no sense of embarrassment. I wondered what it would be like to feel so safe inside my skin — to be so accepting of myself. Could I be like her one day?

*Of course you could.* Unexpectedly, my inner demon believes in me. *You dealt with that douchebag in the park. Why should this be different?*

'There's a party I'm meant to be going to,' I said. 'I suppose that was my reason. The thirtieth anniversary of my last year in high school. I wasn't so happy in high school. I didn't make the most of it. And I want —'

'You want to show them,' she said.

'That's right. I want to —'

*Make them look.*

By the time we reached Victoria Park, the street lamps were already lit. The others had lights, some clipped to their belts, some on straps around their head. Alex handed me a spare, and made sure I fixed it in place. 'Don't want you tripping when it gets dark.' Then she ran off ahead of us, leaving the three of us together.

'OK,' said Leonie. 'Now to begin your first run. You'll run for just a minute, then walk for two to recover. Don't take it too fast at first. Just an easy jog.'

'I'll try.'

They were right about everything else but this. Jogging isn't easy. It was fine for the first few minutes, but after a while it got tiring. *This is when they start to laugh*, my inner critic told me. *This is when they show who they are.*

Except that it didn't happen. Salena and Leonie stayed with me, one at each side. Sometimes Leonie gave me tips. 'Try to hit the ground with your heel.' 'Try not to bounce, it wastes energy.' She herself runs tirelessly, in spite of her size and the fact that she talks constantly as she runs. She ran the London Marathon three years ago. She isn't afraid of anyone.

Over the next fifty minutes or so, I learnt all about Leonie, who has a dachshund called Fleagal, and who works for a firm of solicitors. I also learnt about Rahmi, who comes from Leicester, but who moved south to work in the theatre. She's actually a spot operator, but works in the coffee shop three days a week to supplement her income. And I learnt a lot more about Salena, who I've known for nearly five years without finding out that she loves *Star Trek*, has a small tattoo of a rose on her thigh, and has a girlfriend called Sophie, who for complicated reasons she has never introduced to her parents. All this without a single glance into any of their houses.

And yet, I couldn't quite rid myself of the idea that Alex was judging me. So pretty, so athletic – how could she not? Alex was the image of those girls at Mulberry High, who basked and preened for Mr D, and sunbathed by the side of the track in shorts so brief that they might as well have been underwear. Pretty girls like Lorelei Jones. Girls like Katie Malkin. I had to know what she thought of me. Whether she was on my side. So, when she ran back to meet us, looking barely as if she'd broken sweat, and found me tired and out of breath halfway into a minute's run, I looked into her house, to see what she *really* thought of me –

Some people reveal themselves at a glance. Others have hidden secrets. Some people like to project themselves as one thing, while living as something else. But Alex's house was wide open. That isn't to say there weren't secrets, but everything in her was welcoming. There was no sense of judgement there. Just honesty, warmth and encouragement. A little sadness, mostly centred on a place I did not explore: some pictures of a boy who looks remarkably like Alex herself. A lost twin, perhaps? In any case, it was private, unconnected with what I was looking for.

I cast a little further. Here was a room of mirrors. *This is where her self-image lives*, I thought, expecting self-satisfaction, contempt, or – what did Leonie say? *Show ponies and Karens.* But, instead, I only caught reflections of other people. Leonie, running her marathon. Salena, going: *I can't, I'm done*, and Alex

169

pulling her along, saying: *Come on, you're nearly there.* I was there too, in reflection – red-faced, panting, out of breath – but there was no hint of mockery. Instead, there was pleasure, and hope, and belief, and something like recognition –

'You'll be running this circuit in no time,' she said. 'Trust me, Bernie, we've all been there.'

I grinned. 'OK. I believe you.'

'You coming back on Sunday, then?'

I nodded.

'Here, have a granola bar.'

I walked back home with a spring in my step, swinging my sports bag and feeling better than I had in months. I was so absorbed in my thoughts that at first I didn't notice the car parked just outside the house. Afterwards, I did, of course. A little red Mazda with bright alloy wheels. But because I didn't see it, I walked into the house without thinking.

'I'm home!' I said, and went into the living room, where Martin was sitting watching TV. It smelt of takeaway pizza and booze. And on the sofa opposite, there was a man with a can of beer, wearing a T-shirt with the slogan: *This is Not a Drill.* I had barely time to register who it was when he turned to look at me, opened his mouth and collapsed onto the living-room floor.

It was Woody.

# 6

It was past midnight by the time the ambulance arrived. Woody was awake by then. I remember making cups of tea, and listening as Martin tried to explain to the helpline what had happened. *No, he hasn't been drinking. No drugs. No allergic reaction. It looks like some kind of narcolepsy.* A growing irritation in his voice as he realizes that the person at the other end doesn't know what narcolepsy is. *Look, he needs an ambulance. Yes, his breathing's fine. So why do I think he might need help? Well, let me see. Maybe the fact that he keeps passing out for no apparent reason?*

In fact, the episode had been relatively short. Half an hour, that's all. I helped lay Woody on the sofa, with a pillow to prop up his head. I used the opportunity to take a look inside; to check for damage; to rearrange recent memories, to file away what had happened instead of letting it take precedence. You can't make a memory go away. Not forever. Not completely. But you can push it into a quiet room, file it under *Irrelevance*. That way, there might be a better chance of his seeing me without a reaction.

I was right. When he awoke, he seemed almost back to normal. His house showed no visible damage; no guilt, no tendency to self-harm. That was good. I made some tea, and let him talk. It was pretty easy. Men like Woody seldom want to know what the woman in the room thinks. He drank his tea, ate pizza and gave me unsolicited advice when he learnt I'd taken up running. When I told him I had plenty of guidance, he frowned and said:

'Those amateur clubs don't teach you much. You'll need a proper trainer. At your age, you don't want to overdo things.'

Funny, how men like Woody like to tell women what they want. But I just smiled and nodded, and wished for the ambulance to come so that I could have a shower. I took a few minutes away from him to change into some fresh clothes (and because I didn't like being around him wearing those skin-tight leggings) and found that Martin had come off the phone. From their conversation, I guessed they were discussing me.

'You'd think it would have put her off, but no. She wants to start running. That's good, right? She needs to lose a bit of weight.'

'She wants to do a spin class. Or maybe a Nifty Fifties. Give her something better to do than running around the park at night.'

'I've told her not to go out alone. That running club sounds like a good call. And it's an all-women club, so –'

'Yeah, well, as long as they're not a bunch of fucking le—'

And there he goes again. *Poof.* Out like a blown fuse – or rather, like a Rohypnol victim. I'll admit, it's almost funny. And it's very interesting to see what might trigger his episodes. I considered searching his house again, but decided against it. *Let him be. Maybe this will fix the thing that makes him want to rape women.*

By the time the ambulance finally came, Woody had passed out three more times. The third time was during a conversation about cancel culture in publishing; specifically, at the word *woke*. How strange. I wonder how many other words or thoughts are linked to his behaviour. I faked concern for Martin's sake, but I can't find it in me to feel either guilt or sympathy. The thing I introduced into his mind isn't dangerous. It's more like a circuit breaker that will trip if he thinks of doing bad things. So no. I don't feel guilty at all. He isn't my responsibility.

I took my shower and went to bed, and for once there were no night sweats, or nightmares, or cramps, or anything but sweet, untroubled, restful sleep. I think I'm getting the hang of this.

Menopause is a piece of cake.

# TRACK 6:

---

# The Beast in Me

'I am half sick of shadows,' said
The Lady of Shalott.
*Alfred, Lord Tennyson, 'The Lady of Shalott'*

# I

*Extract from Class of '92, by Kate Hemsworth*
*(published by LifeStory Press, 2023)*

I took me another seven years to link Mr D's death with Bernie. Even then, it was hard to believe that a schoolgirl could have driven a grown man to this strange end, alone in a house of relics. I wouldn't have believed it myself, but for that memory locked away, waiting at the back of my mind. But, on some level, I always knew. I have always been waiting. Waiting for the end of a phrase begun when we were just thirteen, left suspended all this time, awaiting its conclusion. And, finally, it came, last year, as part of a story I read online, and I knew. I just *knew* it was Bernie.

What you now call the *Third Incident* began as a trivial story. A comic aside to the main news; a piece of online clickbait. A forty-two-year-old personal trainer from London had developed a condition that had doctors baffled. Whenever he came into contact with certain words or phrases, the man would fall into deep sleep, lasting between two and six hours. The man – Jim 'Woody' Wood, from Crouch End – showed no physical symptoms to account for his condition. Tests on him were still under way, but it was known that the trigger words included: *woke, feminist, females, abortion, pills, pro-choice, transgender, relax,* and, most bizarrely, *doughnut.* Doctors could find no reason for this sudden narcolepsy, but Mr Wood claimed that the illness had 'ruined his life'.

The story was an oddity that barely made the national news. The *Daily Mail* ran it under the headline: *Woody's Woke-ing Nightmare,* and a thread in the Comments section online launched the theory that feminists had somehow created a new drug, to silence men and to force them into submission. This theory eventually found its natural home on various conspiracy websites, where it became quite a phenomenon. The fictional drug, named MK2 by unnamed 'experts' on mind control, was said to be rife in the capital, and men were advised to be on the alert, to stay in groups, to check that their drinks were not tampered with, and to avoid contact with women they'd met online. A prominent male commentator complained about these suggestions, saying that the Metropolitan Police wasn't doing enough to combat the problem, while a prominent right-wing woman activist launched a virtual campaign in support of Jim Wood. A comedy Twitter account was launched, calling itself *@ThatDoughnutGuy*, attracting over two hundred thousand followers. And I wished – how I *wished* –

Wished what, do you ask? That I'd been kinder to Bernie Moon? That neither of us had ever known a boy called Martin Ingram? It doesn't matter now, of course. I'm just telling the story. For thirty years, Bernie Moon stayed locked away inside my head. I've always been good at compartmentalizing. Little Tupperware boxes, filled with fragments of things past. I've never felt the need to talk about those things to anyone. Who would I have told, anyway? Lucas isn't the kind of man who would understand how it happened. My husband likes to go out with his friends from work, drink beer, go to matches.

We used to call that being 'a man's man'. I liked that we were different. And I have my own social circle; my friends, some of whom I have known since school. Lorelei Jones is one of them, though we never had much in common. But both of us ended up teaching: Lorelei at Chapel Lane, me part-time at a theatre school called Stagestruck, on the Malbry Road.

It isn't the kind of friendship you see on *Sex and the City*. Given a wider choice, I probably wouldn't have chosen her. But Malbry is a shallow pool. Habit holds us together. Coffee mornings, book groups. Church. Yoga classes twice a week. Sometimes we go for drinks with the girls. These are my friendships. They are not close. Not close enough for discomfort. But they are the safety net of my life; the thing that reminds me that I am still pretty, and popular, and a success, even though I never became the famous actress I wanted to be; even though Lucas is cheating on me with the wife of a friend from football.

None of that really matters, though. I never felt deeply about Lucas. I loved how I felt standing next to him, and how other people looked at us. I love our house on Peppercorn Row, and our garden with its neat little beds. I love our children, Sadie and Ben, both popular at their respective schools. I love the order of our lives; the sense of continuity. That's why, when I looked at that online piece about the narcoleptic man, and saw Bernie Moon looking out at me, my first thought was of the impending reunion, and of how I could avoid it.

*30-year sixth form reunion! Pog Hill, class of '92! Cocktails, fashions, music and more!*

The reunion party was Lucas's idea. Of course it was. He and his friends had been planning it together for the best part of a year. A midsummer dinner-and-dance party at Pog Hill Sixth Form, just like old times. Bringing the gang together again. Cocktails and karaoke. *It'll be fun*, he told me. *Just like 1992. You could even do your act – what was it? Do you remember?*

A shiver, delayed by thirty years. Oh yes, I remember. I remember Pog Hill Prom, as we (rather pretentiously) called it. Our A levels were over, and the end of term was days away. We were filled with dreams of university and beyond. The world was ours. We were beautiful: the girls, in evening frocks and heels, the boys, in tuxedoes and bow ties. The band, a four-piece combo with Martin Ingram on bass, played all the hits, and we posed for the photographer, looking fantastic (or so we thought), except for Bernie Moon, whose weight had really ballooned over the summer term, and who hadn't even touched her champagne.

Yes, I remember. Which is why, when the Third Incident happened, I pushed it to the back of my mind. I told myself she wouldn't come to the school reunion. And even if she did, I thought, what could she do? We'd both moved on. *House* was a game that only belonged to a distant childhood. And yes, of course, I was wrong about that. As the Third Incident demonstrates, the game was only beginning.

# 2

*From the LiveJournal of Bernadette Ingram (marked as Exhibit BI 1):*
*Friday, April 1st, 2022*

I woke to four texts from Iris, sent between midnight and three-thirty. One reads: *Can't sleep. You?* Another says: *Don't forget our date tonight!* The other two are just lists of names. Men's names, with addresses.

Iris, it would seem, has a plan.

I met her, as we had arranged, at a cocktail bar half a mile from the house. I'd chosen our table with some care. A little alcove, set apart, allowing for discretion. I need not have troubled myself. Iris was late, and her entrance caused some considerable interest. She'd chosen to wear a black tank with a plunging neckline, and skin-tight jeans. Her pink hair was artfully tousled; her slim, bare arms were sleeved with tattoos. Earrings shaped like lightning bolts dangled from her earlobes. She looked like the lead singer in an indie band. She saw me waiting for her and gave an exuberant wave. A middle-aged man with a bad moustache glanced at her from his seat by the bar, then turned to his friends. I caught his look and turned away, as I had always turned away, in the days when I was visible.

But Iris didn't turn away. Instead, she swerved and made for the group, moving in so fast and so close that for a moment I thought she might actually knock the man with the bad moustache from his seat.

'Don't you stare at me,' she said, loudly enough to make heads turn. 'Stare at me, and I'll fuck you up.' And then, as the man flinched back in shock, she laughed and smacked him on the arm. 'Ah, come on, I'm just playing with you. Banter. Can't you boys take a joke?'

The men were still staring after her by the time she arrived at our table. She gave me a big smile, sat opposite, and said: 'So, have you ordered?'

I shook my head.

'Let's start with margaritas.' She ordered a pitcher, ignoring my protests. 'And maybe some wings. And some cheesy fries. And – ah, fuck it, let's have pizza.'

The waitress returned with a laden tray of food and a pitcher of margaritas. Iris ate heartily, and I joined her, feeling suddenly ravenous. I usually skip lunch at the shop, or maybe just eat a sandwich. And alcohol always makes me eat – more so since I hit the menopause. My inner demon smiles and says: *So what? Being hungry's hardly a crime. Go on, have the pizza. It beats DeeDee's Goddess Recipes, anyway.*

Iris ate the chicken wings quickly and unselfconsciously, using her fingers, and with sounds of appreciation. I sipped my cocktail. People were looking at us. Well, men. Men were looking at us. I fought the urge to tell Iris to be – *What? Less hungry? Less herself?* I told myself that at least my fear that she might have been traumatized by what had almost happened to her was unfounded. She looked fabulous. Beautiful, relaxed, unfazed. No nightmares for her. No feelings of guilt, or anxiety that it might happen again.

I texted Martin I'd be late home, and sipped my margarita. It was half ice, and blissfully cold. I held the glass to my burning cheek. Iris sucked her fingers clean, looked up and said:

'So, Bernie. Tell me everything.'

I shook my head at her. 'Not so loud.'

'Who cares? It's fucking sci-fi, anyway. They'll think we're talking about a movie we watched, or something.' She lowered her voice and grinned. 'Is that better?'

'Fine. Just keep it down, OK?'

I ventured a side glance into her house to make sure she really was OK. It was easy; all the lights were on. Apart from the ones in her beloved superhero comics, there were no monsters lurking. The memory of a recent tattoo was the only slight pain I could find; at least, without searching deeper. I sighed. She was going to be OK. That's all I cared about, anyway.

'How have you been?'

'Fantastic.' Iris grinned at me through a mouthful of chicken wing.

'You said you weren't sleeping.'

'I'll sleep when I'm dead.'

I nodded. She certainly looked all right; what I needed now was to somehow tone her down, which meant deflecting her interest in what had happened to Woody.

'He's in the news. Did you see him?' she said, and, reaching into her handbag, pulled out a page torn from yesterday's *Metro*. Just a squib, with his photograph. Eight lines of print and a strap-line. Damn.

*Asleep On the Job!*
*Until last week, Jim Wood (42) was in perfect health. Now he falls asleep without warning between five and ten times a day. Doctors suspect narcolepsy, a rare brain condition that causes*

*someone to suddenly fall asleep at inappropriate times. This time,*
*it was at work. Not in a boring Zoom meeting (we get that!), but*
*at a spin session, packed with attractive young women. Jim Wood*
*is a fitness instructor at The Bodyworks gym in East Finchley.*
*Now that's what we call a nightmare.*

I should have seen it coming, I thought. Stories like Woody's
always come out. What had triggered that episode? Was it
just the presence of those attractive young women? Or had
I opened one of those doors that led to the dark places in his
mind? In any case, I told myself, there was no reason to link
him to me. And if he were going to name Iris, then surely he
would have done so by now.

Iris waited patiently for me to finish reading. 'So how did
we make him do that?' she said. 'And how come I can't do
it now? I mean, there are men all over the place. Why can't
I flip them, like we flipped Woody?'

*Oh, God. She isn't going to give up until she has the whole*
*story,* I thought.

'You didn't do anything,' I said.

'The fuck I didn't! Bernie, it was like – somehow we turned
the tables on him. Hoist him with his own *bast*-ard.'

She was getting louder again. I glanced into her open
house. I think perhaps I was hoping to do what I'd done
with Woody; to gently sideline the memory, to file it under
*Irrelevance*; to send it to the Quiet Room. But Iris was awake
to me. There were no quiet rooms in her house. All her lights
were on, and she showed no sign of keeping quiet. Worse
still – and perhaps because of the presence of those superhero
narratives – there was an instinctive understanding of what
I'd done, unmarred by fear or disbelief, and hungrily, cheerily
eager for more.

I said: 'Look, Iris. I'll tell you. But you can't tell anyone else. And you can forget us doing it again, because this was a one-off emergency. And because when you're feeling angry, or hurt, you never know what damage you'll do.'

And so, at last, I tried to explain about the mirrors, and the game. Iris listened attentively – hungrily, like a feral cat that has been fed once, and will not leave. 'I get it,' she said. 'Like Empath. Empath, from the comics?'

'I don't read comics,' I told her.

'Oh, well. Empath was one of the Hellions, the White Queen's original students, and –' She stopped. 'What do you mean, you don't read comics?'

I shrugged.

'Jesus, Bernie. If you're going to have a superpower, you could at least take an interest. You mean you reflect whatever you feel? Whatever you see in someone else?'

'Broadly speaking, yes,' I said.

'That's amazing. Do it now!' She glanced over her shoulder at the man with the bad moustache, who was still sitting with his friends in the same place by the bar. 'Do it to *that* guy. He looks like a creep.'

'No,' I said. 'Weren't you listening? It's dangerous.'

'Not to us,' said Iris. 'Go on, Bernie. Check him out. Go up to the bar, or something, and order us another jug. This one's nearly done, anyway.' She emptied the last of the frozen margarita into my glass. 'Go on, do it. Do it now. I want to see you in action.'

'Seriously, Iris –'

'You said it was only dangerous if you were feeling angry or hurt. But you're feeling fine, right? No reason to think you'd fuck him up.'

'Iris, no. This isn't a game.'

She put a hand on my arm. 'Come on. Just this once. I want to see.'

And maybe it was the tequila, or maybe my inner demon, or just the peculiar force of her personality, but I stood up and made my way to the bar, and, as I passed, just allowed my hand to touch the stranger's shoulder —

A crackle of connection. The reflection of Iris' gaze, like something seen through a window. His house is dark. A single light illuminates the mantelpiece. He has had a row with his wife, and some of the bitterness lingers. The door that leads to her stands wide. I don't want to go in there, but I do, reflecting the scene back at Iris. And there she is, in the corner, sitting with her head on her knees, *looking very ugly today, not that she was ever much. And the tears. Oh, man. The fucking tears. It's enough to drive a man to drink.*

That's his voice. I hear him now. It's like an echo in his mind, except that the echoes are memories. No, not memories. Thoughts. But you can tell that they will soon become memories. Right now, they're retelling his story. *His* story. *She was wrong. She always is. He is the real victim here. He pushed her into her corner. She pushed her way out, with violence. She's always been the violent one. Not that the woke fucking liberal elites would ever believe something like that. They'd take her side in an instant. Everyone takes the woman's side. No one ever cares about the male victims of violence. No one launches a hashtag when a man gets murdered in the park. But when it's a woman, it's all #MeToo and #IStandWithJoPerry.*

Jo Perry. Her name in his mind makes me flinch. But this man isn't a murderer. He *is* an abuser, though, in his way, although he would never admit it. What I see in him suggests a man who is skilled in self-deception. See how, already, the scene has changed. It's all about misdirection. The Great Carovnik knew about that. That, and mirrors, and lighting.

I ordered another pitcher of frozen margaritas, and brought it back to our table. Iris was waiting impatiently, her eyes filled with lights and reflections.

'So?' she said.

'So yes, he's a creep. But that doesn't mean we should interfere.'

'Why not?'

Once more I tried to explain. 'What you find in a person's "house" can be misleading. We all have hidden, ugly stuff that never shows itself outside. The man – whose name I don't even know – has no more of this than anyone else. He makes his wife unhappy. So what?'

'So you could change him,' Iris said. 'You could make him appreciate her.'

I thought of Mr Davis. His house. Those cuts on his arms. I shook my head. 'You don't understand. It's not as easy as –'

*Bullshit. It is.*

My inner demon's voice is as clear as if Iris had spoken aloud.

'Bernie, he's a creep, and he's been staring at us all night. Tell him to go home to his wife.'

'I can't,' I said. But I knew I could. All it would take would be a small rearrangement of mirrors. No more than telling a man to buy his books in a bookshop, instead of online. No more than suggesting to a mother that reading a book about a girl presented no danger to her son's masculinity.

I reached for a slice of pizza. I hadn't meant to stay this long. I'd meant to get home by eight o'clock and have a late dinner with Martin. Too late for that now. I finished the slice. It would be very easy, I thought, to adjust the man with the bad moustache. All I would need would be to –

I glanced into his house once more. The door to his wife was closing. I moved in close, and turned up the lights, and angled them onto his image of her. Her name is Marjorie, by the way. A pretty name. And she *is* pretty. Not as young as she was, perhaps, but she loves him. And he loves her. Maybe not enough, though. He thinks about himself a lot more. Maybe I can, with a delicate hand, push away his selfishness, and turn the mirrors onto her. Maybe with a tiny hint that he should go back home *right now*, perhaps with a box of chocolates and a promise to do better.

It's actually pretty easy. I think I'm getting used to this. There's no sense of disturbance, no trauma to the man's mind. Just a little suggestion that pleasing his wife makes him happy. Just a little touch of remorse. And it worked: he left almost immediately, to the great surprise of his friends, who called after him, laughing, but could not make him reconsider. He gave me a curious look as he left, as if my face seemed familiar, but otherwise, he looked just like a man in a hurry to get home.

Iris grinned and refilled my glass. 'Who's next on the list?'

I shook my head. 'Iris, we can't keep doing this.'

'Why not? You got my text, right?'

'You mean the list of names?'

'Yeah. It's a list of all my douchebag exes. I thought we could pay them a visit, and –' She rolled her eyes dramatically. 'You know. Do what you do best. Use your secret sci-fi superpowers.'

'Er, *no*.'

'Why not?'

I lowered my voice. 'Well, for one thing, I'm not a character from a comic book. Second, if all your exes suddenly changed personality after a visit from both of us, don't you think that pretty soon someone would link us with Woody?'

'Ah. Good point. Hadn't thought of that.' She picked at the last slice of pizza. 'God, I'm starving. I always am whenever

I've had a new tattoo. Want to see? It's not gross, or anything.' And before I could answer yes or no, Iris had bared her shoulder to reveal a monochrome tattoo so fresh that it still had the cling film. 'I wanted to mark the occasion,' she said. 'To remind me of what nearly happened. Do you like it?'

For a moment, I couldn't move. A hot flash crackled like lightning from the back of my heels to the roots of my hair. I stared at Iris' new tattoo, still pink around the edges, and felt a spinning sense of fear so great that I almost stopped breathing.

It was a garland of heart-shaped leaves and tiny, pointed flowers, over a scroll with two words in a delicate, feminine script.

'*Woody* nightshade. Get it?' she said. But I was looking at the scroll tattooed under the nightshade wreath, and the words that Grace Oyemade had spat at Mr D by the playing fields that day; the day the spotlight of puberty had finally pinned me powerless.

*Never Again.*

# 3

*Friday, April 1st*

Memory goes deeper than words. Shame goes even deeper. A mirror, reflecting a mirror, creates an infinite ladder of images, and Mr Davis, seeing them, had fallen down it to a place where even I couldn't reach him.

And yet, it came from a friendship. The friendships we make in childhood are so much more intense than any we make as an adult. What I had once shared with Katie had coloured every part of me. And even when we stopped being friends, I couldn't help wanting to share in her life. But after that birthday party, Katie had locked me out for good. And so I had to watch her from Lorelei's house, or Grace's, or Jenny's, or Linda's, or any one of the other girls lucky enough to be her friend.

That was where it started, I think. With Mr D, and his *Special Squad*. Katie was among them, of course, and so was Grace Oyemade. Those girls who used to watch him run. The ones who sat by him at lunchtime, who came to his training sessions. There's always a teacher in every school to whom the pupils congregate. Sometimes, they're entertaining, or funny, or approachable. Sometimes they run a lunchtime club. Most

of the time, their influence is positive, benevolent. And Mr D
certainly didn't *look* suspicious. He didn't make inappropriate
comments. He seemed to care about his girls. He gave them
advice about training, and encouraged them to be supportive
of each other, as well as competitive in their chosen sports.
He was aware that some of the girls saw him as a heart-throb,
and was gently self-mocking in response.

But *inside*, there were secrets. Inside, he was making plans.
I knew, because I'd seen beyond the spaces he made public.
I'd looked into the wings: I'd seen his magic, his trickery.
Not that they would have believed me: Mr Davis had a way
of making a girl feel special. Grace Oyemade, in particular.
He spoke to her like an adult. He told her she was different.
He gave her little gifts when the other girls weren't around
– a bar of chocolate, a book. And yes, she liked it, of course
she did, because she was only thirteen, and didn't know
any better. But I knew where all this was leading. I knew,
because he'd done it before. There were whole rooms in his
house devoted to his conquests. All of them girls like Katie,
like Grace, dazzled by his glamour. All of them hopeful and
naïve, and certain of their power.

And so, on Sports Day, I intervened. I reflected his secret
back to her, like sunlight from a polished shield. I didn't
mean to do any harm. I only meant to show the trick. To
prove he wasn't worthy. And it worked – it really worked.
I saw the moment it happened. Grace was running towards
him, humming like a tuning fork; every muscle, every nerve
exquisitely tuned to his frequency. There was no doubt in
her mind that she would win the race. It was effortless. She
was barely out of breath, and the others were far behind her.
And I was there. I was sharing it. My heart was pounding
like a machine. And when at last I was ready, it felt just like

the Great Carovnik's trick – the table turned, all the dishes in place, and only the tablecloth missing.

Except that Grace didn't understand. All she got was the sudden blast of that image in her mind; the dazzle of reflected light. And it felt like a violation. It felt like a betrayal. And she lashed out – not at me, but at *him* – with all the force of that borrowed light, so that everything came crashing down – dishes, vases, silverware, glasses of wine all over the floor, and Mr Davis with them, like something from a slapstick show, gone from funny to terribly wrong.

I never saw Grace again after that. Never got to put things right. And Mr D was unreachable. I *might* have had a chance to help if he'd allowed me to touch him. But he made it impossible. He didn't want to touch us, not even accidentally. You could see it in the way he flinched if a girl approached him; in the way he avoided busy corridors at Break. Somehow, Grace and I had set off a kind of cascade in the teacher's mind; a sequence of movements that sooner or later would send all the dishes crashing down. And I realized, as that dreadful term came to an end, that something had also changed in me. The mirror that allowed me to see into other people had also been broken, leaving nothing in its place but fragments and uncertainties.

And blood, of course. The blood that marks. That signals the end of innocence. Suddenly, with puberty, I was no longer invisible. Every pimple, every frown, was suddenly under the microscope. And though I'd been an attractive child, puberty made me feel ugly. I hated my breasts. I hated my thighs. I felt both horribly visible and ludicrously unattractive. Who could possibly love me now? Who could ever be my friend? Worst of all, I felt I *deserved* it for what I'd done to Mr D. I was under a curse of blood, a curse that would last nearly forty years –

But not anymore. My talent is back. And my *new* friend has no fear of the potential side effects. Mr Davis died because he couldn't face what he'd seen in himself. Just as Woody's episodes were just reflections of his mind. As a child, I'd assumed the blame. I'd taken *Never Again* as a command. But talking to Iris, I can see that she understands it differently. The tattoo on her shoulder is a warning to men – *all* men.

*Fuck with me at your peril.*

I have to admit that last night was the best evening I've had in a long, long time. Iris is so different to women of my generation. So young, so profane, so filled with energy and enthusiasm. It's catching, I think. I find myself responding with a teenager's eagerness. I wonder if Dante would like her? Dante is very private. He never mentions a girlfriend. There are no pictures of girls on his Instagram, or his Facebook. Sometimes, I allow myself to wonder what might happen if he met a girl like Iris – a girl who loves comic books, fried food and raucous conversation. Someone to provide a foil against my mother's influence. Someone I could understand, and who might even bring us together again –

I got home after ten o'clock, long after I'd said I'd be home. Martin looked disapprovingly from his laptop as I came in. 'Are you drunk?'

I shrugged. 'A bit. We ended up having dinner.'

'Who's *we*?'

'Just Salena and me.' The lie came out automatically. 'She's having some trouble at home,' I said. 'I thought she needed cheering up.'

That look again, almost of censure. Martin doesn't like Salena. He especially dislikes the fact that she never stocks books by LifeStory Press. 'I thought you'd be tired of seeing her. After all, you see her all day.'

I shook my head. 'I like her. She's fun.'

'OK.' He went back to the screen. His posture looked stiff and angular. It suddenly occurred to me that my husband was jealous – jealous of a twenty-two-year-old barista with pink hair – and I gave a crow of laughter.

'Oh, lighten up, Martin,' I said, and kissed his unresponsive cheek. 'I'm not cheating on you with Salena.' I looked over his shoulder at the screen and saw that he was on Facebook. I said: 'How's the party coming on? How many people are going?'

'I wondered when you'd mention that.' He still sounded defensive. 'Lots of people have already signed up. Lucas Hemsworth, of course. Paul Black. The band. Andrew Whelan. Joss Lively. The gang from St Oswald's. Your crowd, of course, from Mulberry House. It could be a night to remember.'

I nodded. 'Yes, I think so.' I noticed he hadn't mentioned Kate. To him, I suppose, she comes as a part of the package with Lucas.

'So. You like the idea, then?'

'Of course. We haven't been back home for years. We haven't been to a *party* for years. I want to remember what it was like to dance with you and drink champagne.'

'Right. I'll put your name down.' I thought his voice was softer. 'We can go out and buy you a dress if you like. Something elegant, in black.'

I thought of the black dress I'd worn on the day of the original Pog Hill Prom. A shapeless thing, from a charity shop, designed to conceal as much as possible. Then I thought of Katie's lamé dress, and how it had mirrored the stage lights.

'Maybe I'll try something different this time,' I said.

Martin shrugged. 'Black suits you.'

# 4

*Saturday, April 2nd*

Thirty-two customers today. Thirty-nine books between them.
Salena gives Kafka the credit for this, and has bought him not
only the catnip mouse, but also a treat-dispensing ball, which
he has taken to chasing exuberantly all over the shop in the
hope of persuading it to dispense. Salena's Books is doing well,
and if some of this is my doing, then perhaps what Iris referred
to as my *secret sci-fi superpower* isn't such a bad thing at all.

How strange. I'd never intended to share my gift with Iris.
But now it feels as if a mass of toxic clutter has gone from
my house. Guilt is corrosive; and loneliness. I had no idea
how much, until now. But Iris understands. She says I don't
have to fear my power. As long as I keep control of it, and
don't use it when I'm upset. Mr Davis was a mistake. Woody
was better. I stayed in control. The man in the baseball cap
proves that. And I am learning all the time; learning through
experience. Of course I am. It takes practice. The Great
Carovnik must have spent thousands of hours perfecting her
craft. Maybe she started when she was small. Maybe she broke
dishes. I don't break things. Not anymore. I only suggest that
people buy books by underrepresented groups. That selfish

men treat their wives gently. That parents teach their sons respect. But with power comes responsibility. I've learnt that already with Iris. Salena, too, I realize, is becoming my responsibility. And Woody – well. Woody is on the way to becoming a problem.

He was meant to be coming round tonight – I'd assumed, to collect his car. I'd hoped that Martin would deal with him, and that he'd be gone by the time I got home. But at six o'clock, when I returned, the car was still parked outside the house, and Woody was there in the living room, watching TV with Martin. They'd had curry delivered instead of pizza, and his T-shirt said: *Blink if you want me*, but otherwise it was just like the other night, and I felt a kind of shiver. Menopause has broken my inner thermostat, so that I often feel hot when I should be cold, and cold when I should be sweltering. But that shiver was something visceral, like a premonition of death, and it slid into my belly like a snake into a basket.

Martin gave me an apologetic look. 'I told Woody he could stay with us for a few days, till he feels better,' he said. 'You don't mind, do you? We've got the guest room going spare, and he's still having those panic attacks.'

Of course, there was nothing I could say. He'd already answered my question for me. Woody will sleep in the guest room, the one that used to belong to our son. It is also tacitly understood that I will change the linen, and make the bed, and ensure that our guest has fresh towels and clean underwear. After all, I made him this way. I am, after all, responsible.

I went to bed early, while Martin and Woody stayed up late. I heard their voices for a while, and then they watched a movie. I opened my laptop and went online, feeling strange and empty. Recently, social media hasn't felt like the dopamine hit it once was. Nowadays, it feels more like an expression of loneliness. But when reality fails to satisfy, a life of shadows is better than nothing. And so I went back to my usual haunts, in hope of finding some relief.

Dan had posted on Instagram: *Saturday night: nachos and cheese.* DeeDee was *Getting Her Goddess On* (something to do with sheet masks). And the Finchley Fliers Facebook group was discussing the park run tomorrow.

*Alex Foster: It's looking good. Nearly 200 signed up so far. Raised over £500!*

*(Leonie Chapman likes this)*

*(Salena Wicks likes this)*

*(Rahmi Arain likes this)*

*Rahmi Arain: Will the family be there?*

*Alex Foster: Stephen says he'll say a few words. He's putting the money towards a memorial plaque.*

Did Alex know Jo Perry? It certainly would seem that way. I wonder if Jo ever ran with them. The thought gives me a shiver. Soon, we would be running for her (well, I'd mostly be walking). Two hundred women, running; and people like Alex to urge them on. I wonder what Martin would think of that.

*Bernadette Ingram: Wow! It sounds a little daunting.*

*Alex Foster: Don't worry. We won't leave you behind.*

Suddenly, I am almost in tears. She makes it sound so simple. For the first time, I really feel as if this could work. That we could be friends.

*Bernadette Ingram: Sounds good!*

*Alex Foster: See you tomorrow!*

I closed my laptop and turned off the light, feeling absurdly comforted. From downstairs, I could still hear Martin and Woody watching their film, but that hollow feeling was gone. Interaction with others really does produce dopamine.

I reached for Alex's house across the distance between us, and caught a gleam of humour, like a smile through a rear-view mirror. I couldn't reach any further. Still, with practice, I'm sure I could. Like my pelvic-floor exercises, I should make it a daily routine.

I went to sleep and dreamed – for the first time since child-hood – of running in my own skin, feeling the steady beat of my heart, and the soft wind blowing through my hair, and my slow and regular breathing.

# 5

*Sunday, April 3rd*

This morning, I got up early to buy croissants and fruit for breakfast. Woody may be many things, but he is also a guest in our house, and as such, my responsibility. By the time I returned, he was already sitting in the kitchen, drinking coffee with Martin.

'We're just about to go to collect a few things from Woody's place,' Martin said. 'Don't bother about breakfast; he's on a special diet.'

'Oh.' I put down my shopping. Six croissants: I always buy too many. And peaches from the roadside stall. I thought of the doughnut we'd shared last week in Priscilla's Pantry, and said: 'That's fine. I'll eat them.'

Woody gave me a sideways look, as if to suggest that he had thoughts, but said nothing. Maybe he's learning. I considered looking into his house, but the idea of going in there again made me feel a little queasy. As long as he isn't a danger to himself or to anyone else, I have no need to intervene. But the thought of him here, in *my* house – and for how long? – makes me nervous. I don't like the way he looks at me. That narrow, calculating smile. Does he suspect me? I think not. And yet, he doesn't like me. Perhaps he senses I don't like him.

By now, it was almost nine o'clock. I changed into my running things, then headed out to Victoria Park. A small crowd had gathered in anticipation of the morning's run. A woman with a loudspeaker was calling out instructions. Another was handing out laminated cards, each printed with a number.

Salena spotted me in the crowd and waved me over. 'Come on, don't be shy!'

I smiled. 'I think I must be insane.'

'Don't be silly. It isn't a race. Well, maybe it is' – she pulled a face at Leonie, who was wearing pineapple-print leggings – 'but I'll stay with you all the time. Just walk as much as you need to. OK?'

And then we set off; Salena keeping just ahead of me, occasionally encouraging me to speed up to a light jog. I ran as much as I could, and was cheered to find that I'd finished the circuit in just over fifty minutes. 'Not bad,' said Leonie, hugging me. 'Next time, I promise you'll be able to run the whole course.'

By ten o'clock, most of the runners had started to drift away. A soft, fine rain had started to fall. I still felt strangely elated by the afterglow of the crowd. So many people, in such close proximity, make for easy access. Their houses are open, their minds within reach. It's easy to snatch at a passing thought, even without physical contact. This woman is pregnant, just six weeks on. She hasn't told anyone. She runs in the warm glow of knowledge. This girl is in love. It shines out of her. Her house is ablaze with reflections. This woman is thinking of Jo. She runs because Jo Perry cannot; she means to enjoy every moment. So many women. So many lives. Beautiful pieces of broken light reflected from their houses; making connections, releasing their thoughts, provoking that surge of euphoria.

The cordoned-off place where Jo Perry died has been lined with floral offerings. A teddy bear. A handwritten card that reads: *Dear Mummy. I love you.* I find a nearby bench and sit, in spite of the needling rain. *She was a mother too*, I think. I wonder about her children. I wonder what they will remember of her, apart from the fact that she was murdered. Will her husband – Stephen, is it? – will he make sure they remember that she used to make pizza? That she always used to arrange the toppings to look like faces? That she liked nineties electronica? That she used to wash her hair in something that smelt of pineapple? That she once farted audibly when they were watching *The Lion King*, and they never let her forget it, and sometimes called her Pumbaa? That she loved to dance? That she'd once spent a summer working in a jam factory, and had never eaten jam since? That she was terrified of wasps? That she used to sleep with one foot hanging out of bed, whatever the climate or season?

The rain felt hot against my face. I realized I was crying. *What's happening to me?* I thought. *How can I possibly know these things?* It was almost as if my experience had opened a window into her house. Suddenly, I *knew* things. Her daughter Maddy was named after a character in a favourite book. She would be six on July 3rd. She had insisted on leaving her teddy with her little card. *Teddy will look after her. Teddy will make sure she's OK.*

This was too much, I told myself. Too much, and yet too little. Nothing I have seen so far would be useful to an inquiry – even if I could persuade the authorities to believe me. All my talent gives me is a glimpse into their minds.

But what good can my talent do, unless it shows me who killed her?

*Don't be ridiculous.* The voice sounded a lot like my mother again. *Life isn't like that, Bernadette. Sometimes bad things just happen.*

But sitting there on the bench in the rain, I could feel a connection. So many voices, so many hopes, so many women running for Jo. It had to mean something, I told myself. It had to make a difference. Otherwise, what was the point? And why would the blood tell me otherwise?

I stood up, already feeling my muscles starting to stiffen. The rush of dopamine from the crowd had receded like the tide. I wanted a shower and a snack, and some time to decompress, away from Woody and Martin. How far was it to Woody's place? With luck, I thought, they wouldn't be back with his things until lunchtime.

Arriving home, I showered, changed, and made a cheesy pasta bake, along with a big bowl of salad. And then I switched on the radio, in the hope of some relaxing music, and instead heard that an arrest had been made in the case of the Jo Perry murder.

# 6

Sometimes the body responds to news before the mind has time to engage. *A fifty-seven-year-old man from East Finchley has been detained in connection with the murder of Jo Perry, the mother-of-two found dead after going for a run in the park.* It struck me like a hot flash, sweeping towards my hairline, bringing with it the scent of damp earth, and engine oil, and burning, and blood.

*They've found him.*

I put down the salad bowl and sat at the kitchen table. The hot flash ignited my face and neck and raced across my scalp. Sheathed in flame, I couldn't tell whether I felt anger or grief. I laid my head on the tabletop and sobbed from sheer frustration.

They've found him. Of course, there are no details yet. But online, there are already rumours. A quick search through Twitter reveals the man to be Graham Crawley, an English teacher at a school outside London. Nicknamed 'Creepy Crawley' by pupils, he had a reputation. Other rumours suggest that the man had a history of domestic violence. On the Jo Perry hashtag, I find *@whitey2947* and *@drdoodad816* arguing with *@irisnoir23*.

*@whitey2947: This is a disgrace. They shouldn't even be talking about an ongoing inquiry.*

*@irisnoir23: It's certainly a disgrace. That a man with that kind of history should ever have had a job in education.*

*@whitey2947: People are far too quick to assume guilt without knowing the full facts. This man hasn't been charged with anything yet.*

Of course, he's right. The man *hasn't* been charged. So why does my body feel this way? Why am I on the alert like this? The medical website calls it *emotional lability,* and describes it as: *quick, often excessive changes in mood, with strong emotions, such as uncontrollable laughing or crying, or heightened irritability.*

DeeDee is more upbeat. *If you're feeling feisty today, then maybe you need some alone time! Punch a pillow. Scream a song. Make like a banshee, and HOWL!*

I wondered what the neighbours would think if I followed her advice. And *feeling feisty* doesn't begin to express this sensation. But yes, I needed to be alone. I needed space to reflect. I didn't know Jo Perry, and yet her death has been so much a part of everything that has happened to me that I feel her loss like a part of myself. I know her home, her children. I know what she ate for breakfast; the kind of clothes she liked to wear. I know that she left a bookmark in *The Hundred Thousand Kingdoms,* to which she will never return, because a man decided that he was entitled to take her life –

*Stop it. Anger won't bring her back.*

The eminently sensible voice of my inner critic was like a glass of the cucumber water DeeDee recommends for stress. (I've never tried cucumber water. To be honest, it sounds vile.) But my inner demon's voice was like a shot of tequila.

*Pay him back. You know you could.*

And today, the thought is not only frightening, and shameful, and wrong, but also strangely intoxicating. *You could do it, Bernie*, it says. *Fuck him up. Send a message.*

I won't, of course. That's Iris' voice, steeped in comic-book lore. Superheroes, solving crime in a world without justice. But we have a legal system here. We have a police force. If this is their man, they will prove it, and he will be imprisoned for life. That's how it works, in the real world. That's how grown-up justice works.

*Except that it doesn't, Bernie.* Justice doesn't serve men and women equally. Men who commit crimes against women are too often depicted as victims. A man was provoked. A man was disturbed. A man was *failed by the system*. A man has lost his career, his life, for the sake of one, ill-considered act. It's almost as if men expect to be shielded from the consequences of their violence. And yet –

I thought back to Adam Price, that poor little boy from Chapel Lane. So out of place in that nice little school; so filled with anger at the world. I hadn't understood it then, but *he* was failed by the system. What had Katie seen in his house to make her react as she did? To make her reject our friendship? Perhaps Adam Price grew into a man who projected his hatred onto women. Perhaps, in Jo Perry's killer, there is the ghost of a sad little boy. That makes me think of Dante. I wish I could say all this to my son. That I know how childhood marks us. That I wish I had been better.

There came the sound of a car outside. I wiped my face with the back of my hand. Martin was back, with Woody's things, and somehow I had wasted an hour online. I stood up and rinsed some dishes as they carried Woody's things upstairs. *Rather a lot of things*, I thought. I wonder how long he's planning to stay? Martin mouthed an apology behind Woody's back as I watched them carry a big box of electronic gear upstairs: laptops; screens; cameras.

*Sorry.*

I shrugged. It looks as if Woody may stay for more than just a couple of days. A week, perhaps. Maybe longer. So much for the possibility of a quiet Sunday with Martin, or evenings, just the two of us, in pyjamas, watching TV. I hate the thought of that man in our house, making himself comfortable. I hate the thought of cooking for three, when the third is not Dante. Most of all, I hate the thought of Woody in my son's room, sleeping in his childhood bed, watching the view from his window. But I have only myself to blame. My intervention made him this way. By evicting him from Iris' house, I have brought him into mine. Perhaps that means *he*'s my son now.

# 7

*Wednesday, April 6th*

After four days in Dante's room, Woody seems very much at home. From what I understand, he spends most of his time lounging in bed, watching TikToks on his smartphone. He has suffered several 'episodes', in spite of being on anti-seizure medication, and is currently on sick leave from his job at the gym.

The Press have got hold of his story now, as have social media. The list of words that make Woody pass out has attracted a lot of hilarity. Salena spent most of the afternoon reading quotes to me from a spoof Twitter account calling itself *@ThatDoughnutGuy*, purporting to be Jim Wood, and sending out hourly reports on the state of the chemical gender war.

Yes, I suppose I could fix him. But I don't want to be inside him again. The man is in no danger, and, more to the point, neither is any woman in his company. That doesn't mean I like him being here. I can't relax with him in the house. I spent most of my day off in cafés and at the library, because I just couldn't bear being alone with him. I hope that his problem settles down soon, and that he can go back to his old life. I'm sure it's just a question of giving him time to readjust, and to unlearn his bad habits.

Checking his social media, I see that he has a TikTok account, as well as a YouTube channel, devoted to conspiracy theories about his mysterious condition. These theories range from 5G masts, to alien abduction, to mind-control drugs delivered by vaccine, and have gained him many new followers. His tendency to pass out at some point during the broadcast only makes him more plausible among the conspiracy theorists. Martin has been trying to get him to see a therapist. But Woody refuses, maintaining that all he needs is a rest and a health kick, including a change of diet. To that end, he spends hours pumping ten-pound hand-weights from his reclining position, and lives on four servings a day of *RippedinSix*, a protein shake, made up in a plastic bottle.

It's very strange, how quickly our lives fall into new patterns. Woody has only been with us four days, and already we have a new routine. Morning: I get up and shower before the boys take all the hot water; make breakfast – *RippedinSix* (chocolate flavour) for Woody; coffee and toast for Martin and me. Then I load the washing machine; do my pelvic-floor exercises; score some dopamine in the park; and go to work at Salena's Books. I try to make sure I am ready to leave at the same time as Martin. Although I know Woody isn't dangerous, I don't want to be alone in the house with him. Then, after work, I kill time until Martin is almost due to come home. Sometimes I go running, or sit and watch reflections of the world go by. Then I go back and make dinner: *RippedinSix* (chicken) for Woody; pasta and salad for Martin and me. Later, we watch a movie – or rather, Martin and Woody watch a movie. The only time Martin suggested putting on something I liked (*The Piano*), Woody passed out, so now they watch movies like *The Punisher* and *300* and *First Blood*, while I read, or work on my laptop, or look through my social media.

I've been somewhat neglectful of my online communities. It has been a couple of days since I last checked Martin's Facebook. Of course, there has been a lot on my mind, not least the Jo Perry suspect, and, of course, my pursuit of the dopamine rush that is my *real* social media. But Martin's Facebook reveals nothing much other than his concern for Woody, and a few conversations with Lucas about the reunion party in June. A hundred and forty people have accepted the invitation so far. Lucas is delighted. Lots of stuff about catering, retro cocktails and music. Nothing more about Katie. And Lucas wants to bring back the band. He still has all their gear, he says, stored away in his loft space. Martin got rid of his bass long ago, but Lucas has one he can lend him. He even has a copy of their original set list, as if either of us could forget, and a recording, taken from the back of the hall. Martin seems excited by this. *Man, I'd love a copy*, he says. *I had no idea. Send one over!* I can't help wondering if it's because he wants to hear Katie's voice again. I find myself hoping that the recording will be terrible, out of tune. That his memory of her will fade away like a Polaroid.

Meanwhile, the Jo Perry suspect continues to cause speculation. We have a name – Graham Crawley – and the details of the school in which he was Head of English, but as yet no official statement. However, a search of the internet reveals his Facebook account, as well as that of his ex-wife, as well as a plea for privacy from his friends and family. But the internet is no place for that, and speculation is growing. One site names an ex-colleague, who claims Crawley harassed her. Another speaks of his recent divorce, and the change it triggered in him.

*@irisnoir23: So, it turns out that a man nicknamed 'Creepy' turned out to be a creep. If only people had known – oh, wait.*

*@whitey2947: Disgusting how this man's life is being pulled apart before he's even charged. Who the fuck knows why his marriage broke up?*

*@irisnoir23: A woman died, by violence. You think the suspect's history of violence towards women isn't relevant?*

*@whitey2947: Hearsay, based on an estranged partner's words. Hardly a history of violence.*

Iris (I know it's Iris) is quick to respond angrily. The conversation degenerates. Someone calling themselves *@Try_To_Stop_Me* links to an article in a Delhi newspaper about a woman arrested for adding psychiatric drugs to her husband's food.

*@whitey2947: It's happening everywhere. MK2 already doing the rounds in London.*

*MK2.* I've seen that reference before. Google reveals a sinkhole of dark conspiracy theories, the principal one being that women are poisoning men by stealth, using drugs that attack the 'masculinity centres' of the brain. Once the drug is delivered, the victim can then be 'triggered' by the use of certain code words. Feminists across the globe are using this drug on men in preparation for a *gender coup* (and yes, there is a hashtag), after which they will take over all positions of power, reducing men to slavery. Even wives and girlfriends are being radicalized by the feminists, which makes all women suspect. The best defence against MK2 is to only eat food one has prepared oneself, or better still, *RippedinSix*, made up with bottled water.

I wonder if Woody's health kick is linked to this conspiracy. His name is certainly spoken in these circles of the internet. Still, this shouldn't affect me or Iris. He has moved on from us. His TikToks veer between plaintive rants against the doctors who have not helped him, and extravagant claims about his physique. Apparently, he is a *total beast*, thanks to clean living and *RippedinSix*, and urges men to strengthen their minds and to build their perfect bodies through training and exercise.

At night, in bed, in whispers, Martin and I discuss what to do. 'We can't keep him here forever,' I say, after another movie (*Fight Club*) with bottled beer and *RippedinSix*.

'I know. But try to understand. He feels cut off from everyone. He can't go anywhere on his own. He could pass out anywhere: on the Tube, in the pub, in the gutter. He'd be completely helpless. He could be robbed, or anything.'

I avoided saying the obvious. This is a man who once specialized in making women helpless. 'He needs to see a professional,' I said, trying to sound sympathetic.

He nodded. 'Easier said than done. But yes, he's not in a good place.' He turned over and put his arms around me, and kissed my hair at the temple. It's been a while since he did that. 'You've been really great about this. Just thought I ought to tell you.'

And there he is. The man I love. Not given to fulsome compliments, or grand gestures, but decent; sincere. I know it doesn't always sound that way, but we do OK together.

*Then tell him*, says that inner voice – critic or demon, I couldn't say. *Tell him what's been happening.*

*Er, no. I don't think so.*

*Why not? Don't you trust him?*

Good question. I don't really know. Maybe I haven't *trusted* anyone since I was a child. It's still there, you know; the gap that Katie left in my life. For a while, I really believed that Martin had filled it. But that wasn't true. First love is a potent drug. It occupies every moment. But as it settles into a more quiet kind of companionship, we realize how much those hormones obscure. There are so many rooms in my house into which Martin has never even glanced. So many doors that are locked to him; so many secrets unspoken. It isn't a question of trust. I mean, every couple has secrets. But the thought of trying to explain my gift – my *curse* – to Martin –

*So? You could just show him instead. Show him, the way you showed Iris.*

Now I *know* it's a demon voice. That way lies damnation. It seemed the most natural thing in the world to share my gift with Iris. But the thought of sharing with Martin fills me with something like panic. Once more it occurs to me that I have never looked into Martin's house. Now that my gift has returned, I wonder why I've never tried. Is it Woody? Is it me? Or is it rather Adam Price, the boy who never went away?

# TRACK 7:

# Little Plastic Castle

But who hath seen her wave her hand?
Or at the casement seen her stand?
*Alfred, Lord Tennyson, 'The Lady of Shalott'*

# I

*Extract from Class of '92, by Kate Hemsworth*
*(published by LifeStory Press, 2023)*

Trauma is a curious thing. It doesn't always feel violent. It can even pass you by almost without registering, except for that taint it leaves in the air, a pollution you don't even notice. What happened with Adam Price was like that. It lingered like the aftershock of a half-remembered dream, then vanished, along with the memory of everything that we had shared, so that by the time I started at Mulberry House, I'd forgotten all about Adam Price, and the things that had seemed so important to me when Bernie and I were seven.

My father was concerned that I was growing up too quickly. But I couldn't grow up quickly enough: all I wanted was to be just like the adults around me. Adulthood meant security – rules – a world in which everything made sense, stories weren't real, games were just games, and children were safe from monsters.

A school report from my third-year English teacher, Mrs Platt, reads: *Katie is hard-working and conscientious, but she lacks imagination.*

It was an understandable mistake. I was an avid reader, but of non-fiction and real-life narratives. I no longer had any patience with tales of the supernatural. I liked the kind of literature that teaches us about real-world events, and history, and relationships. I enjoyed theatre and drama; but I favoured *Julius Caesar* over *A Midsummer Night's Dream;* the historical over the occult. Adam Price had broken me somehow from the inside, and it took a second trauma, thirteen years later, for me to even remember how.

But what I'd seen in Adam Price went far beyond just trauma. It was like stepping into a house in which every room had the radio on, all tuned to different stations and cranked up to head-splitting volume. The result was a kind of dreadful white noise filled with angry voices; a disco-theque of hate and abuse, and guilt, and shame, and fear, and self-loathing. And there were monsters in there, too, more frightening than any story. Monsters with human faces, and dreadful, inhuman appetites.

I had no words for what I found; but I knew as soon as I entered his space that this was a violation. I wasn't meant to see this, I knew. I'd overridden Adam's consent. And I sensed how hard he had tried to hide the damage, the darkness within him. He felt it too, which was why he reacted as violently as he did, grabbing me by the hair and shoving me onto the ground, shouting, *Stop it! Stop it!* even though, as far as any witnesses knew, *he* was the one attacking *me*.

By the time Mrs White intervened, I'd forgotten most of the details. All I remembered was guilt and shame, and the sense that I was bad inside. I didn't want to discuss it. I didn't even want to think about it. A part of me blamed Bernie – Bernie, who would have understood if only I had confided in her. But all I wanted was to forget what I had seen in Adam Price, and to banish the strange tinnitus that hearing his thoughts had awakened in me. And as that memory faded with time, the sense of trauma faded too, leaving a buried part of itself in my undeveloped mind, where it stayed hidden for thirteen years, before revealing the monster's face —

But I said I wouldn't speak of him. I never have until now; not to Lucas, or anyone. Some secrets are too much to share, even with our loved ones. Then there's the fear at the back of my mind that if I told Lucas what happened that night, it would change the way he sees me. And I *like* the way he sees me. I like my reflection in his eyes. Just as I like the way I look when I appear on Instagram: airbrushed, pretty, carefree. Of course it's an act. But we all do that. We cover up our damage. We make ourselves presentable. We put out the knick-knacks and photographs and hide away the trauma. Except perhaps for Bernie Moon. Bernie speaks for all of us, whether we admit it or not. Which is why I am telling this story now, after everything that has happened. Because, in spite of everything, Bernie Moon was on our side.

They say not all men are capable of damaging a woman. You see them on social media, flying their hashtags like banners. And whenever a man commits a crime — a murder, a violation — they come out to protest their innocence. To distance themselves from the criminal — or sometimes even excuse him — just as women instinctively see themselves in the victim. Why is this, I wonder? Not all men find guilt in their hearts. And yet, all women find damage. Yes, I read about Jo Perry, too. I'd noticed where in London she lived. I even wondered if Bernie —

But no. Let's stick to the facts as I know them. I'd seen the Facebook invitation to the Class of '92 reunion. I'd already seen Martin Ingram's response. I had no desire to go. But Lucas and Martin were best friends from school. They'd been at Pog Hill together. Lucas was Dante's godfather. He talked to Martin all the time. There was no way I couldn't attend this party. I told myself there might be enough other people there to avoid being around Martin and Bernie – as long as I was careful.

I suppose you think that was naïve. But really, it seemed possible. That after so many years apart, we could put the damage behind us. But damage doesn't work that way. Damage tells you it was your fault. That you did something to provoke it. It teaches you you're worthless. It laughs at you during the night. It eats away at you until something gives – your heart, your soul. Even maybe your marriage. If it's a marriage built on a lie, perhaps that's the happiest outcome. But I'll leave that to you to decide, once I've finished telling my story.

After Mr Davis left, Bernie dropped right off my radar. It had been years since we had shared any kind of friendship, and now I had my own circle of friends, my own developing interests. I became increasingly involved with the Drama department at Mulberry House, and in the fifth form, was cast as Juliet in the school play, alongside a boy from St Oswald's. That was Martin Ingram. Dark hair; soulful eyes behind little wire-framed glasses; some adolescent acne that would linger on until sixth form. The boy who played Tybalt was more my type, but Martin was playing Romeo. Inevitably, we were thrown together. I wouldn't say that we became friends, but for the next three years or so, he was a part of my social group, which consisted of girls from Mulberry House and boys from nearby St Oswald's. I would see him from time to time at our local youth club. He was rather shy with me – many Ozzies were awkward with girls – and I was barely aware of him, except as a gangly presence in an oversized Army Surplus coat, which he wore winter and summer.

Once or twice, he came to events organized by Mulberry House – a concert, an end-of-term disco – but I never saw him with a girlfriend. He always came alone, or with his friend, Lucas Hemsworth. Lucas played Tybalt in the play, and we were an item for a while, but it was nothing serious. Later, we reconnected, of course. After university. But then, we were young. We were playing the field. The whole world was ours – or so we thought. I hadn't worked the truth out yet. I hadn't understood that the men who asked for my number, who took me on dates, who carried my shoes as we walked back at night, were not at all who I thought they were. Those men, who said they loved us. Who lied. Who knew that the world wasn't ours at all. The world belonged to them. And yes. Although not all of them *did*, *all* of them were capable.

# 2

*From the LiveJournal of Bernadette Ingram (marked as Exhibit BI 1):*
*Thursday, April 7th, 2022*

Not everyone gets to keep their first love. I did; that makes me lucky. It didn't turn out quite as I'd hoped, but we are still together. This is what I tell myself, on those nights when he holds me. And Time has made us strong, so that we know each other very well – far too well for me to need to look into his house to see what's running through his mind.

We met at Pog Hill, in the sixth form. I'd never had a boyfriend before. At Mulberry House, I was weird and shy – too shy to talk to boys, too weird to appreciate attention. But Pog Hill was a fresh start. No one cared about Mulberry House. No one remembered *Weird Bernie*. In defiance of the other girls who teased their hair and wore florals, I created a look of my own: black jeans and Converse boots and an Army Surplus parka I'd picked up from a second-hand shop. I'd decided that if I was going to stand out, I would do it on my own terms.

I was studying English, History and Philosophy. Martin was in my English class. He was in a band with some friends, which made him one of the cool kids, so I was all the more surprised when he found me in the rec room one day and asked if I'd ever considered being a singer in a band.

'What kind of band?' I said.

He explained – with an awkwardness I found faintly familiar – that his band, while working on original songs, was playing covers on Saturday nights at a pub in Malbry, and that a female vocalist would help them broaden their repertoire.

For a moment, I stared at him. I knew about the band, of course. And I knew from the grapevine that Martin played bass, which I found somehow comforting. My limited knowledge of pop music had left me with the impression that bassists were somehow reliable, while lead guitarists and singers were vain. I have no idea if this is true, but it gave me the courage to answer him.

'I don't know if I *can* sing,' I said.

'Most people can sing,' he said, with a smile that made me want to smile back. His eyes were grey, and surprisingly warm. I'd always thought grey eyes were cold.

'Why me?'

He shrugged. 'You've got a style. Have you ever sung before?'

'Just in the choir at church,' I said.

He laughed. 'That's cute. Let's try you out.'

I followed him to the music block, which was an old Victorian house set apart from the main body of the college. Here were the practice rooms, each with their own piano; most of them in poor repair, but good enough for students. As we walked, he talked to me about his poetry; his ambitions; his desire to get out of Malbry and to see the world. By the time we'd reached the practice room, I already knew that he loved Ted Hughes, Tori Amos and Kate Bush. I knew about his favourite films (*Alien, The Lost Boys, Yojimbo*). I knew about his peanut allergy. He was unlike anyone I'd ever met: candid, mercurial, funny.

'Here. Stand by the piano.' He spoke as if he were ten years older than I was, instead of only six months. 'What can you sing?'

I looked down at the keyboard, which was as yellow as old dentures. 'I don't even know if I can.'

He opened the piano stool, revealing a cache of sheet music. He reached under the pile, and came out with *The Kate Bush Songbook*. 'Let's see, shall we?' he said. 'I've been practising this one.' And, sitting at the piano, he launched into the opening chords to 'The Man With the Child in His Eyes'.

Of course, I was a disaster. I thought I knew the song, but realized, as I started to read the lyrics, that I'd confused it with something more recent – 'Manchild', by Neneh Cherry. I faltered and struggled. My voice swooped and fell. My face and neck began to burn. I said: 'Hang on. Let me try this again.' I opened my mouth, and found myself croaking at him like a frog.

Martin stopped. He looked at me for a moment, then grinned. 'You're right,' he said. 'You *can't* sing.' And then he stood up, and kissed me very gently on the mouth, and such was my astonishment that it never occurred to me that this moment would shape the dynamic of our entire relationship.

We spent the rest of lunchtime talking in the garden, and when school was over, I went by the local record shop and spent all my week's lunch money on a Kate Bush CD, and spent the evening in my room with that song – *our* song – on repeat.

Funny, how things alter with time. Thirty years ago, that song had a different meaning. I was in love with the thought of a man who was different, childlike, vulnerable. To me, Martin represented that. Beneath his confident, energetic persona, I thought I could see the boy he had been: a fellow outsider; unpopular; weird. It never occurred to me to think that perhaps what he saw in me was the new Bernie, the one I had created from scratch when I had first come to Pog Hill. For a long time, it never occurred to me that perhaps he believed in my fiction. And for a long time, I didn't realize that our love had begun with my ignorance, and with his disappointment.

But now, the wind is changing. It feels ripe with possibility. I've lived too long in the shadows. It's time for me to step into the light. With my power has come a desire to reinvent myself again, just as I did when I came to Pog Hill; to over-write Old Bernie, and to make of myself something different.

Salena knows a woman who could give me singing lessons. 'Anyone can sing,' she says. 'It's just a question of choosing the right song, in the right range. I could give you her number.'

I left my name and my details, and arranged a lesson for next week. I have eight weeks before the Pog Hill reunion party. Eight weeks to learn how to sing my song. A month ago, I would have laughed. The thought of singing in public – and in front of *her* – would have terrified me. But things are changing. I have changed. And the thing is, I always liked singing. I liked it in the choir, and when I thought no one was listening. I don't have Katie Malkin's voice, but I bet I could do something. And I really think that, this time, with the right combination of confidence and killer heels, I could finally make Martin look.

Iris is wholly in favour of this. I have fallen into the habit of meeting her a few times a week and having a couple of cocktails. Between that and the Finchley Fliers, I might almost have a social life. Not that I do much flying yet, but I already feel stronger. Even my hot flashes and night sweats are growing less troublesome.

Martin thinks that I'm meeting someone from the running club. How can I tell him that my friend is a twenty-something coffee-shop employee I rescued from a predator? Plus, Iris isn't a common name, and Martin might get suspicious. Martin is clever. Martin makes connections, and invisible though she is to him now, it wouldn't take much to expose her. Woody has to go, and soon. The question is, how to do it?

'Just tell him to piss off,' says Iris, in her usual way. 'Better still, just fuck him up.'

I've tried to make her understand. But Iris is totally fearless. In her world, *fuck him up* is the solution to every problem not solved by tequila or Mexican food. In some ways, it's very refreshing. I wish I had her attitude.

Still – Woody, though. His presence has moved from annoying, to something approaching unbearable. A few days ago, I could still just about tolerate being in the same house, as long as we weren't in the same room. Now, even the sounds of his occupancy fill me with dread. The sound of his toilet flushing. The sound of him, ranting into the night from whichever of his social media platforms he happens to be on. He has a daily newsletter, too. He writes it in a special code, so as not to be triggered by seeing the words that make him pass out. (That's what he calls it, *triggered*, as if he were the victim of trauma here, instead of the women he has attacked.) I smell the animal reek from his room, like that of an unwanted dog.

Martin feels the pressure, too. I think he misses our routine. It makes him defensive and brittle, although he never shows any impatience with Woody. With Woody, he is cheerful and calm, even when Woody isn't. He has been drawing up an extended list of the words that make Woody pass out, and is working to find a connection. It's a slow process, based on trial and error, but certain words have already been banned from our conversations.

'*Doughnut.* Why doughnut?' Martin says to me when we're lying in bed one night. 'There must be a reason somewhere, but I can't make out what it is.'

Martin has a theory that Woody's condition is based on his distrust of women. He isn't wrong; but after a day of deferring to Woody's needs, of pandering to Woody's moods, of making excuses on Woody's behalf, I'm starting to lose patience.

'You're not a counsellor,' I say. 'He needs to see a professional.'

'You don't understand,' he says. (I do.) 'He's always been fighting fit. He doesn't know how to express weakness. All this is bringing back memories he doesn't know how to cope with.'

I take a deep breath to try and push down the anger building inside me. It comes out over my skin instead, flashing its warning signals. 'Has he said when he's going to leave?'

'Jesus, Bernie!' He's angry too, and, under pressure, anger flies out at the only available target. 'You're fucking cold, do you know that?'

*I'm* cold. That's hilarious. I can feel my own anger now, building up like lava. Just for a moment, I think about looking into Martin's house. I banish the thought in horror. There is too much anger between us right now. Too much buried resentment. Imagine what might happen if I looked into Martin's house and saw her looking back at me –

'I'm sorry,' I said. 'I know he's your friend.'

Martin's silence was glacial. I could feel him next to me, taut as a bundle of barbed wire. This too is Woody's fault – *my* fault, by association.

*Just tell him to piss off,* said Iris at the back of my mind. *Or better still, just fuck him up.*

I wish it were that easy.

# 3

*Thursday, April 7th*

Forty-three customers today. Salena still assumes that Kafka is to thank for our popularity. Good. Let him take the credit. My life is complicated enough. But since Woody's arrival, I have turned my attention increasingly to the pursuit of dopamine.

This man is cheating on his wife with a woman the age of his mother. He likes her to hold him in her arms and gently stroke his thinning hair. Sometimes he asks her to sing to him. He doesn't see it as cheating, but he feels a compulsion he can't ignore. He loves his wife, but it isn't enough. His mother died thirty years ago. I send him the taste of Ovaltine, and the message that she loves him. He buys four books, including Michelle Obama's autobiography.

This man had sex with two women last night. He filmed them on his mobile phone. Tonight, he means to upload the footage onto a revenge porn website. I send him a strongly worded instruction to delete the footage, as well as a suggestion to buy *Nobody's Victim*, by Carrie Goldberg. While I'm at it, I also enjoy the bacon sandwich he just ate, as well as absorbing the memory of his satisfaction – I don't have time for lunch today.

And still they keep coming – the people who on another day would just have walked by, but for that little voice in their mind, suggesting that books are the answer.

This man is young. He still lives at home. He follows Woody on TikTok. His house already has a shrine to Woody in the front room. He thinks Woody talks a lot of sense. I leave a little note suggesting that Woody is unreliable, and that MK2 is a myth. But this shows how fast his poison has spread. It's faster than social media. A squib in the paper has given rise to a number of other pieces. A piece in *The Spectator* links Woody's case with suicides in young men, and suggests that this is all because of the erosion of gender roles. Even sales of *RippedinSix* are mounting: I noticed a huge display of it in the window of the health food place opposite Finchley Allsports. Alex doesn't stock *RippedinSix*. With its aggressive marketing, bold lettering, and industrial-sized tubs of products, it seems aimed exclusively at men. The slogan – NO DISTRACTIONS! – reinforces its message of total commitment.

In the real world, I have finished my first week with the running club. Salena keeps time with a stopwatch, and tells me when to run and when to rest. Rahmi makes conversation. Leonie provides encouragement, and tells me I can do it. Surprisingly, she seems to be right. I think I'm making progress. Alex comes with us, and runs the course, then runs back to meet us. She sometimes brings a snack at the end – a handful of muesli bars, satsumas, some cans of lemonade. She's slim, but does not mention weight. A glance into her house reveals a history of eating disorders, although that part, like the vanished boy who could be her twin, is securely boarded away. It makes me feel slightly guilty at having misjudged her initially. She's nothing like the girls I knew when I was at

Mulberry House. She's happy to welcome anyone, as long as they're supportive. The small fee each of us pays every week is barely enough to cover the snacks. After our run last night, I asked: 'Why do you do it?'

Alex said: 'Because when I was young, there was no one to tell me how to become who I wanted to be. I was terrible at sports —'

'You were?' I couldn't imagine it.

She shrugged. 'Running was only useful when it came to evading bullies. And, believe me, there were a lot of those at my school.'

'*You* were bullied?' I was surprised. It's hard for me to visualize Alex being unpopular.

She smiled at my reaction. 'I went to a boys' school till I was sixteen. It wasn't a pleasant environment.'

For a moment, I wondered why a girl would be in an all-boys' school. Was it because of Alex's twin? Then —

'Oh.'

*Oh. That wasn't a twin.*

Alex was still watching me. 'It's hard to be a girl,' she said, 'when everyone wants you to be a boy. It's hard to feel your body even really belongs to you. But we're not just the way we're made. We're also what we make of *ourselves*.'

I thought about that for a moment. It felt new and refreshing. The idea that you could make yourself into the person you wanted to be was suddenly very bright in my mind. *You can clean your own house*, I thought. *Throw out the stuff you don't want to keep. The things people gave you to carry. Their dreams. The weight of their expectation.*

'I'm so happy for you,' I said. 'I wish I could be brave like that.'

Alex gave a gentle smile. 'Survival isn't brave,' she said.

'Sometimes, it's the only choice.'

Leonie ran up to join us. 'Please tell me there are still peanut bars. I medically *need* a peanut bar.' She held out her hand for the peanut bar that Alex was holding out to her. 'All mine,' she said to me. 'Unless you want to race me?' And, grinning, she started off at a run, back towards the gates of the park.

I'm always surprised at how fast she is. She only runs slowly when she's with me. But Leonie has taught me that you can be a runner at any size, any age. Her house is a comfortable, warm place of bright colours and laughter and cooking and joy, and the pleasure of having a body that is fat, and strong, and healthy. Leonie has identified the toxic places in her house. She has shut off those rooms of self-doubt and needs no social approval. I like her, and this family. I like that she has a place for me – not a whole room, of course, but a place where her running mates' achievements are proudly displayed.

*Maddie: first half-marathon! Steph: 20K on 2/6/21.* And here I am, too. *Bernie Ingram: started running with us today, beating 40 years of shame.* I can feel her pride in that, which is also now my pride; and now, whenever I feel as if I couldn't run another step, I think of her, and keep going.

As I caught up with her at the gates, she grinned and hugged me. It reminded me how little physical contact I've had in the past two years or so. Martin isn't really used to hugging people. At Pog Hill, the other kids hugged all the time. But Martin was physically distant, which made him different, romantic. At sixteen, in love with the Brontës, I yearned for drama and chilly romance. Now, at nearly forty-eight, I would prefer affection. Leonie's hugs are full-bodied and warm, like the rest of her. I like that. And I like the fact that I am part of a group, for the first time in my life.

I practise saying: *These are my friends* in front of the bathroom mirror. Some days, I almost feel ready to say it aloud to someone. But when I try, I always feel something like a hot flash shooting into my hairline, and I hear the voice of my inner critic saying: *Don't be stupid. You don't have friends. People like you don't deserve friends.*

Whose *is* that voice? I've often thought that it was the voice of my mother. Or Mrs Harding. Or Lorelei Jones. But lately, it sounds more like Martin's voice; Martin, whose friend Woody is currently living in our house. I wonder what he would say if I brought one of *my* friends home to stay? Iris, Salena, or Leonie? It sounds impossible. Martin would never allow it. And yet I find myself wondering who put him in charge of our household. Who gave him the authority?

*It doesn't have to be like that, you know,* says the voice of my inner demon. *You could take charge. You know what to do.*

It is a cold and beguiling thought. I banish it to the Quiet Room. Martin's house is off-limits to me. And yet I can't help wondering: is this because I am afraid of the damage I might do, or is it of what I might find there?

# 4

*Friday, April 8th*

It has been a week now since Woody moved into the guest room. I'm beginning to feel the strain. His diet of *RippedinSix*, combined with his exercise, and the fact that he lives in week-old underwear, gives the room a hamster-cage fug. He has installed a webcam and a laptop on Dan's old desk, from which he makes his broadcasts to a growing audience, both on TikTok, and YouTube.

It seems that people love to hear about the things that most frighten them. Secret cabals of aliens. Paedophiles in high places. Satanists; extraterrestrials; sinister conspiracies, mostly involving marginalized groups. Woody himself is increasingly drawn to the MK2 theory. A drug, created by womankind to eliminate masculinity. It all makes perfect sense to him. He is, once more, a victim. A woman must have drugged him, he says, to have made him the way he is. So far, he has not named Iris. I don't think he remembers her.

He's taking some kind of stimulant. I know, because he orders it to our address, via Amazon. Whatever it is, it keeps him awake. I can hear him, recording his daily slices of insanity. I can't bear to watch him. And yet I must, or look into his house, and submit myself to the horrors there. *They've stolen my words*, he rages impotently to his audience. *They've installed a limiter into my brain.*

Well, to be fair, that isn't wholly inaccurate. We know the use of certain words tends to bring on his episodes. I'm not sure why that is, or how these associations work. Either way, it has made him cautious, and now he speaks in a kind of code. Women have become *Exes*. I think this refers to the XX chromosome, but my mind persists in seeing them as women he has discarded and used. Feminists are *Genderbombers,* or sometimes just *The Enemy* (this includes the feminized men, or *Handymen*, who, according to his theory, will be the ones to survive the impending Gender Coup, and serve the new world order). His broadcasts are divided between the practical (how to keep fit from the safety of your bedroom; how best to protect yourself against a potential MK2 attack) and the personal (how he hasn't been able to achieve a climax since it happened, not even using online porn; how his mysterious episodes have affected every part of his life). He speaks of the terrible feeling of never knowing when it will strike; the terrible uncertainty of not knowing if a woman is a Genderbomber, or just an ordinary Ex.

*It's like PTSD*, he says. *It's eating me up from the inside. Exes can never know how this feels. This helplessness. This uncertainty. One day I'll be OK, and then – Wham! That's the worst part of it. Nobody knows when it's coming. Nobody knows who to trust anymore.*

It's almost amusing, isn't it? The man who specialized in drugging and raping women now feels he doesn't know who to trust?

Martin doesn't believe in MK2, but he sympathizes rather more than he ought to. He tells me over and over again that I should try to understand. I wish I could tell him the truth; that I understand it only too well, but I can't. Where would

I even begin? Woody's experience reflects what every woman has been through. Not all men are abusers, but every woman has reason to know what that abuse feels like. Perhaps that's why I don't want to fix whatever is broken inside him. Perhaps he needs to understand that all actions have consequences.

Last night, we had half an hour alone while Woody recorded his podcast. It felt like listening to Adam Price, raging and crying from the Quiet Room at Chapel Lane. The thought makes me feel guilty and strange. Sitting next to Martin felt like a kind of betrayal. I'd made us both a cup of tea, but the guilt was so overwhelming that I couldn't bring myself to drink mine. Instead, I checked my watch, stood up and said:

'I think I might go for a walk.'

'I'll come with you,' Martin said.

That was unlike him. I didn't know whether it was a good thing or not. *Maybe he wants to be with me, away from Woody's influence.* The thought made me feel warm inside. I don't remember the last time we went for a walk together. For a moment, I allowed myself to imagine us, hand in hand, alone in the park. But Martin didn't hold my hand. Instead, he walked beside me, his glasses reflecting the street lights, his expression unreadable.

'Is everything OK?' I said.

'Why shouldn't it be?' said Martin.

'Well, there's Woody. Stuff at work. I don't know. I thought you seemed – *stressed.*'

He looked at me. Under the street light, his face was all planes and angles. '*I've* been stressed? Bernie, have you seen yourself? You're like a crazy person. I hardly recognize you anymore.'

That took me by surprise. It should have done; Martin has always been very good at reflecting his own state back at me.

And he *is* under stress; I can see it. Between his fraught relationship with LifeStory Press – and Jared Noonan Philips in particular – and now, his anxiety over his friend. Nevertheless, I found myself saying:

'I'm not the one with the problem. Woody's putting us both under stress.'

He made a sound of exasperation. 'This has nothing to do with Woody. It's like some kind of mid-life crisis. I mean, I understand about – you know – *the change*. But this is getting out of hand. These friends you go out with. Who are they? What do you talk about? Because when you get back, it's like you're a different person.'

I shrugged. I was starting to prickle with heat. 'I don't think that's fair. I'm trying to be as patient as I can. But your friend makes me really uncomfortable.'

'Oh, yes. Let's make it all about *him*.'

The hot flash was coming. I pushed it down. 'It's not about him,' I said. 'It's about the way you ignore my feelings about him. There's something wrong with him, Martin. I know you don't see it, but there is. He's aggressive. He's paranoid.'

'You've never liked him.'

'*No!*'

He sighed. 'Listen, Bernie. I know what this is. That Jo Perry murder upset you. It's understandable. It was a terrible thing to happen right on our doorstep. But to blame *all* men for the actions of one –'

'I don't blame *all* men,' I told him. 'But if people had listened to what women said, then maybe Jo Perry would still be alive, and people wouldn't be saying: "*A guy his friends called 'Creepy' turned out to be a creep. Who knew?*"'

'Your mother thinks you should see someone,' said Martin.

'You spoke to my mother?'

'She phoned up on Monday night. You were out. I ended up having to talk to her.'

Damn. He was right. In all the upset over Woody moving in, I'd forgotten my weekly call to my mother. The thought of her discussing me with Martin made my skin flash like a neon sign.

'She said she'd had a bad time, too, when she was your age,' Martin went on. 'Hormones all over the place. She gave me a number, in case you needed to talk to someone.'

*Someone from church.* Of course. My mother thinks all my problems stem from not going to Confession. But I didn't want to talk about my mother to Martin. Instead, I said: 'I'll bear it in mind.'

'As long as you know,' said Martin. 'I mean, if even your *mother* thinks —'

I nodded. 'I'm fine. It's just hormones.'

# 5

*Saturday, April 9th*

At last, Graham 'Creepy' Crawley has been charged with Jo Perry's murder. The fact that he is an educator has already caused outrage. Protests and calls for more security in schools have joined the vigils in support of the victims of male violence. Another group of protesters have used the case to protest against self-identification, apparently on the basis that the guilty party might attempt to be fraudulently placed in a women's prison. Others have suggested (seemingly without evidence) that the murderer might have been dressed as a woman in order to pass unnoticed. Trans groups have (quite rightly) pointed out that this has nothing to do with them. So far, what we do know of Graham Crawley is that he lives in Archway, was Head of English for four years at The Murray School, and that his ex-wife used to go to the same gym as Jo Perry. A photograph shows him in casual dress, laughing with some friends in the pub. He could be anyone. He could be you. He is divorced, with two teenage sons, which earns him the label *Family Man* in today's edition of the *Metro*. Neighbours describe him as *outgoing, friendly, always ready to share a joke.* An ex-colleague describes him as: *An old-fashioned man's man. Liked a drink. Can't see him hurting a woman.*

I wonder if I could find him if I looked hard enough for his house. After all, I did find Jo – but then, I'd had previous contact with her. Finding Graham Crawley would be a different matter – but could I find him? Confirm his guilt? Or maybe even more than that?

No. That's Iris talking. Iris has a strong belief in personal justice. She thinks we should go out and right wrongs, like proper superheroes. I tell her it doesn't work like that. But I know she doesn't believe me. Still, she can't do anything. Except maybe argue on Twitter. All the same, I've taken to dropping in at Priscilla's Pantry every morning before going to work, for tea and, if it's quiet, a chat. Sometimes I have a doughnut. It's better than breakfast with Woody, and besides, I need to keep an eye on her. Iris is far bolder than I am. Her energy tends towards the confrontational. And yet, she too, like Alex, is becoming a part of my life. Not quite a friend, although she knows more about me than anyone.

*Meet me at our place tonight*, says a text from her today. *There's something I need you to do for me.*

*Our place.* She means the cocktail bar. I had no choice but to agree. Iris already knows too much. And if I'm honest, being with her is easier than being with Martin right now. And where Martin goes, Woody goes, at least up to the bedroom door. With Iris, at least, I don't have to hide the dust under the hearthrug. Iris sees me perfectly. And she actually *likes* what she sees. This too, is appealing.

I know what you're thinking. That I have '*unresolved maternal shit*', as Martin likes to put it. Only this could possibly explain why I'm drawn to a young woman who could easily be my daughter. But you would be wrong, and so would he. What I value is friendship. Friendship, like the one I had as a child, with Katie. Friendship, like the one I had – or thought I had – with Martin. But when I met Martin, we were sixteen. We were both dazzled by hormones. At the time, I thought he saw me, but Love is a two-way mirror. We saw what we most wanted to see: idealized images of ourselves. Now the mirror is broken. That's how we see the magician's trick. That's how we see the world now; through the fragments of the past.

Iris was late. She always is. While I was waiting, I looked at the cocktails menu. Then, seeing the place begin to fill up, I ordered a Cosmopolitan. They're out of fashion now, of course, but it seemed somehow very sad and wrong that I'd managed to live for forty-seven years without ever even tasting one. Cosmos, I thought, were for women with friends. Women who meet in big, noisy groups and talk about their sex lives. Women like Alex and Leonie. Women who are at ease in their skin.

A young man brought my drink on a tray, with a dish of Japanese rice crackers.

'Waiting for someone?'

I nodded. 'A friend.'

I felt the start of a hot flash, like burning rain across my skin. The inner voice that often says mean and angry things doesn't like the fact that I have a friend. That inner voice is always quick to point out how ridiculous it is that a woman my age should imagine being friends with a girl like Iris. And yet, the young man doesn't think it strange.

'I hope you have a nice evening.'

I drank my Cosmopolitan. It was pink as Iris' hair, and tasted dangerously innocuous. I ordered a couple more cocktails: one for me, one for Iris. Mistake. By the time she rocked up, late, I'd managed to drink both of them.

'Sorry I'm late. I had a thing.'

Once again, I marvelled at how cool Iris managed to look. Tonight, she was wearing a fluffy pink biker jacket that matched her hair, black high-heeled boots, and a pair of black jeans that looked as if they'd been dragged through a shredder. She looked at my empty cocktail glass.

'OK. We're going to need more of these.'

Over a couple more cocktails, Iris told me the details. She has a new boyfriend. His name is Nic. He's an actor, though his only role so far has been in panto. But her close escape with Woody has made her somewhat suspicious of men, and Nic just seems too perfect, somehow. Too handsome, too attentive. She wants me to check him out, she says. Make sure he's boyfriend material.

'Er, no. After what happened last time?'

'You mean with the creep?'

'You mean Woody.'

'He was a rapist and a creep. Plus, he was fragile as hell. If you hadn't flipped him, something else would. That guy has serious issues.'

And yes, she is right. But nevertheless. Playing *House* isn't a game anymore. Perhaps it never really was. We didn't see it at the time, but Adam Price was our early warning of the damage we could do. That's because Adam Price was already damaged, of course. We just didn't know it, or suspect what might happen if he was pushed. But as people grow, so does their damage. So does their instability. Any change to their house becomes increasingly likely to cause harm.

'I know he did,' I said. 'And yet –'

And yet The Great Carovnik's voice still whispers quietly in my ear. I'm supposed to *make them look*. She chose me for that reason. She saw something in me. She wanted me to understand that if men get to stare at us, we can stare right back at them.

*Just take a look inside,* she says. *Just make sure he's cool. You don't have to do anything complicated. Just make sure he isn't getting ready to –*

'Pull some kind of stunt,' finished Iris. 'He's due here any minute, so let's get a pitcher of something in and get you doing what you do.'

I wanted to protest, and yet the three Cosmopolitans I'd drunk seemed to be in agreement with her. I was practising my skills. Why not do as Iris asked? It might save her some heartbreak. As long as all I did was *look* –

'Here he is now!' said Iris, standing up to greet a young man of about thirty. Dark-haired, dark-eyed; a smile that made him more than ordinarily good-looking. An actor, she'd said. That didn't mean much. Actors are ten a penny here. What I wanted to know was this: Was he honest? Was he kind?

His front room is impeccable. Tasteful, well-furnished and orderly. No sign of excessive ego, or of unsavoury habits. A neat collection of anterooms devoted to friends and relatives. No sign of obvious monsters.

I glance at Iris. She grins back. I can see she likes him. That's good: she deserves to find someone. I delve a little deeper, looking for the door marked *Sex.* Everyone has one, and as a rule, I tend not to look inside. But this is a special circumstance, and Iris is still vulnerable. She needs to be sure that the man at her side will be on her side at all times.

It doesn't take much. A glance, that's all. I don't intend to change him. Just a glance behind the scenes, to make sure Iris will be safe. And, for a moment, I almost believed that this man had no vices. He likes women. Respects them. Admires their strength and resilience. Loves their bodies. He also likes to choke them, not always with their consent. Nor is he entirely averse to a bit of stealthing.

*Shit.*

And there it is. The damage. The crack that shows up the illusion. This is a man whose secret life only shows up in certain lighting. Could I have fixed him? Left a sign, saying something like *Consent Matters*? Maybe I could, I told myself. But this was the hidden part of his house, the part where complications arise. It wasn't like suggesting that someone buy a children's book. Whatever I move here has consequences that cannot be predicted. What happened to Woody proves that. *Besides, this is about Iris*, I thought. *She's the one you're protecting. And even if you fixed him, would you trust him with your friend?*

I left his house, and looked at her, and shook my head. *He isn't cool.*

She mouthed at me: *Why?*

I gave a shrug. *Later.*

'OK.' She jerked a thumb in the direction of the bathroom. I followed her across the room, leaving Nic sitting alone at the table. As soon as we were out of his line of vision, Iris turned to me and said: 'Well?'

I told her.

She nodded and turned for the door.

'Wait a minute! Where are you going?'

Iris gave her troubling smile. 'We've established he isn't a keeper,' she said. 'And you don't want to take any risks. But he might as well pay the bar bill. Right? Even a douchebag can manage that.'

'But don't you want –'

'Proof?' She shrugged again. 'Why? There are plenty more men out there. But there's only one of you.'

How very matter-of-fact she seems. How very unlike other girls of her age. Could this be a result of what happened that night, with Woody? Did I reflect more of his image into her house than I'd meant to? Have I damaged Iris, too?

She seemed to sense my discomfort. She smiled again, looking suddenly both very young and very old. 'Babe, you worry too much,' she said, dragging me towards the door. 'Let's get burritos. I'm starving.'

# 6

*Monday, April 11th*

More news of Graham Crawley today. An ex-colleague has given an interview to the Mail Online. Four years ago, Emma Button was a teacher trainee at The Murray School. Graham Crawley, then newly divorced, had asked her out for a couple of drinks. Emma refused. She describes what ensued as a *barrage of emails, texts and letters*, plus unsolicited flowers and gifts that made her feel uncomfortable. Finally, Emma Button had complained to the deputy head. He had told her that Graham was going through a bad patch, and that she should be more understanding. But after weeks of harassment, during which Graham Crawley had spent whole evenings parked outside her house in his silver Audi, she had complained to her tutor, who had quietly transferred her away from The Murray School into a different post. *I read about the arrest*, she says. *I recognized the name straightaway. They knew he was a problem, even then. I can't help thinking, that could have been me.*

The photograph they have chosen to use shows Emma in a bikini. I wonder what that's meant to say. That she was fair game? Presumably she didn't wear it when teaching. Already the replies to the piece are filled with misogyny and hate. Many address her directly, as if she had written the article:

*Get over yourself, love. You're not even a 5.*

In other news, Woody's car was clamped. Later, a tow truck took it away. Of course, there's no question of him driving until we know what brings on his episodes. But this does not help his condition, or improve his temper. Martin was away when it happened, but I was in the kitchen, and caught the whole of the altercation.

Woody thinks that the police are in on the conspiracy. They know all about MK2. Even their Chief is a woman. Over banana *RippedinSix*, he explained it all to me, in short, staccato sentences that made him sound as if he was giving dictation. *To them, masculinity means crime. Destroy masculinity, they think, and crime will be a thing of the past. And so, they're poisoning the men. It's chemical castration on a massive scale. That's why there are so many kids who don't know what they are anymore.*

'I don't see what this has to do with your car.' He was so angry that I feared it would trigger another episode, and I had better things to do than spend my morning cleaning banana *RippedinSix* from the sofa.

He gave me a look of contempt. 'It's a Mazda RX-7. Cherry red, in perfect condition. Do you think they would have been so quick off the mark if it had been a fucking Prius?'

I thought of telling him that sometimes a cigar is just a cigar, but I suspect that in his case, it isn't. Instead, I said: 'I'm so sorry that happened to you. I hope you get your car back soon.'

He gave me a suspicious look, but settled down to drink his shake. I made myself a coffee and retreated back to the kitchen. Woody seldom follows me there. I think it's where he thinks I belong. I checked my social media. Dante first. I miss Dante. But this is nothing new; I've missed him every day for the past ten years. Last night, he went to a movie with

friends. *The Batman.* Popcorn and tortilla chips. No pictures
of his friends, but there is a picture of Dante, holding two
enormous cups of crushed ice and soda. He has grown a beard
since I last saw him. He is laughing. I haven't heard my son
laugh since he was a boy. I wonder if my mother has. He'll
be at her house for Easter. I sometimes imagine what that
must be like – the friends, the food, the laughter. I wonder
what it would have been like if –

*Stop it.*

I know. It was decades ago. But with the resurgence of my
gift, my guilt has also resurfaced. The potency of a woman's
blood has always been a symbol. Maybe it's what's left of my
Catholic upbringing.

DeeDee has posted a feature on dressing after the menopause. According to her, women don't want to be constrained
by fashions. *Dress like a goddess!* she bugles. *Throw away those
painful heels and try some glittery flip-flops instead! Invest in some
timeless pieces, like this featherlite cashmere shrug from Céline, and
this linen skirt from Dimity! Granny chic is in right now, so get
raiding those attics, girls, and see what treasures you can find!* There
follows a series of photographs of DeeDee, dressed in 'granny
chic', which, to her, seems to consist mostly of long, flowing
dresses and gossamer knits with price tags that would make my
mother gasp. I sense that grannies in DeeDee's world mostly
lounge around their decks in pastel-coloured linens and silks,
looking like supermodels. For a moment, I try to visualize
myself as an extra in DeeDee's world, looking behind that
perfect façade –

I feel the pinch of connection, like static electricity. A hot
flash rakes across my scalp. And with it, a bright gleam of
knowledge, unexpected as a seam of silver through a piece
of coal.

*DeeDee and Jules are splitting up. She wonders how she will explain his absence to her followers. She wonders whether the bitch will allow him to keep his Instagram account, or whether that's part of the settlement. Perhaps I'll get a dog, she thinks. A cute little Pomeranian. Everyone loves dogs, she thinks. That should play well with the socials.*

Of course, it's really nothing like this. It's more like trying to piece together shards of a broken mirror. And yet, for a moment, I touched her house across the space between us. I must be getting stronger. These occasional touches – the one by Jo Perry's murder site, and now this new reflection – are as yet involuntary. Like the hot flashes themselves, I cannot control what I reflect, or focus my vision accordingly. But even fragments of light can reveal things that were once in darkness.

I closed DeeDee's Instagram and looked for Katie's Facebook. A selfie of her at the gym, with her daughter Sadie. Sadie looks just like Katie when she was a teenager: slim, dark-haired, athletic. But there's no spark, no connection here. No reflection of her house. No contact with Martin, not even in his private messages. There's plenty more in there about the reunion party, though. Lucas and Martin are talking about reprising the band's original set. *It's going to be great!* Lucas exclaims. *Do you think we should get Katie to sing?*

*Hell, yeah!* Martin says. *Get her to wear the same outfit. That backless dress. The sandals.*

This is a private message, of course. He doesn't know I can read them. If he did, he wouldn't have said that. Not that he was fucking her then – that was still a year away – but he still knows how it hurts me. Does Lucas know he fucked her? He and Katie had become an item shortly after Pog Hill. Isn't there a code that forbids men to fuck their friends' girlfriends?

*You keep saying that ugly word*, my inner critic tells me, sounding just like my mother today. *Foul language is unlady-like, as well as being an insult to God.*

*Good*, says my inner demon. *Let Him be insulted. Where was He when Jo Perry was killed? Where was He when Martin fucked Katie?*

It's childish, I know. But it still hurts to see how often Martin thinks of her. *Get her to wear that backless dress.* It was silver lamé, with a halter neck, and she wore her hair up, in the kind of artless, messy bun that hairdressers take hours to achieve. And she sang – how had I not known she could sing? – *our* song, 'The Man With the Child in His Eyes'.

And, once more, comes the dreadful urge to take a glance into Martin's house. Just a glance – to see where he is, and how much of him still dreams of Katie. It's only like checking his Facebook. It's not as if it means anything. Except that it does, it means *everything*, and I find myself consumed in a flash so hot that it actually burns, it rages like a forest fire, eating up everything in its path –

Upstairs, a toilet flushes. Woody has gone back to his room. The hot flash – and the memories – have left me feeling ravenous. I head for Priscilla's Pantry like a drowning woman for the shore. To feel that rush of dopamine.

I could suddenly kill for a doughnut.

# 7

*Tuesday, April 12th*

That lamé dress. I can't somehow seem to get it out of my mind. And the reunion party, too – designed to copy the Pog Hill Prom – fills me with a kind of despair. I am travelling back in time. Memories that were dormant till just a couple of weeks ago are now returning to baleful life. Katie. Martin. Mr D. And Adam Price, that angry boy whose voice has followed me across the years –

If only someone could do to me what I did then to Katie. Remove those useless memories. Insulate them with marshmallow fluff. But even that attempt didn't last. And there's no one to do the same for me. Martin knows there's something wrong. I've seen the way he looks at me. Woody's perpetual presence has driven a new wedge between us. Martin thinks I'm angry with him because his friend has not gone home. He's wrong. I'm angry with myself. For carrying that vision of her inside me for so many years.

I mentioned the Pog Hill reunion again this evening, at the running club. Leonie and the others are always so easy to talk to, and when we're running (at the gentle pace Alex says should allow for conversation), I find myself confiding in them rather more than perhaps I ought. Maybe it's because it's still so dark. Darkness is confessional. Darkness encourages secrets.

'It sounds like it's going to be lots of fun,' said Salena.

I shook my head. 'I doubt it,' I said. 'It wasn't a great time for me. I'm not in a rush to revisit Pog Hill, or anyone who went there.'

'But isn't that where you met Martin?' she said. I can feel her puzzlement. Looking into Salena's house reveals her romantic nature. The legend of Martin and Bernie has coloured her own relationships; given her a benchmark that she believes she can never reach. She herself has had so many tries at finding the perfect match, but has never found *The One* – and, secretly, thinks she never will.

I slackened my pace to a walk and said: 'Relationships are weird. You think you know someone, and then they turn out to be someone else completely.'

'Not you and Martin, though,' she said. 'You're the exception that proves the rule. Childhood sweethearts, still together after all this time. Isn't that what everyone wants?'

'Is it?' said Leonie.

I shook my head. Alarmingly, I was close to tears. I said: 'I honestly don't think Martin's noticed me – I mean, *really* noticed me – in years.'

'But that's because you're *comfortable*,' said Salena, whose faith in *The One* is still strong enough to override reality.

'Fuck comfort. Give me great sex,' said Leonie, whose sex life is as joyous and demonstrative as the rest of her. '*Is* it great sex, Bernie?'

I couldn't help smiling. 'I'm struggling to remember the last time we had sex at all.'

'Er, sounds to me as if your guy needs a reminder of what he's got,' said Leonie. 'Why don't you get yourself a knockout dress, and a knockout pair of heels to go with it, and dance all night with all the men you should have fucked in high school?'

I was almost out of breath by then, but not enough to stop myself from laughing.

'I mean it,' she said. 'Give him the works. Don't creep into that dance hall like a frightened little mouse. Sashay in there like a queen! Give yourself the evening you should have had thirty years ago. Make that man of yours sit up. Give him the surprise of his life.'

I smiled, and started to run again, Salena on one side, Leonie on the other. The thought of *surprising* Martin is curiously pervasive. Could I do it? It's certainly true that over the past couple of weeks, something has changed inside me. Even Martin senses it, although he isn't sure what it is. Have I lost weight? Done something new? In any case, he disapproves. He doesn't like surprises.

'I once tried to *surprise* him with a set of black lacy under-wear, and he laughed. He actually laughed.'

'He did *what*?'

Until that moment, I hadn't realized I'd spoken. But in the dusk, with their faces bobbing beside me like lifebuoys, I'd said the quiet bit aloud. And now, it all came rushing back, in all its hateful detail, and my face was burning salt, and I took a breath that felt like a sob. I've kept this story to myself for thirty years, but now it's free. Perhaps this rage that I can feel has released something more inside me. Perhaps I am really beginning to change.

Leonie stepped into my path. 'OK, this workout's over.' She put her hands on my shoulders. It wasn't dark enough to need lights, but all the same, night was falling, and the scent of blossom from the trees was like a benediction. 'I need to understand what you said. He *laughed*?' she repeated. 'What the fuck?'

'He doesn't think of me in that way.'

Leonie made an explosive sound. For a moment, there was silence.

Then Salena said: 'Bernie. You deserve to be with a man who loves you, thinks you're beautiful. If he doesn't think of himself as the luckiest man in the world, then why is he even with you at all?'

'Dante –' I began to say.

'Dante's thirty. He can cope. Seriously, when *was* this?'

'I don't remember.'

*Yes, you do.* The inner demon, ever alert, is quick to respond to such a lie. I remember everything. Every word; every gesture. I remember the date – March 26th; the year, 1994. Martin was back for the Easter break: we had plans to celebrate. Just a long weekend by the sea, while my mother looked after Dante. We went to Scarborough by train; neither of us had a car. We stayed in a bed-and-breakfast place over-looking the sea. It was cold, but sunny, and the sky was that impossible blue that only exists in memories. We ate fish and chips, and walked on the beach, but Martin was strange and distant throughout. When we went back to the B & B, he had a long shower, and when he got out, he found me lying on the bed, dressed in black lace and satin, and –

*He laughed.* He laughed and laughed, like it was a poison he had to spit out. And afterwards, when at last his face had turned from angry red to pale, he said: *Bernie, what the fuck? What's this?*

But we both knew what it was. It was my last, sad, pathetic attempt to win him back from Katie. To win him back, the way women do in movies and in pop songs. And my mother's voice in my mind was like an earworm that wouldn't let go.

*Look at you. Cheap. You sold yourself cheap. And now you're behaving that way, too. You're cheap, and you're ridiculous.*

He'd told me what had happened when he came back for the Christmas break. Tearfully, brokenly, he'd confessed. *I'm in love with someone else. But it's all right. I'm not going to leave you. I'm going to stand by you, and Dan.* And now it was clear that what he meant was: *Be a mother to my child. Be a companion. Be a wife. But don't try to be my dream girl. That role is already taken. We're both grown-ups. We'll both survive. Just don't do that. Ever again.*

I didn't tell the whole story. But it was enough to make Salena gasp. 'He said that to you? He actually said that?'

I nodded. *That isn't all he said.* But I don't want to tell them the rest. I think perhaps I am still ashamed. Not of buying lingerie. Not of wanting to have sex. But maybe of letting him off the hook. Of accepting to take second place to her. Yes, perhaps that's at the heart of my shame. Remember, I was nineteen. The stretch marks on my stomach had barely even started to fade. I still believed that time would change what he thought he felt for her. And besides, he'd promised me: *It's over. It was only the once. She knows it can never happen again.*

'So why did you stay?' Salena asked. 'Why didn't you just leave him?'

It seems very simple to someone her age. Young people think in absolutes. But love is a trap that closes very, very slowly. Not like the Venus flytrap, in spite of its more suitable name, but more like the cobra lily, that guides its victim gently downwards into the killing jar. And yes, I thought I could change him. Girls in stories so often do. Through strength and perseverance, they tame the beast; they rescue the boy from the embrace of the Snow Queen. But not this girl. She just got old, and the boy stayed just as he was, seeing the world through a shard of ice that could not be melted.

'I'm sorry,' said Salena. 'I shouldn't have asked you the question. Leaving isn't always a choice.' She put her arms around me. Leonie joined her, then Rahmi, who had been running some distance ahead, but who had stopped when she understood that something had happened. I started to cry; not quiet tears, but great big ugly, honking sobs. I felt as if I'd been drowning, and these women had saved me. All I had to do now was to purge the salt water from my lungs along with that dreadful memory.

We stayed there until Alex arrived, picking up the stragglers. She didn't ask what was wrong, but instead, produced a bottle of juice. 'Here. Don't forget to hydrate.'

I wiped my eyes. 'I'm sorry.'

'No need to be sorry,' Leonie said. 'Men can be such douchebags.'

Salena said: 'Whatever you do, it's OK. Whatever you feel, it isn't wrong. But if ever you want a place to crash, or to think things over, or just to lie down and watch Netflix, I'm here. And so are the others.'

I nodded. 'Thanks.'

We walked back slowly through the park. The night air cooled my burning face. Until tonight, I'd never imagined telling that story to anyone. But tonight, I told my friends. And tonight, the inner voice that tells me I'm ridiculous was completely silent for the first time since that night, when I stripped off the black lingerie and crammed it into the pedal bin, and changed into a nightshirt, and did not – *could* not – walk away. And tonight, after my run, while Martin and Woody were watching a film, I ran a luxurious bubble bath, and poured myself a glass of wine, and googled cocktail dresses, and lingerie, and dancing shoes.

# 8

*Wednesday, April 13th*

I had my first singing lesson today. It wasn't what I'd expected. First of all, I'd expected the teacher to be older than I was, perhaps in her sixties or seventies. I'd imagined her looking something like Mrs Clarke from Mulberry House, with cat's-eye glasses and tight grey perm. I don't know why I thought this. Perhaps because of her name – Charlotte Hyde – or her address in a nice part of Hampstead. Perhaps because the concept of singing lessons is still so strange to me – even stranger than *running club*, or *going for a drink with friends*. That's what I'll have to tell Martin when I go out on Wednesday nights. *Going for a drink with friends*. The singing lessons will remain a closely guarded secret.

She asks me to call her Charlie. She's young – about Salena's age – and sings in a band called Bad Karma. It's a kind of alternative band of the kind Dan used to like: they have a YouTube channel and an account on Bandcamp. She lives with her friend in the basement flat of her parents' big house overlooking Hampstead Heath. She has bleached hair and a pierced nose, and ten years of classical training. She gets all kinds of people coming to her, with all kinds of different requests. Some are semi-professionals; some are complete amateurs. And she tells me *anyone* can sing: all I need is practice.

'And confidence, of course,' she said. 'Let's start with some warm-up exercises.'

I'd expected a kind of audition. I'd even printed out my song, from a page on a lyrics website. But Charlie barely looked at it. For our first lesson, all I did was repeat assorted vowel sounds in different vocal registers, while she played the accompanying line on her grand piano. It wasn't singing. It wasn't even music. I felt uncomfortable. I knew I sounded ridiculous. I didn't sound at all like myself – I didn't even sound human. And yet a glance into Charlie's house revealed no scorn, no judgement. Charlie's house is at variance with her punkish appearance: a place of order on every side, smooth and cool and disciplined.

'Ba, ba, baaa. Come on. After me.'

*Ba, ba, baaa. I sound like a sheep.*

'Ba, ba, baaa. Come on, Bernie.'

*Ba, ba, baaa.* My voice is a tiny, ridiculous croak. My throat is dry. I feel too hot. In a moment, she's going to say: *You're right, Bernie, you can't sing. You're the exception that proves the rule.*

'Louder! Bernie!'

*Ba, ba, ba –*

The hot flash is tremendous, sweeping over me like the sea. I feel the sweat stinging my scalp; my throat is dry and scratchy. For a moment, I'm back at Pog Hill Prom, watching Katie sing on stage. I can smell my teenage sweat; the scent of my Impulse body spray; the hot smell of the stage lights and the sawdust of the scenery. I can hear the sigh of the crowd, like waves of the seashore, and above it, her voice, so high and sweet, swooping like a seagull –

'I can't do this. I'm sorry,' I said.

Charlie looked at me and smiled. 'Can't do *what*, exactly?'
'Sing.'

She nodded. 'I see.'

I was surprised. I hadn't expected her to agree so quickly.

She stood up, went into the kitchen and came back with
a glass of iced water. 'Hot flash?' she said.

I nodded.

'Thought so. Menopause can change your voice. It sometimes reduces your vocal range and gives you a dry throat.
Take a drink.'

I took the glass and drained it. *This is where she tells me*, I
thought. *This is where we say goodbye.*

Charlie closed the piano. 'Why did you come to me?' she
said.

'Because I'm an idiot,' I said.

'Not so. You told me you wanted to sing a song at your
high school reunion. *This* song.' She picked up the printed
sheet I'd brought with me to the lesson.

I nodded. 'But I can't,' I said.

'No, you can't,' said Charlie. 'You have a lovely contralto
voice. Forcing it into that high soprano register will only
make you sound weak. Over the next few weeks, I'd like
us to explore your *real* voice. The one you've been hiding
away all this time.'

For a moment, I struggled to understand what she was saying.
I was expecting: *No, you can't sing.* Or maybe: *It's too late for
you.* But Charlie thinks, not only that I have a lovely contralto
voice, but that with training and exercise I can combat the
vocal fatigue that so often comes with menopause.

My *real* voice. I like that. Martin was wrong. Just because I
don't sing like Kate Bush doesn't mean I can't sing at all. And,

in only one lesson, I'm already learning that there's power in my voice, a power I never suspected. Singing in the choir at Mulberry House has given me some good habits. Running has already taught me something about breath control. And the Great Carovnik has taught me the most important lesson of all: that I can take the spotlight, and that I can control their gaze.

And so I've chosen the song I should have chosen thirty years ago, a song that has followed me all the way from Pog Hill to East Finchley.

When I told Charlie, she shrugged and said: 'An oldie, but let's try it, right?'

And so I did. And yes, I can sing. And when finally I take the stage at the Pog Hill reunion, I'll be singing a song from my teenage years, the song I should have sung from the start. Not 'The Man With the Child in His Eyes', but Neneh Cherry's 'Manchild'.

# 9

*Thursday, April 14th*

Tonight, I went out with my new friends from the club. Alex has a tradition of going out every week with some of the girls for drinks. She calls them our *Yowza nights*, when we get to celebrate our achievements. It doesn't have to be much. A PB from one of our runners. Someone got a promotion at work. Kafka got a mention on some influencer's TikTok. We talk about anything we like. We drink tequila shots, craft beer. Rahmi doesn't drink, but she likes virgin cocktails with parasols.

We laugh a lot. It's still quite strange to hear my own laughter mixed with theirs. It feels almost dangerous, as if someone's going to stand up and shout: *That's Weird Bernie from Pog Hill, what the hell are you doing with her?* But we are all weird in different ways. Even Alex, who seemed at first to be a version of the sporty girls who gave me such a tough time at school, has had her share of damage. She still struggles from time to time, but has mostly grown beyond it. I like her. I like *all* of them, but most of all, Leonie, who takes no shit from anyone, and whose cheery self-awareness comes from half a lifetime of therapy.

Today was Salena's birthday. Her girlfriend Sophie was there, too, and Rahmi's partner, Asma, and Alex's boyfriend Danny. Sometimes the others bring partners, which makes me self-conscious that none of them (except Salena, in passing) have actually met Martin yet.

'Forget Martin,' Leonie says. 'Let's see that gorgeous son of yours.'

I smile. My phone screen shows Dante, as he appears on Instagram. Bearded, smiling and handsome, showing his best face to the world. You might even believe that I was the one he was smiling at – except that I have no idea where the picture was taken, or who provoked that gorgeous smile that lights his face all the way to his eyes.

Leonie pulls the kind of face she makes when she's eating chocolate. 'He's lovely.'

I have to agree. I wonder what he's doing now.

Leonie is the only other person whose partner has not joined us. We've heard plenty about him, though. His name is Joss, he's a solicitor, and although Leonie likes him, she doesn't think he's a keeper. Today, with a bravura designed to deflect from her real disappointment, she announced that she had finally decided to end the relationship once and for all.

'I should have broken it off months ago,' she said. 'But the sex was fantastic. All the same, he was a dick. I should have known. I've had a few.' She speaks about it with cheery disdain, but I can tell from looking into her house how much the break-up has hurt her.

'What happened?' I said.

Leonie shrugged. 'Turns out he was one of those guys who love to have sex with me, who say how gorgeous they find me, but won't come out and admit it to any of their circle,' she said. 'Finally, after weeks of hearing him say how he can't wait to introduce me to his friends, after weeks of going to supposedly favourite restaurants where no one knows him, after weeks of great sex and expensive food in strangely deserted locations, we ran into someone he knew at work. And he blanked me. He fucking *blanked* me. Talked for fully five minutes to this guy – whoever he was – without even acknowledging the fact that he was sitting right next to me, the woman he fucks three times a week, but suddenly – *poof!* – I'm invisible. And he said to me – do you know what he said? Oh, hang on –' She waved a hand. 'More shots here, please! I'm celebrating!'

The waiter, a young man with beachy hair in a topknot, came over. 'What's the occasion?'

Leonie smiled. 'You'll see,' she said. She has a smile that starts with her eyes and fills the whole room. 'What's your name?'

'Ben.'

'Well, Ben. I hope you can help me. I'm expecting a friend in a minute, and I'm planning a little surprise for him. When he comes in, I'd like you to accompany him to our table. Can you do that? He might be shy. But I'd like you to do it anyway.'

'Sure.' Ben looked confused, but game.

'So, I'll give you this sign when I want you to – Oh, speak of the devil. That's him, Ben. See him? Over there. By the door.' She indicated a man in a suit. Thirties, handsome. Suit and tie.

Alex gave a staccato laugh. 'You did *not!*'

I looked at Leonie.

'Meet Jocelyn,' Leonie said, still with that infectious smile.

By then, we could all see Ben escorting the newcomer towards our table. He looked confused, but when he saw Leonie, surrounded by the rest of us, he froze, then took a step backwards.

'Hey, don't go!' called Leonie. 'Everyone, meet Jocelyn. Jocelyn, this is everyone.' Her voice was loud enough to cut through the buzz of conversation. Jocelyn stood pinned by the lull, looking stunned and out of place.

'Joss keeps saying how much he'd like to meet my friends,' said Leonie. 'But he's not so keen on me meeting his. In fact, he told me just last night that although he loves having sex with me, he needs to consider his profile. Publicly dating a fat chick would make his colleagues lose respect. "You're great in so many ways," he said. "But I need to be with a woman who looks good next to me at parties." She took a breath, then belted out at the top of her voice: 'So – let's have a big cheer for Jocelyn Moore, of Morgan, Moore and Brammall; solicitors, family law, property, wills and probate.' She raised her voice even further, and, motioning for the room to stand, yelled: 'Big cheer for Jocelyn, dick of the week. *Welcome to my party!*'

At this, the whole of the bar began to laugh and cheer and catcall. The rest of us stood and joined in the applause.

Leonie lifted her glass and tipped it ironically at Joss. 'Here's to fat chicks,' she said. 'And yes – in case you were wondering – Jocelyn, you've been dumped.'

Jocelyn Moore gave her a look that combined hatred and horror. I didn't need to look into his house to see what he was thinking. But he was close by. So easy for me to step forward, physical contact. And it was so easy to look inside that place of glittering surfaces and find the man who had hurt my friend.

I probably shouldn't have done it. But who tells a woman he's sleeping with that she's bad for his public profile? And all this to Leonie – Leonie, of the laughing eyes, and the generous heart, and the big, warm hugs, and the dirty laugh, and the total refusal to play the role of the funny fat girl who hates herself? Leonie *loves* her body. She loves the strength and thickness of her muscular thighs, her soft round breasts, her glossy hair. She loves the fact that she can run, and the endorphins her body creates. She loves the fact that she can wear fifties-style dresses and low-cut tops. She loves sex with men *and* women, and has no problem finding partners. But glancing into her house just then, I saw what no one else could see. I saw doors that had been nailed shut suddenly starting to open: whole floors that had been locked away begin to stir into dreadful life. Leonie's mother first took her to Weight Watchers when she was seven. When she was twelve, her grandmother said: *You'd be so pretty if only you lost weight.* When she was at Cambridge, she had a liaison with a young man on her Law course, who, after three years of companion- ship, conversation, and great sex, dumped her at the end of term because he'd *needed to get serious.* When she was in her first job, she was passed over for promotion twice in favour of less qualified newcomers. When she finally summoned the courage to ask why, her boss spoke vaguely of *work ethic* and *health issues*, in spite of the fact that she worked hard, and had taken fewer days' sick leave than he had.

What the hell is wrong with these men? Leonie is intel- ligent, beautiful, funny, charismatic, successful, healthy, and yes, she is fat. Why is that a problem? Fat is not lazy. Fat is not sick. Fat is not unprofessional.

And so I lashed out. Much as I had done with the man in the baseball cap who had snatched my bag, I reacted instinc- tively. I never thought. I saw his perfect projections – his highly paid job, his collection of shirts from Jermyn Street, his cabinet of first editions and his carefully curated circle of not-quite-friends. And behind them, I saw all his doors – his secrets, his insecurities, the mirrors reflecting his true self – and flipped them all like playing cards. I showed him how small he really was. I showed him the worthlessness of his peers, the hollowness of his values. I felt like the Great Carovnik, surrounded by mirrors, claiming the stage, smiling, swimming in applause.

*Abracadabra.*

For a moment, Jocelyn just stood there, swaying; dazzled. I can relate. I have grown stronger over this time: stronger, more perceptive. And Jocelyn Moore was already in a state of heightened sensitivity; surprise and humiliation made him easier to access. I withdrew, feeling triumphant. The noise in the bar had died down to a hum. Jocelyn was watching me, looking somehow arrested, like a man who has just experienced a revelation out of the blue.

For a second, I was afraid that I'd done something terrible.

But nothing happened, except that, then, Jocelyn very carefully took off his tie. Sky-blue silk, with a faint stripe, and an Italian label. For a moment he smoothed it out, using the tips of his fingers. Then, he rolled it into a coil – a strangely mystic spiral – and handed it to Leonie, a formal, almost courtly gesture, like a knight with his lady's token. Then he turned and left the bar, still without speaking a word, to the bewildered almost-silence of the many patrons.

When he was gone, Leonie looked up from the coil of blue silk in her hand. 'What the hell just happened?' she said. 'And why was he staring at Bernie?'

I shook my head. I could feel the hot flash overwhelming me. Sweat began to trickle from my hairline down my face.

'Ah, dammit,' I said. 'Does it show?' By now the heat had spread from my face to my chest, from my armpits, to my belly. 'Hot flash. Hello, menopause! Some men don't know it's rude to stare.'

'Oh, right.' Leonie nodded. 'Of course. Do you think that's what it was?'

I shrugged. 'What else?'

'He looked as if he knew you.'

'Nope. Never seen the man before.'

I wanted to slip inside her house and close all those doors of uncertainty, but I was already starting to feel discomfort. I'd never used my skill before in such a very public way, and I was already wondering what form the man's reaction would take. The mind is a labyrinth, filled with beasts. Who knew what I might have unleashed? Would he pass out at certain words? Cut his wrists? But Iris tells me repeatedly that I mustn't blame myself. I didn't make these men who they are. I should not feel guilty.

And so I ordered a fresh round of shots, and we drank, and we laughed, and we hugged, and then I went home to find Martin with Woody, watching TV, and opened my social media to find that Graham Crawley had killed again.

# IO

*Friday, April 15th*

It was thirty years ago. He was just a student then, reading English Lit. at Leeds. Apparently, he was there between 1992 and 1995, just like Martin and Katie. Born in Manchester, studied at Leeds, moved to London later. One among thousands of students there, but still it raises my hackles to think that Martin could have known him.

Maybe he stood next to him in the cafeteria queue, or shared a drink at a party. Maybe he even spoke to him. Passed him a joint. Brushed up against him in a crowded passageway. Stood next to him in a urinal. Shared a conversation, however benign or unmemorable. All these possibilities seem dreadfully plausible to me now, as does the likelihood that Crawley – the manchild into whose mind I slid to witness Jo Perry's murder – was also responsible for the unsolved murder of Anna Symonds, a Chemistry student walking home through Woodhouse Moor from a party one Saturday night in 1993, her body discovered by children on their way to Sunday school.

The police had suspected one of the addicts and homeless people who slept on the Moor. But the presence of 'Creepy'

Crawley, and the similarity of the attack, has triggered a new inquiry. And we now learn that Crawley was already known to his lecturers: two women students reported him for sexual harassment. But university pastoral care tends to be sporadic. Crawley had escaped with nothing more than a warning from the dean, and the investigation that followed Anna's murder had mostly been assumed to be the work of an outsider.

Poor Anna. The photograph they're using shows a pretty, blonde girl, not unlike Jo Perry, wearing a gingham halter-neck top and a smile of heartbreaking optimism. Graham Crawley has a type. The details of her murder are there if you want to look for them, but I see no reason to go there again. Graham Crawley was there, and it seems more than likely he killed her. But the thought that Martin could have known him – even in passing, not even by name – is an itch I cannot satisfy.

'So ask him,' says Iris.

'I already have. He swears he doesn't remember.'

We were having pizza in one of our usual places. Cheap food, cheap drinks and little to no chance of meeting Martin's friends. It occurs to me that this is almost the same technique used by Jocelyn Moore with Leonie, but when I tell Iris this, she just laughs.

'Oh, please. It's nothing like that,' she says. 'Besides, I don't have the faintest desire to meet your douchebag husband.'

'He isn't a douchebag –' I began.

She raised an eyebrow. 'No? I seem to remember you telling me all kinds of shit – not least, him forcing you to put up his rapey friend for God knows how long –'

'Martin doesn't know what he did.'

'You think? Is he a moron? Because, unless he is, if they've been friends for as long as you say, he must have noticed something.'

I don't believe that. You can know someone well and still not know their secrets. And Woody was careful for a long time: he didn't even know himself. But to think that Graham Crawley and Martin might have crossed paths – even fleetingly –

*You could find out*, says the inner voice.

Don't think I haven't considered it. The police, in their slow, painstaking way, are starting to move in on Crawley's friends. People he knew at university. People from his literature course. What's left of his family – a brother in the Army, a mother in a nursing home. His ex-wife. Two ex-girlfriends. One of them (another blonde who would have been pretty in 1993) has already sold her story to the *Daily Mail* – a story of emotional abuse, and controlling behaviour, and anger. It's not an uncommon story, but the media's fascination with Graham Crawley has grown since the death of Jo Perry. The possibility that he might now be a serial killer excites them. He even has a fan account now, with pictures of him as a student, where young women admit to the world that he has become their *guilty crush.*

Iris shows me on her phone a photo of Crawley at twenty-one. He was handsome. That comes as a surprise. It shouldn't: most young people are. Slim, dark hair, good cheekbones. He looks like the youthful hero of a Hollywood werewolf movie. Now, of course, he is different. Now he shaves his head, and works out, and his body has thickened. But the eyes are the same: still very blue, surrounded by fine laughter lines under strong, dark brows. So yes. He is still attractive to a certain kind of person. It shouldn't be the case, but it is. He's the kind of man who, even in jail, gets proposals of marriage. We've seen it before. Beauties, innocents, drawn to beasts in the hope that they may be princes in disguise.

In most cases, this does not end well. And yet, we believe in the fairy tale. We mark ourselves as prey in the hope that we can tame a monster.

It shouldn't be happening. He shouldn't become a hero or a person of note. There is already talk of a TV documentary about his life. His ex-wife has signed an exclusive deal, serializing her experiences. Some internet sites are clamouring that his treatment has been unfair; that he will be denied a fair trial; that women are somehow responsible for the crimes of which he is accused. Some claim that he has been framed for the crime. Some are even claiming that he is a victim of MK2 and the Genderbomber conspiracy.

*@whitey2947: It's happening everywhere, no one's safe. #Genderwars*

*@manpower999: That's part of the plan. Getting women into the police, the army, everywhere men are traditionally been strong. #Genderwars*

*@chemically_castrated6: You don't know who to trust anymore. Women are everywhere. Nothing's safe. My 13-year-old keeps going on those sex change sites. I'm shitting myself he's gonna turn.*

*@whitey2947: Oh man, that's bad. I hear that a lot. Maybe get him to join a gym?*

*@manpower999: Yeah just make sure its single sex.*

Woody's latest podcast suggests that he, too, shares the belief that Crawley has fallen victim to gender wars. I do not often listen to his rants, but this one drew me in, not least for its tone of desperation. *They're spreading the net,* he says, in the hoarse and shell-shocked tone of a man who has been under fire for weeks. *The Exes. Genderbombers. Them. There isn't a day when you don't hear of some man falling victim. They're clever, you see. They work from the shadows. They're underhand. And if you try to fight them, they'll play the victim card every time. They say you're being an abuser. Someone has to do something, and soon. They're winning. They've already changed the world. They started with the language. You know what I mean. There are things we can't say anymore. You know what happens when we do. We're chemically cancelled now, we're chemically castrated. But actions speak louder than words. So stand tall. Stand tall and take the world back, before the Genderbombing turns into a gender genocide.*

That's worrying. It sounds as if his delusion has escalated. And now he, too, has a new slogan. He posted a picture on Instagram of a tattoo that caught his eye. A picture of a pin-up girl, topless, winking provocatively; adorned with the words that have haunted me since childhood.

*Never again.*

# TRACK 8:

---

# Unchained Melody

She left the web, she left the loom,
She made three paces thro' the room.
*Alfred, Lord Tennyson, 'The Lady of Shalott'*

God's house is as packed with secrets and lies as
any other abuser's.
*From the LiveJournal of Bernadette Ingram (marked as
Exhibit BI 1): April 16th, 2022*

# I

*Extract from Class of '92, by Kate Hemsworth*
*(published by LifeStory Press, 2023)*

We stayed at Mulberry House until after we'd finished GCSEs.
After that, some of my friends stayed on, but most of us went
to Pog Hill Sixth Form College to do our A levels. Pog Hill
had a lot going for it. First, it was a good school, with a good
academic record. That kept the parents happy. Second, it was
a state school, which made it free, as well as ticking one of the
boxes top universities look at when trying to fulfil their diver-
sity requirements. Third, it had boys as well as girls, which was
all we really cared about. Well, maybe not Bernie. As far as we
knew, Bernie Moon had never had a boyfriend. Some of the
other girls said she was gay, and Lorelei Jones made a big thing
of never being in the changing rooms or the toilets when she
was around, which was kind of ridiculous.

But in sixth form, everything changed. I guess when you've
been the awkward kid at school, it's best to go somewhere
else and try to reinvent yourself. That's what Bernie did.
She arrived on the first day of term with a new haircut – a
choppy bob that suited her – in black jeans and brand-new
Converse and a Fred Perry shirt that showed off her curves.

I don't think I'd seen Bernie out of school uniform since her eleventh birthday party, so it came as almost a surprise to find out she even had curves. I mean, she was actually pretty. And although the girls from Mulberry House still thought of her as *Weird Bernie*, we were only little fish now. Pog Hill was the big pool. Pupils from a dozen schools all around the region. They didn't care that we'd been popular, or that we'd played hockey for Mulberry House. To all the others at Pog Hill, we were all just first-year students, trying to fit in. So Bernie Moon got a fresh start, just like all the rest of us. Just like Martin Ingram.

I'd first known Martin as a shy, awkward boy with terrible acne, who only came to life on stage. Now the acne was mostly gone, and he'd grown another four inches. His hair was dark and rather long, and he wore John Lennon glasses and a long black raincoat, which gave him a faintly bohemian look. He still wasn't really my type – I liked outgoing, athletic boys – but I caught some of the other girls checking him out. None of them seemed to interest him, though. Not until Bernie Moon.

It happened some time after Christmas. I don't think I really noticed at first. I'd been too busy fitting in and building a circle of friends of my own to see that Bernie and Martin were spending time together. Martin had started a band with a couple of friends from St Oswald's, and they spent lunchtimes in the music block, playing the piano and hanging out. Lucas Hemsworth was one of these, but by then I was seeing Nigel Morris, a second-year music student, and Lucas was very far from my mind. So when Bernie and Martin hooked up, it came as quite a surprise, both to me and to the rest of the Mulberry girls, who couldn't get used to Bernie Moon being one of the cool kids.

Not that she cared. She was in love. The two of them were inseparable. They went everywhere together. They met up between lessons. They had their own little meeting place at the back of the locker rooms, a kind of window seat, in front of a long panel of marbled glass. I think they thought it was all theirs; in fact, it was a well-known spot (or so Nigel said) for making out. The funny thing was, the marbled glass only blurred the view from the inside: from the outside, you could totally see everything that was happening. That's why only first-years ever met in the locker rooms. By the time they reached the second year, they already knew better.

But by the time Bernie reached the second year, she and Martin had already gone further than just making out. I didn't notice at the time. By then I was dating John Weaver, an English student with a conditional offer from Cambridge, and applying to Drama school. And although I kind of noticed that Bernie Moon was getting fat, it never occurred to me to think that maybe there was a reason beyond too many doughnuts at lunchtime.

Of course, I should have noticed. But I was too absorbed in myself, and my plans, and my ambitions. And there was something else, too; something that burrowed into the heart of my nice new little community.

Adam Price was back.

Of course, Adam Price had never got even a single GCSE. There was no way he'd have got into Pog Hill, not even to study metalwork. But we found him there anyway, working as an apprentice to the Pog Hill caretaker, courtesy of some kind of scheme to rehabilitate young offenders. Because yes, that's what happened to him. It all made the papers eventually. Behavioural problems, went into care, tried to burn down his foster home. Now, at seventeen, he was back, like a dog you thought had been sent to the farm, watching us from his place in the wings, just waiting to make trouble.

I know how unkind that must seem to you. But he was everything I feared. I was a nice girl, from a nice home. He was a starving animal. It wasn't his fault, but his childhood had rotted him away inside, so that by the time he got to Pog Hill, he was rotten through and through. Anyway, that's what I thought. And he did nothing to change my mind. It didn't help that he looked just the same as he had at infant school. The same greasy yellow-white hair; the same pinched look; the same way of scowling at you from under those tinselly, colourless eyebrows. He'd grown, but not well; too tall for his build, like something that has grown in the dark. And he used to go out of his way to stare at us – at me especially, I thought – in silent, baleful hostility.

At first, I assumed he was like that with everyone. Some people are like that, I thought. Adam Price was hostile and rude. But as time went on, I realized that I was his principal focus. It was almost as if he were stalking me, watching everything I did. Whatever I did, he was somewhere close by. On the playing fields. With my friends. In the rec room. At Drama club. It was like having a scratchy label in the back of your collar. It was a low-grade discomfort, but I felt it all the time. Adam Price had it in for me, though why that would be, I had no idea. But his gaze was a reproach, and a promise of payback.

Payback for what? I scarcely remembered the incident that he had provoked at junior school. All that remained was a sense that Bernie Moon had been somehow responsible. But by the time we got to Pog Hill, Bernie was so wrapped up in herself and her new boyfriend that I doubt she even noticed him. Bernie Moon was so in love that she didn't notice anything.

And that made me resentful of her. Maybe. Just a little. Just enough to feel no remorse for the thing that came later.

Remember this. I was seventeen. What did I know about anything? How could I possibly have known that I would be responsible for something that, thirty years later, would shatter so many of our lives? All I knew was that I could sing, which was something Bernie couldn't do, and that her boyfriend was in a band, and looking for a singer . . .

# 2

*From the LiveJournal of Bernadette Ingram (marked as Exhibit BI 1):*
*Saturday, April 16th, 2022*

Tomorrow is Easter Sunday. No chance of a visit from Dante. Easter belongs to my mother, because I no longer speak to God. I speak to them both instead on the phone, before church, to say Happy Easter. Dante always sounds strange on the phone, like a man selling insurance. I remember him as a small boy, hunting for chocolate eggs in the garden. I remember his round, rosy face, his excitement at finding the eggs. There's none of that boy left now. I don't recognize him in there at all.

Martin gave all his old things away when Dan went off to college. There's not a toy left, or a pair of skates stored at the back of a boot cupboard, or even a pair of baby shoes hidden in a sewing box. It's exactly as if he was never here. That he was someone else's son. But my mother – she sounds like the cat with the cream. She is practically purring.

'We'll all be praying for you,' she says. 'Then afterwards I thought we'd pop over to see Katie and Lucas, and the kids.' My mother never misses a chance to remind me that Katie has stayed near her family. That she has two children, younger than mine. That she is popular and liked in the community.

*A Catholic can always come home*, or so my mother tells me. All I need is to confess my sins, and then I can take Holy Communion. But that would mean confessing to things I can't put into words. And who would I confess to? There's no one here I trust. God's house is as packed with secrets and lies as any other abuser's.

'So what have you been doing this Easter?'

'Oh. You know. The usual.'

'I see. You could come, you know.'

'Maybe next year.' (We both know I won't come next year.) 'But we'll be heading north in June. For the Pog Hill reunion.'

'Yes, Lucas mentioned it. What will you wear?'

'I don't know, Mum. I haven't thought about it yet.' This, too, is a lie. I've thought about it ever since I saw the invitation.

'Make sure it's something loose,' she said. 'Fitted dresses don't suit you.'

'I'm sure I'll find something, Mum.'

'All right. Happy Easter.'

I fled to Pricilla's Pantry, to escape the weight of Martin's expectations. I always cook a special meal at Easter – roast lamb with all the trimmings – but this time the thought of spending hours in the kitchen, while Woody and Martin watch TV next door, makes me feel hot and angry. When he is with Woody, Martin barely speaks to me, unless he wants something specific, or unless he is making a joke. It's as if the Martin he becomes in Woody's presence is deliberately excluding me. The *real* Martin – the one I know – speaks to me when we are in bed, or when Woody isn't around. But with Woody, he is boorish; putting his feet on the furniture; leaving his crockery for me to pick up. I mentioned this the other day, as I picked up a half-empty bag of tortilla chips, left over from the previous night, and Martin looked at Woody, rolled his eyes and said:

'Yes, *Mum.*'

It was a joke. I know it was. And yet it brought that dangerous heat welling to the surface. My face felt hot to the roots of my hair.

'I'm not your fucking mum, Martin.'

I know. It wasn't like me at all. I so rarely lash out at anyone. For a moment, I was afraid that Martin would be angry, but Woody laughed, and Martin joined in. I went into the kitchen to get a glass of water, and their laughter followed me, strange as footsteps behind you at night; loud and faintly tribal. Since then, Martin has been cold. I think he feels I belittled him. And so I haven't bought anything in, and now it's too late to book a place anywhere for Sunday lunch, and the guilt of it overwhelms me.

*What kind of hostess are you?* said the voice of my inner critic. *You were supposed to look after things. Be a good wife and mother. Instead, you're out all hours with your friends. Is this what I brought you up for?*

There's no pretence today that this voice belongs to anyone but my mother. Today, I know she'll be baking for the feast tomorrow. Apple and cardamom pie; Simnel cake; and Dante's favourite, treacle tart. Lunch will be a leg of lamb, with rosemary and garlic, served with green beans and roast potatoes, home-made relish and mint sauce.

*You should have been here.* Her voice is like a splinter in my conscience. *You should be with your family, instead of going off on your own, doing harmful, dangerous things.*

I sent her to the Quiet Room. She won't stay there for long, but talking to Iris always helps.

Priscilla's was empty when I arrived, but Iris was at a table with a pot of tea and some muffins. Her phone was charging at her side: I saw the little screen flickering.

'It's my break,' she said. 'Sit down. Muffins and tea, on Priscilla.'

I sat down and took a muffin. 'You can't imagine how much I need this right now.'

'Woody being a douche?'

I shrugged. 'I think maybe it's catching.'

'Fuck 'em both.'

Sometimes, I envy Iris. Her world seems so much simpler than mine. Men fall into one of two categories: keepers and douchebags. Women are even easier, being split into fighters and quitters. Her world is a combination of working, going out, being fabulous on a budget, reading comics, playing with her guinea pig, watching movies and drinking too much tequila. Her solutions to most problems tend to be refreshingly basic. *Fuck him up. Let's have wings.* I don't mean to be dismissive; it's just that Iris doesn't seem to care much about life's subtleties. And, to be fair, it's refreshing to be with someone who really understands, who doesn't judge, and who doesn't overthink everything.

'You should find yourself a toy boy,' said Iris. 'You look good for your age –'

'Ouch.'

'I mean it. You really do look good. If you dressed up a bit –'

I looked down at my outfit. I'd made an effort today, I thought. Not quite DeeDee's *Granny Chic* level, but my jeans were well cut, and my jumper could almost pass for cashmere. 'What's wrong with what I wear?'

She laughed. 'Oh, you sweet abandoned thing. You need to come shopping with me one day. Get yourself a new wardrobe. Granny chic is not for you. Well, not if you mean to get some, that is.' She glanced at her mobile, grinned suddenly. 'Oh, this is amazing.' She pushed the mobile towards me. 'Just take a look at this guy. He's giving all his stuff away. He gave this girl a *Rolex* –'

I looked across at the little screen. A TikTok of a homeless guy sitting by the side of the road. Except he isn't a homeless guy. And he isn't asking for cash, he actually seems to be handing it out. He's sitting cross-legged on the pavement, throwing money to passers-by. Some people hurry past him, alarmed; others linger and hesitate.

*Take it*, he says. I can read his lips, though TikTok has given him an upbeat musical soundtrack that jars with his earnest expression. Someone takes a note from his hand and lifts it to the light. Someone else accepts a watch.

*God bless you*, says the man. His eyes are shining with gratitude.

'What do think?' says Iris. 'Mad millionaire? Publicity stunt? Religious freak?'

I shook my head. The quality of the clip was poor, but even so, I knew who this was. I'd seen him just a few days ago, in a pub with my running mates. Suitless now, in T-shirt and jeans, his face pinched with anxiety.

*Here, take this. Take this*, he says, handing out money to passers-by.

I stared at Iris in dismay.

'What's wrong?'

'I think I know him.'

'You do?'

A nod. 'His name is Jocelyn Moore. He used to date a friend of mine.'

She gave me a look. '*You fucked him up!*' I shook my head, but she went on gleefully. 'Don't deny it. I knew it, Bernie!

You fucked him up good and proper. What'd he do? Get her pregnant? Cheat on her?'

'Shh, for God's sake, Iris —'

'Oh, relax. There's no one here.' She gave me one of her brilliant smiles and poured me a cup of tea. 'Bernie, you're amazing! You fucking *legend*! You *hero*!'

Once again, I tried to explain. But Iris wasn't listening.

'Babe. You *have* to do it again. It's like poetic justice. They think they're in charge, but you can get inside their heads. Imagine what you could do if you really put your mind to it. Imagine getting close enough to the douchebag who sits in Number 10. Or those douchebags in Texas, making abortions illegal. Or the douchebag in Russia. Or the one in South America. I mean, I could start you off with a list.'

'Iris. *Iris!*'

'Yes, I know. But if ever you got a chance, don't tell me you wouldn't try.'

'No, Iris!'

'Whatever. But some vows are made to be broken.'

And although I smiled back, I couldn't help but feel uncomfortable. I've come across that phrase before, and seen that grin on someone else. It's not an uncommon phrase, of course, nor are the words unusual ones, but how many twenty-two-year-olds really say *babe*, or *douchebag*, or *you fucking legend*? It's almost as if a splinter of Woody has become lodged in Iris; a shard like a piece of mirror glass. And I wonder – not for the first time – what else did I turn when I turned the tables on Iris?

# 3

Dante called by this morning. He arrived with some flowers, and the kind of vaguely sheepish look that he always assumes when he has spent time with my mother. Of course, she makes him feel guilty. That is, after all, her specialty. She suffocates him with her love, while simultaneously making him feel as if he should be married by now, with children of his own. *After all*, she tells him, *I won't be here forever.*

*Good*, says my inner demon.

Of course, I don't mean it. (*Yes, I do.*) And yes, it is ironic that, after so many years of living under the shadow of my mother's disapproval, I should now find my own son equally disappointing. That isn't to say I don't love him. That I wouldn't die for him. But Dan is the son I should have been, not the son I dreamed of having. And today I could smell her on him like the frankincense at Mass.

'Happy Easter, Mum,' he said. 'Granny sends her love.'

*Of course.*

'Come in. Have some coffee.' He followed me into the kitchen, where Woody was having breakfast. Salena's Books was closed today, but Martin was back at the office. I found a vase for the flowers and put them on the table.

Woody was sitting in T-shirt and boxer shorts – neither of them very clean – drinking *RippedinSix* from a plastic jug. He looked up when Dante came in, and smiled. I have come to hate that smile. Of course, I know what's behind it.

'Dan, this is Woody. He's been staying with us for a few days.' More than a few. I try to smile, but I can already feel the dirty heat of a hot flash working its way towards my face. It happens when I'm tired, or stressed, or when I don't like someone. *I can read your face like a book*, Martin used to tell me. Nowadays, I think my book is in a different language.

'You're Jim Wood,' Dante said. I could hear something in his voice that was almost admiration. 'I've seen your TikTok. Bloody hell!'

Woody said: 'Nice to meet you, Dan. I must be getting famous.'

Dan shook hands and sat next to him. I passed him his coffee. He likes it sweet. I saw the way Woody looked at him, taking a drink from a woman. When Woody makes coffee, he takes it black, and always fills the kettle himself, in case of an MK2 attack. But he didn't say anything: I'm assuming that, as the wife of his friend, I am, if not quite beyond reproach, then at least above open suspicion. This, I suppose, is a good thing. Less good is the fact that Dante knows all about him.

'I've been watching everything. I mean, that list of words – *my God*!' Dan is alight with enthusiasm in a way I haven't seen since he was a teen, obsessed with computer games and *Guitar Hero*. Dante's enthusiasms now include: crypto (which he thinks is the future), more computer games (he now does something to do with game design) and –

It occurs to me that I no longer know what my son is obsessed with. Politics? Conspiracy theories? I've never met his girlfriend, assuming he has one at all. I don't know how he spends his time. Does he like clubbing? Going to pubs? Playing tabletop role-playing games? Listening to theories about MK2, and Genderbombers, and women taking over the world, and drinking *RippedinSix*?

*You could just look*, says Iris' voice. *Deploy your sci-fi powers.*

*No. I know how that sounds, but it would feel like a violation.*

*Babe, wake up. It is a violation. Call it playing House, if you like, but it's trespass. And you've done it before. So don't go all soft because this is your son. Go in, and see what's happening.*

If this had been Martin, I wouldn't have looked. But the thought that my son could have been infected by Woody's lunacy overrode all my other concerns. When Dante was a little boy, I used to look under his bed for anything that might do harm. Drugs. Flick knives. Fireworks. I never found anything dangerous, but I looked. Looking put my mind at rest. And I'm on edge about Woody, and the space he takes up in our house. In our lives. And so I looked into Dan's house; into the nice front room he has, all decorated with photographs. *Just to check he's safe*, I thought. *Just to check that Woody's poison has not spread to my son.*

His house feels both strange and familiar. So many things I recognize. Toys I'd thought he'd forgotten; books I didn't know he'd read. My picture is there on the mantelpiece, but I am dwarfed by the giant face of my mother. Of course. But I knew that already. I look for the things I don't already know. Hobbies. Work life. Girlfriend –

*Aaaaand –*

*So.* My son is gay. That's why he's never mentioned a girlfriend. There's a young man, though. David. He's never spoken of him, either. But there's a whole room devoted to him, to the things they do together –

*Never going in there. Nope.* There are things you never want to see. Watching your son have sex is one. That doesn't mean I think it's bad. It's just that some perfectly normal things are perfectly uncomfortable. But why did he never tell me? Did he think I would love him less? Did he think I would disapprove? He feels my disappointment. It's there in every part of the house. It's like a kind of miasma. It's in his childhood; his memories of all we shared together. And he's hiding so many things from me, still. A tattoo of an octopus – just there, on his right shoulder. The fact that he smokes. That he sometimes smokes dope. How unhappy he was at school. How much the others ridiculed the fanciful name I'd given him. I'd always thought my son fitted in. I'd always thought he was popular. Now I see that he tried his best to conform, hating every moment. My father saw it early. *You'll make the boy into a sissy.* Dan saw my early absence and linked it with my father's words.

How little I know my son, I thought. How little my son knows me. He has no idea how much I care. How much I miss him. How happy I am that he has found love –

Among the cascade of images that come from Dante's house comes the realization of how much my talent has *grown* since I last explored it. Glancing into strangers' rooms, trying to persuade them to buy books is one thing, but this is something else. It feels like an enormous appetite that has never been fully slaked. It wants to send its hungry roots into every room in Dante's house (even that one, with David). And it just keeps coming, reflecting his thoughts: like mirrors, reflecting infinity –

I pull away before I can do damage. I'm bleeding inside from what I've seen. A hot flash grazes my body. Sweat trickles into my underwear. Dante's feelings and my own are tangled in each other like string.

No, I can't let him feel this way. I can't let him carry this guilt for me. I have to do something to stop him. But imagine what would happen if I broke something. Imagine if I trod carelessly and cracked his inner world open.

I poured a glass of water, and waited for the hot flash to subside. I could tell my face was red. Beads of sweat ran down my neck.

'Are you OK, Mum? You look –'

'Yes.' I wiped my face with the back of my hand, and saw a streak of mascara there. 'I'm fine. It's – just –' I gave a ghastly little laugh. *'Hello, menopause!'*

I say that far too much, I know. I do it to make a joke of the fact that my body is doing frightening things, things that are outside my control. Meanwhile, my mind is also doing frightening things; expanding its potential for vision and destruction. But I needed to talk to my son, and Woody was playing gooseberry. I didn't want to touch him again, not even accidentally. If only there were *another* means of just making him go away –

*'Doughnut,'* I said.

Woody passed out.

'That's better,' I said. 'Now we can talk.'

Dan stared in astonishment as I manoeuvred our unwanted guest into the recovery position.

'It's fine. He'll wake up in a couple of hours.'

Then I stood up and gave Dante a hug. It must have been a year since I last did that. He feels solid, and warm, and clumsy, and his height always surprises me. I hugged him for a long time. After a while, he hugged me back.

'Oh, Dan. I've missed you so much. Sit down, and tell me *everything*.'

# 4

Dan and I talked for a long time, with Woody asleep between us. He told me about his boyfriend, his job, his life, his octopus tattoo. It felt as if, for the first time in years, we had made a connection. I know there's work to be done here, work that can't be covered in a couple of hours, but it's a start. A chance to break this deadly ice; the hope of a relationship.

My Big Fat Menopause puts it this way: *Hey, goddesses! Missing the patter of tiny feet? Now's the time to reconnect with babies who have flown the nest! Why not plan a girls' night in, or a trip to a baseball game? Who knows, your grown-up son or daughter could become your new best friend!*

Martin thinks it's unlikely. According to Martin, Dan now thinks I have a terminal illness. He cannot believe that menopause can account for the change he has seen in me. 'She told me she was *proud* of me. She's never, ever said that before.'

Poor Dan. And yet, I hope he feels better. My gift has done that much, at least. Dan is whole. And Iris is safe. And Salena's business is thriving. Now that I'm running three times a week, even the headaches and mood swings have receded. I've had three lessons with Charlie so far, and I'm just starting to find my voice. At last I'm starting to understand what I can do, and how to control it. I can do this, I tell myself. The memory of Mr D does not need to define me. I have my friends, my plans, my life. I don't think I've ever been happier.

Only two shadows remain. One is Leonie's ex-boyfriend. Over the past few days, Jocelyn Moore has become an internet curiosity. *Rolex Guy*, as they call him, now lives in a hundred TikToks, giving money to passers-by. Rahmi says Leonie thinks he's having a nervous breakdown.

'She says he came by the other day and tried to give her his Audi. He's giving all his stuff away: suits, shoes, money. He's even trying to get on some kind of list, so that he can donate a kidney. He says the more he gives away, the less empty he feels. How does that make sense?'

It makes perfect sense, if you think about the way mirrors reflect in reverse. I flipped him, just like I flipped Woody. Turned his emptiness outward. But Jocelyn seems happy, she says. Perhaps he's had an epiphany.

My second remaining problem is currently still occupying our spare room, and spends most of his life online. His daily broadcasts have become a kind of therapy for him. I listened to a minute of today's offering before closing the app. I can't bear it. I can't bear the thought of him, in our house, in Dante's bed. Martin still doesn't understand. I knew he's as desperate for Woody to go as I am, but he feels sorry for him. But I can't bear it anymore. The stink of his obsession, his food, his sweat, his rage – has gone beyond unbearable. I could perhaps have fixed him once. Now, I can't. My power has grown. The anger inside me would tear him apart if I even glanced through a window.

On the Finchley Fliers Facebook group, I ask the advice of my new friends.

*Bernadette Ingram: He's been here three weeks already. Seriously, short of murder, what the hell do I do with him?*

*Leonie Chapman: Give your guy an ultimatum. You've been way too patient so far. Tell him if Woody doesn't go, you'll change the locks on both of them.*

*(Salena Wicks likes this)*

*(Rahmi Arain likes this)*

*Alex Foster: Be kind, but firm. Don't let him draw you into a fight. And if you need moral support, I can be there. Just say the word.*

Iris has a more forceful approach. 'Chuck him out! You know what to do. You're not his mum. Jesus, Bernie, what's the good of being a superhero if you never use your powers?'

And yes, I know. My friends are right. But making him leave of his own accord, without doing further damage – there's the challenge. I have been patient, for Martin's sake. But now I must act. I hope I can do the trick without resorting to Iris' favourite tactic. But one way or the other, *Jim from the Gym* has to go.

# 5

*Monday, April 25th*

I spent most of Sunday and today cleaning out the guest room, airing it out, getting the grime and the stink of him out of my son's old bedroom. Tonight, at last, it feels as if most of the miasma is gone.

At last. You can't imagine my relief. And no. I didn't go into his house, not even to leave a suggestion. I'm actually very proud of this. I didn't even get angry. I confronted him on Friday, after work, not from the shadows of a haunted house, but as Leonie would have confronted him, or Iris, or Rahmi, or Alex.

I found him in the living room, watching TV in his underwear. He looked up briefly as I came in, then turned his attention back to the screen. I said:

'Jim, can we have a talk?'

Martin had gone to his study as soon as he realized what I was doing. I wasn't surprised. All the same, I felt a little pang of disappointment. This was going to be hard enough without my having to do it alone. I imagined my friends beside me: Iris, and Alex, and Leonie. I summoned all my courage. Kindly, but firmly, I told him:

'Listen, Jim, you've been here three weeks. I know you're Martin's friend, but it's time for us to claim our house back, and for you to get back to your life.'

For a moment, Woody looked at me, feigning not to understand. I know that look. I've seen it before, when Dante was a little boy. *Step one: pretend it's not happening.*

'I'm sorry? Bernie, are you OK?'

'I know it's not what you want to hear. But it's time you heard it anyway. You can't stay here forever, you know. We all have lives to go back to.'

*Step two: wheedling.* 'I promise I will. But I need to get back on my feet. Just another week, OK?'

'Another week won't change things. You need to get back to your home. Your *life*.'

*Step three: guilt.* 'But I'm sick! You can't throw me out when I'm still sick.'

Of course he knows I'm not *throwing him out*. Nor is he actually sick. But he wants to manipulate me, to take the conversation into a direction of his choosing. And so I refuse to follow. Instead, I think about Alex's advice, and wait for him to run out of steam.

'What if I pass out? What if I *die* when I'm passed out? That would be on you, Bernie. That would be on both of you.'

*I'm sorry, but –*

No. No apologies. I've looked after him long enough. He should be grateful for that. He should be thanking me, instead of trying to make me feel guilty.

'You've lived with your condition for weeks,' I told him. 'You need to start addressing it. You can't do that from our guest bedroom. You need to see a professional.'

'I tried.'

*No, you didn't. Step four: debate.* 'What about the counsellor you were meant to be seeing?'

293

'She's useless. She thinks I have some kind of problem with women.'

She's on the money with that one. But I'm not here to argue the point. 'Woody,' I said. 'You need to grow up. You can't blame the world for your problems. You have to take control of your life. Try to work with your sickness, if you can't cure it completely.'

He looked at me with open dislike, then played his final gambit. *Step five: ask the other parent.* 'Let's see what *Martin* thinks, shall we?'

'Martin thinks you need to go. He just doesn't know how to tell you.'

'Or maybe Martin's just too blind to see what game you're playing. Don't think I haven't noticed. You're one of those women who *pretend* the man's in charge, but still somehow manage to get everything they want.'

'I'm sorry you feel that way, Woody. I'll help you pack your things if you like.'

'I don't need your help!'

'I understand.'

Eventually, it descended into the kind of ranting that even Martin could not ignore; a kind of distillation of his paranoia. *Step six: rage.* The kind of screaming, transcendent rage that gets children sent to the Quiet Room.

*I know it was you. I've always known you were slipping it into my protein shakes. Maybe you injected it with a superfine needle. I know what you are. You and your friends. Pretending to be so harmless. Getting into the minds of men, stealing their testosterone. You've done it to Marty, too. I can tell. He isn't the man he used to be. In the old days, he would have known how to deal with a bitch like you –*

And that was where he lost Martin. At last, he'd reached his breaking point. Thrown open his house, with all its madman's clutter, for the world to see. And the best part was that I didn't have to go in, or do any damage. This time, it was all self-inflicted. I stayed where I was, and held my ground, until he broke into pieces.

*Abracadabra.*

Well, *someone* had to do it. Martin should be grateful. He'd already shown me that he wasn't able to do it himself. He was always like this with Dante, too; standing on the sidelines while Mummy played the monster. Because, in spite of their bluster, men are pitifully weak when it comes to standing up to their friends in support of a woman's argument.

But Woody went too far this time. A direct attack, not just on me, but on *him* by association. No man likes to be made to feel less of a man by his friends. And so Martin drove Woody home that night, and on Saturday morning drove back with all his paraphernalia – dozens of jugs of *RippedinSix* and the shakers that come with them, plus clothes, and the equipment he uses for his broadcasts. Martin's private Facebook reveals a half-hearted apology, and a promise to stay in touch. *You know what Bernie's like, mate. She has her problems, too. Just know I'm always here for you. Let's get together soon.*

On Saturday, when I got home, Martin was in his study. He didn't respond when I got in, or when I called him for dinner. Martin sometimes has dark moods, during which he withdraws completely. I used to dread them. Now I know to leave him alone until he decides to engage. That used to be so very hard, especially when it lasted days. Now, it seems less important, somehow. Perhaps it's because there's someone to share it with.

Text to Iris: *I did it! He's gone!*

🖐 *Celebrate?*

*Not tonight, though. MARTIN.* 😠

*If he's being a dick, you know what to do*

😊 *er no*

🔥 *FHU*

I know what she means. And yes, I could. I know that too well. Of course, I'd never do it. But tonight, the temptation to just look inside his house was stronger than ever. *Does he blame me for Woody's tirade? Resent me for forcing him to leave?* It would be easy to find out. But that would be cheating. A trespass. Instead, I waited quietly, reading my social media, until at last, at around ten o'clock, he emerged and said, almost apologetically:

'Do you want a cup of tea?'

I looked up from my phone. 'OK. Thanks.'

Martin brought up the tea from the kitchen, then sat down next to me on the sofa. I could tell there was something on his mind, but I forced myself to wait. I could hear the clock on the wall ticking away the seconds. This time, the silence was comforting. I hadn't quite realized how much noise Woody generated, and how much accompanying noise Martin made when they were together.

'You're very quiet,' Martin said. 'Are you OK?'

I nodded. 'I'm sorry I sent your friend packing,' I said. 'But it was either that, or beat him to death with a tub of *RippedinSix*.'

He gave a little laugh. 'That bad?'

'Worse,' I said. 'Who'd clean up the mess?'

He sounded a little easier now. 'That stuff was rank. You know, he was trying to get me to drink it, too?'

'I hope he gets help.' (I meant it, too.) 'But we were never the ones who were going to provide it. And I really didn't like the way he was starting to look at me. It was beginning to feel as if he was getting obsessed with me.'

Martin nodded. 'I know.'

'You knew?'

'He used to bend my ear all the time. Telling me you were poisoning me. Trying to find out where you go when you're out of the house. He was convinced you were either having an affair, or that you were going to secret meetings with Genderbombers, planning to smash the patriarchy.' He laughed again, and I wondered what he would say if he knew the truth. Not that I could ever explain. Where would I start? 'To be honest,' he said, 'I'm relieved to see him go. To have the house to ourselves again. It's been too long. And now, you don't need to spend your time in coffee shops just to avoid him.'

I managed to conceal my surprise. Could Woody have been following me? Could Martin?

I shrugged. 'What can I say? I like doughnuts.'

He laughed. 'Now I know your secret.'

Was there the slightest edge to his voice? You never know with Martin. I've always felt that potential in him, like a piece of glass in an apple.

'I know you didn't like him,' he said. 'Thanks for bearing with him so long.'

I shrugged.

'I mean, he isn't politically correct, but there's no real harm in him. It's just his way. Underneath, he's a pussycat. And whatever he might have said in anger, you know he'd never hurt a woman.'

I know nothing of the sort, but I didn't say so. Men are so very fragile, you know. So quick to feel emasculated. So quick to blame women for the cracks in their ego. I didn't break Woody. I'm proud of that. But I did defend my home.

'He didn't mean those things he said,' Martin went on. 'You know that, don't you?'

Funny, how often men tell us these things. Funny, how quickly men will excuse the kind of behaviour in their friends that makes women feel unsafe.

'I mean, he's just not capable. I know that for a fact.'

'OK.'

He looked relieved. 'As long as you know.'

It's almost funny, isn't it? I wish I could have told him. But the thought of trying to explain my gift to Martin is impossible. To Iris, yes. But not to him. Why is that? I ought to trust him. I *do* trust him. But Martin has always had issues with trust. Ironic, that the man who fucked my friend should be the one with trust issues. But that's the way it is with him. *It isn't personal*, he says. But I am unreliable, too emotional to be trusted. This, from the man who has spent the last month watching Woody unravel. But women are stronger than you think. I am stronger than you think. My friends have already taught me that. And we don't need superpowers. Together, we are strong enough to make the world pay attention.

Not that I want to change the world. I'm not a campaigner, like Iris. All the things I want are small: to help Selena's shop stay open; to encourage parents to let their children choose their own books; to run 5K without stopping. And maybe, to surprise you. Just a little. To make you look at me again. I've known you such a long time. You stopped really seeing me years ago. But now, the Pog Hill reunion has given me this opportunity. The chance to revisit our shared past with a new and powerful energy. This time, I will not sit by and watch, and wish, and wonder. I will not let you make this into your personal fantasy. I will dance, and I will sing, and most of all, I will be seen. I will take the spotlight, and I will make them stop and stare. Not through my gift, but my own hard work, and courage, and power. I will turn the tables, and smile at you, and whisper:

*Yes, I made you look.*

Just like The Great Carovnik.

# TRACK 9:

---

# I Missed Again

Out flew the web and floated wide
The mirror cracked from side to side.
*Alfred, Lord Tennyson, 'The Lady of Shalott'*

*Extract from Class of '92, by Kate Hemsworth*
*(LifeStory Press, 2023)*

Give me credit for this, at least. I didn't steal Bernie's boyfriend.
I had a boyfriend of my own – Simon Naylor, whose family
owned property on Millionaire's Row – and he was taking
me to the prom in his dad's Lexus. Of course, it wasn't really
a prom. Not like in American films. But Pog Hill had preten-
sions. It was a grand old building, with a grand old history. It
had once been a girls' grammar school, which had closed down
in the seventies. It had a good reputation, both socially and
academically. And the Head, who was a throwback from the
old days of the grammar school, rather liked the idea that we
were more than just a sixth form college.

Thus the Pog Hill Summer Prom took on a gilded quality,
something like the Oxbridge May Balls of the Head's student
days. It took place during the last week of term, when all
the exams were over. The tickets were quite expensive, but
everything was included: food, drink, entertainment. The
dress code was black tie; the teachers were there to supervise.

There are pictures of me still on the Pog Hill Facebook
page. I looked a knockout. I was wearing a backless lamé

dress cut low to the very small of my back, and although it had quite a high neckline, I knew it was making people stare. Bernie Moon looked frumpy in a black dress that looked like it belonged to her mum. I didn't know she was pregnant then. All I knew was that I felt invincible, ready to face the future with head held high, and a smile on my face.

And maybe I felt resentful of her. Maybe a little jealous. Everything was so easy for her. She was top in all her subjects. And while I bounced aimlessly from one boyfriend to another, never really feeling anything, she was in love.

To be in *love*. People talk as if it's the greatest feeling in the world. Songs and stories make it out to be more important than anything. But I don't think it's ever happened to me. I feel as if I'm colour-blind in a world of rainbows. It's not that I don't love Lucas, or our children. But I'm aware that being *in love* is something else; a kind of divine madness. Nowadays, I'm mostly grateful that I never went through that. But in those days, I felt as if everyone knew something I didn't; and Bernie was the worst of them all, because she had the real thing; the bells-and-whistles, *Wuthering Heights*, *Casablanca* drama of it.

But I could sing; and she couldn't. Martin had already told me that when he recruited me for the band. It was a four-piece, with Martin on bass, and Lucas Hemsworth on guitar, and Andrew Whelan on piano, and Joss Lively on drums. Martin sang – quite well, I thought – but what they really wanted was a girl to front the whole thing. A pretty girl, with a pretty voice, to make them shine more brightly.

The songs were mostly old torch songs, easy to learn and to perform. And I loved being onstage. I loved it more than anything else I'd ever known. I wanted to be a performer – an actress, a singer, anything – to be on that stage, to see those lights. And so I stepped in. I accepted the role. Three weeks' practice with the band was all we really needed, and during that time, I got to know Lucas Hemsworth a little more. He was supposed to be dating Amanda Bond, but she'd broken her ankle playing hockey, and wasn't coming to the prom. I liked him better than Simon (who was a bit of a dick, actually), and I could tell he liked me. And so I pulled out all the stops: the dress, the voice, the whole shebang.

And for an hour, it was magical; gilded in that luminous way that certain memories evoke. I was eighteen. I was beautiful. I had all my life ahead of me. I was *Promise*, personified; sparkling in silver lamé.

Of course, I wasn't to know then that this would be my finest hour. The promise never materialized. I never made the West End, or even a bit part in *Coronation Street*. Thirty years after the Pog Hill Prom, I'm still right here in Malbry. Teaching Drama to children who – if they're lucky – may one day perform in a charity gala for the local hospice. If I had known then, maybe things would have turned out differently. But that night, I felt invincible. Carried away on their applause. And even when I looked into the wings and saw Adam Price looking back at me – Adam, with his oldman's hair, and his jack-o'-lantern scowl – I felt only a faint and momentary flicker of discomfort. I was the star of the evening. He was only the caretaker's boy. What could Adam do to me now?

Looking back, I realize that I was asking the wrong question. It had never been a case of what Adam Price could do to me. But riding high on their applause, I missed the truth entirely. And when it finally came clear, the harm was done, and there was no going back, not for him, or for any of us.

# 2

*From the LiveJournal of Bernadette Ingram (marked as Exhibit BI 1): Sunday, May 1st*

Graham Crawley made the news again. This time, by confessing to the murder of Jo Perry, then attempting to hang himself with his prison trousers. He has been placed on suicide watch. Iris, as always, is merciless.

> *@irisnoir23: Another cry for attention? Pity the bastard didn't succeed.*

> *@whitey2947: So he's already guilty, then? You're that sure?*

*Whitey2947* has a point. Some people *do* confess to crimes they haven't committed. I can't help thinking that if only I could see into his house, I could find out for certain whether Graham Crawley is guilty. I should be able to do that, now that my talent has been refined. But try as I might, I can't manage to summon the killer again. His light always eludes me. I've tried, but in vain. And yet, my skill has grown so fast in every other way. I can summon Iris, and Leonie; Alex, Rahmi, Salena. I can look into every customer at Salena's Books. I can glance across the park, and summon a dozen strangers. I even see

DeeDee LaDouce, and share in the aspects of her life that she doesn't post on Instagram. And yet, Jo Perry's murderer remains completely out of reach.

Maybe I need to access that dream. Go back to where he killed her. But dreaming on demand is a skill that I have never mastered. Even sleeping is hard enough, on these nights as I lie beside Martin. I'd thought that with Woody gone, I could sleep. But now, the house is too quiet. I sometimes get up, and quietly walk from room to room in the dark, like a ghost in my own haunted house. Sometimes, I go to the guest room and lie down on Dante's bed. *Ghost* and *guest* are such similar words. Which one am I, now Woody has gone?

Martin seems more relaxed, though. The toll of living with Woody has been higher than I'd suspected. He even cooked dinner yesterday, for the first time since Dan was at home. Nothing too ambitious, just linguini and a salad, but it was nice to come home after my run to a meal that someone else had prepared. And there was a bottle of wine, too, and candles on the table. It's not like Martin to do those things. He doesn't care much for gestures.

'Is it our anniversary?'

That was a joke. I knew that, of course. Martin doesn't do anniversaries, just as he never buys flowers, or sends me a card on Valentine's Day. He'd rather be spontaneous, he says. There's something distasteful about these fabricated holidays. Except that this wasn't spontaneous. It felt obscurely furtive. As if he'd been doing something wrong. Has he been talking to Katie on Facebook, or on WhatsApp? Has he been talking to Woody? Following me? Discussing me? Does he still suspect me of something that requires investigation?

'I just thought it might be nice,' he said.

And it is, Martin. It really is. It makes me almost want to cry. It's such a simple thing, making food, and yet it's on the list of *Things that Bernie Always Does*, like making the beds, or watering plants, or buying Christmas presents. When we first moved here, we silently split the house down the middle. Domestic issues fall to me. Everything else falls to Martin.

'I know it's been weird lately, with Woody being here and everything. I wanted to give us a chance to – you know. Have some time together again, just you and me, without anyone else.'

'Have you seen him?'

'He texted me. Wants to meet up somewhere and talk.' He grinned. 'I think I'll give it a miss.' He poured a glass of wine. 'Sit down. I've hardly seen you.'

I sat. This was new. Martin never seems to notice when I'm not around, unless he needs me for something. Could he be jealous? Surely not. And yet it almost feels that way. I helped myself to pasta. I get so hungry when I run.

Martin gave me a sideways look and said: 'I'm glad you're still eating carbs, anyway. A lot of people won't touch them when they're trying to lose weight.'

'I never said I was trying to lose weight. I said I was trying to run.'

He shrugged. 'Whatever; it suits you.'

Stranger still, I told myself. Martin doesn't give compliments. If he comments, it's usually because he has noticed something wrong. *Is* something wrong? The temptation to just take a look is almost overwhelming. Martin's house is so *very* close, and all my anger has all vanished.

'You might even be able to fit into that cocktail dress you wore at the Prom. Remember?'

And there it is again. Not vanished, but pushed under. Martin doesn't mean it that way, but he's an expert at breaking my confidence. That vision of me at the Pog Hill Prom – so young, so raw, so insecure – returns like a vicious outbreak of hives.

'I was pregnant, Martin.'

'Oh. I must have been thinking of something else.'

And yet, the urge to look remained. Why haven't I used my power on him? Is it only anger? We've been together for thirty years. We are one unit. One heart. One soul. He was my first. My only. I have never kissed another man. Other people tend to think that this is sweet; romantic, even. I'm not so sure. We're like two trees growing from the same root; twisted around each other. Why do I not look inside him? Why have I not confided in him? Is it really because I'm afraid of what my anger might do to him? Or am I secretly afraid that if he sees who I really am, he will know that I am a monster?

These were my thoughts as I lay on Dan's bed in the small hours of this morning. I used to lie there when he was small, reading to him, or just talking, surrounded by his stuffed toys: dinosaurs, elephants, sharks, dogs. Now this room is filled with ghosts. Dan at six; Dan at nine; Dan at ten, just starting to thicken like a young tree. Perhaps that's why I like it here. Ghosts should stay together.

I was just about to drop off to sleep when Martin came in. 'Are you OK? I heard you get up.'

'I'm fine. I just couldn't sleep. I didn't want to disturb you.'

He kissed my forehead. 'Come back to bed. You'll catch cold.'

This concern is unusual. Martin is rarely demonstrative. Maybe there's something on his mind, I thought. Maybe he needs to talk to me. And so I followed him back to bed, and lay with his arms around me.

'Are you OK?' he said at last.

'Of course.'

'Are *we* OK?'

'Of course.'

Even more surprising, I thought. It isn't like Martin to feel insecure. We haven't really been OK for years, not in the way he means, but I know he needs reassurance. I can tell he still feels guilty about bringing Woody into the house. I find this strangely touching. I held his hand and promised him that everything was fine, and at last, we fell asleep together, still holding each other like children.

You see, it isn't all bitterness. I don't want you to feel it is. Sometimes it's just good like this, and I could cry with relief at the knowledge that we're still together. And sometimes the thing that binds us is like wild roses and razor wire, all tangled into something that bites and bleeds and never, ever stops bleeding.

I understand nobody's perfect. I never expected that of you. But all I want to know is this. Which one will it be tomorrow? The man who kisses my forehead and holds me till I fall asleep? Or the man in the castle on the cliff, with its rooms all filled with secrets?

# 3

At last, I called my mother today. I've been putting the call off since Easter. Martin, being an orphan, doesn't have this problem. I sometimes find myself envying him. And then I feel guilty, because she tried. She did her best to shield me. But a shield is hard. It has to be. And I needed her softness. So now we are both hard, and polished, and bright, reflecting back at each other.

On good days, that brightness reveals itself in her sharp wit, and her laughter. But on bad days all it does is hurt. Today was one of her bad days. I sensed it almost as soon as she picked up the receiver. No feigned surprise today. Instead, there was a barely concealed aggression, beginning with the words:

'So, you *finally* decided to get in touch.'

I tried to explain about Woody. Then I tried to speak about Dante, and Martin, and the bookshop. But she closed down every opening, every conversational path, with the same, dry, toneless snap.

'There's always something. Some excuse. Two years, it's been, since you visited.'

'Mum. That's hardly fair. I —'

309

'Dan told me all about it. He says he saw you a few days ago. Says you were behaving like a completely different person.'

'We had a talk,' I said. 'That's all.'

'Well, at least you're talking to *someone*.'

Ouch. That's my mother; sharp as a tack left in a slipper by mistake. I thought about saying: *I have friends now*, but the idea of talking to her about the running club, or Iris, or Alex, or Charlie, was unthinkable. I can live with her displeasure – I've lived with that for most of my life – but the thought of her *approval* is somehow more unsettling. I remember her cleaning up after my eleventh birthday party. All those little sandwiches, and fairy cakes, and goodie bags. She took them all to Father Tom, for the church coffee morning, so that by the end of it everyone knew that no one had come for my birthday.

'You'll still be here for that party, though.'

'Yes,' I said. 'We'll be coming up then.'

She gave a sniff. 'That would be nice. Katie and Lucas will be there.'

I sometimes wonder if my mother suspects Martin's infidelity. I sometimes wonder if she guessed, maybe after that Scarborough break, when he went back to university. She has never mentioned it, but it's there in her voice when she speaks of him; a kind of studied indifference.

'You used to look so pretty together, you and Katie Malkin. People at church even used to think you were sisters.'

*Here it comes.*

'Dan always favoured Martin, though.'

This, too, is a frequent complaint. As if I purposely chose my son to look as little like my side of the family as possible.

'Sadie and Ben look just like her. They call me their *Adopted Gran*.'

*How nauseating of them*, I thought.

'I always wondered when you'd give Dan a brother or sister. I suppose it's too late now. I'm going to have to wait for Dan. Assuming he even wants children. That's what you get, when you put all your eggs into one basket.'

By now I could feel the beginnings of a hot flash gathering somewhere in the region of what DeeDee LaDouce calls *Your Sacred Chakra*. This is a regular feature of my mother's conversation; and right now, all I wanted was to jump into her house and scream: *Shut up! Shut up! SHUT UP!* –

Well, that's the question, isn't it? I know I could make it happen. But I can also imagine the carnage that would follow. Those doors are closed for a reason. I dare not take the risk with her. I broke off a full ten minutes before the end of our allocated time, and went for a run in the park, on my own, out of sheer frustration.

It wasn't enough. I doubled back towards Priscilla's Pantry, where I ate a doughnut out of sheer rage, then ordered another and burst into tears.

Iris gave me a look. 'Don't blame me. I don't bake them.'

I tried to smile. 'I'm OK. I am. It's just my bloody mother.'

'I thought you said she lived up north.'

'She does. But I called her this morning. I wanted to tell her –' I stopped. I realized I can't tell my mother anything. Not about Dante, or his octopus tattoo, or the small but crucial victory of the other day. Not about Woody, or Jocelyn. Not about my headaches, and the hot flashes that still strike whenever I feel tired or upset. Certainly not about my running, or my singing lessons, or my little party plans.

'We don't have a single thing to say to each other anymore. It makes me so sad,' I said at last. I didn't mean to say it aloud, but Iris has looked inside me. She knows. 'When did that happen? I always thought we'd find – I don't know – some kind of common ground one day.'

Iris looked sceptical. 'Why's that?'

'Well, she's my mother.'

Iris shrugged. 'But you told me you hardly see her. What kind of common ground will you find if you only visit once a year?'

I thought about that for a moment. Iris, for all her youth, can be remarkably worldly-wise. 'I suppose you're right,' I said. 'But every time I see her, it's –' It's just like thirty years ago. It's as if no time has passed, and I am still that pregnant girl, too fat to fit into *The Dress*. Nothing I have done in the time I have been away from home has tempered her disappointment; the feeling that I should have been someone other than myself; someone who fitted into her space. Someone like Kate Malkin.

'You fixed it with Dante,' said Iris. (It wasn't quite true, but I knew what she meant.) 'Why don't you do the same with her? Sci-fi superpowers, yo!'

With Iris, it's always so simple. She watches a lot of movies. In movies, there's always motive. Things happen for a reason. Conflicts are resolved at the end. Lovers are reunited. In a movie, I would use my sci-fi superpowers to fix all my relationships, to solve Jo Perry's murder, and then settle down with my newly appreciative partner, having finally realized that my superpowers are simply the reflection of my lifelong craving for love.

Not so in real life. Real life is dull, and messy, and random, and chaotic. Real life is broken dishes. Real life is failure, and unborn dreams. Real life is lying in the muddy grass of a London park at night, and realizing that a relatively lesser-known piece of eighties hip-hop will be your closing credits. And yet –

*I could, couldn't I? I could fix my mother. Maybe not today, but later, when I feel better. Look inside her house and fix whatever went wrong between us.*

It's a dangerous thought. Like all of the darkest fairy tales, it hovers between *Never Again* and *Happy Ever After.* I've never looked into my mother's house. Or my father's. When I was a child, they seemed like giant fortresses; huge and dark and threatening. Playing *House* with Katie was tiny teacups and teddy bears. Playing *House* with my parents would have been Jack in the giant's castle; Theseus in the labyrinth; Ariadne, the seventh bride, opening Bluebeard's chamber. Children are raised with these stories; these grim warnings not to intrude into the world of adulthood. The child in me still sees my mother as the beast in the labyrinth; but maybe we could find a common ground, now that I too am a monster?

'I'll think about it.'

'Good,' she said.

*Perhaps in June, when we go north.*

'What, for the reunion?'

She read my mind. Iris does that sometimes, in a way that seems almost unconscious. As if I'm somehow reflecting images of myself at her. Katie used to do that, too. Maybe that's why I'm so drawn to her. That, and because she's the only one who really understands. She does not judge. She accepts me.

'So, have you decided on a dress? What are you wearing to the do?' We're back on the subject that interests her. As soon as we stray too far into issues of relationships, Iris' attention flags. But when it comes to outfits, hairstyles or make-up, she comes alight. 'I see you as a blonde, somehow. Or maybe we need to wait until you've chosen the dress.' She narrowed her eyes. Today, her hair is a faded version of the fuchsia-pink she wore when I first met her. It looks like the fairground candyfloss I never got to eat as a child.

'I haven't really thought about it yet.'

That's a lie. She knows it is. I think about it every day. It has been years since I bought a dress; years since I went to a party. I don't know how to choose anymore. I think maybe I never learnt. My mother used to choose my clothes. That's why I still dress like a Catholic girl. Thanks to Iris, I can almost understand how it feels to wear skin-tight jeans and plunging tops, with dangling earrings and neon-pink hair. But as for trying it in real life –

'We need to take you shopping.'

I like that *we*. It makes it sound as if I have a daughter. Dante's idea of a shopping trip is buying five pairs of the same kind of jeans online, then maybe having a pizza.

'Let's go shopping this afternoon. Get you kitted out properly. Monday's a slow day anyway. Rahmi can handle things on her own.'

'But –?' Martin and I share a bank account. If he sees me spending unexpected money on clothes, he'll wonder what's happened. He might think –

'Who cares what he thinks? I mean, you can always change that. Leave him a note, saying: *Everything's fine*. Plus I've seen where you live, babe. It's not like you don't have the money.'

I tried explaining to Iris that the concept of just *leaving a note* isn't as simple as she assumes. And I have already put aside my reserve of personal spending money on singing lessons with Charlie. I have no secret savings account, nothing to sell on eBay. What's the point of finding the perfect evening dress if I can't afford it? And then I'll need shoes, and make-up. Oh God. It must have been ten years since I last bought a lipstick.

'Oh, relax,' said Iris. 'Trust me. All we're going to do is look. Come on. It's a shopping trip, not the fucking *Italian Job*.'

And so it was that, an hour later, I found myself in Selfridges, still in my leggings and sweatshirt, looking at designer evening gowns with Iris, who seemed wholly impervious to the disapproving looks of the shop assistants.

'I don't like the looks we're getting,' I said.

Iris sniffed. 'Ignore them. It's not our job to impress the staff. It's the other way around.'

And then she began, with no embarrassment, to pull out dresses from displays. When approached by a shop assistant, she said, with frightening glibness: 'My friend needs something nice to wear for the MTV Awards next month. We'll need help here. And maybe some drinks? I think we're going to be quite some time.'

The shop assistant looked doubtful. He was young, and impossibly elegant, and it was clear from his face that he didn't think I looked the MTV type. But Iris has an energy that sweeps away objections. Within five minutes, she had not only won his allegiance, but somehow also managed to make him believe by implication that we were stars. Soon, I found myself swept away, talking about designers and styles, trying on dresses far, far out of my price range, while Iris and her assistant (whose name turned out to be Florian) each scrutinized the effect from a red velvet armchair, drinking a glass of Prosecco.

There were evening gowns of every kind: black organza; silver lamé; white satin that draped to perfection. There were beaded cocktail frocks, and barely-there wisps of layered tulle. There were sheaths of midnight velvet, and Grecian drape, and shimmering moiré. There were plunging necklines, demure boat-necks, spaghetti straps and bustiers, not to mention clutches, and shoes, and scarves, and shrugs, and shawls, and stoles. And in the middle of it all was Iris, giving instructions; Iris passing judgement; Iris in jeans and scuffed Converse boots, giving orders as if she were born to it. Her confidence was infectious; even I could almost believe that she was a fashion professional. And for a time, I forgot myself, and plunged into the fantasy.

'No, not black. Everyone wears black. You need something that makes you stand out.' Iris has a keen interest in clothes, in spite of having little to spend. Instead, she seeks out vintage stuff in charity shops. The slightly distressed look suits her, although I doubt I could pass it off. She waved away a creation in floaty yellow silk. 'Dude, no. Do you want her to look like Big Bird? I said stand out, not fly away.'

Florian, awed into submission by her imperious manner, ventured to suggest that she might also like to try something on.

Iris paused. From the changing room, I could hear her gentle reply. 'Oh no,' she said. 'Dude, I don't buy off the peg. I go to the designer.'

I suddenly thought of Adam Price, and Katie, and the dressing-up box, and felt a finger of unease raise the hairs on the back of my neck. I glanced at myself in the mirror – it was full-length, and showed me my reflection. The dress was very simple: red, floor-length, and made of some kind of jersey that draped so perfectly that it looked as if I'd been dipped in blood. *That's the one*, said my inner voice (definitely the demon today). *That's the dress you're going to wear at the Pog Hill reunion. That's the dress that's going to ignite the enemy's ships at Syracuse.* Then I glanced into Iris' house, and everything came crashing down.

*Oh, no. Iris. Oh, no.*

'*What did you do?*' I hissed at her, pulling her into the cubicle.

'You're always so dramatic. Relax.' Iris gave her brilliant smile. 'You look a knockout in that dress, by the way. It's definitely a keeper.'

'It costs over a thousand pounds!' I mouthed. 'How did you even get me to –'

'Bernie, listen to me. You seriously need to relax.' Iris grinned again, and once more I was reminded of Woody, in front of the coffee shop, miming: *Let me in, I'm a friend.* 'We're here to make you fabulous. Forget about the price tag. Just concentrate on what you do.'

'But I'm not doing anything,' I said in a tiny, whistling voice.

'I know,' she said. 'But you're going to.'

I knew it. I'd suspected it, deep down, since we'd stepped off the escalator. And, looking into her house, I could see all her justifications. Iris steals things. She always did. Comics, at first, then CDs, then cheap jewellery from Accessorize. And now Iris steals things not just because she could never afford them, but because it's obscene, to charge so much for something you might only wear once. And now that she has learnt the trick –

*Learnt it, just like Katie.*

*Look at me! I'm a pirate princess!*

I pulled off the red dress frantically and scrambled back into my clothes. It was ridiculous. I was ridiculous. How had I even allowed myself to be talked into doing this? But, of course, I already knew. Katie had already shown me. Katie had moved into Adam's house and rearranged his furniture, without my even showing her how – as if simple proximity to me was enough to teach her. Now Iris was doing the same thing with me, manipulating my feelings, making me accept a scheme that could only end in disaster.

*How long has she been doing this? How long have I been her unwitting accomplice?*

'Stop it!' I hissed. 'Iris, don't you *dare*!'

But Iris was unstoppable. Before I knew it, she was outside the cubicle, talking to Florian, accepting another glass of

Prosecco and congratulations on our upcoming (and wholly fictitious) MTV award.

'I'll be watching on the night,' promised Florian. 'I'll be cheering you on!'

Iris gave him a hug. 'I know. We wouldn't have managed without you.'

'I'm so *excited*!'

'So am I. Thank you, Florian. You're the best.'

Then, she calmly picked up the dress, slipped it into a garment bag and marched serenely out of the store, head high, like a pink-haired warrior queen, triumphant, from the battlefield.

# 4

'Don't think of it as stealing,' she said. 'Think of it as doing your bit to redress the balance of inequality. You know all that high-end stuff's made in a sweatshop in China or somewhere. Besides, everyone knows that designers are falling over each other to get stars to wear their dresses. That guy was practically begging me as soon as I mentioned the MTV Awards.'

'Iris, there *are* no MTV Awards! Well, there probably are, but –'

Iris waved a dismissive hand. 'Bernie, you deserve a chance to show those high school bitches you can rock an evening dress. And you looked amazing. It would have been a crime to turn it down.'

I tried to tell her it *was* a crime, but she had already moved on to shoes. 'What were you thinking? Heels or flats? I'm thinking –'

'Iris, you have to listen to me. That's not how it works. That's not how you use it. It's –'

'Why not?' she said. 'Bernie, don't you get it? You do it because you *can*. Isn't that why we do anything?'

My inner demon says she is right. We do these things because we can. That's how the balance of power works.

319

All my life, I've believed that certain things were immutable. They simply were, like me making the beds, and Martin taking the car to work. Or taking the hot water. Or offering his friend the spare room without even consulting me. Who taught me these things? Who told me that women have no power? And why do I still feel so hateful, so culpable in proving them wrong?

'Iris, these things all have consequences.'

'Everything does,' she told me. 'You can't blame yourself for everything. It's the chaos effect, babe. A butterfly on a flower in Kent can cause a tropical cyclone. Do we exterminate butterflies? Mow down all the flowers? Nuke Kent?'

I was still shaking, but Iris' calm had started to have an effect on me. Or maybe it was Iris, in my house, rearranging my furniture. I couldn't tell anymore. All I knew was that I felt suddenly better.

'Look, there's a tea shop. Come on,' she said. 'Little sandwiches, fairy cakes. Fancy tea that tastes like perfume. My treat. OK?'

I nodded. The shock of seeing Iris manipulate the sales assistant was beginning to subside. Even the suspicion that she might have been manipulating *me* had become less of a shock, somehow. And the dress, which only a moment ago had seemed an albatross around my neck, was quickly regaining its glamour. I couldn't help it. Stolen or not, it was the most beautiful thing I had ever worn.

I followed her into the tea shop and sat at a window table. No one seemed to notice me. No one thought I didn't belong. Perhaps that oversized garment bag, stamped with the Selfridges logo, acted as a passport. Perhaps it was Iris' larger-than-life personality that eclipsed me. Either way, it seemed that, once more, I had become invisible.

Iris ordered for both of us. She knows all my favourite things. Cucumber sandwiches. Spicy cheese puffs. Lemon cake, Victoria sponge. Jasmine tea, with flowers that unfurl like sea anemones. We ate, and drank, and I found myself laughing at our adventure; discussing make-up, and hair, and shoes, as if we did this every day.

*Why don't you?* says that inner voice. *It's not so unusual, after all.*

I try to explain that having friends isn't something I'm used to.

*Friends, is it, now?* The inner voice sounds amused, but not unkind. *Finally, Bernie, I think you're starting to make progress.*

Well, maybe I am. I realize now that I have spent most of my life believing I didn't really deserve nice things. Because of what happened to Mr D. Then, Martin came along and I was so grateful for his love that I let him consume me. I became a speck in his world, circling in his orbit. His friends became my friends. His dreams became my dreams. I lost myself in him, in Dan. I exchanged my house for a labyrinth. And he drew me in with promises, made me think that one day I would find him. But thirty years later, Martin is still perpetually just around the corner; still hidden in the labyrinth that he has built around himself, and I am still a lost child, vainly chasing shadows.

Iris, on the other hand, has opened her house. She is welcoming, and generous, and in her way, she wants me to keep growing. Iris has become my friend. Not like Katie, but perhaps –

'You've gone quiet again,' she said. 'What is it? Need more sugar?'

I looked at her. 'Let me see your tattoo.'

She shrugged and bared her shoulder. The design was already perfectly healed: a wreath of nightshade, bearing the words, *Never Again*. It was beautiful.

'Can I touch it?'

'Be my guest.'

I think I'd expected the spiky design to be detectable by touch, but the skin was perfectly smooth. It was as if the flowers had been pressed between two Bible pages. 'I like it,' I said. 'It's – compelling.'

'You didn't like it before,' she said.

Well, of course, there's a reason for that. The story of Mr D, and Grace, and his subsequent disintegration is one I've avoided telling her. Now I did, over cooling tea, and in a voice that trembled.

'So now you know,' I told her at last. 'That's what I mean by consequences. Not quite a tropical cyclone, but –'

'The bastard had it coming.'

That's Iris, I told myself. Combative, practical, without remorse. Good for her. If only I could have half her certainty. But, of course, she hadn't seen him. She hadn't seen the way he flinched whenever a girl got too close to him.

'No one deserves that, Iris,' I said. 'Listen. I obliterated him. I made him cut words into his arms.'

'No, you didn't,' Iris said. 'You showed him what he was, that's all. It's not your fault if he hated it. You were a child. He was a man. He was the one responsible. Why are you trying to make out it was the other way around?'

I shook my head. 'But Iris, there's more.' I started to tell her about Jocelyn Moore, and the young man with the baseball cap, but she put a finger to my lips.

*Shhh. Bernie. Watch me.*

Iris' voice in the back of my mind was like a gentle hand on my shoulder. I found myself drawn into her house, beyond the front room with its coloured lights and its arrangement of kitsch little memories, into the secret passageways of her deeper experience. A door marked: *Men* – half open now, and a mirror reflecting what was inside.

I could feel a hot flash clutching at my lower back, and I closed my eyes and breathed deeply until the heat had gone away. But Iris had showed me something that I would have struggled to put into words; something like a giant ball of yarn, made up of oddments, and filled with sharp things: needles, shards; the secret expression of damage.

*This is the man who called me a slut when I wouldn't give him my number. This is the man who touched my breast when I was on the school bus. This is the man who messaged me, pretending to be a fourteen-year-old boy. This is the man who followed me home when I was only twelve years old. This is the man who wouldn't stop, even when I asked him to. This is the man who dated me for a year, then dumped me the first time I slept with him. This is the man who filmed me in bed and put the results on a dating site. This is the man who drugged me because he only likes unconscious girls. And this is the man who knew, who watched, but didn't do a thing to help.*

Oh, Iris. Now I understand. Not all men have done these things, but all women have experienced them. Not all men have taken part, but all men have looked away. I opened my eyes, and saw her watching me with a little half-smile.

'You see. I get it,' she told me. 'They make us feel guilty for what they do. That's how they operate. A man finds himself attracted to a twelve-year-old. Straightaway, it's: *What was she wearing? Did she look older? Did she remind him of someone else? How can we make her responsible, and make him look like the victim instead?* Fuck's sake, Bernie. You've been carrying this – this pointless guilt – around for nearly all your life. Let it go. It was never yours to carry in the first place.'

And yes, she's right. I took a breath and let it out, very slowly. It felt as if for all this time I'd been breathing through a straw. It was as if she'd opened a door, and let a roomful of poison balloons float out into the blameless sky. And it felt good, so good: so free –

'Thank you,' I said. 'Oh, thank you.'

She grinned. 'About bloody time. Now, finish your tea, and let's go steal some fucking shoes.'

# 5

I hid the red dress and the shoes at the back of the guest bedroom wardrobe. Martin won't look in there. Martin doesn't notice much unless it affects him directly. And right now, this week, Martin has problems of his own to deal with, mostly concerning LifeStory Press, and the latest in the controversy surrounding Jared Noonan Philips.

I don't usually get involved with Martin's business, but unlike most of the authors published by LifeStory Press, Jared Noonan Philips is a man with a large following, and his controversial memoir has garnered some attention. Recent allegations on social media and elsewhere that his departure from a previous publishing house was prompted by complaints of bullying and sexual assault have not until now been made official, although the staff in question have all spoken out against him on various social media.

The *@YoungPretenders* Twitter account has recently been reinstated, and has followed Philips's cancellation tour, which so far includes nineteen interviews, as well as a spot on GBTV. Over the last couple of weeks, Martin has been under increasing pressure to comment on why LifeStory chose to publish Noonan Philips now, when so many others had distanced themselves in the wake of the scandal.

'I think we have to remember that no charges were ever brought,' says Martin in a recent interview with *The Bookseller*. 'Are we to condemn him because of a few complaints from junior staff? The *#MeToo* movement has created a climate of accusation. High-profile men are always at risk. But that doesn't mean readers should be denied this important memoir.'

And besides – he doesn't say this, but – a controversy is just the thing to push sales. Because of this, LifeStory Press has already sold ten thousand copies of the new memoir, entitled: *One Man, Adrift*, and which stands at No. 1 in the Amazon Practical and Motivational Self-Help chart. People are talking about it all over social media. Many have bought it simply because they are outraged that his previous publisher did not. And in a recent interview with the *Daily Mail*, Jared Noonan Philips spoke at length and in detail about the Genderbomber debate, declaring that not only is MK2 real, but that it has created a climate of fear in men, and heightened aggression in women.

'We're seeing the rise of the hashtags,' he says. 'A war that began on social media, but which is now continuing on our streets, in our cafés and pubs – even maybe in our homes.' Since then, he has created his own hashtag – *#NotMe* – which has been trending on and off since last week. He even cites Woody's podcast, describing Woody as *'chemically cancelled'*. This phrase too has become a hashtag, a flag for conspiracy theorists, who have embraced it wholeheartedly.

*@whitey2947: So women want equality? Let them go fight a war see how they like it #NotMe*

*@irisnoir23: Women have been fighting in wars for centuries.*

*@whitey2947 I mean with actual guns and shitt*

*@chemicallycancelled121: Men created MK2 women only exploited it.*

*@whitey2947: Yes, mate, the real war's right here right now.*

*@irisnoir23: MK2 isn't real. It's just another excuse for weak men to blame women for their own failings.*

*@whitey2947: It's real, you need to educate yourself.* (At this point, he inserts a link to Woody's YouTube.)

*@irisnoir23: Thanks, pal. I already know that guy. He's full of shit, and so are you.*

Oh, Iris. Be careful. Through Jared Noonan Philips, Woody's story has reached a new audience. Words like *Genderbomber* have become, if not actually household terms, then terms with a nodding acquaintance with a man you might know at the pub. *UnHerd* and the *Spectator* have both run stories about MK2, with dubious links to testosterone in women's sports, and speculation about what would happen if it got into the water supply. The Graham Crawley case has somehow become linked with this again, with the Twitter account *@ThatDoughnutGuy* helping drive the satire.

Martin doesn't think it's funny. I came in tonight after my run to find him on FaceTime with Woody. He broke off almost as soon as I came in, but I overheard something about *RippedinSix*, and Martin saying urgently:

'Don't talk to them. They only want to stitch you up – and me, by association. Just let it go, man. Take care of your health.' And – I opened the door. 'Uh-oh, here's the wife. Got to run, man. Talk soon.'

*The wife.* I don't like that. It makes me sound like a kitchen appliance. No other close relationship uses the definite article; you wouldn't say *the son*, or *the friend*. But the wife is acceptable. *The wife*, like *the dog*. Like *the postman*.

'Oh, don't start,' Martin said. His face looked drawn and tired. There was a red mark on the bridge of his nose where he'd been wearing his glasses. I wanted to reach out and touch it, but Martin has clearly defined territorial zones, into which I am not always allowed. 'I've already been on the phone for an hour.'

That was hardly my fault, I thought. I offered him a cup of tea.

'No. I have to get on with some work.' And at that, he withdrew to his office, closing the door behind him.

It was a lie. I can always tell. He just doesn't want to be near me. I wonder what happened with Woody; if that was what made him turn away. To me, it sounded as if he has been approached by the newspapers. Maybe, at last, Woody has remembered something important. Or maybe he simply hit a nerve. Either way, Martin's office is out of bounds to me. When he's in there, it's understood that he wants to be left alone.

I showered, and changed, and made myself a little salad, and a grilled cheese sandwich. I wonder what's on Martin's mind. He rarely shares his feelings. He used to, back in the Pog Hill days. We used to read each other's minds without the need for mirrors. Or so I thought: perhaps I was wrong. I certainly can't do that anymore.

*But you can. But you could.*

Well, yes. But it's easier just to check Facebook. Looking into his house is a risk. I know how that sounds: I've done it before – to my friends at running club, to Iris and Salena. None of them ever suffered any harm. But the *men* – the men are different. Woody, and Nic, and Jocelyn, and Mr D –

Not Dante, though. Not Dante. Not all men are predators. Dante is good. Martin is *good*, in spite of all that has happened. But don't all women think this way? Did Crawley's ex-wife suspect him? The media often blames the wife of a man who has been an abuser. She must have known, they tell us. But even if you knew, would you dare to make the knowledge public? Would you dare, if you really knew the things of which he was capable?

On Facebook, things seem to be quiet enough. Still no contact with Katie. I'm beginning to think that perhaps my fears of Martin resuming his relationship with her have been exaggerated. Instead, there's an ongoing (and very public) conversation about Jared Noonan Philips with a number of colleagues in the book world. Another about the dietary bene-fits of *RippedinSix* (Martin isn't a fan), then a series of private messages between Martin and Woody, apparently in response to whatever passed between them tonight.

*Jim Wood: I'm sorry, man. She's one of Them. You should watch your back from now on.*

*Martin Ingram: I hope you know how ridiculous that sounds. Not to mention ungrateful.*

*Jim Wood: You don't understand. She was there when it happened. I saw her in the mirror.*

*Martin Ingram: So what? You saw Bernie in a pub?*

*Jim Wood: It wasn't like that, dude. I can't explain. But she was there, and she was with*

*Martin Ingram: Woody? Are you still there?*

*Martin Ingram: Woody?*

*Martin Ingram: Woody?*

# 6

*Wednesday, May 11th*

No sound from behind the office door. No answer when I knock. It's late, and Martin has not left the room, not even to get a sandwich. He does this sometimes; I assume that he is working on one of his manuscripts, but he could be playing a game online. (*Or looking at Katie on Facebook*, says the demon voice inside my mind. *Maybe imagining her face instead of mine, next to his on the pillow.*)

Ridiculous. I know that's not true. And yet it makes me uneasy.

'Martin? Did you fall asleep?'

There is no answer from inside. He doesn't like to be disturbed. I know this, but it's midnight. Maybe he has earphones on. Maybe he's had a heart attack. Maybe he's lying there, dead, on the floor.

'Martin, I'm off to bed now.'

Still, no answer. I know he's inside. I know he hears me calling. But sometimes he just doesn't answer. He chooses to be absent. It occurs to me that Martin has been absent in one way or another ever since Dante was a boy – and the thought makes me sad, and angry, and ready to cry

– except that Martin has always made clear how much he despises women who cry, which is why I never do. *Although if you're going to despise someone*, says the little voice in my head, *then why would it be the woman, and not the man who makes her weep?*

I remember him telling me once, when we were still such a part of each other that I didn't know where Martin began and where Bernie ended: *Love always reminds me of death. The more you love, the more you lose, the more you come to fear losing it. That's why I'm sometimes cold with you: because I can't bear to think of a time when we won't be together.*

At the time, I thought that was the most romantic thing I'd ever heard. Now the memory ignites a flash of unexpected rage. *Grow up, for fuck's sake. I had to.*

That anger. It still surprises me. Is this menopausal rage? Or is it something long-suppressed, finally finding its voice? I was so happy, the other night. I thought we'd made a connection. Now, he has withdrawn again. Whatever connection we made has gone. But when he's like this, all I can do is leave him alone, be patient, and hope that, like a stray cat, he somehow comes back of his own accord.

And he loves me, doesn't he? He told me all those years ago. He said it means he loves me. Except that it doesn't feel that way. It doesn't feel a part of me, the way it did when we were young. When I was eighteen, I thought that his aloofness was romantic. I told myself he wasn't cold – he was complicated. He wasn't like other people. The things that other people do – the cups of tea, the holding hands, the little everyday kindnesses, like making lunch, or running a bath, or a bunch of flowers on Valentine's Day – we were beyond those common things. Now I sometimes tell myself that I should have settled for something commonplace.

Iris' voice, inside my head: *Maybe you deserved better. Maybe you stuck with him for so long because you didn't believe that.*

No. That's not the reason I stuck with Martin for so long. Love doesn't have to be deserved. Nor does it have to be happy. It just is, like a rock on a beach. Sometimes covered by the sea, swept by winds, buried in sand, but always there. It isn't a pretty rock, or an especially interesting one. But it's there. It's part of my landscape, and I live with it every day.

I went back into the front room and messaged Iris on my phone.

*Martin's being a dick. How are you?*

No answer. She must be asleep. I tried Leonie, with the same lack of result. Eventually, I did what DeeDee LaDouce would have advised from the start: I ran a bath. It means there won't be any hot water for Martin tomorrow, but for once I didn't care. I locked the bathroom door, and lit some little tea-lights. Then I got into a bath that was scented with rose and patchouli, and closed my eyes, and considered the reflections in the window glass of a haunted house.

*Oh –*

I only looked in for a moment. I didn't even mean to. It just happened as I was thinking of him. Cloud shapes in a summer sky. Reflections in the water. And then I was there, like a sudden flash of light into a darkened room.

I told myself I should leave at once. But it was too late. And I wanted to know – oh, so many things. If he was happy. Troubled. Asleep. I wanted to see if my photo was still there on his mantelpiece, or if Katie was there instead. But what I saw was nothing like that. There was no mantelpiece. No front room. No pictures; no welcoming furniture; no souvenirs; no knick-knacks. Most people have a public place in their house to welcome their friends. A little like a Facebook page, with snapshots of their public life. But Martin's front room was a set; a flickering image of himself projected against a bare blank wall. There was no effort to convince anyone of its reality. Cheap props discarded on the floor. A half-painted background, abandoned to dust. And beyond that, there was – nothing. The dark. A silence worse than damnation.

I took a step into the dark. Just like all those high-school girls in slasher films who just can't stop themselves from exploring the basement of the haunted house. Just like Bluebeard's wife, who must have suspected something. I was afraid, not for myself, but for what I would find down there. For what might change how I saw him. I shone a tiny pencil of light into the emptiness beyond –

Still nothing. No severed heads. No shambling, faceless monsters. Simply a giant, abandoned space of devastating bleakness; littered with pieces of broken glass and incomprehensible machinery. It looked to me like a spaceship, stranded on a planet of leaden skies and barren soil; with a row of featureless doors far away in the distance; every one of them airlocks; every one unreachable –

I'd never seen depression before. Not in that way. But I knew it. That bleakness, like fields in February, a hundred years from springtime. The gunpowder silence. The double-locked doors. He does not think of me, because he does not think of anything. Except maybe for the thing that I can see mirrored in every reflective surface; in every piece of broken glass. *Love always reminds me of death. The more you love, the more you lose, the more you come to fear losing it.*

Martin's parents both died when he was a child: his mother of cancer, his father of a heart attack, nine days after the funeral. His Yorkshire grandparents raised him, but there was always that sense of loss, and with it, the guilt. *Did I drive them*

333

*away? Did they love me? So why did they leave me?* And here it is still, this inner space; this yawning, cosmic, emptiness. This sense of badness. The inner voice, saying: *None of it lasts. No one is listening. Nobody cares. They're dragonflies on the skin of a lake: all they see is reflections. Pretty colours. Distractions. I see the dark. The winter. The deep. How can anyone bear it?*

There's the Martin I knew as a boy. Even then, he was trying to tell me. I thought he was being poetic. But, even then, he was trying to show me who he really was. *All these things are distractions*, he said. *Everything dies. Even the stars.*

*Except for love.*

'Except for love,' he echoed, and smiled. Marty Ingram from Pog Hill, forty-nine, but still only five: the man with the child reflected there in the windows of his eyes.

I went back to the office door and entered without knocking. Martin was sitting at his desk, his laptop closed in front of him. He looked up in surprise: I never come in when the office door is shut. He seemed about to say something, but I just put my arms around him. And then I reached for the door in his house – that distant door marked *Bernie*. Distance has no meaning here – unless you want it to mean something. In the same way, the doors are not doors, except when we choose to portray them that way – doors marked *Bernie*, or *Katie*, or *Mum* – but I opened it anyway. Not very far: just a crack. But sometimes, a crack is all we need to let the light come shining through.

And I saw myself. That girl from Pog Hill. That sad girl in the too-tight dress. And I saw how he'd seen me then, illuminated with his love; the brightest, most beautiful light in his world –

He looked at me. 'You're back,' he said.

'Oh, love,' I said. 'I've always been here.'

He followed me up to the bedroom.

# 7

*Thursday, May 12th*

Don't get me wrong. With human beings, there are no easy
solutions. Martin woke up this morning just as he'd been every
other day, except that he made me a cup of tea. There was no
great epiphany. And yet, it somehow feels as if we've turned
a corner. I still feel we're connected, somehow. That maybe
I can get him to agree to some kind of therapy. And now, of
course, I'm all the more determined to surprise him. To show
him that love is more than just dragonflies on a summer lake.
Dream girls are ephemeral. Katie is an illusion. But I'm right
here, and I am real, and I will make him see me.

Leonie texted me in answer to my text of last night: *Sweetie,
all men are dicks. Sending love.*

Iris' response is even more succinct. *FHU, man.*

I will, of course, do no such thing. But it made me smile
all the same. When Martin had gone to work, I put on the
red dress and the stolen shoes (patent red, block-heeled, and
tall as a giant redwood), and looked at myself in the bedroom
mirror. I actually think I look pretty good. With better hair
and some make-up, perhaps –

*Fuck perhaps. You're gorgeous.*

Online, *#NotAllMen* is trending. Graham Crawley has been charged with three more murders over the past fourteen years. The victims are: Anna Symonds, the young Chemistry student from Leeds; Julie Lovett, an ex-pupil from Battersea Park; and Candace Thorn, a sex worker from Brighton. There are calls to tighten up the rules on who is allowed to enter the teaching profession. The Education Secretary has made a statement, as has the Chief of the Metropolitan Police. The phrase 'one bad apple' is overused, prompting me to wonder whether any of these people have ever arranged a fruit bowl.

*@Irisnoir23* maintains that the police are part of the problem, rife as the organization is with toxic masculinity. To this, *@whitey2947* says: *All girls say that until they need protection.*

Iris, as you can expect, has nothing but scorn for this.

*@whitey2947* goes on to say: *It's men who need protection, love*, and posts a link to Woody's YouTube. It already has a hundred thousand views. This is madness. But it is a madness as catching as violence. Woody's rants against the Genderbombers are potent, and vicious, and hateful. And his theory – nonsense as it is – is like a plague. It goes everywhere.

'You could stop it,' Iris says. 'You could stop them *all*, if you wanted to.'

'No, I couldn't.'

*Yes, I could.* I have grown much stronger. My gift is no longer a bludgeon, but a rapier. And yet, it is still so unpredictable. Jocelyn Moore, for example. TikTok knows him as *Rolex Guy*. Channel 5 did a feature on him, entitled: *The Man Who Gave Away Everything*. The *Guardian* and the *Telegraph* have both published articles about him, one presenting him as an old-style philanthropist, the other as a delusional menace of the radical Left. Ironically, several publishers have offered him large advances for his autobiography. And the portion of the internet that remains obsessed with MK2 brings dark significance to the fact that Jocelyn Moore's bizarre change of personality occurred right after a break-up with his girlfriend.

*@whitey2947: It's funny how when a man breaks down, there's usually an Ex behind it #chemicallycancelled #gendercide*

*@drdoodad816: I hear you, man. It's like these things are happening as part of an orchestrated campaign. #BelieveTheMen #NotMe #IStandWithJNP*

And yes, to a certain extent, they are right. Except for the orchestrated campaign. But a splinter of mirror in a boy's eye can change the way he sees the world. *You did that*, says the inner voice. *You made them look. Didn't you?*

I don't feel bad about Jocelyn. He seems perfectly happy. The urge to give away money seems to have given him a purpose. No, what I want now is to make Martin stare; to make him see me, look at me, perhaps for the first time since that day in Scarborough. I want to make his jaw drop. To make him remember. To knock him dead.

But Martin isn't looking. Martin doesn't see anything right now, except his most famous client, doggedly trashing his legacy in the Press and on social media. One of Jared Noonan Philips' ex-publicists has finally made her complaint official. Francesca Adom, 26, claims that Philips groped her three years ago, after a party. When she complained, he is reported to have said: *Come on, love. It comes with the canapés.* The *Daily Mail* has already run a feature, deploring the earnestness of young people in publishing and their inability to understand the language of flirtation. The *Mirror* ran a piece entitled: *Sphinx Author in Sex Row.* And Sheffield Hallam University, where he was due to give a talk, have cancelled his appearance, thereby fuelling the wrath of the internet, and the further rise of the *#NotMe* hashtag.

Jared Noonan Philips seldom uses Twitter. He does have a Twitter account, with a blue verification tick and over a hundred thousand followers, but he follows no one in return, and rarely engages in dialogue. Today, he posted:

*@TheNoonanPhilips: In my day, women engaged with men, listened to what we had to say. Nowadays, they spend all their lives watching themselves on TikTok. Perhaps if they looked up from their phones once in a while, there wouldn't be a #GenderWar.*

Predictably, his tweet has provoked some anger. But it has also generated thirteen thousand likes, as well as approving comments from some of his friends and colleagues.

*@AmbrosePetersonAuthor: Being a white male novelist of a certain age is to be at the bottom of the pile. We need to start a campaign to help young white men be seen and appreciated again.*

*@CarolinePJoyce: Absolutely. Editors can't even get publishers to look at books by white male authors anymore.*

*@theberniemoon: Not true. My husband is an editor, and his authors are still largely white men.*

*@TheNoonanPhilips: If so, then your husband is in a minority. My experience of publishing (which spans over fifty years) tells me that the literary world is falling into a new Dark Age of misandry.*

*@wakandajo: Your use of the phrase "Dark Age" is – er,* 🙄

*@pinkiepie2298: U all white hon?*

Oh, I sense a pile-on. Step away, Bernie. Make some tea. Social media can sometimes be very far from sociable. A man who has lived for most of his life on a pedestal may feel actively victimized by the thought of equality. But I can tell that Martin is stressed. He has tried to persuade Philips to avoid social media for a few days. But he keeps compounding the damage. Now, as well as the accusation of misogyny comes that of racism too – which is not helped by the fact that Francesca Adom is a young woman of mixed race. I feel an anxious prickling at the edge of my hairline. Not quite a hot flash – at least, not *yet* – but a signal to disengage.

I make myself a cup of tea. There are doughnuts in the bread box, and I take a couple, too. When I return, I find that Philips's tweet has already attracted over fifty replies. I also see that *@irisnoir23* has liked *@pinkiepie2298*'s tweet. I can almost see her now, frowning over her mobile phone; her pink hair pushed back from her forehead; her house agleam with furious energy. And maybe because I am thinking about Iris and her anger, I feel a sudden rush of heat, and find myself looking into the house of Jared Noonan Philips.

A strong emotion can forge a link, or the need for something specific. Perhaps in this case it is my continuing need to protect Iris, as well as my need to shield Martin from the backlash of this scandal. Either way, it was wholly accidental: one moment I was on Twitter, the next I was looking into his house, searching beyond his narrow façade and into the labyrinth beyond.

The man has a high opinion of himself and his status. There is a whole room devoted to *Britishness*, which is linked to *Saying Things As They Are*, and also to *Posterity* and *The Legacy Novel*. His own novel is placed high in this area, alongside such writers as Pinter and Nabokov. A marble statue of himself overtops the rest of them.

As for *Women*, there is a whole nymphaeum devoted both to their conquest and to their worship, in which his titanic mother stands enshrined in dreadful majesty. Two tumbled statues on the marble floor below represent his ex-wives, both harpies who proved themselves undeserving of his love. He has a daughter, whom he never sees, and whose room is no longer open. He has raped two women, though he doesn't think of it as rape. After all, they agreed to it. The fact that they were juniors, much further down the chain of command, has nothing to do with their consent. *And besides, some women use men as a ladder to the top. It's all about choices, and getting by. They've done well out of the deal. I'll bet neither of them regret it.*

I caught the ghost of Iris, like a reflection in a mirror. A series of flashes from her house, heliographing her sentiments. *Go on. Fix him. You know you can. Use your superpowers.*

I tried to concentrate on my tea, but it suddenly tasted foul, like pennies steeped in vinegar. I felt the hot flash gathering like a flock of birds at the roots of my hair. Soon they would become a murmuration. I took a bite from my doughnut, but that was a mistake, too; it reminded me of Woody.

Meanwhile, the ghost of Iris was heliographing furiously. *Go on, Bernie. Fuck him up.*

No, I won't do that. But it might be possible to make a change. Something about respect, perhaps. Something about boundaries. Something about privilege, and how, to the man who has always viewed the world from a lofty pedestal, equality feels like a step down. That image of his mother in the room marked *Women* is striking: so much larger than everyone else, rising above the rest like the sun. Maybe I should insert a suggestion that all women deserve respect; that his mother is not a goddess, nor are his ex-wives harpies.

There's an illusion, often used by stage magicians. They call it the *Sphinx Principle*. Like so many magic tricks, it's based on mirrors, reflecting the sides of the stage to create the impression of empty space. Perhaps I could use my own mirrors, I thought, to make the Sphinx disappear. A tiny alteration, that's all, but I hope that it will help deflect his thoughts from their current path. 1 can do this. I'm in control. Just watch me.

*Abracadabra.*

# TRACK 10:

---

# Another One Bites the Dust

He was a douche, and now he's dead.
Isn't that better for everyone?
*From the LiveJournal of Bernadette Ingram (marked as
Exhibit BI 1): May 21st, 2022*

# I

*Extract from Class of '92, by Kate Hemsworth
(published by LifeStory Press, 2023)*

The printed invitations said: *Carriages at midnight*. My carriage
was Mr Naylor's silver Lexus, driven that evening by Simon,
who was therefore barred from drinking. Not that there was
much drinking that night: there was a bar, but it mostly served
pale ale and light cocktails, to be limited to two drinks per
ticket. I'd had two fake-champagne cocktails, and was feeling
pleasantly floaty, but the Head, Mr Allright, was serving at the
bar, and although he was funny and friendly and great, he had
a way of knowing if anyone was going too far. I briefly considered asking my date to get me a drink, but Simon was dancing
with Lorelei Jones, and I didn't want to disturb them.

I wasn't jealous. Simon was just one boy among many.
And Lucas Hemsworth had kissed me, gently, in the darkness
backstage as we waited for the curtain call, and the touch of
his lips still lingered on mine as if I'd eaten chillies. Could
Lucas Hemsworth be the one? The thought was not quite
idle. I told myself that it would be a nice story to tell our
kids one day: that *this* was the moment I'd known for sure.
In the darkness behind the stage, with the applause of the

345

crowd in my ears, and my eyes all filled with electric stars. In that moment, I was sure where my life was going to lead. True love, stage school, then the West End, and maybe even Hollywood –

I suddenly wanted to be alone. The magical evening had grown thin, and was starting to dissolve. The band had packed up their equipment, and the stage looked dark and empty. I could see Simon and Lorelei Jones necking on the dance floor. My silver sandals were hurting my feet, and I wanted to sit down. There was a garden alongside the hall, accessible through a pair of French doors hidden by a curtain. I drew back the curtain and slipped outside. There were a few raised flower beds and some wooden benches here, under an avenue of trees that were garlanded with fairy lights. The night was still warm, and I could smell cut grass and night-flowering jasmine, and the sleepy scent of the linden trees that lined the paths through the gardens. Through the half-drawn curtain, I could see right into the hall, with its soft rosy lights and the couples softly entwined on the dance floor, now imbued with romance again by the night and the distance. The music from the PA was timeless and orchestral, all strings and sweeping cadences. It all felt so innocent and safe, like looking into a snow globe. I remember thinking: *You'll remember this for the rest of your life.*

And then a shadow detached itself from one of the linden trees. Adam Price had always looked like a skinny little goblin to me, but now, with his face in shadow and his hair torched silver by the lights, he looked like a creature from a dark fairy tale, all scrawny limbs and shock-headed spite.

For a moment, I was frozen in place. Adam's stillness mirrored mine. I wanted to run for the French doors. But I couldn't turn my back on him. Instead, I started to back away, very, very slowly.

346

Adam grinned, showing deeply stained teeth. 'You look pretty,' he said. 'Like a princess.'

It was the first thing I'd heard him say since we were children at Chapel Lane. He sounded just the same, too: both pleading and aggressive. I'd always seen rage in Adam Price, a rage that I'd thought was aimed at me. Now I realized that what I'd seen as rage was really a dreadful confusion; that of a child lost in the woods; orphaned, beset by monsters. It was a strange but compelling thought. I was suddenly sure that I was listening to a seven-year-old trapped inside a man's body.

'Don't you remember me?' he said. 'I remember you.'

I nodded. 'I remember.'

'You were friends with Bernie Moon.'

'Not really,' I said.

He looked at me. In the fairy lights, his eyes looked enormous, filled with stars. Once again, I had the feeling that he was an inhuman creature. A changeling; a goblin; a troll. I'd told him I remembered him. But most of me didn't remember the incident that had provoked his departure from Chapel Lane. That memory had been shut away, and I didn't want to revisit it.

'You did something to me,' he said. 'That day, by the dressing-up box.'

'I don't remember,' I said. 'We were kids.'

He gave a ghastly kind of smile. 'Your house was nicer than mine,' he said. 'I wanted to stay in yours, I think.'

I didn't know what he meant at first. *Your house?* He'd never been to my house. I kept thinking of him as a boy, and how he'd ended up in care, and how he'd tried to burn down the house of the people who had taken him in. But there was something else there, too. Something like a distant dream. I'd been a princess, then, too. Except that it didn't feel that way. It felt like being –

347

*A monster.*

I shook my head. That wasn't right. *Adam* was the monster. Adam had set fire to his foster parents' house. He'd hurt me. He'd hurt both of us.

'I didn't mean to do it,' he said, as if he'd read my mind. (Or had he put the thought in there, like a note left on the mantelpiece?) 'I just wanted to stay inside. I just wanted –'

But suddenly, I didn't want to hear what Adam Price had wanted. I put out my hands, as if to ward off an attack. It felt as if he were on me again, smashing my face into the floor, although he hadn't moved from his spot.

*I'm a princess,* said a voice in my mind. *Look at me! I'm a pirate princess!*

How could I have forgotten that? And yet, somehow, I had. The memory – the *guilt* – had wound itself tight into a little ball, and had remained in hiding for years, waiting for this moment.

I said: 'Go away! Leave me alone!'

He took a single step forward. 'What's wrong?'

'Don't touch me!' I said. 'Leave me alone!' And all at once I was screaming at him, screaming just as I had that day, screaming and crying and feeling my memories unravel like string –

'What the hell is going on?'

The voice came from the French doors, and I turned towards it in relief. 'Thank God. Take me away,' I gasped. I was aware I was shaking; my face was hot; my throat was raw; I put a hand to my eyes and it came away black with mascara. But he was there, and I clung to him as if he had saved me from drowning. I vaguely remember thinking how it should have been Lucas there, Lucas who had saved me, but I clung to Martin now, smudging mascara onto his shirt, sobbing into his shoulder. I didn't think about anything else. I mean, he could have been anyone. I barely even noticed him until later, much later, by which time I had almost lost sight of what had happened with Adam, or why I had panicked in that silly way. But by then, the Head was involved, and Adam was nowhere to be found, and Martin Ingram had already told everyone that Adam had assaulted me, and Lucas Hemsworth had driven me home and told my parents, who called the police, and there was no way to stop it by then, or for me to take it back −

# 2

*From the LiveJournal of Bernadette Ingram (marked as Exhibit BI 1):*
*Thursday, May 19th*

I find that menopause dreams are sometimes especially, gruesomely vivid. This time, I was in a house; no house I'd ever seen in real life. No house that could ever exist: all built from scraps and fragments, poised on the edge of a yawning sinkhole that seemed to go down forever.

*Where am I?*

*Whose house is this?*

I came in through the front room, but there was barely anything left. It was as if the whole façade had been blown in by an explosion, all glass and debris everywhere. The doors were the same; some blown right in, some hanging from their hinges, and beyond them, I could see levels and floors; impossible perspectives; some hanging by precarious threads, some tilting out into darkness. Here there were walkways of shredded steel, and banks of dead-eyed monitors, and gates into disused warehouses, and piles of discarded rubble.

And it stank: like food left out to rot, but so much worse. And there was a sound like white noise and electronic feedback. Except that it wasn't a noise, of course. That's just my mind's way of processing it. But something was broken in there all the same; something terminally unhinged; something cold and shivering, screaming perpetually into the void.

*This is a dream*, I told myself. *I can leave it any time.* But all the open doors seemed to lead to somewhere else within the house. A dressing room full of mirrors, reflecting emptiness within; a room filled with sports equipment, all of it buried under fat sheets of dust. A room of children's toys, all eyes; a room of magician's tricks – top hats, red-lined capes, magic wands, garlands of silk handkerchiefs in every colour imaginable. And in my dream I realized that this was The Great Carovnik's house, and thinking of her, made her appear just as I'd remembered her: silver jacket, top hat, smile like a cutlass, reflecting a clamour of voices.

*It was you! You did that to me!*

*Feminism is cancer!*

*All I want is for you to relax!*

*Mother? Are you watching?*

Whose are those voices? They fly at me from all angles, like lethal pieces of broken glass. And they speak all at once, in a rising clatter of voices that is all one voice. It is the voice of *#NotAllMen*; the voice of the patriarchy. The rage and terror of men when women learn to deploy their power.

And in my dream, I know that I can turn my mirrors onto them all. I can turn the table around without breaking even a single glass, because all their doors are open now, and looking into the mirrors, I see that I *am* The Great Carovnik: silver jacket, black top hat, high-heeled boots and dazzling smile. And because this is a dream, I have candyfloss-pink hair, and earrings shaped like lightning bolts.

*I am The Great Carovnik*, I say to my reflection. And in the mirror, she smiles at me, a smile like the edge of a sheet of paper just beginning to burn, and says: *Little girl. You always were.*

Then she takes off her big top hat, and beckons me to look inside. And inside, I see the sinkhole again, like a rabbit hole to hell. And inside, in the darkness, I can see them all: the men. Jim Wood. Graham Crawley. Jocelyn Moore. Mr D. Jared Noonan Philips. All of them falling, all of them damned, all of them caught in that magic hat. And then I am falling with them, falling into the darkness, because pride comes before a fall, and the Fall came with sin, and the blood is a sign –

I start to struggle, then to scream. I'm falling into the emptiness. I realize that I have been tricked. The tables are turning, without my consent. Mirror fragments explode like clouds of angry wasps all around me. I hear a voice – not a man's voice this time – saying:

*I'm a pirate! A pirate princess!*

And then another. *Fuck them up. Fuck them up, Bernie. Once and for all.*

And then I awake, soaked with sweat and shivering, to the scent of sour earth and spilt loose change, and daylight through the window, Martin, saying: *Fuck, not again* – and blood drenching the mattress.

# 3

That was the day before yesterday. Since then, it has been all over the news. *London Man Dies in Yoga Class Rampage.* That was the headline. It makes it sound as if he were the victim. The *Sun* puts it more succinctly: *Doughnut Guy's Lethal Workout.* In any case, you already know what he did. Turned up to an all-women yoga class, weeks after leaving his job at the gym, then barricaded himself inside and pulled out a commando knife.

Imagine that for a moment. Imagine the confusion. The furious ranting of the man, screaming about Exes and MK2. Some of the women tried to flee. Some tried to confront him. Jim Wood, slashing and stabbing. The screams. The blood on the parquet floor.

And then, after how many terrible seconds of turmoil, and screaming, and panic, and blood, one woman finally remembered the words, the magic words that made Woody pass out.

'She started screaming: "Feminist! Woke! Abortion!" Then: "Doughnut! Doughnut! Doughnut!"' an eyewitness told the Metro. 'And at that he just collapsed onto the floor, as if she'd pulled the plug on him. We couldn't even believe it was real. But there he was, on the floor, asleep, with the knife right under him.'

She is less clear on *who* caused his death. As are the others, apparently. It was an accident, it seems. No one claims to have seen anything. There are so many prints on the knife – and in the blood on the polished floor – that there was no hope of determining whose hand (if any) was responsible. Statements are understandably confused, occasionally contradictory.

*'After that, we all rushed in – to tie him up, or something.'*

*'I think maybe the knife must have slipped.'*

*'I don't recall what happened next.'*

*'I just saw the blood.'*

*'All that blood – I didn't know where it was from.'*

Of the nineteen women in the group, only one suffered serious injury. The rest suffered defence cuts, mostly slashes to hands and arms. Woody, with his frequent boasts of knowing how to handle himself, turned out to be less than an expert, even against unarmed women. No one seems to know how he got that slash to the femoral artery, and although the internet is rife with rumours about the murder of a vulnerable man by a conspiracy of women, no further action was taken by the police.

Of course, by then, they had more on their plate than the death of a known troublemaker. Jim Wood was just a footnote that night. At eleven-fifteen, less than an hour after Jim Wood's body was removed from the crime scene, Graham Crawley was found dead in his cell. The cause of death is uncertain, but no foul play was suspected. No drugs were found; no weapons; there was no violence to the body. It was a puzzle. A man with no history of heart disease, stroke or epilepsy appeared to simply have died in his sleep. The media suggested sleep apnoea, or Sudden Adult Death Syndrome. The dark places of the internet whispered that he had been *silenced before he could tell the truth*, whatever that meant.

Not that anyone should care. He'd confessed to one murder, and had probably committed three more. It saved the state some money, some said. And if there was any link between his death and the accidental stabbing of a troubled conspiracy theorist, the connection is only made by malcontents, right-wing pressure groups, performative misogynists and vocal proponents of toxic masculinity.

*Two men, dead on the same night. Murder looks good on you, Bernie.*

Of course, I didn't kill them. And yet my dream was so vivid – as vivid as the one in which I witnessed Jo Perry's murder – that I can't help feeling I was there; watching from the wings, somehow. Maybe that's because of the blood. Good thing I bought some more Maxi Pads.

Martin blames himself, of course. For not realizing that Woody was about to combust. And he blames himself for not being there to talk him out of whatever he did. He is keenly aware of having neglected his friend recently; partly because of the controversy over Jared Noonan Philips, and partly because of Woody's insistence, verging on paranoia, that somehow *I* knew something about his mysterious attacks.

It sounds ridiculous, doesn't it? And how could I have possibly known that those two men would combust in this way? I was fast asleep at the time. Fast asleep, and dreaming. But the blood on the mattress thinks otherwise. The wise blood, that remembers. Remembers all the way to that time when Katie turned Adam Price. Remembers all the way to the time when Iris somehow turned *me*.

As soon as we saw the news today, Martin immediately phoned the police, presenting us both as witnesses to Woody's fragile mental state. That meant making a statement, of course. We went to the station together. I could feel my heart racing, even though

I'd done nothing wrong, and hot flashes raced all over my skin like tiny electrical charges. I asked for some water. The officer who came to take my statement was a young woman, no older than Dante. I fought the urge to ask her what had happened to Graham Crawley. But this wasn't about Graham Crawley. I had to remind myself of that. Instead, I told her about Jim Wood; about his fixation with protein shakes, his panic attacks and his growing conviction that women – *all* women – were part of a mass poisoning conspiracy. Martin gave his own statement to a different officer, and when we had finished – it didn't take long – we left, with no sense of whether or not our testimony had confirmed anything they already knew.

Martin spent the rest of the day following the news online, and arguing with people on Twitter, who saw Woody's attack on those women as a kind of heroic gesture. One Substacker described Woody's death as *Suicide By Cunt*, and predicted a rise of MK2-related deaths. A prominent literary author compared Jim Wood's death to that of Orpheus, torn apart by the Maenads. *The speaker of truth*, she writes in the *Spectator, has often been a lonely voice. And as the blistering sun of cancel culture rises over our land, the voices of the truth-tellers and prophets fall silent, one by one.* There is a great deal more in the same vein, but what it amounts to is this: Jim Wood, driven mad by the women of the woke, has fallen martyr to the culture wars. It might even be funny, if so many people didn't believe it.

On Twitter, his name is trending. The spoof account, *@ThatDoughnutGuy*, has been suspended. Even Graham Crawley's death has been eclipsed by the news; except in those circles in which both events are seen as deeply, mysteriously interlinked. One of the women injured in the gym class stabbing has been named as Charity Brown, a trans woman from North London, provoking a violent response from the

Gender Critical movement, and a renewal of their demands for women-only spaces, in spite of the fact that when a man actually *had* entered a women's space to perpetrate a violent attack, no one had stopped him from entering, and he'd seen no need to dress as a woman to do so.

The only silver lining is that Jared Noonan Philips is silent. His Twitter account shows no activity, nor has he made any comment on social media, or elsewhere. His daily emails to Martin have ceased. Perhaps my intervention has actually done some good. I hope that this means Martin will be free to concentrate on processing the death of his friend, and moving on quickly to other things.

Iris had already heard the news about Woody when we met at our usual place, but she was typically unmoved. 'He was a douche, and now he's dead,' she said. 'Isn't that better for everyone?'

On any other day, I might have let her wave away my fears. But the blood on the mattress had ideas of its own. And my dream of The Great Carovnik, with Iris' pink hair, made me feel increasingly uncomfortable. Could she have been inside my house without my being aware of her? Could she have used my mirrors to intervene? To do something bad? It seems all too possible. I keep thinking of Katie, and the way she flipped Adam Price. The way she made him dance to her tune. The way she absorbed his memories. And that, too, makes me think of how Iris has somehow managed to make me accept things that I would never have accepted, *if I'd been completely myself –*

I looked at her. 'Did you do it?'

'Do what?' Iris sipped at her cocktail. Today she was wearing a white halter top emblazoned with the words: *COULD YOU NOT?* Her hair was like a candyfloss cloud. She looked so young – and so innocent – that I could hardly bear it. But she knew what I meant. I could tell by the gleam of humour that heliographed at me from her house. And the shadow of suspicion that has hovered over our relationship almost from the first now sharpened into certainty.

'Graham Crawley. Was it you? And Woody – did you –'

'Fuck them up?' Her eyes were shining with laughter. 'Bernie, you worry far too much. They were both fucked up anyway.'

'But did you? Were you *there*?' I said.

She grinned. 'How could I have been there? Graham Crawley died in his sleep. Some might call it a blessing. Now he's no burden on the state. And as for Woody, he was nuts. He could have gone deeble any time.'

*Gone deeble.* Such a typically Iris expression. And yes, I know I didn't make Woody attack those women. But I did create the circumstances for him to do so. Would he have done it anyway? Or was he pushed?

*Pulled*, my inner voice. *That's how he went under. Because once she gets inside your mind, she can do whatever she wants. She can move your furniture. She can turn the tables. And whatever she breaks – well, that's on you. Because the person you save becomes your responsibility forever.*

I looked at Iris. Her sleeve of tattoos; her fluffy pink hair; her bright, yet somehow predatory smile. I like her so much; and yet there is something unsettling about her; a place of shifting sands. Like Woody's, her charm is dangerous. Like Woody, she knows it.

'Let's eat,' I said. 'Hot wings, French fries. Order anything you like.'

Iris gave me that killer smile. 'Yo, Bernie! *That's* my girl.'

# 4

I hardly slept at all last night. Turns out that night sweats are nothing compared to the kind of insomnia triggered by worrying who your friend might kill next in your dreams. I have no doubt now that she was the cause of both Woody's and Crawley's combustion. I also know that it wasn't her fault. This is what I did to her.

Nor is she the only one. A search on social media reveals that Jocelyn Moore has gone dark. Having given all his possessions away, as well as donating a kidney, what does he have left to give? A further, deeper search reveals that he has joined a monastery. There, he has no possessions; no family; not even his name. His loved ones are bewildered. No one suspected that he might do this. And yet we must hope for his happiness.

Jared Noonan Philips, too, has gone as dark as midnight. No tweets, no blog posts, no interviews. Martin is cautiously relieved; but he was getting anxious when a quick email from the man himself revealed that he has gone to stay with his mother in Bath for the foreseeable future. Martin hopes that this means Philips is working on a new book. I don't think so. I wonder if my intervention triggered this.

Meanwhile, another favourite has emerged from TikTok. This one, an otherwise nondescript young man, has made it his task to apologize to everyone he meets. I haven't seen the footage yet, but I think I would recognize him. A young man in a baseball cap; twisted with uncertainty; rooted to the spot as he whispers his apology. Spinning plates, now out of control. How soon till they are broken?

It's less than three weeks now until the date of the Pog Hill reunion party. Some days, I can hardly wait. On other days, it's like a storm, with thunderheads about to collide. I feel as if I am juggling plates, each one higher than the last. With Salena's Books; the party; my running club; social media; singing lessons; watching over my son; understanding Martin; and now, keeping Iris under control, I feel as if this magic show is seconds away from catastrophe.

Iris says I should just go with the flow, get laid, get drunk, *whatever, babe*. Charlie thinks I should let rip. *You have this secret voice*, she says. *This voice, that no one else has heard*. Leonie thinks I should stop apologizing for things, assuming guilt for things, and *just be my authentic self*. Of course, Leonie doesn't know what there is inside my house. Two more men are dead, and a third is – well. Whatever Jocelyn Moore is now, it's because I changed him. And Iris – I keep thinking back to my dream. The falling men. The sinkhole. The top hat and the cutlass smile. Just as Katie and I were linked, so has Iris come to be linked to this power inside me. But while Katie shrank at what she found, Iris has embraced it. And I know I have to stop her somehow; otherwise she will kill again. She has a list. She told me so. Where are her douchebag exes now? Where will she find her next victim?

On Twitter, @irisnoir23 writes in response to a tweet about Woody's death: *Why should there be a conspiracy?*

*Some men just deserve to die. He went out to kill women, and got himself killed instead. It's poetic justice.*

*@francinefoofoo: He was mentally ill. What's wrong with you? Where's your sense of empathy?*

*@irisnoir23: celebrating with champagne* 😃

*@whitey2947: This is what feminism looks like now. Name-calling and #misandry*

*@HB82323434: Makes me so angry. 'Be nice,' they say. Some victims are going to be so pissed off they will be unable to 'be nice' anymore.*

*@irisnoir23:* 🔥 😃

Of course, it isn't the real world. It's only social media. But a combination of Iris' lack of empathy and her '*fuck them up*' attitude means that no man in her orbit is safe. I wonder who she is dating now. Since Nic, she hasn't mentioned anyone. But I know that she goes on Tinder, and that she has a healthy appetite for sex as well as food. How long will it be before she tries to sound out a new boyfriend? How long will it be before she decides that he deserves to be put in his place?

Message from Iris: *What's up?*

*Not much. Pizza and a movie.*

*What, with the douchebag husband?*

In actual fact, Martin is still struggling to process what happened to Woody. And as if that wasn't enough, the Jared Noonan Philips situation is rapidly deteriorating. Two more young people have come forward over the past few days to accuse him of sexual misconduct. LifeStory Press is under growing pressure, and although Philips himself remains mercifully silent, it is getting increasingly hard for Martin to ignore or contain these rumours.

*That guy who wrote* The Sphinx, *right? I always thought he was a pervert.*

*He's not a pervert, Iris. He's just a guy in publishing.*

*You could fix him.* 🔥

I change the subject in haste. With Iris, you never know when she might get it into her head to be helpful. She is the wildest of wild cards, and any intervention of mine – a suggestion, for instance, to leave him alone – might trigger one of her impulses.

*Seriously, Bernie. What's the point of superpowers if you never use them?*

And there you have it. To Iris, the solution is clear. Everything is a joke to her, to which the punchline is murder. I try to explain that it isn't so simple, but she only laughs. It's concerning. I glance into her house from afar. Her front room is flooded with laughter. The big sign over the mirror reads: *BERNIE, YOU LEGEND!* Of course, that's just a translation of what I see inside her. But it means she sees me. She knows that I am watching. I must take care; make myself small; make myself inconspicuous. And when I move, it must be swift. I only have one chance with her. It's just that –

*You love her*, says that voice.

And yes, I do. But I see now that I have been very selfish. Iris doesn't belong to me. Neither did Katie, or Dante, or even Martin. Perhaps I hold on to people so hard that I end up breaking them. But this time it won't happen. I swear. This time, and for the first time, perhaps, I am in complete control.

# TRACK 11:

———

# Changes

What's left is the space between the two, that breathless space where you can pretend – if only for a few seconds – that everything's still possible.
*From the LiveJournal of Bernadette Ingram (marked as Exhibit BI 1): June 4th, 2022*

# I

*From the LiveJournal of Bernadette Ingram (marked as Exhibit BI 1):*
*Tuesday, May 24th*

Record sales at the bookshop today. At last, Salena tells me that we are making a profit again. The debts we accumulated last year have been paid off, and we are now officially out of the red. Last weekend, *The Bookseller* named Salena as one of its Indie Heroes, and since then, a string of publicists from various publishing houses have contacted us, wanting us to host book events. Next week, a young Black children's author is booked to do a reading: we have already sold over two hundred copies of her new book in readiness.

'It's like a miracle,' said Salena today, as we were unpacking the new stock.

'This miracle took a lot of hard work,' I said. 'You should be proud of that.'

She looked at me. '*You* should be, too. I've watched you. You've been amazing.'

I shrugged. 'I'm nothing special,' I said.

'Oh, but you are,' she said. 'Bernie, you've changed. I don't know what it is, but since you started running with the Fliers, you've had this new kind of *energy*. You're like a completely new person.'

'Well, I have you to thank for that. Running has given me confidence.'

She shook her head. 'It's not just that. I don't know how to describe it.' She smiled. 'Anyway, whatever it is, I'm glad. You deserve it, Bernie.'

Her faith is oddly touching. But I'm glad she feels this way. Two months ago, I would not have believed that she and I could ever be more than just work colleagues. Then again, two months ago we were not connected. Now we share so much, she and I. I know what she is thinking. I can see when she is anxious or depressed. I know the tensions in her home, and the problems she has with her parents. I often see these things without even having to use my gift, and it makes me happy to think that maybe she likes me for *myself*, and not because I changed her.

But yes, I *have* changed. I am changing. Even Martin sees it now, although he doesn't know what it is. And since I looked into his house, I have been more understanding of his moods and behaviour. He is under a lot of pressure still regarding Jared Noonan Philips; but once it's over, I hope that he will agree to go to therapy. I mentioned it at dinner tonight, and for the first time he didn't reject the idea out of hand. In fact, he looked at me and said:

'Bernie, you're always so sensible.'

I was so surprised that I hardly knew how to answer. But in spite of his praise, I felt a small disappointment. Because, though *sensible* is good, I'm planning for so much better. I'm planning for *spectacular*, and *sexy*, and *surprising*. So hang on to your hat, Martin; because in just over two weeks, I'm giving you the surprise of your life.

# 2

*Wednesday, May 25th*

This evening, I managed to run the whole of our five-kilometre circuit without stopping. Everyone cheered as I approached the top of the last long incline that marks the end of the run, and even though I was certain that I wouldn't make it, I did it, on a wing and a prayer, and even managed to speed up a little as I rounded the last bend – which was all downhill – without collapsing in a heap under a stray rhododendron.

'You made it!' said Salena, jumping up and down.

'This bend shall thenceforth be known as *Bernie's Bend,*' said Rahmi. 'In honour of Bernie, who kicks ass!'

Then Leonie gave me one of her hugs, which made me actually want to cry, and Salena took a photo of me just as I crossed the finish line, and posted it on her Facebook page, under the heading: *Small Victories.*

I had no idea this would mean this much. My friends. My new and marvellous friends. They helped me to this, and to so much else. They gave me this new confidence. Isn't it strange, how for such a long time I thought I didn't deserve this? That I was somehow responsible for everything that had gone wrong? That if Martin didn't want me the way he wanted Katie, it meant that it was my fault, that I must have failed him?

*You want to change, Bernie? Then change.*

And I did. I *have* changed. Not in any silly, superficial way, but deep inside. I feel different. I even *look* different, although I'm not sure exactly what has changed. My body feels better aligned, somehow. I'm no longer afraid of their judgement. And there's something that has been nagging me; something that I want to do –

'I want to celebrate,' I said. 'I want to mark this occasion.'

Alex said: 'How about a Yowza night? Pizza and shots? Does that sound good?'

I nodded. 'But first –'

I told them my idea.

'A *tattoo*?' said Leonie. 'Hell, *yes*! Do you know where you're going?'

I named the place Iris uses. *You can just walk in*, she says. *No one will rush you, or anything*.

'I'm coming with you,' Salena said. 'Unless you want to go in alone?'

As it happened, I didn't, and *everyone* came with me: Rahmi, and Leonie, and Salena and Alex; all of my wonderful, messy friends, sprawling onto the armchairs in the waiting area. The tattooist was a young woman called Rosie, with shaved hair and a beautiful smile. I explained what I wanted, and she listened attentively. It was only a small design. She didn't think it would take very long.

'Just that?' she said. 'Just those words?'

I nodded. Now that I was in the chair, I wasn't feeling so confident. The instrument in Rosie's hand looked frightening and alien. My friends were still in the waiting room; I wished they could have been next to me. I wondered what Rosie thought of me, still in my leggings and running top, hair in my face, nearly fifty. Did she find me ridiculous? Did she –

*Does it matter?* The inner voice was neither critic nor demon.

*I mean, maybe* – I began.

*No it doesn't,* said the voice. *It's yours, not anyone else's. And look, your friends are right next door. They think you kick ass. They said so.*

And suddenly, it *was* OK. I wasn't nervous anymore. The needle hurt a little, but not as much as I'd feared, and when she showed us the design in the mirror, I laughed aloud with pleasure.

'Keep it covered for a day or two,' said Rosie. 'Then just keep it hydrated with a little unscented lotion. It should heal fast – it's only small – but come back if you have any questions.'

I told her I would, but I doubt if I will. It's hardly even sore tonight. And Martin won't notice the new design – I'll hide it under my nightshirt. But on the night of June 4th, I'll be watching his face as I slowly take off my new red dress, to reveal nothing at all underneath but the three little words etched on my skin just above the bikini line:

*Made You Look.*

# 3

Friday, May 27th

Just one week and a day to go. It feels like being a child again. My overnight case is already packed. The red dress; the skyscraper shoes; the tiny sequinned evening bag; the make-up from Fenwick's on Bond Street, which I bought from a friendly assistant, who showed me how to apply it, and who presented me with the receipt – for what seemed like a staggering sum – in a small silver envelope, like the invitation to a ball.

I don't really have any jewellery. Only a little enamel pendant that Martin gave me years ago, when we were both still at Pog Hill. I love it, but it won't match my dress, and I daren't ask Iris, because knowing her, she'd try to rob a jeweller's. Instead, I asked my running friends if they had anything they could lend me. It feels somehow wrong to be doing it, but they've all been so supportive of me since I told them my plans, and besides, as Leonie says, *Fliers stick together.*

This morning, she dropped into the shop, and gave me a little square box, stamped with the name of a Bond Street jeweller.

'Take this. Jocelyn gave it to me. I can't bear to look at it anymore.'

Inside was a ruby pendant like an angry cube of fire. 'My God, is that *real*?' I lowered my voice. 'What am I supposed to do with it all day? Keep it in my handbag?'

She grinned. 'Why don't you wear it, you dope?' And, reaching under my ponytail, she clasped it in place around my neck.

I felt my cheeks go red. 'I can't. I can't borrow this. I'd be worrying about it all the time. What if I lost it? I'd never forgive myself —'

Leonie gave me one of her looks. 'Bernie, it's a *gift*,' she said. 'I have more bling than I'll ever wear. And the last thing I want right now is to keep something that reminds me of him.'

DeeDee LaDouce swears by the healing power of crystals. According to My Big Fat Menopause, the ruby is: *a perfect stone for you warriors, as it stimulates your survival instincts. Rubies bring love and confidence, loyalty and courage. So treat yourself! Forget menopause rage! This is the only way to see red!*

DeeDee LaDouce is appalling in so many ways, and yet maybe she's right about this one. I do feel stronger; more confident. I do feel like a warrior. That's good: because there are things I must do this week that will require courage.

I took off the ruby when I got home and hid it in my overnight bag. I don't want Martin to see it just yet. Not that he's paying attention right now. Even the drama at work has been eclipsed by his plans for the reunion. He talks to Lucas on FaceTime every day. Sometimes, they chat on Facebook, or send each other visuals. From these conversations, I have learnt that there will be a starry backdrop on the stage, a decor comprised of huge glass jars filled with strings of fairy lights, and that the band will play their original set, with Katie as their special guest.

It's perfect. Martin has been under strain over the Jared Noonan Philips affair. The book is selling reasonably well, but not because the public cares about an author memoir.

Instead, it is the author's views on MK2, and #*Gendercide*, and the dangers of being a man in today's world that have attracted the media. Martin has been assailed by daily calls from journalists, asking for comment. He looks tired and depressed. He needs a change of scenery.

'Why don't you go up to Malbry?' I said. 'You could use some time away. Hang out with Lucas and the band. Get in shape for the party.'

'What? On my own?'

We were lying in bed. Darkness is confessional: and it allows me to look into his house, at the same time floating a tiny hint, like a butterfly, past his window.

'You're due some time off from work,' I said. 'Why don't you go and stay with Lucas for a few days? You could drive up north with your stuff. Maybe take Dante up with you. He could stay with my mother. Have a practice night with the band. I'll come up later, on the train. I've booked us a room at the Premier Inn for the Saturday night, just the two of us.'

I sensed his surprise. His resistance. Martin likes to plan things quite carefully, and sometimes gets upset when things change. I floated the idea again, very softly, into the air, while at the same time suggesting that perhaps it had been *his* plan from the start, a plan that suited everyone. And Katie would be there, of course. Face-to-face, and in the flesh –

Of course, I'm playing with fire. I know. But I know what I'm doing. Let him have his week with her. Let him have his fantasy. And then, on Saturday night, I'll be there, ready to eclipse her . . .

'You wouldn't mind?' he said at last.

I smiled to myself in the dark. 'Not at all.'

'OK,' he said. 'I'll give it some thought.'

He's driving north on Monday.

# 4

*Friday, June 3rd*

It has been a strange kind of week. Being in the house without
Martin is a new experience. Who knew that another human
being could leave so much space in their absence? Of course,
his things are all still here: his books, his clothes, his work
things – the things I'm not supposed to touch. There are whole
rooms – office, basement, loft – into which I am not supposed
to go. I wonder how that happened. How could the house –
*our* house – have become *his* house so easily? Of course, I know
we could never have afforded this house without his great-
aunt's inheritance, but even so, I clean it; I buy furnishings;
I put things away; I plan and design the decor. Without me,
it would have remained just as his great-aunt left it; carriage
clock on the mantelpiece, china dogs, chintz wallpaper and
all. And yet, I feel like a ghost here, wandering from room to
room, marvelling at the life we had, never quite together.

I spent most of Monday evening in his office, at his keyboard,
trying not to feel guilty as I searched through his computer
files. On Tuesday, I sat on the sofa, eating cake and drinking
wine and watching TV in my pyjamas. On Wednesday, I had
my final singing lesson with Charlie. She wished me luck,

taught me a new breathing exercise, and told me she knew I'd be fabulous. And, on Thursday, I invited the girls here to an evening of cocktails, and laughter. It felt both thrilling and dangerous, like the midnight feasts at boarding school we used to read about in books. We talked about running, and music, and men, and when Martin finally phoned to find out why I hadn't phoned him earlier, we all shushed and giggled like schoolgirls so that he wouldn't suspect anything. And today –

Well, today, I went to the hairdresser's, and had my hair cut, not into my usual shoulder-length bob, but into a daring pixie cut, and coloured, not my usual brown, but a strident, joyous red. I love it. I might be someone else. And then I went home, and waxed my legs, and did my pelvic-floor exercises, and put on a black dress and patent heels, and Leonie's ruby at my throat, and went out to meet Iris. Not to our usual place, this time, but to the West End, and a tapas bar I'd read about in *Time Out*.

I'd chosen the place very carefully. Somewhere we wouldn't be recognized. I wanted it to be a nice place, because this would be our last meeting, and I also needed it to be safe, for what would happen afterwards.

Of course, Iris had no idea of what I was intending. My house was open, its mirrors bright; its doors flung wide and welcoming. It wasn't easy. It's hard not to see this as an act of betrayal. *And yet it must be done*, I thought. *There is no other solution. But how I'll miss her. How it hurts to lose the friend she has become.*

She came in late, as always, blithely turning heads as she came, in a lime-green minidress and boots. I'd already ordered cocktails. But my cocktails were alcohol-free. I needed a clear head tonight. I needed to be ruthless. I knew that the more she drank, the less she would notice my intervention. And

I'd kept myself so small for so long that she had no inkling I'd been hiding in her house for nearly two weeks, biding my time, secretly planning my strategy.

'Fuck me, Bernie, you're a redhead!' Iris is never subtle. Her greeting rang across the room, cutting through the ambient sound of many conversations. But her face had lit up like a slot machine, and I couldn't help laughing as she made her way through the crowded area towards our table.

'What does Martin think?' she said.

I told her Martin didn't know.

'Being single suits you. Are you sure you don't want to make it permanent?'

I laughed at that. But she has a point. Martin and I have been together for so long that for a time it was hard to believe that I could function without him. But recent events have made me feel that I could have another life. A different – maybe a *better* – life. It's not that I want to leave Martin. But I've enjoyed my freedom this week. I've enjoyed reclaiming our house. I've enjoyed reclaiming *myself*.

*It doesn't have to end,* says the voice of my innermost demon. *You don't have to go back to that life. You don't have to end it with Iris.*

And yet I do. I know it now. Iris is a problem. A problem only I can solve.

'How about the singing lessons?' she said. 'Ready for karaoke yet?'

'Not quite.' I've had nine lessons with Charlie so far, and at long last, I'm finding my voice. Using it still feels unsettling. As if it belongs to someone else. Before that, I'd never dared sing anywhere but in a choir. But it's like the running, I think. The hardest part's accepting that perhaps I'm a person who can sing.

'You'll be fine,' Iris said. 'What's the big deal with singing, anyway? You just open your mouth and make a noise.' She herself has no inhibitions at all about singing in public. She goes to a karaoke in a bar on Saturday nights, and can often be heard there singing 'I Will Survive' in the style of a punk Debbie Harry. 'Your problem, Bernie,' she went on, 'is that you have too many inhibitions. But stick with me, and we'll soon have you standing on tables and belting out "Dancing Queen" with your knickers round your ankles.'

I grinned. *God, I'm going to miss her.* 'Perhaps I just haven't found the right cocktail yet.' I sipped at my virgin mojito.

'Then let's make it our mission to find it,' she said. 'But first, let's order. I'm *starving*.' She waved a hand at the waiter. 'The sharing platter, please, my good man. And hurry, it's an emergency!'

I'd already tried the Sphinx Principle on Jared Noonan Philips. Of course, he'd been unaware of me then. This was more of a challenge. But I'd considered my plan for a long time, working out all the angles. And now, I meant to use this trick to solve my Iris problem.

*Now. While she's distracted. Now.*

I took a breath and reached for the part of myself that I had left dormant. I thought of it as a tiny splinter of reflective glass; a mirror, left inside her house, now ready to be deployed. A spyglass, that would allow me to search her mind while she was otherwise occupied, and make such changes as were necessary without alerting her to my presence.

I'd done it before, with Katie, after the business with Adam Price. In her case, it had been to shield her from the memory of what she had seen; with Iris, I was looking for more. And while she was ordering the food, I closed my eyes and went searching.

Iris has changed since the last time I looked. The little front room, with its knick-knacks, and pictures of hamsters, and pastel shades, is still in place, but behind it, her house has expanded, and its character has changed. The walls are concrete, emblazoned with slogans in neon colours. Some of the slogans read: *#YesAllMen*, or *#KillerQueens*, or simply, *NO*. And the doors at the back of her house – the doors that lead to damage – yawn open at deadly angles, revealing the grinning darkness beyond. From the darkness come flashes of sickening, red-neon light, revealing an interior built around a sinkhole –

*Oh, Iris. What have I done to you?*

There are rooms here, too; impossible rooms, held in place by nothing but air, and filled with the debris of a disintegrating personality. It's as if the fragment of Woody that has been lodged all this time in her mind has finally worked its way to her heart, causing destruction all the way. I know now what I have to do. I did it before, with Katie. But with Katie, the damage was small. With Iris, it is frightening. Can I hope to repair it now? Pull her back together? Close that yawping hole in her mind, from which come the voices of chaos?

For a moment, I wonder if I can. The damage seems catastrophic. But my skill has grown with use, and practice has empowered me. I start with closing some of those doors. Each one resists. The Iris I know does not want to go back into her box. And yet, it must be done. I have to extract the splinter from her heart. This Iris has no remorse, no shame. Her world is built on simple lines. Powers need to be deployed. Some people just deserve to die. And now that she knows how to deploy the power I ignited in her, how far would she take that theory?

*Please. I want to live*, whispers Iris' voice from the sinkhole. *You made me this way. You fixed me. You can't just walk away from me now.*

And now comes the plaintive voice of Jim Wood: *This is on you. You did this to me. Please, Bernie, don't kill me again.*

And finally, the voice of my inner demon: *This is what you get when you start believing you can change things.*

I bite my tongue and try to ignore the voices. Only closing the doors matters now. It's hard, but my powers have grown so much that all it takes is focus. One by one, the doors swing shut, cutting off that sickly light. Doors marked with the names of men, scrawled in neon colours. Doors with the names of Twitter trolls, and creeps, and douchebag exes. With every door, the house contracts, slowly resuming its original shape. The sinkhole narrows, the voices recede. I close the door marked *Crawley*. It protests like an infant. Then, the door marked *Jim from the Gym*. It closes with a whimper.

The light has changed. So has the ominous rushing of air from the sinkhole. Now I can see her front room again, its pastel shades; its clutter. The slogans on her walls have gone. *@irisnoir23* has disappeared. So has the damage that unleashed her rage; the memory of her assault and everything that followed it.

Last of all comes the door with my name. The room beyond it is cavernous. It's touching, to see how important I have become in Iris' life. But this is where the sinkhole lives. This is the source of the danger. This is where my mirrors reflect; where they have deployed their deadly heat. And yet, it's the seat of our friendship; of everything she has meant to me. Our nights out together. Our shopping trips. Our friendship. Her transformation. All these things will be lost, as soon as I close the door marked *Bernie*. I push against it, hard. It resists. The light above it flickers like the *Exit* sign at a nightclub door. I push against it once again. It sobs like a woman, then closes. The red light flickers one last time, then fades away. I seal it.

*Goodbye, Iris.*

The food had arrived. A sharing platter of hot wings, and fries, and pizza slices, and jalapeno poppers. Iris looked up at the waiter. Already, her expression had changed. The part of her that had become Woody's reflection has been eclipsed. She looked at the mountain of food with the air of someone awakening from sleep. Then she looked at me with barely a gleam of recognition.

'Wow, you must be hungry,' I said.

'Do I know you?'

I shook my head. 'You work in Priscilla's Pantry, right? I'm one of your morning regulars. I *really* love your hair, by the way.'

'Thanks,' said Iris, with a smile as innocent as it was heart-breaking. 'Yeah. I thought I'd treat myself.'

# 5

It feels like a bereavement. Iris has been such an important part of my life over the past couple of months that it's hard for me to imagine going on without her. I'll still have my friends from the club, of course, and Salena at the shop; but Iris was the only one who ever saw the whole of me. Who accepted the darkness as well as the light. But now she is herself again. She won't even remember me. Maybe she'll wonder what happened to the last two months of her memory; but she will recover in the end, and will suffer no permanent damage.

I left her in the tapas bar, and watched her from a distance. She thinks she has suffered an episode of alcoholic memory loss. The barman asks where her friend has gone, but she does not remember me. Nor does he – I took from his mind the details of my appearance. His name is Nathan. I check his house. He's kind. His concern is genuine. He makes sure Iris is OK, then gets her to a taxi. He does not ask for her number, though I sense he would like to. Maybe, if she decides to come back, they will meet up for a drink. I hope so. He's her type. And he has no secret vices. If she were to ask my advice, I'd tell her Nathan isn't a creep. He might even be a keeper.

Back at the empty house, I feel a quiet sense of completion. I take a shower, and apply body lotion to my tattoo. Rosie was right: it has healed rapidly, without even leaving a layer of dry skin. I wonder what Martin will think of it. I wonder if he'll see me.

*And if he doesn't? If he laughs? If he thinks you're ridiculous? If he sees your tattoo and thinks you're off your fucking trolley?* The words are brutal, but in Iris' absence, the voice is calm and rational.

Well, if that happens, I tell myself, I will not go quietly back to my box. Whatever I do, I will not do that. Never again will I be a ghost in my own house. Never again will I take second place to a decades-old fantasy. On Saturday night, I will make him look. It's up to him what happens then. For now, I'm very tired, and I have a train in the morning. Let's see what happens on Saturday. On Saturday. *Tomorrow.*

*Tonight.*

# TRACK 12:

---

# Mirrors

Which will it be tomorrow? The man who
kisses my forehead and holds me when I fall
asleep? Or the man in the castle on the cliff,
with its rooms all filled with secrets?
*From the LiveJournal of Bernadette Ingram (marked as*
*Exhibit BI 1):*
*May 1st, 2022*

The truth was a mirror in the hands of God.
It fell and broke into pieces. Everybody took a
piece of it, and they looked at it and thought
they had the truth.
*Rumi*

# I

*From the LiveJournal of Bernadette Ingram (marked as Exhibit BI 1):*
*Saturday, June 4th, 2022*

Don't lie. You knew it would come to this. You, in your party dress, sitting there, a glass of champagne in your hand. This room. This sound of breaking glass. This light. This scent of blood and roses. And me, in my magician's disguise, caught in the spotlight as the drum rolls, and the crowd holds its breath, and hopes, and believes, even though they already know that everything will come crashing down . . .

There's a word for this feeling. *Svaha.* It means the interval of time between the completion of an act and its inevitable consequence – the space between lightning and thunder. When I was a little girl, head under the blankets during a storm, I used to hold my breath and count, and wait for the sound of thunder. Thunder was what frightened me, although I knew the lightning was worse. Lightning can kill you faster than you even know it's happening. That's because light travels faster than sound. As soon as you see the lightning flash, the strike has already happened. You just haven't heard it yet. You have to let it take its course. What's left is the space between the two, that breathless space where you can pretend – if only for a few seconds – that everything's still possible. You can even manage to fool yourself that, this time, it won't happen; that somehow the universe will stop, keeping all the mirrors intact, suspending the crystal in mid-air, never to fall, never to smash, like stars hanging in the vacuum of space.

But you always knew, didn't you? It has taken thirty years, but you always saw this coming. The future – our future – was already here. And here you are, in your high-heeled shoes and lamé dress, and Mother's pearls, looking like a child again with your Dutch-doll face and bobbed black hair reflected in the mirror glass, and a wall of flames in your smoke-dark eyes. Nothing else is real anymore.

Everything else is *svaha*.

# 2

*Extract from Class of '92, by Kate Hemsworth*
*(published by LifeStory Press, 2023)*

You think you know what happened on the night of the Pog Hill reunion. Over the past twelve months, the Press has rationalized everything, put it all into neat little compartments. The truth is messier than that. The truth always is. And yet, we all know the timeline. That has been well established. Bernie travelled north on the train. She went first-class – there are deals at weekends. The trolley assistant remembers her largely because she was so polite. Not everyone is polite to trolley assistants on trains.

*She seemed like such a nice lady*, she says. *She just sat there and read a book. I brought her tea and biscuits – they're complimentary in first class – and she seemed so surprised. I remember thinking: there's a woman who deserves more nice surprises.*

She took the train from King's Cross to Wakefield Westgate, then took a cab to the Premier Inn a few miles outside Malbry. It's about a half-hour drive, and she took the cabbie's number so she could call him later. Then she texted Martin.

*I'm running a little late. Meet you there?*

Then, she took a long bath, did her pelvic-floor exercises, put on her make-up and her dress while doing the vocal exercises her singing coach had taught her – by now it was getting towards 7.00 – and took a selfie. Yes, *that* one – the one you've seen again and again. She sent it to four of her friends on WhatsApp, along with the message: *Yowza night!* – and then sent it to an inactive Twitter account named *@irisnoir23*, with a more cryptic message:

*@theberniemoon: Here I am now. This is me. Time for me to take the stage. Whatever happens, thank you. I think the Great Carovnik would be proud.*

And then, as you know, she called her cab and made her way to Pog Hill Prom, the ruby at her throat sending out tiny flashes of secret fire.

# 3

*Extract from Class of '92, by Kate Hemsworth*
*(published by LifeStory Press, 2023)*

Some places are just magical. Perhaps it's the style of the archi-
tecture; or the breadth of the gardens; or the sense of history
that hangs like scented wisteria over the doors. Pog Hill House
was one of those; a large, late-Victorian red-brick pile that
had once been a girls' school. It stands in its own grounds,
surrounded by paths of azaleas and rhododendrons, with a long,
sweeping entrance of iron gates that leads to the grand stone
steps by way of an avenue of cherry trees. The cherry trees
were no longer in bloom; but the azaleas were blossoming, and
the avenues between the trees were garlanded with strings of
sparkling solar lights.

I'd thought it pretty in '92. But now the magic had grown,
somehow, from something purely aesthetic to something
steeped in nostalgia. I'd expected to feel nostalgic, of course –
doesn't every woman feel that for the girl she was at eighteen?
But what I hadn't expected to feel was this potent grief for
who I once was. Of course, I hadn't been back since the day
all of us came in for A level results – all of us except Bernie
Moon, whose pregnancy made her row of As as useless as the

wedding dress passed down from her mother. But coming back to Pog Hill now, I found it practically unchanged. The trees are a little taller now; the doors a different shade of paint. But the places that matter – the theatre, the gym, the little lake, the playing fields – all those were just as they'd always been. A reminder, perhaps, of a state of grace.

I'd kept my distance from it all until the night of the party. Lucas and his friends from the band had been planning it for months, along with some old friends on Facebook – Martin Ingram included. I pretended support, while hoping that something would happen to make the planned reunion impossible. But weeks passed, then months, and the plans had become increasingly hard to escape. The band assembled (minus Martin, of course) to practise in our basement. The front room began to fill with brochures from Lorelei's party planner's. Lucas spent hours every day on the phone – or on FaceTime, or WhatsApp – talking to friends about menus, and cocktails, and fashions, and games. He got our children involved, and engaged the local crèche to set up a side room for younger attendees. He really tried to get me involved, and when I still remained aloof, assumed I was shy about singing. Of course that wasn't why. But the thought of getting back up on that stage, and wearing my lamé dress again, was enough to give me the shivers. And yet he kept pushing me. *Wear the dress. Sing for us. You were so brilliant last time.*

But Lucas isn't very bright. I don't mean that in a cruel way, but Lucas is a simple soul, who likes rough and tumble, and nights out with the boys. And being the way he is, he assumed my reluctance had something to do with Adam Price, and what happened between us at the original Pog Hill Prom.

*If you're worried that freak'll be there, you can rest easy*, he told me. *He wouldn't dare show his face again. He knows I've got his number.*

Poor Lucas. It was never his fault. And he never knew about Martin. It would have changed things if he'd known; made them complicated. Why hurt him that way, when we could just go on as if nothing had happened? And, to be honest, I hadn't even thought about Adam Price for years. I know how that must make me sound, but I promised to tell you everything.

After what happened at Pog Hill Prom, he lost his job at the college and was put on a sex offenders' register. He wasn't prosecuted, but the conditions of his release after the fire at his foster home meant that even a small infraction could mean serious trouble for Adam. I understand he spoke to the police on the night of the prom. They told me he'd admitted to stalking me on campus. They told me he'd even admitted to following me home, saying; *I wanted to be in her house, that's all. Her house was so pretty.*

I didn't ask myself at the time what he'd really meant by that. I was simply glad to be rid of him. To me, he was a reminder of an unpleasant moment in an otherwise wonderful evening, and a memory of something that made me feel uncomfortable. Where he went after that; what he did, and whether or not he survived, it was really none of my business. Except that it was. I see that now. I see it all so clearly.

Sometimes, trauma shuts you down. The memory of trauma. In Adam's case, what happened that day around the toy box at Chapel Lane had been too much to process. Not the things I'd seen in his mind – those awful pictures of abuse, hunger, hatred and neglect. Not even what Adam had done to *me* in his rage and confusion. The thing I couldn't accept was what I had done to Adam Price. I had violated him. Overridden his consent. And yes, I was a *nice* girl. Adam was the *bad* boy. And yet, I had done the terrible thing. I had taken over his house. Robbed him of all agency. Taken his body and made it do anything I wanted. I'd made out it was a game at first, just like any other abuser. But I had always known what it was. And after that, I'd pushed it down so far that I'd convinced myself that *I*, and not *he*, was the victim.

It all began to unravel when Martin came to stay with us. Lucas had embraced the idea, mostly because it would help with the band, but also because he imagined that Martin would persuade me to sing. 'You've always got on with Martin,' he said. 'You always had that chemistry.'

And so I agreed to sing on the night, and threw myself into the planning. Bernie's mother was helping with the catering – she'd always liked that aspect of social gatherings. And Dante had come to stay with her – it was her eightieth birthday the following week, and she was having a party of her own. And so, between various party plans, I was able to make my space. And as the Saturday grew close, I started to think that maybe I could even enjoy it a little.

I got to the party at seven o'clock. The band had finished their sound check. Martin was on bass – he'd had to borrow a guitar from a friend – and he was wearing his usual black, though his hair was greying now, and short. Otherwise, he looked startlingly similar: grey eyes under small wire glasses, prominent cheekbones, wry mouth. As I said, not really my type; but I suppose you could see the attraction. Lucas has gained a lot of weight over the past thirty years. He played rugby when he was young, and still has that rugby-player's frame, but a lot of the muscle has turned to fat through too many pizzas and pitchers of beer. I don't mind this. I like it, in fact. It feels like the sign of a life well-spent. Lucas is soft and comfortable. Martin, by comparison, is awkward, brittle, gangly.

He smiled at me as I came in. I pretended not to see. He'd been staying with us since Monday, sleeping in the studio Lucas uses as a rec room. It was less awkward than you might think. I was out most of the day, so we were never alone together, and as soon as Lucas got home from work, they would go and sit in the studio, drink beer, play games on the PlayStation. It was like hosting a kids' sleepover. And Lucas – he was over the moon. He was just like a child again. I left them to it, and made my own plans. But now, at the reunion, there was no escaping them. And Martin had told us that Bernie would be meeting us later –

The band wasn't due to play until nine, but there would be a DJ, and drinks, and canapés, and dancing. Lucas was Master of Ceremonies. After all, it had been his idea to have the reunion in the first place. We'd had over three hundred replies to the original Facebook post; over five hundred tickets sold. Everyone I'd known at Pog Hill, and all the old crowd from Mulberry House; Lorelei Jones, Kate Lindsey, Jenny Ashford, Linda Kite. Even Ms Langley was there – the old Headmistress, now retired, but still active on the Board of Governors – as well as a smattering of some of the younger Pog Hill members of staff.

I scanned the faces from the stage. I recognized some, not all; but the one I was seeking wasn't there. There was no sign of Bernie Moon. Not then, as the party began, and not at nine, when the band was to start. I wasn't altogether surprised – Martin had already told us that she was running late. Besides, I knew there were reasons she might not want to see me. And so I danced, and drank cocktails, and tried very hard not to listen for the sound of approaching thunder.

# 4

*Extract from Class of '92, by Kate Hemsworth*
*(published by LifeStory Press, 2023)*

Meanwhile, Bernie Ingram – or Bernie Moon, she was that night, according to the photoboards that lined the Pog Hill entrance hall – was standing in the shelter of a bank of azaleas that bloomed against the falling dusk like the shoulder of a thundercloud. Perhaps she was waiting to make her entrance. Perhaps she just wanted to enjoy the quiet of the evening. It was still quite light, and the air was filled with the scent of smoke and roses. I know; just as I know that there was a single ardent point of light in the sky; the evening star was rising. I know she was thinking about a night thirty years ago, when the same fairy lights hung from the trees, and the same music filtered through the open French doors of the concert hall. I know she was cold, just as I know she also told herself: *One minute more. One minute more, before it begins. One minute more, before the show.*

There's no point explaining how I know. Just stay with me for this. OK? Bernie Moon and I have the kind of history that can never be erased; the kind that dates to when magic was as easy as maths. She took out her phone and checked Martin's Facebook. Then she checked Twitter, where *#Gendercide* was trending.

*@drdoodad816: 53% of the mothers of boys with GENDER IDENTITY DISORDER have Borderline Personality Disorder or symptoms of depression. Crazy mothers mess up little boys regarding their male gender identity. #Gendercide*

*@whitey2947: i know right they start with the kids then fuck up the men #Gendercide #FeminismIsCancer*

He then goes on to post a picture of himself, aged seven or so. It's a small, grainy, dog-eared photograph, which has been cut from something else. From a class photograph, actually, taken that winter at Chapel Lane. I have one of my own, although it isn't on display. But then, I had other photographs of myself at seven years old. Adam Price did not. He had kept this one with him all this time. Bernie Moon had kept hers in a little silver frame at home. She has it still, though the silver frame has since been used for something else. But it shows the whole of 1W – Adam Price included – sitting cross-legged on the story mat, with Bernie and I looking like twins, sitting together on the far right.

'Are you not going in?'

The voice made her look up from her mobile screen. A woman – in her seventies – was standing on the footpath. White-haired, thin, high-cheekboned, and wearing a beaded black cocktail dress that looked like twenties vintage.

'*Mum?*' said Bernie.

The woman frowned. 'I think you must have – *Bernie?*' For a moment, the two of them stood, each watching the other, in silence. 'Your *hair*,' said Bernie's mother. 'I almost didn't know you. You look so different. Have you lost weight?'

Bernie smiled. 'I don't think so.'

'Well, it suits you, whatever it is. Come here. Let me give you a hug.'

Bernie's mother felt to her like an armful of birds in her cocktail dress. She smelt of a floral perfume that reminded her somehow of Iris. And the dress; it looked familiar, like something from childhood, and the memory of the cedarwood with which she lined her wardrobe. 'That dress. I think I've seen it before. Is that –'

'*The Dress?*' Her mother shrugged. 'I had it dyed black for tonight. I thought I might as well wear it, given that no one will need it now.' She paused and looked at Bernie. 'You could have told me. That Dante was – you know – *same-sex-attracted.*'

'Mum, it wasn't for me to say.'

'I suppose not.' There was a long pause. 'I'm glad you decided to come,' she went on. 'I didn't want Dante to tell you. They found something in my pancreas. It's probably nothing. You know what they're like.'

For a moment, they both stood in silence. Then Bernie took a step forward and took her mother once more in her arms. 'Why didn't you tell me?' she said. 'All those times we spoke on the phone –'

'You know I don't like phone calls. And anyway, I knew you'd be here. I thought you'd be coming with Martin. I nearly didn't recognize you.'

Bernie sighed. *Here it comes*, she thought.

'I think a woman can really come into her own at meno-pause. Look at you. You're blossoming. I hope that man of yours understands just how *fucking* lucky he is.' She gave a surprisingly dirty laugh, as if to acknowledge the irony. From inside came the sound of the band as it launched into the first number of the evening.

'They're starting,' said Bernie's mother. 'We should go in and listen.' She saw Bernie hesitate, and went on: 'Come on, love. Let's do this. We can have a proper chat tomorrow.'

# 5

*Extract from Class of '92, by Kate Hemsworth*
*(published by LifeStory Press, 2023)*

I'd made an effort for Lucas, but I was feeling my age that
night. Perhaps because of that lamé dress, which was a little
too tight for me; perhaps because of Martin. And when I sang,
I didn't hear the whisper of future audiences, but the way my
voice wavered on the high notes. Unlike Bernie, I hadn't had
time for vocal exercises. But I was with friends: the audience
was prepared to be lenient. I walked up to the mike and sang
the four songs I had sung the night of the original prom, and
everyone hooted and whistled, and it should have been magical.

But it wasn't. It felt horribly flat. My head hurt, and Lucas
was raucous in his introductions, and Martin's bass was much too
loud, and the keyboards were overwhelming. My vocals through
the backline sounded like the voice of an unhappy drunk singing
'I Will Survive' at a staff social. I hated it. I hated *them*. Most of
all I hated *him* – still so much alive in my memory that at first
I failed to notice Adam Price watching me from the wings, his
tinselly eyelashes shining in the greenish glow of the exit sign.

Adam Price. The ghost in the wings. His presence was inevitable. We'd all slid effortlessly back into our eighteen-year-old

selves: Lorelei Jones, making bitchy remarks about how fat her friends had got over the years; Kate Lindsey, who'd always worshipped her, laughing even though the joke was on her; and Lucas playing the joker; and Martin Ingram, all dark and aloof, and looking almost amused at it all. All of us had partners and friends, family members and spouses there. Bernie's mother was in the crowd. Dante was there somewhere, too. My mother, Maggie, was there as well, watching me, and telling everyone how I could have been a famous actress if only I hadn't devoted my life to looking after my family. Everywhere you looked there were familiar faces, neighbours and friends, and people we had known from school, looking both different and unchanged, touched with that special magic. And then there was Adam, watching us all from his hiding place backstage, a harlequin of reflected light, his hands clenched into desperate fists over nails bitten down to the quick.

Some people are almost invisible. Adam Price was one of them. We'd never noticed him much when he was working as the caretaker's help, and we didn't notice him that night, even when he was standing so close that you could have reached out and touched him. Why would we? We were gilded. Adam Price wasn't one of us. Adam Price had never been anything but ugly and dull. Adam Price had never had friends with whom to be reunited, or family to applaud him, or any talent to applaud. Adam Price had never had anyone see him properly, or look beyond his ugliness and anger to the heart of him.

Except maybe one person. She too had been an outsider. She too had been unhappy and shy. She too had been robbed of some part of her childhood. She saw him standing in the wings, looking old, and yet so young, like a boy under a curse from some cruel story. And he saw *her*, from his shadows, and something passed between them. No one else recognized her at first − no, not even Martin. People stared, though. How could they not? Nothing was left of that awkward girl we used to call *Weird Bernie*. In her blood-red evening dress, her hair dyed a screaming scarlet, she stood out in the audience like something from a fairy tale. And when she stepped up to the stage, parting the crowd like the Red Sea, I suddenly saw who she was. I *knew*, just as everyone else suddenly *knew*; and the crowd fell silent in her wake like an avenue of fallen trees.

*Abracadabra.*

I know. You think I'm imagining it. You think all this tragic episode comes from some kind of mass hysteria. But that's how it has always been, with women and their power. Women's voices, so often dismissed as weak or unreliable. But there was no hysteria then. We looked at each other. I saw her. And seeing her, I saw myself; older now; disappointed; wearing an outmoded lamé dress that was too tight to be flattering. I saw my life − so small, so safe − as precious as a snow globe. And I knew that she could take it all. Smash it open, blast it apart with one glance of those black-light eyes, and I felt so close to extinction that I could almost smell the smoke −

But none of that happened. She didn't stop. She didn't hesitate at all. Instead, she simply walked on past me, and, pausing only to drop a sheet of music in front of the piano, she took my place in the spotlight, and smiled, and said to the silent audience:

'Last time, I sat and watched this show from the shadows. I was ashamed. Ashamed of being pregnant, ashamed of being plain, ashamed of forsaking my power. This time, I'd like to put it right, if you'll excuse the drama. I've spent my life waiting for someone to see who I really am. Whether he will, or whether he won't, I thought I was here now because of him. But I'm here tonight because of me: because of Bernie Moon, as was. I owe it to her to sing this song; the song I should have sung years ago. Thank you for this moment, and for giving me my chance again.'

And then she looked at Andrew Whelan, who was sitting at the piano, and he nodded, and started to play the intro to Neneh Cherry's 'Manchild'. A few seconds later, Joss Lively on drums joined with an easy hip-hop beat. It wasn't quite like the record – but Andrew could sight-read, and he gave it his best shot. Even Martin joined on bass – the beat was easy to follow, and the chords were simple enough. And she sounded *good*. Not professional, but in tune, expressive, in control. I could see everyone watching her – my mother, Dante, Lorelei; Martin, from his place on the stage – as if they just couldn't believe it.

And yes, for a razor-slice of time, everything was as it should have been all those sunlit years ago: every piece of crockery, every crystal dish in place, the lights reflected in her eyes like a falling chandelier. I want you to see that, before I go on. Really see it. *Look* at her. Look very hard at Bernie Moon, being herself for the very first time since Life took the spotlight away from her and gave it to another. Before we hear the thunder, I want you to imagine that it was good, and the lightning flash was only the flash of mirrors, heliographing applause –

*Svaha.*

# 6

*Extract from Class of '92, by Kate Hemsworth*
*(published by LifeStory Press, 2023)*

Now for the part you've been waiting for. You'll probably not believe it. It's already filtered through so many layers of horror and feeling and sorrow and fear that, as a witness statement, it probably has no value. But it's *our* story – hers and mine. So here I am telling it in her place, even though some parts are missing.

I'd been feeling bloated and hormonal all day. I'd assumed it was because I'd slept badly: approaching menopause has caused a number of symptoms, which my GP is trying not to address, by telling me to *wait and see* before I opt for HRT. Wait and see for what? you ask. But that's the disadvantage of having had the same doctor for so long. He still treats me like a child who needs to be told what's good for her. But as I began my part of the set, I'd begun to feel a familiar cramping in my lower abdomen. *Damn.* I'd had irregular bleeding over the past twelve months or so, but for the past three or four there had been no flow at all. In a way, it was a relief. But I still knew the symptoms. Those cramps. The bloating that made my lamé dress feel so tight that evening. Even the changes in my voice. *What fucking perfect timing.* It might have been why I felt angry, too. Angry at Lucas for making me sing; angry at Martin for being there; angry at all the rest of them for their ridiculous applause; angry at myself. And most unfairly of all, angry at *her*, for making such an effortless connection with the audience; for looking so good; for having survived the pain of adolescence.

I felt a rush of blood to my face. *Oh wonderful. A fucking hot flash.*

I had to stay: I couldn't just walk off as Bernie was taking her bow. But now the sweat was trickling down from my hairline into my eyes, and I could feel my carefully applied eyeliner heading south. And the applause for her song went on and on, longer than for any of mine, and then she turned and looked at me. Not at Martin, who was still staring as if he'd been turned to stone, but right at me. *Into* me. And I could see my anger there, reflected in her shining eyes, and feel the heat coming from her like a lightning strike of energy –

*Hello, Katie.*

And then I was there. There in her house. As if I'd never gone away; as if we were still magical. And she was in mine; I could feel her there, thinking: *Oh you bitch, how you hurt me. Can you see how you made me feel? Do you see me, Katie?*

I'd known her house forty years ago as a small and comfortable place. Now it was almost unimaginably vast. Of course, we grow. All of us do. We collect mountains of baggage. And here was Bernie's, in the form of this space that could hardly be called a house anymore. It was like a cathedral of memories; treasures hoarded and kept within; ossuaries of buried bones; spires and stairways and chapels and crypts. I wasn't afraid. I know it sounds odd, but I knew those doors would open for me; even the doors that were sealed away. And I could feel her sorrow, her rage, like a blast of inner heat, and the sweat came in sequins onto my arms, and all her doors swung open –

And I saw Grace, and Mr D, and myself, all so very young in there, all so very gilded. And I saw Bernie Moon as was; *Weird Bernie,* with the haunted eyes. And I saw the Great Carovnik, the magic show we'd seen as kids; how deeply it had marked her. And I saw her mother, and *The Dress* put away in a wardrobe; and Father Tom's disappointment; and Mrs Harding's lectures. And I saw women with names like Salena, and Iris, and Leonie, and Alex; women whose faces were friendly and kind, dancing like fireflies in the dark. And I saw Adam Price, and the way she'd tried to shield me from what I'd seen in him, and how she'd tried to take away the horror of that trespass. And I saw Dante as a boy; Dante as a young man; a thousand memories kept under glass, unfaded in his absence. And, of course, I saw Martin. I could hardly have avoided him. He was everywhere; every part of her seemed devoted to him. He was in the stained glass, and in the statues, and in the floors. In the cathedral of her mind, Martin's presence sounded out like a giant organ; his voice was like incense pouring from the censers. It was astonishing. Like being in the belly of the whale. And it was terrible, as well. Terrible that *this* is how she saw him – how she saw *me* – how she saw what had happened between us, all those years ago.

So many years of longing. So many years of aching guilt. So many years of wasted friendship and comfort, forgiveness and warmth. I couldn't bear it. She had to know. I couldn't carry its weight anymore. And so I opened up to her, those doors I'd thought were gone for good. I let her see what had happened, the night Martin Ingram walked me home, when we were students together.

# 7

*Extract from Class of '92, by Kate Hemsworth*
*(published by LifeStory Press, 2023)*

*She knows he likes her. She always has, ever since that night at the*
*Pog Hill Prom. The time he saved her from Adam Price. Her knight*
*in shining armour.* Except that it was all a fake, and Adam hadn't
done anything wrong. His only crime was to be there at a time
when she was feeling vulnerable.

It's funny how we often reframe our trauma as third-person
narrative. It's so much easier to think of oneself as a fictional
character than admit to events that happened to us in the real
world. And we tell these stories to ourselves over and over,
until, at last, even we believe they're true.

I remember it all. It was the time of that dreadful murder
on Woodhouse Moor; the big public park near the centre of
Leeds. Her name was Anna something, and her body had been
found less than a mile from the student house I was sharing
with four other girls. Martin had been watching me dancing
throughout the evening, and I knew that if I asked him to,
he'd walk me back safely over the Moor. I also knew that he
had a bit of a crush on me – had had it ever since that night –
and I was young enough to enjoy the power I had over him.

It was one of those warm spring nights that sometimes come out of nowhere. Even then, late as it was, there was still a trace of that warmth in the air, and besides, I'd been dancing; my cheeks were aflame; the stars were like a wheel of light all across the midnight sky.

'Walk me home?' I said, and smiled.

'Of course,' he said; ever the gentleman.

And so we walked back over the Moor, and he talked; and I watched the stars, and danced to my own inner music. And then, he came in for a coffee, to the sleepy surprise of the girls, who were sitting in the common room listening to music, and he and I went into my room, and stayed there until morning.

*I think it's time you left*, she says, seeing him taking his shoes off. There's something indecent about it, she thinks, although she herself has been barefoot for the past half-hour. *I've got a lecture tomorrow at nine.*

*Shhh*, he tells her. *Shhh, come here. Let's just talk.*

And yes, she tries. Really she does. She tries to say: *What about Bernie?* But words don't seem to stop him. *Bernie isn't here*, he says. *You're here, and you're astonishing.*

And now his hands are all over her, and she pulls away from him. She starts to say: *No, Martin*, but the thought of his reaction, and the looks on the faces of her friends as he walks back through the common room, is enough to give her pause. He pulls her back into his arms, and kisses her neck, and whispers: *Bernie isn't here, Kate. She never was. It was always you. My dreamgirl. Dreamgirl Katie.*

Something in her shuts down at that. She knows she's drunk too much to talk back. And then she thinks of Adam Price, and how hard he protested his innocence, and of what the others will say if Martin decides to tell his friends about his date with Kate Malkin. And she thinks maybe she asked for it, and maybe she isn't the good girl her mother always said she was.

*It's only sex*, she tells herself. It's not as if she's a virgin. And some dates are bad. That's all, she thinks: there is no need for drama. One bad date in exchange for the thing he did the night of the Pog Hill Prom. One bad date, that's all. Not rape. Just one, silly, trivial incident.

I'd pushed the memory deep, deep down. Right to the very back of my house, bound up in spider silk, like a cocoon. But Bernie found it all the same. I felt her unpicking the woven strands with delicate, inhuman fingers.

*It wasn't rape*, they whisper to her. *It wasn't his fault. It was mine.*

But isn't that what all victims say? Don't we all try to blame ourselves? Victimhood is all about shame. We both know that, Bernie and I. And shame and blame are sisters, so close that they might almost be twins. Maybe that's why we push these things down. We build secret rooms to contain them. But sometimes, the poison spreads. And sometimes it bursts open –

He left in the morning, just before nine. I made him a cup of coffee. And then I took a long, long shower, and made the bed, and felt just fine – until I found the condom where he had dropped it on the floor, and I began to tremble. *At least he used a condom*, I'd thought. *That proves it can't be rape. Right?*

They call it *stealthing* nowadays. The slipping off of the condom during intercourse, without telling the girl, or asking for consent. Some men think of it as a game, although it's a violation. And when, four weeks later, I realized my period was overdue, I made all the arrangements without a word to anyone, and had the unwanted packet of cells flushed out of my body, and never looked back, or gave it a thought –

I believed I'd banished the memory. But now I see that all I did was bury it deep, and hope it would die. I buried it deep in the place where I had buried Adam Price, along with the guilt of what I had done. And in that place, I buried the feeling that I'd deserved it, deserved the violation because I'd done the same to Adam. And then, instead of facing my guilt, I'd let them accuse an innocent. I'd let an innocent take the blame for the fear I'd pushed down inside me.

And now I can feel those cramps bite deep under the belt of my lamé dress, and the shame and self-hatred that comes with the blood makes me want to curl up and die. *It was Martin,* I tell her. *Martin, and not Adam, who stole away my childhood. I'm not the Katie you thought I was. She was only ever a dream.*

And then her presence is gone from my house, and I am fully myself again. The whole exchange has taken seconds, that's all, although it feels as if we've been on stage together, awaiting this moment, for thirty years. She turns towards me. She opens her arms. The crowd is still applauding. It feels as if it could go on forever.

And now, at last, comes the lightning strike. The figure from the darkened wings. It's Adam Price, who has watched us both throughout this strange performance. Adam Price, whose house I'd seen when magic was as easy as maths.

*Your house was nicer than mine,* he'd said, on the night of that other prom. And yes, it was true. My house *was* nice. My life was nice. Adam's was not. Horribly abused as a child; passed from one foster home to the next; friendless; unhappy; his anger had grown; a monster in a labyrinth. And I had violated his space, I had trespassed without his consent; looked into his house and mocked the stunted secrets that grew there. *Look at me! I'm a princess!* Poor Adam. No one looked at *him*. Forced into my house, seeing the life he'd been denied – the loving parents, the good marks at school, the best friend, the many toys, good meals, the stories at bedtime. No wonder he'd been angry. No wonder he'd tried to recapture that. No wonder he'd watched me, longed for me, finally grown to *hate* me, first throughout my days at Pog Hill, and then, to this stage, to this audience; to this thunderous resolution.

The *Malbry Examiner*'s headline reads: *Local Man in Pog Hill Attack 'May Have Been Radicalized', Say Police.* The *Daily Mail* presents it as *Death By Social Media.*

But what everyone agrees on is this: that Adam Price had fallen deep into the MK2 rabbit hole. Poor Adam – or *@whitey2947*, as he liked to call himself – believed in the Gender Wars and chemical cancellation; drank *RippedinSix* by the jugful, and had, until recently, subscribed to Jim Wood's newsletter and YouTube channel. *A troll*, they called him, who'd taken his dispute out into the real world. Others maintain that he was just expressing his freedom of speech.

*He wanted to make a difference*, says Jared Noonan Philips, writing for *UnHerd*. *That gesture ended in tragedy. But who is to say who bears the ultimate responsibility for this act of desperation? Price, the convenient scapegoat, or a society already riddled with the cancer of toxic femininity?*

Whichever it was, the man had a knife. Only a box-cutter, but it was sharp, and in his hand, it looked big enough to contain a whole world. He *sidled*, rather than charged at her, with that look of confusion and rage that had so characterized him as a boy. He looked a lot older than we were then. His hair was white; his face was red; and in spite of my fear at the knife in his hand, I felt a terrible pity for him, although it was hard to understand whether the feeling was Bernie's or mine.

For a moment, he stood there, wavering, pinned like a moth in the spotlight. The silence around us was deafening. The blade of the knife seemed to reflect everything I'd ever lived.

'You were the one,' he said, in a voice that seemed to belong to a small child. '*You* did this. You fucked me up. You and the other *Exes*. Jim Wood knew the truth. He said so in his final blog. He said you'd got to him at last. *He* knew who the monsters were.'

For a moment, Bernie looked at him. She seemed completely unafraid. In her high-heeled shoes, she towered over him like a monolith.

'I know it feels that way, Adam,' she said.

'How the *fuck* can you know how I feel?' His voice was a shapeless, angry wail.

*Trust me. I just know*, she said.

And for a second – which felt like so much longer than that – we were both in Adam's house. And I was surprised, because Adam's house hadn't really changed. It was still small; so small that I was surprised at how huge it had seemed when I was a child; how frightening. Now all I felt was pity, and a surge of terrible sadness. Because Adam, too, was a victim. The poor, stunted victim of both of us. Blamed for everything as a child; blamed for being bad; for being hungry; for seeking something better. And when he didn't find it, blamed for being angry; blamed for being dull; forever unloved and forsaken; Adam, the scapegoat, the monster; the troll in a house of strangers.

'How the fuck can you know?' he said. Now there were tears running down his face. The blade in his hand was scary-bright, and shining like a mirrorball.

*Come here*, Bernie said to him. I don't think she was using words.

For a moment, he wavered, the tears on his face reflecting the coloured stage lights. And in those reflections I saw Bernie's house, running like we used to run when magic was as easy as maths. And I saw the realization there of what Martin had done to us, and of what we'd done to Adam Price, and of how the cycle perpetuates. And I saw the stained-glass windows running down the cathedral walls, and the statues sifting into sand, and the words going up like incense smoke. And Bernie said: *Come here*, and it felt almost like forgiveness.

Then Adam lunged forward, and Bernie Moon gathered him gently into her arms, and they fell together onto the stage in a billow of scarlet fabric.

# 8

*Extract from Class of '92, by Kate Hemsworth*
*(published by LifeStory Press, 2023)*

After that, everything happened at once. I remember the lights going down; the safety curtain crashing. Martin, at the top of his voice, shouting for a doctor. Lucas saying: *Is that blood?* in a voice that sounded high and far away; the cramps in my belly twisting like a vicious corkscrew in my gut. Andrew and Joss had already pinned Adam to the ground, but there was no sign of a weapon now, and Adam wasn't moving. I tried to get to Bernie, but there were already too many people there, crowding the apron in front of the stage. I closed my eyes and reached for her: and there was her house again, just as it had been years ago, when we were friends.

*Thank God, Bernie. I thought you were —*

But something was happening inside Bernie's house. It felt like a kind of gorgeous cascade; a splash of suspended crockery. Dishes, vases, bon-bon jars, chandeliers, cut-glass goblets. All The Great Carovnik's show: the banqueting table, the table-cloth, the banks of hidden mirrors reflecting the salvage ten fathoms deep, throwing doors and windows open. It felt like being inside a great kaleidoscope of coloured glass; mirrors at every angle; every one reflecting a world. For a second, it hung there, as gorgeous as a raindrop on a rose.

*Look. Now. Look at yourself.*

Her voice in my mind was very clear. And I knew that every person there had heard it just as I had. Some of them denied it, of course. *Most* of them denied it. But none of them could deny the changes that happened afterwards. The men, who for the first time *really* started to think about the lives of the women in their lives; their lived experience. The damaged women, whose fear of men had made them blind to their own bigotry, now seeing for the first time that our bodies need not define us. Shy women who feared to speak out, suddenly finding their voices. Secretly abusive men, brought to their knees by the realization of what they have done. Even bewildered little boys, hating women for laughing at them, and hating themselves even more. Everyone in that room heard the voice. Everyone saw the kaleidoscope. A perfect circle in the air, like a cathedral rose window.

And then it shattered. It pulverized; sending out shards of consciousness to every person in the room. I found myself falling backwards. So did every person there. It felt like an explosion, as if a bomb had gone off on stage. There came a sound like the thunder of a million doors blowing inwards at once – and then there was nothing at all but the sound of sirens, and the hum of the crowd, and the sudden blurt of menstrual blood running down my inner thigh. I didn't need to move closer now. I didn't need to see Martin's face, or hear him calling out her name in a voice as raw as childhood: I knew. My friend was just an empty house. Bernie Moon was already gone.

*Gone where?* I knew you'd ask, but I don't think you'll like the answer. You see, there are no answers here; only more reflections. Hundreds, thousands, millions of them, stretching out across the years. Hundreds and thousands of changes; of tables turned; of lives reversed. And those changes extend far beyond this school hall in Pog Hill. In a pub in East Finchley, the Finchley Fliers feel the crash. In her little bedsit flat, Iris half remembers. Jared Noonan Philips stops to wonder for a moment why his daughter never speaks to him. An unknown man in a baseball cap suddenly feels that maybe he has been forgiven.

The Persian poet Rumi says: *The truth was a mirror in God's hands. It fell and broke into pieces. Everyone took a piece of it, and looked at it, and thought they had the truth.* Well, maybe Bernie was something like that. A mirror in the hands of God. She could make people see themselves in ways no other person could. And when she finally saw the truth – the truth about Adam, and Martin, and me; the truth about herself – she shattered into pieces. Beautiful pieces of broken light, like fragments of a kaleidoscope, that flew into everyone who was there: men, women and everything in between. Everyone in the hall that night; everyone behind the scenes.

Into Lorelei Jones, a shard of unexpected empathy; into Martin Ingram, a shaft of long-delayed self-knowledge. Into Bernie's mother, the thought that maybe perfection is not the aim, and that people are born to be themselves, and to be perfectly human. Into Dante, the feeling that he was loved more than anything else in the world, and that love matters more than conforming. A piece of the truth for everyone. For Adam Price. Even for me.

Everyone in that room was changed in more or less important ways; some barely grazed by the glimpse of truth; some turned wholly upside down. That's how mirrors work, you see. They show you different perspectives. What it feels like to

413

walk on the sky; to look down from the ceiling. Ask anyone who was in that room, and they will tell you how it feels; how every one of them has felt something subtly different – a *change* – over the past twelve months or so.

This is how it spreads, of course. This is how we change the world. Not in violence or in war, but in clarity and contemplation. Change is the thing that waits; that hopes; that sometimes skirts the shadows; that hides under the bedclothes; that tidies up the leftovers; that whispers to your children; that looks at you from polished doors and in reflective surfaces; that sometimes bleeds; and yet is strong, maybe stronger than anyone. That was the taste of a strawberry sweet exchanged for a mouthful of pork pie; the stage magician's assistant taking the spotlight in his place; the woman in the mirror striking out like a bolt of lightning. That was Bernie Moon, who lives now in every woman who was there, and in whose tale I hope you'll find something that will make you look.

# ENCORE:

## The Man With the Child in His Eyes

*From the LiveJournal of @whitey 2947 (marked as Exhibit BI 1): June 15th, 2023*

Of course they tried to pin it on me. They even said I had a knife. But there was no knife. No one was cut. Even the coroner said so. That didn't stop them from trying, though. If not murder, then GBH, or assault, or something. They even brought out my juvie records. Tried to make it look as if I was stalking Kate Malkin. But Katie didn't press charges. In fact, she even came out and said she'd lied about that time she accused me.

I think that's what fixed it in the end. Kate Malkin came out and said I never did a thing to her. For all those years, I thought she was such a bitch. But she did that. She did that for me. It can't have been easy. They tried to get me for trespass then, or for anything else that might stick, but I told them straight. I'm clean now. The caretaker hired me to sweep up the hall. *Disorderly conduct it is, then,* they said. But I don't remember. I think I got a knock to the head. I hadn't been drinking, or on drugs. The blood tests came back negative. And I don't remember being on stage, or any of that other stuff. It was scary for a bit. I even made the papers.

But now it feels as if some junk got cleaned out of my head, somehow. I used to feel angry all the time. I used to spend all my life online, reading up about MK2 and Gender Wars, and everything. It's funny, but now a lot of those things don't seem important anymore.

Lots of things have changed since last year. I've moved away from Malbry into some sheltered accommodation in Leeds. I've got a counsellor called Mike, who listens to what I've been doing. I go to Group on Wednesdays. And I've got a proper job, mowing lawns and verges for the Council. Sometimes I plant flowers too. It's nice. It gets me working outdoors. That's where I met Mel. My girlfriend. I never had a girlfriend before. It's funny, but I'm doing a lot of things I never used to do before. And it feels good. Really it does. Things are looking up, at last.

I sometimes think about the lady who died at the Pog Hill party. They say she died from a blood clot. Something to do with hormones. Her name was Bernadette Ingram, *nay* Moon. I used to be at her school, but I don't remember knowing her. I do remember hearing her sing. That's all I really remember from that night. She did a song called 'Manchild', an oldie by Neneh Cherry. You can hear it on YouTube now, or download it on Spotify. There's a video that goes with it. The girl who sings it is mega hot. I think she looks a bit like Mel. And the lyrics are interesting. It's all about wanting to be someone else, and miracles, and respect. You don't think a song can mean all that much, but this one does. At least, it does to me. I got it as a ringtone. And last week I got a new tattoo. Not a home one, with a compass and ink, but a nice one from a shop. It's a little red heart on my wrist, to remind me that I deserve nice things. It makes me happy to look at it. It makes me remember I'm still alive.

Last week was the anniversary of that Pog Hill party. I went back to Malbry on the train. I went to the cemetery to see if I could find Bernadette Ingram. I don't know why. I don't know her. I guess I just wanted to see where she was. When I got to St James', there was a woman already there. It was Katie Hemsworth, who used to be Katie Malkin. She was standing by a grave and holding a bunch of flowers. She looked up as I arrived. She wasn't surprised to see me. She said:

'Hello, Adam. I thought you might come.'

I wonder how she knew. And yet it seemed to make perfect sense. Katie had her hair in a braid and was wearing some kind of summer dress with shoulder straps and flowers. There was a jewel around her neck. I think it was a ruby. I thought she looked pretty, but didn't say so in case she thought I was being weird. I said:

'You must have been good friends.'

She nodded. 'Yes. I think we were.'

I looked down at the grave. It was simple. No angels, or planters, or anything. Just a slab of polished dark stone and an inscription: *Bernadette Ingram: 1973–2022: Beloved Wife of Martin. Mother of Dan.* Nothing else. Just that piece of stone, all speckled with pieces of shiny stuff, reflecting my face like a mirrorball. It was kind of weird, in fact. It made me feel kind of funny. Like someone was shining a light in my eyes, all the way to the back of my mind.

I said: 'What was she like?'

She said: 'Don't you remember, Adam?'

And just for a minute, yes, I did. Remembered a little girl with black hair, wearing some kind of a pirate suit. The memory came from deep down in my mind; from a place I don't often go anymore; but it felt somehow safe and comforting. And there was a smell, too: like strawberries, and books, and blankets fresh from the line; the smell of a child-hood I never had, and yet I somehow remembered.

And I said: 'It was a long time ago. I wasn't happy in those days. But you were OK. I remember that. You were one of the good ones.'

She smiled, a little sadly, I thought. 'I'm sorry for what happened,' she said. 'I didn't mean it. Things got out of hand. I hope it wasn't too hard for you.'

I shrugged. 'We were kids. What did we know? Water under the bridge, man.'

She held my gaze for a moment. 'Yeah. Water under the bridge.' And then she bent down and softly laid her flowers on the graveside. And then she walked away down the avenue of trees lining the cemetery, and left me looking at myself in the polished granite slab, where, for a minute, I *think* I saw the smiling face of a little girl, hanging suspended in mid-air, like a Christmas bauble.

# Acknowledgements

To be a writer is to be a strange kind of contradiction. It feels uncomfortably *visible* and yet at the same time, *invisible*. It moves between worlds. It conjures the illusion of intimacy between strangers. And yet it would have no substance without those working behind the scenes. Magic needs the conditions for magic to be possible.

And so, my very heartfelt thanks to everyone who helped bring this strange and unexpected book from the shadows into the world. My kind and helpful agent, Jon Wood; my fantastic editors, Sarah Benton, Lucy Brem and Fred Harris; copy-editor Marian Reid; designer Charlotte Abrams Simpson for her bold and imaginative cover concept. Thanks too to the publicity and marketing team: Katie, Francesca, Yadira and Alex, for all their encouragement and enthusiasm. Thank you to the booksellers, to those who keep my books visible; to the bloggers and Tubers and TikTokers, to the tweeters and tooters of the book world and of the writing community.

And thanks to you. You know who you are. If this book made you feel seen, then I wrote it for you most of all. I hope you found something in there to make you see the world in a different light – not broken, but filled with reflections, and maybe a little magic.

# Credits

Joanne Harris and Orion Fiction would like to thank everyone at Orion who worked on the publication of *Broken Light* in the UK.

**Editorial**
Sarah Benton
Lucy Brem

**Copyeditor**
Marian Reid

**Proofreader**
Jade Craddock

**Audio**
Paul Stark
Jake Alderson

**Contracts**
Dan Herron
Ellie Bowker

**Design**
Charlotte Abrams-Simpson
Joanna Ridley
Zane Dabinett

**Editorial Management**
Charlie Panayiotou
Jane Hughes
Bartley Shaw
Tamara Morriss

**Finance**
Jasdip Nandra
Nick Gibson
Sue Baker

**Marketing**
Katie Moss
Yadira Da Trindade

**Operations**
Jo Jacobs
Sharon Willis

**Publicity**
Francesca Pearce
Alex Layt

**Production**
Ruth Sharvell

**Sales**
Jen Wilson
Esther Waters
Victoria Laws
Toluwalope Ayo-Ajala
Rachael Hum
Anna Egelstaff
Sinead White
Georgina Cutler

# DISAPPEAR INTO THE WORLD OF *SUNDAY TIMES* BESTSELLING *CHOCOLAT* . . .

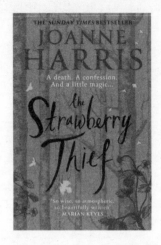

## Faith. Secret. Magic. Murder . . .?

Vianne Rocher has settled down. Lansquenet-sous-Tannes, the place that once rejected her, has finally become her home. With Rosette, her youngest child, she runs her chocolate shop in the square, talks to her friends on the river, is part of the community. Even Reynaud, the priest, has become a friend.

But when old Narcisse, the florist, dies, leaving a parcel of land to Rosette and a written confession to Reynaud, the life of the sleepy village is once more thrown into disarray. Then the opening of a mysterious new shop in the place of the florist's across the square – one that mirrors the chocolaterie, and has a strange appeal of its own – seems to herald a change: a confrontation, a turbulence – even, perhaps, a murder . . .

*'So wise, so atmospheric, so beautifully written'*
**Marian Keyes**